SPELL BOUND

F.T. LUKENS

SIMON & SCHUSTER

LONDON   NEW YORK   SYDNEY   TORONTO   NEW DELHI

First published in Great Britain in 2023 by Simon & Schuster UK Ltd

First published in the USA in 2023 by Margaret K. McElderry Books,
an imprint of Simon & Schuster Children's Publishing Division,
1230 Avenue of the Americas, New York, New York 10020

Text copyright © 2023 F.T. Lukens

1 3 5 7 9 10 8 6 4 2

Simon & Schuster UK Ltd
1st Floor, 222 Gray's Inn Road
London WC1X 8HB

www.simonandschuster.co.uk
www.simonandschuster.com.au
www.simonandschuster.co.in

Simon & Schuster Australia, Sydney
Simon & Schuster India, New Delhi

A CIP catalogue record for this book
is available from the British Library.

PB ISBN 978-1-3985-2147-6
eBook ISBN 978-1-3985-2148-3
eAudio ISBN 978-1-3985-2149-0

Printed and Bound in the UK using 100% Renewable
Electricity at CPI Group (UK) Ltd

MIX
Paper | Supporting
responsible forestry
FSC
www.fsc.org   FSC® C171272

To anyone who feels like
they don't quite fit:
maybe it's time to break the mold.

SPELL BOUND

ROOK

Hex-A-Gone.

The name didn't quite inspire visions of magical greatness. It was a pun. A *bad* one but funnily apt for a local emergency on-call curse-breaker. And while I could appreciate the humor on a campy level, the name definitely was not what had drawn me there. I wasn't cursed. I wasn't hexed. I wasn't in need of a magical service, but I stood outside the nondescript office front that had the name emblazoned in simple white letters across the glass door, and a "Consortium Sanctioned" certificate tucked into the corner of the window.

A wilted potted plant leaned mournfully toward a sliver of sunlight on the other side, and beyond that, the lights were dimmed, making it difficult to see anything other than the reception area. The whole image was the epitome of depressed office park chic, down to the plain black welcome mat on the other side of the threshold, and not what one would expect from a magical business owned by the supposedly most powerful sorcerer in Spire City.

Ignoring the dour exterior, I pulled on the door handle and stepped inside. I had a freshly printed high school diploma in my backpack alongside my newest invention and a deep desire to work with magic, and I wasn't going to be put off merely because the office appeared abandoned. A frisson of excitement or terror—I couldn't tell which—swept down my spine. The inside was somehow less impressive than the outside, filled with typical dull office decor, including an empty receptionist desk and a room of prefab cubicles.

I fidgeted, hands digging like claws into the straps of my backpack, unsure of what to do next. Should I call out a "hello" and hope that someone heard me? Should I ring the little bell on the desk? Should I turn around and walk back out because what the hell was I even doing there? A teenager with no magical ability at all about to beg for a job in a magical profession.

I gritted my teeth. No, I was not going to run. I could do it. I could totally do it. I was *going* to do it. I had to do it. I literally had graduated from school the day before, and I needed a job. But beyond that, I needed to find out if I belonged. The worst thing she could do was say no. Right? Well, she could turn me into a frog. She was a sorcerer after all. But I doubted she would because she was in the business of helping people, albeit for a price. Huh. Hopefully not only for a price. I wasn't exactly swimming in riches, hence my search for employment.

Regardless, the chance of potentially being turned into a frog was one I was willing to take to be able to talk to Antonia Hex.

I shuffled forward, my heels scraping across the mat. I glanced toward the coatrack in the corner, which sagged against the wall. It turned in my direction. I blinked. What? The coatrack straightened from a slouch and regarded me much like how I regarded it. I bit down on my startled yelp as it moved, hobbling over on three legs. It bowed deeply at the waist, or what counted as the waist for a coatrack. Then it gestured toward my backpack, holding out its spindles in invitation.

I clutched my bag with white knuckles and took a step backward, as I had the abrupt and stark realization that my judgment and my self-preservation instincts were not as honed as they probably should be for a nonmagical almost-seventeen-year-old.

For one, I should have freaked out at the sight of a helpful coatrack, and while I was slightly wary, because *weird*, I somehow stayed outwardly calm. I wanted to poke it to see what would happen, curious about the mechanics of an obviously magical coatrack, but self-preservation did kick in and I resisted the urge.

For two, I had willingly walked into the business owned and operated by a formidable sorcerer. I was sure many customers had come and gone in the agency's tenure—otherwise it wouldn't still be in business. But I was also sure that few of them were penniless, utterly powerless humans like myself. And three, while the coatrack tapped its stand, impatiently waiting for me to hand over my bag, I became achingly aware that this was *magic*. Real and powerful magic. Something I hadn't been allowed to experience in so long. The elation of feeling the slightest tingle of it prick along my skin chased away all the apprehensions clamoring in my stomach and replaced them with a bone-deep reverence.

I sucked in a breath as I squirmed in the doorway. Despite the name, Hex-A-Gone was a well-respected business that responded to magical emergencies and specialized in breaking curses, hexes, and jinxes. I had done my research. The owner, the aforementioned Antonia Hex, was a powerful sorcerer, and the rumor was that though she wasn't *evil* per se, she wasn't what one would call *lawfully good*, either. And if she ever wanted to turn evil, there wasn't much anyone could do to stop her.

I should have been terrified or cautious at the very least. And I was, but it wasn't going to keep me from trying to get a job there, because I wanted so badly to learn from her.

The spelled coatrack made another gesture toward my bag. I shook my head. Wait, was it spelled or cursed? I wasn't sure the terminology other than that it was an inanimate object that had been imbued with magic to act as some sort of welcoming committee to the office. If a coatrack could be judgmental, this one was, and it crossed its skinny arms, spun on its base, and hobbled back to a position by the door. Uh-oh, I had offended the coatrack. Maybe I should've given it my bag? Was that some kind of test?

I cleared my throat. I might be in over my head. Just a little bit. Because as much as I *could* research the business itself and dig up a little about the owner, the actual magic involved was hidden away under lock and key, available only to a select few.

I shifted nervously on the welcome mat, my tattered sneakers squeaking on the rubber. I had the terrifying and fleeting thought that maybe the welcome mat was spelled as well, and I was basically dancing on its face, when a small crash followed by a string of expletives emanated from deeper in the building.

"Son of a bitch," a woman muttered as she stepped out of a small break room beyond the partition and off to the side, dabbing at a large rapidly spreading coffee stain on her blouse with a tiny napkin. She was tall, especially in the red heels she wore, and had long dark hair, golden-brown skin, and an intimidating aura.

"Modern appliances just aren't meant to . . ." She trailed off when she looked up and saw me standing by the door. She was undoubtedly beautiful, with berry-colored lips, perfectly shaped eyebrows, and thick lashes, but her most striking feature was her violet eyes. They pierced through me like I imagined arrows would. Her long fingernails were painted black, and they curled around the soaked napkin crumpled in her hand while the stain wicked through the fabric of her sleeve. Her brow furrowed as she looked at me. Then her gaze cut to the coatrack brooding in the corner.

"Why didn't you alert me that someone was here?" she demanded.

The rack's shoulders drooped, and it turned away from her like a scolded puppy.

"Now, don't be like that," she said, tone softening. "But what is the point of having spelled furniture to watch the door if it doesn't do its job?"

The coatrack seemed to sigh, then teetered back over to me and gestured an arm, beckoning me into the office.

"Well, it's a little late now," the woman said, shaking her head. "Just go . . . clean up the coffee. The brewer combusted again." Somehow the coatrack conveyed annoyance in the shrug of its wooden body. "Yes. I'm aware," she said, frowning. "I'll figure it out eventually."

The coatrack slouched off, and the woman turned back to me, her previously white sleeve now brown and damp and clinging to her arm.

"Don't mind him," she said with a shrug. "Herb is moody on his best days."

"Herb?" I asked. It was the first thing I'd said since I entered the office, and the woman's lips quirked.

"That's his name. I take it you've never met a spelled coatrack before?"

Spelled. It was spelled, not cursed. "No. But my grandmother had a temperamental teapot."

She nodded. "Sometimes convenience isn't worth the trouble. Anyway, who are you, and why are you here?"

Oh. Well. Abrupt. But sure. I pulled back my shoulders, adjusting my posture. "My name is—"

She raised her hand and cut me off. "Stop." Her violet eyes glittered. "Let's leave names out of this for now. Tell me why you are here first."

I didn't know how to take that. But I swallowed. "I'm here to meet with . . . the owner, if possible."

"Really?" she said, pulling out the word. She looked me up and down. "Have you been cursed?"

"No."

"Hexed?"

I swallowed. "No."

She snapped her fingers. "Jinxed, then. Don't worry, sweetheart. Jinxes tend to run their course and wear off. You don't need to employ Antonia for a simple jinx if it's fairly mild." She looked around the office, then cupped her hand near her mouth and stage whispered, "You probably couldn't afford the rates anyway."

As I figured. "Um . . . no. That's not why I'm here." My knees shook. "I want to ask her about a job."

The woman's eyebrows shot up. "A job? With the most powerful sorcerer in the city? Possibly in the world? You?"

My heart pounded. "Yes?"

"Is that a question?"

"No."

"So, you don't want a job?"

"No, wait, I do. Yes, I want a job."

She snickered. "I'm just messing with you, kid. Come on," she said, spinning on her heel, her hair whipping behind her. "Follow me to the boss's office. We'll get you squared away."

I stepped off the welcome mat to follow, and the corner smacked me in the ankle. Surprised, I scrambled after her, beyond the entryway and into the office proper.

"Oh, and beware the welcome mat," she said, glancing over her shoulder and giving it a narrow-eyed look. "It's cursed."

Oh. Wonderful.

She flicked her wrist, and an inner door opened. She led me

deeper into the building, past a row of cubicles, and into a massive office. The office had a large tempered glass wall and door on one side and a claw-footed desk in the corner next to a huge window. The nameplate said ANTONIA HEX in big letters. There was a computer, but it was set off to the side, as if it wasn't as important as the hefty, old leather-bound book that took up the majority of the desk's surface. Next to it was a small cauldron on a hot plate and a row of vials in a wooden stand.

The woman walked around the desk and settled herself in the high-backed office chair. With a mutter and a wave of her fingers, the air shifted, and the coffee stain on her arm disappeared in the space of a blink. I tried not to stare wide-eyed, but I'd seen more magic in the last few seconds than I had in the last year, and giddy excitement bubbled beneath my breastbone.

She leaned back in the chair, tented her fingers, and cocked her head to the side. "Sit and tell me why you want to work for me."

Oh. *Oh*. She wasn't some random office worker. She *was* Antonia Hex.

I awkwardly fell into the seat, forgetting about my bag, which crammed between my spine and the chair. I became tangled in the straps for an embarrassing moment until I was finally able to free myself and drop it at my feet.

"Geez, kid. Don't hurt yourself."

"I'm sorry," I breathed. "I . . . I . . . It's just . . ."

"I'm not what you were expecting?"

I shook my head. "Honestly? No."

"Good. I don't like being predictable. Keeps things interesting." She tapped her lips. "Let me guess. You heard the words 'the most powerful sorcerer in an age' and looked the business up on the internet and immediately thought creepy, old, withered hag or someone's doddering grandma who plays with potions. Am I right?"

Close. I did think of my grandma but for other reasons. I scratched the back of my neck. "Something like that."

"Well"—she opened her arms—"appearances can be deceiving." She smirked. "Now, let's get started. But first you have to stop vibrating."

"Huh?" She pointed to where my leg bounced erratically. I hadn't even realized I was doing it. "Oh, sorry. I'm nervous."

"I can tell," she said with a soft smile. "Don't worry. I don't bite." Her smile ticked up at the corner, turning sly. "Well, I don't bite children."

"That's . . . good, I guess?"

She laughed, a low and throaty sound. "You're cute. I'll give you that. But I don't work with people based on that alone. So, spill, kid. Why are you here?"

Okay, this was my chance. I'd practiced my speech in front of a mirror for the last week. I'd made notecards with bullet points and memorized them. I'd worked on my body language and presentation. I'd even worn my best button-down and newest jeans and used cheap product in my brown hair to make it stay in place.

"I miss my grandmother," I blurted. And oh. Oh no. That was not how I'd meant to start. "She died a year ago." Well, that was even worse.

Antonia's eyes narrowed. "I'm not a medium," she said, lips pursed. "And despite Spire City gossip, I can't bring anyone back from the dead. Well, let's be real, I *could*, but that's considered necromancy and is generally frowned upon in most circles. Not that I care what people think of me. But it's not worth the paperwork or the scrutiny."

"No, I know. I mean, I didn't know that. But that's not why . . . I'm not here for . . . I'm sorry. That's not . . . What I meant was . . :" Come on, self, make a statement. "I'm a genius."

Both of her eyebrows shot up.

Shit. That was not it either.

"Wait. I'm sorry." I ran a hand through my hair, then winced when it came away sticky with gel. My hair probably stood on end, and my face was so hot with embarrassment. And now my fingers stuck to my palm as I clenched my fist. I couldn't meet her gaze and stared at the floor, absolutely mortified.

"Is this going how you thought it would?" she asked, the click of her fingernails drumming on the wooden desk loud in the otherwise silence.

"No," I muttered.

"Well, at least you're honest. But as hilarious as this all is, I do have work to do, so . . ." She trailed off.

I lifted my head and composed myself the best I could. "I want to work with you because I want to help people like you help people. My grandmother was a low-level sorcerer, and she made potions and she took care of everyone in the neighborhood. And that's what magic is to me. And I really am a genius. I graduated from high school early with the highest grades in the class, and I learn difficult concepts very quickly. I'm loyal and I follow through and I'm punctual. I brought references from a few of my teachers if you'd like to see them."

She waved away the offer.

"Okay," I said, on a breath. "I'm enthusiastic and I work hard, and I very much want to work for you."

Antonia leaned forward, elbows on the pages of the book, expression placid, bordering on bored.

"Why curse work and not one of those"—she waved her hand— "flashy spell places downtown?"

Ah, yes. The sorcerers for hire who performed spells for exorbitant fees. I'd heard a few of my schoolmates bragging about how their families had hired sorcerers for their graduation parties to spell

9

chandeliers to hover and sparkle and decorations to change every hour and drink glasses that wouldn't spill. All frivolous and fancy magic that cost more money than I'd see in a lifetime.

"I don't want to work for them. I want to work for you. Apparently, you're the best."

"Apparently?" Antonia scoffed. "Child, I *am* the best."

"Then I want to work for you."

She nodded. "Okay. Makes sense. But did you know that curse work is messy and basically the lowest form of magic for hire?"

I swallowed. I had guessed that was the case, and it made my chances of being hired a little more real, especially if there weren't many others clamoring for employment.

"Then why is the best sorcerer in the city relegated to it?"

Her lips pulled into a sly grin. "Why indeed?"

That wasn't an answer. And my weak self-preservation instincts registered that I should probably be afraid of whatever the answer was and make a hasty exit since she blatantly skirted the question. I stayed rooted in my chair.

"Anyway . . . ." Antonia plowed through the tension, not giving me a second to contemplate further. "What if I'm not hiring?"

I'd prepared for that. "I'll work for minimum wage. And if not, then a mentorship. Or I could be your apprentice!"

Her expression went flat, sour. "I don't take apprentices. I don't teach magic. And I work alone in the field."

That was disheartening. I licked my dry lips. "Not even a volunteer?"

She tilted her head, her eyes burning as her gaze swept over me. "Hold out your hand. Palm up."

It wasn't a request. I gulped, afraid and optimistic all at once. Trembling with nerves, I held out the non-sticky hand. She grasped it and yanked me close, forcing me to the edge of the chair, her fingernails pinpricks against my skin. She stared at my palm intently, smoothing her thumbs over the lines, then pressed the tip of one finger hard, right in the center. It hurt, but I resisted pulling my hand away and clenched my jaw against a whine. I expected that this might happen, that I'd have to endure this test again, and I braced myself for it, gritted my teeth, and bore the pain. I'd failed it once before, and the anxiety of falling short again swirled inside me, made my stomach churn and my free hand shake. But I was also hopeful because Antonia was the most adept sorcerer in the city, and maybe the outcome would be different because maybe she would see that I belonged. It was one of my reasons for coming here, and I hoped against hope that the result would be different.

After an excruciating minute, she released the pressure. "You aren't magic," she said, brow furrowed as she studied my hand. "I can't sense any magic ability within you."

I did my best not to physically deflate right there, but my throat went tight, and the burn of unshed tears gathered behind my eyes.

"Can you even see the ley lines?" she asked.

Ley lines. The source of all magical energy. They crisscrossed the globe, stronger in some parts of the world than others. Some of the thickest and most powerful lines converged right here in Spire City. Sorcerers could see them, draw from them, and use them to perform spells and infuse potions with the magic from them. It was like magical Wi-Fi. The rumor was that some sorcerers were even so adept that they could build a reserve of power from the lines inside themselves for use later. Though it was only rumor.

Antonia snapped her head up and dropped my hand. It fell to the desk with a smack. "Well?"

I couldn't lie if I wanted. "No," I said. "I can't."

She leaned backward, tented her fingers. "Huh. Well, this has all been fun. But without the ability to use magic, I'm sorry to say that there is no place for you here."

Her words were a slap. They weren't mean, just matter-of-fact. But they still stung, picked at the open wound of insecurity in my chest that whispered to me that I'd never fit in anywhere. Too smart for my own good. Too aware of the magical world to live without it, but not magical enough to be included and certainly not wealthy enough to access it. I'd known, deep down, that approaching Antonia was a long shot, a desperate attempt at belonging, but I'd hoped . . . I had desperately hoped that as powerful as she was, she could see magic in me when no one else could, and perhaps she'd sense that I was supposed to be here, a part of her world. But she hadn't. She didn't. My heart sank to the floor, and my cheeks burned with shame.

"None?" I asked, voice cracking. "At all?"

"No, kid. Without magic, employment wouldn't be allowed anyway." She studied me. Her eyes caught the light, shining like two bright jewels. "You're not going to cry on me, are you?" she asked.

I shook my head, frantically trying to rein in my utter dejection. "No," I said, my voice a rasp, blinking back tears. I'd wait until I was on the bus back home at least.

"Look, kid, this line of work, it takes . . . Well, even the girl who manages the office has a bit of magic. This is not something to dive into lightly. It's hectic and can be frightening for someone who has not been around it before. And I just don't have the time to train someone who doesn't know the difference between a curse and a jinx and wouldn't be helpful in breaking either if they did. I'm sorry."

I pressed my lips together and nodded. "I understand."

"Good, because—"

The phone on the corner of the desk rang. It was a typical office phone, but it was so loud and so *obnoxious* that we both flinched.

Antonia cursed and pointed a finger at it, magic bursting from her in a wave that knocked the phone onto its side. It continued to ring, though now more of a dying whale song type of noise than a high-pitched trill. After a moment of torture, the sound finally sputtered out with an eerie dial tone.

Antonia put her hands over her ears. "I'm sorry. My office manager is on vacation, and somehow the stupid phone got turned up to high volume and I have no idea how to turn it down, and I can't magic it, because if I do, it just explodes."

"It explodes?"

Antonia winced and pointed behind me. I turned in my chair to see a plain box in the corner with the remnants of a phone exactly like the one on her desk. There were also fragments of what looked at one time to be a desk lamp and . . . Was that a printer?

Wow. I raised an eyebrow as I turned around. "Is that what happened to the coffee maker?"

She huffed. "Magic and machines don't mix."

I clutched my bag at my feet.

"And I am magic, and I break electronics all the time." She sighed. "I really wanted that coffee."

My heart leaped, and my thoughts buzzed in the face of a potential opportunity. Maybe there was another way in. I cleared my throat. "I can fix that, you know," I said, nodding toward the phone. "And the coffee maker. I wasn't lying when I said I was a genius."

She lifted her chin, straightened from her defeated slump. "You can fix that?"

"Yeah. I have a way with electronics and technology." I leaned over and righted the phone. Taking the receiver from the cradle, I found the volume button on the keypad and turned it down to a less earsplitting level. It was an easy fix, something Antonia could've figured out on her own, but I wasn't above exploiting this newfound weakness to my benefit. I gestured toward the laptop that was pushed off to the side. "Do you even use that?"

Antonia rolled her eyes and crossed her arms, defensive. "I know how to use it. I just don't. It's a preference." She eyed it like it was a monster that would come alive and eat her. "Okay, fine. I don't like it. It doesn't like me. We have a mutual understanding."

"Is it cursed like the welcome mat?"

"I wish. I'd know how to fix it then."

Well, this was a smidgeon of leverage. So, I pushed. "I could take a look at it if you want?"

She gauged me with a shrewd eye, then wagged her finger in my face. "Don't think I don't know what you're doing," she said, lips pulled into a wry smile. "But fine, you fix that computer, and I'll give you a job."

"Really?"

"On a *trial* basis. And only in the office. No magic. No field work. Office staff only."

It wasn't exactly what I wanted, but it was close enough. Better than nothing at all. At least I'd be around magic again.

"Okay. Deal."

She nodded. "Do you have school or something?"

"I graduated."

"Okay. Well, come back tomorrow morning to fix the laptop, and we'll talk."

I smiled wide, my head spinning from the emotional roller coaster of rejection, then acceptance in the space of a few minutes. "Okay. That's great. Really awesome. I'll be here. Thank you. I'm very excited."

"Don't make me regret it, kid. Leave before I change my mind."

I shot to my feet, swinging my bag over my shoulder. "Okay. Yes.

Leaving now." I scrambled out of the office, down the hallway past the cubicles, and to the reception area. I waved at Herb, who ignored me, turning away in dramatic fashion.

"Hey, kid!" Antonia called.

I skidded to a stop and spun on my heel. Antonia leaned in the doorway of her office, yelling across the empty space. "What's your name?"

"Edison," I called back. "Edison Rooker."

She made a face. "That's an awful name." She hummed. "I'm going to call you Rook. Okay. Got it."

Well, close enough. I turned back toward the door.

"And watch out for the—"

As I stepped across the welcome mat, it jerked to the side, sliding my foot out from beneath me. I stumbled but managed to keep from falling to the floor by catching myself on the wall . . . with my face.

"Mat," Antonia finished weakly.

"I'm fine!" My nose throbbed. A trickle of blood wound its way from my nostril. "I'm fine. It's fine."

I heard muffled laughter and a "holy shit" follow after me as I fled out the door, but I didn't turn around, too embarrassed, too bloody, and very aware that my position with Antonia was tenuous enough that an encounter with a cursed rug could potentially ruin everything. Better to make a run for it before she could change her mind.

Sprinting toward the city bus stop, I couldn't help but laugh, even though my nose ached. I felt like I could run a marathon and sleep for a week at the same time. Catching my reflection in the bus window as it slowed to a stop, I could see that I looked a bit deranged and did my best to tame my hair and wipe the blood smears off my face. The bus driver gave me a judgmental once-over when I boarded and swiped my card, but she didn't say anything as I headed toward a window seat near the back.

I slumped into the seat, and my leg jiggled in anxious excitement as I watched Spire City speed past me in a blur of tall buildings and busy streets. The city itself was massive, stretching in all directions, one of the largest in the world, a far cry from where I'd grown up in my grandmother's cottage on the very outer edge of the city sprawl. Antonia's office was a good hour bus ride from my apartment, but it would be worth it. So worth it.

The best part though was that I'd be around magic again. It wouldn't be like living with my grandmother, where she'd conjure sparkling butterflies for me to chase in the spring or spell the fire to heat the house in the winter. Where there was always a bubbling cauldron of something, be it soup or a cold remedy or a sweet fizzy drink for the hottest days of the summer. But it would be something more than the loneliness of the apartment and the absence of any familial affection.

I pulled my cell phone from my pocket and checked the time. I had no messages, which wasn't a surprise. I didn't have friends at school, only classmates and acquaintances, since I was the new kid who moved in at the start of senior year and also younger than everyone I shared classes with. And my caseworker had been clear that while my stipend and rent would continue until I turned eighteen, now that I'd finished my mandatory education, I was well and truly on my own. No more awkward check-ins, no more supervision, and now nothing to stop me from pursuing my own interests and enacting my tenuous plan to gain entrance back into the magical community. The community I'd been cut off from when my grandmother passed.

And with that thought, despite the excitement of the afternoon,

I sank lower in my seat and leaned heavily against the window. I dozed as the bus navigated the busy street, rocking when it went up on the curb, honking the horn at pedestrians, and jerking to a halt every so often at the different stops along the way.

When it finally pulled into my stop, I hopped up and exited, yawning as the events of the day caught up with me and fatigue settled behind my eyes. I quickly walked the short route home, head down, hands twined in the straps of my bag. I lived on the fourth floor, and while the elevator was rickety and the buttons on the panel were burned out half the time, I went with it instead of the stairs because I was on the verge of being worn out. By the time I'd made it to the door, I was well and truly exhausted.

Once inside, I kicked off my shoes in the entranceway and dropped my bag onto the couch, then switched on the TV for some background noise as I rooted around in the freezer. The apartment was quiet and still. Lonely, to be honest. But I'd been lonely for the past year, since my whole life had been uprooted, and it was easy to slip into the comfort of it. It wasn't entirely a bad thing, and now I had work to look forward to since I was going back to Hex-A-Gone in the morning.

Feet on the coffee table, ice wrapped in a paper towel pressed to my nose, I pulled my backpack into my lap. I unzipped it and gently took out the device that I'd been working on for the last year of my life. The Spell Binder.

Its creation was what had kept me going since the day I'd been forced from my grandma's cottage and sent to live in the city on my own. Ever since, magic had been excised from my life when a nameless government sorcerer had pressed their finger into the center of my palm and deemed me not magical and thus not allowed to stay in the home I knew or the community I loved. Unable to see the ley lines, they said. Unable to learn how to cast. Unable to access magic. Banished to the outside looking in with the only entrance being vast sums of money, which I didn't have.

I had hoped that having the most powerful sorcerer in the city— the world if Antonia was to be believed—read my palm, she might see a spark that someone else had missed, that there was fledgling potential within me that she could nurture. She hadn't. The confirmation hurt worse than I thought it could. And even if she had found a smidgeon of magic, she'd been clear that she wouldn't teach me, sending a jagged ache of rejection piercing through me yet again.

But I'd be okay. I'd experienced worse. And while it didn't feel great, it merely meant that I had to recalibrate and adjust, something I happened to be excellent at. So she wouldn't be teaching me magic directly. That didn't mean I still couldn't learn about it. I could learn anything. I was a genius after all. I had learned to live on my own. I had learned to navigate life in the city. I could carve out a place for myself within the magical world. That's why I created the Spell Binder in the first place. I couldn't see the ley lines, so I developed a device that could see them for me.

I checked it over, making sure that it hadn't been damaged in any way. I powered it on, and it blinked to life in my hand, the screen flickering. This was the first step in changing my life, because if I could see the magic myself, then it couldn't ever be taken away from me. Despite the slight setbacks, I held on to hope. I had to because it was *all* I had. And with Antonia's unwitting assistance, I was never going to be without magic again.

2

ROOK

"Have you ever heard of antivirus software?" I asked as I tapped on the keys of Antonia's laptop. It harbored an amazing number of viruses, and I was surprised that it still functioned. She peered over my shoulder; her violet eyes narrowed, but I couldn't tell if her apparent distrust was of me or of the computer itself.

"Is that a thing I need?"

"Yes," I said with a grin. "Especially if you don't want anyone trying to steal your credit card information or spying on you."

"Well, we sorcerers are notoriously secretive, you know."

I spun in the office chair Antonia had set up in one of the empty cubicles while the software I installed went to work. "I've noticed. Why is that?"

She took a sip of her very large coffee, which I'd made after fixing the fancy espresso machine, and tossed the length of her dark-brown hair over her shoulder. Her fingernails sparkled blue today to match her blouse. "I assume you've heard of the Magical Consortium?"

I nodded and pointed toward the front office window. "Like the certificate in the window?"

"The one and the same. They're the magical world's semblance of a governing body. A bureaucratic nuisance, if you ask me. But they make the rules that sorcerers have to follow, even if they are stifling and nonsensical and literally exist just to make my life difficult."

I didn't remember my grandmother ever mentioning the Magical Consortium, but I knew they existed from the whirlwind of events that transpired after her death, including the evaluation that resulted in my banishment from the magical world. Their logo was also stamped on all the certificates in the windows of magic businesses around the city, and when I tried to research magic on the internet, I usually encountered a "This page has been blocked by the Magical Consortium" message any time I got close to real information.

"They sound fun," I said as I went back to fixing Antonia's computer.

Antonia snorted. "They're anything but. And they are not fans of sharing information beyond their 'inner circle.'" She made finger quotes, which was impressive considering she still held her coffee cup. "They have a tantrum if any magical information is shared with nonmagical folk. Which is why you won't find anything about magic on the internet or anywhere beyond the tightly controlled spell books. They have a death grip on the flow of information. And anyone who tries to step out of line is immediately dealt with."

I broke out in a full-body sweat. Dealt with? That didn't sound pleasant. When I was developing the Spell Binder, I'd tried to track down a map of the city's ley lines to compare against its readouts since I couldn't see the lines myself. It had been a fruitless endeavor. The only people who offered to provide some inkling into the inner workings were shady and wanted to meet in dark parking lots or back alleys at odd times and in isolated places. I'd considered meeting up with someone once, but I didn't want to become the next unsolved murder mystery featured on a true-crime TV show.

"Dealt with?" I asked, hoping for nonchalant.

"Handled. Reprimanded. Relegated to curse work." The last bit came out sharp and bitter, and a tingle worked its way down my spine at the implication that Antonia had been on the wrong side of the Consortium before. She drummed her fingers against the side of her cup and continued. "They like to pretend to exert control over practicing sorcerers, but they can't keep an eye on all of us all the time, not even with their scrying mirrors. It's bureaucracy and power under the guise of regulations and safety for everyone." She rolled her eyes. "But in reality, it's to keep the cash flowing. That certificate in my window was very expensive, if you catch my drift."

Oh. That was interesting. "Really? I thought those things were like the health inspector ratings you see in restaurant windows."

Antonia laughed. "Not quite."

"And for a supposedly secretive sorcerer," I said, checking the progress on the software, "you don't seem to have a problem giving the Consortium's secrets away to a nonmagical person."

"Well," she said, pursing her lips, "the Consortium and I aren't exactly friends."

Interesting again. "No," I said in mock surprise. "Really? I hadn't picked up on that at all. You sound like you have a very high opinion of them and their policies."

"Don't say that. I have a reputation to uphold." She smiled, tight-lipped. "They like to pry. Make sure I'm not doing anything I'm not supposed to, though I've been on my best behavior for decades. I made a little mistake when I was young and reckless, and it will follow me for the rest of my life. It's ridiculous."

"Do I want to know?"

"Probably not." She took another sip of her coffee. "I mean, there was some mayhem." She held up her hand and squeezed her thumb and forefinger together. "And some curses. A bit of death."

My eyes widened.

"This is good, by the way," she said, holding up the coffee, changing the subject. "Somehow you've made the coffee maker work even better."

The part of me that was concerned overrode the part of me that preened at the compliment. "A bit of death?" I asked.

She shrugged. "I shouldn't have said anything. Anyway. We need to talk. You've held up your end of the bargain. The computer is fixed. The coffee is great. So, I need to hold up mine."

I did my best not to smile too wide. My leg bounced with nervous energy under the desk. "Okay," I said, voice cracking on the second syllable. So much for keeping my cool.

She had the grace not to mention it, though her lips quirked at the corners. "You will work five days a week. You will answer the phones for me and talk to the customers. And you'll fix everything I break."

That didn't sound too bad. "I can do that."

"I'll pay you weekly."

That sounded even better. "Awesome."

"Great. But to be clear, I'm not a mentor. I'm not a friend. And you are not my apprentice. No magic. You are office staff. I don't want the Consortium to think I'm breaking any rules, so stick to the technology. Understand?"

"Yes? Kind of." Not ideal for my plan. I needed access to magical information. I bit my lip.

She sighed. "Out with it."

"How am I supposed to interact with the customers if I don't know what they're calling about? How will I know if it's something you can handle—"

"I can handle anything."

"Noted. But how do I know what's an emergency and what's something that can wait a few hours?"

She stroked her chin. "You have a good point."

"And you just said that the Consortium doesn't like information being shared with folks who aren't magic, so you know, if you shared a little, it would be a tiny act of defiance."

Narrowing her eyes, she studied me. "I don't like that you already know me so well. But I am a fan of tiny acts of defiance."

"What harm could it do? Like you said, I'm not magical. I can't do anything with the information anyway."

"You drive a hard bargain, Rook. But okay. I'll teach you the bare minimum. But nothing is shared outside this office." She waved her hand at the laptop. "No internet. No documentation. We sorcerers stick to scrolls and books, and they are highly monitored and regulated by the Consortium. So, no taking notes." She touched my temple with the tip of her long fingernail. "It has to stay up here."

"Deal."

"All right, first things first." She sat on the desk next to me. "Curses, hexes, and jinxes."

"Wait? We're starting already?"

"No time like the present." She crossed her legs. "Unless you don't want to learn?"

"No! No, I want to learn. Go ahead."

"Okay, so jinxes are low level, easily remedied, and usually wear off on their own. They're an inconvenience, not necessarily meant to hurt or harm, just annoy. Like, hitting every red light on the way home or stepping on every Lego in the near vicinity. They're not powerful, and lots of times they're cast because someone pissed someone else off and they want to be petty in return. They're my favorite spell because they can be very oddly specific and occasionally hilarious." She giggled. "One time, I jinxed an ex of mine to bray like a donkey anytime he laughed for like an entire week. It was amazing. He couldn't break it, either, because, I'm, well, me," she said with a wink.

"Anyway, that was a while ago, and I've moved on and totally don't have it bookmarked on my calendar to jinx him once a year."

"Wow. Wow. Wowee. So much information there, boss." Note to self, do not allow Antonia to put my name on a calendar. I cleared my throat. "So, they're harmless fun."

Antonia crinkled her nose. "If you've been jinxed that you can't step on any cracks on the sidewalk, and it makes you walk in the road and therefore you get hit by a bus, not so harmless anymore."

"Ah."

"They're not terribly difficult to break, but someone who is jinxed can't break it alone. They must have help, so I get called to be the second in the counterspell fairly often. But like I said, most jinxes only last a short amount of time, and sometimes the person who has been jinxed doesn't even know. Just takes it as a day of bad luck."

"Okay. Got it."

"Hexes are fairly similar. They're a little more powerful, last a little longer, and—" Antonia was cut off by the sound of her phone. She set down her coffee and shoved her hand into the pocket of her tailored trousers. She pulled out a cell phone with a hideously cracked screen and a background filled with icons over a distorted image of . . . Was that a dog?

"Huh. It's Fable Page. They're a fellow curse-breaker. I have to take this. Lesson over for now." She hopped off the desk, hips swinging as she walked back to her office. She answered the call. "To what do I owe the pleasure, Fable? Need me to swoop in and save the day?" She cackled at whatever the response was before closing the door.

Suddenly, I was alone in the office again, except for Herb, who stood creepily in the corner with his spindly arms crossed, obviously annoyed at my presence. At least the welcome mat had only swatted at me as I entered this morning and didn't actively try to vault me into the wall again. My nose was still tender and a little swollen, but luckily the bruising was minimal. With Antonia busy and with the computer doing its thing, I propped my backpack between my feet, unzipped it, and reached in.

I had wrapped the Spell Binder in a soft hoodie to protect it and placed it in my bag that morning. It was about the size of a small tablet and was an amalgamation of a few different pieces of tech, but it had morphed into something wholly different. It powered on, and immediately the light at the top glowed a bright green. The screen flickered to life, and a map of the local area came into focus, with Antonia's office right in the middle. On the screen, a thick green line pulsed right over the top and swept across town before disappearing.

I swallowed. At the apartment, the Spell Binder always showed no data, as there were no ley lines anywhere around where I lived. I knew that. Everyone in the apartment building that I had talked to confirmed the area was barren of magic, part of the appeal to some residents. But now the screen was working. Holy shit. It was actually *working*. And it made sense that Antonia's office would sit on a powerful ley line. I traced my fingers over it and with a slight touch moved the map around, but the presence of the ley line on the screen petered out. Huh. I'd have to work on that, see if I could boost how far the Spell Binder could detect the magical energy, but for now I was just ecstatic that my invention worked. Now all I had to do was confirm that the information it showed was correct.

Antonia's office door opened, and I shoved the device back into my bag.

"I have to head out," she said, shrugging into a light jacket and pulling her hair into a ponytail. "Fable needs my help with a cursed piano. It's apparently highly volatile. Heirlooms usually are if there are strong family attachments and memories."

"Um . . . Okay."

"You have my cell number. If someone calls, take down their information and call me. It shouldn't take me long to deal with this, and if you have to leave before I get back, just make sure to lock up."

"I don't have a key."

She frowned. "Key. Right. To lock the door because you can't set the wards."

I winced.

She waved away the problem. "It's fine. Just don't leave until I get back. Call me if you need me. Don't go into my office, and don't touch anything. Ever. At all. Other than the computer and the phones. Got it?"

I nodded. I was totally going to go into her office and snoop around. There was bound to be some information on ley line locations in there.

"You know what, just . . ." She snapped her wrist and pointed two fingers across the open space to her closed office doors. A blast of light burst from her hand and slammed into the glass. A ripple of purple spread over the area, fizzling with a low hum akin to electricity, then dimming until it was no longer visible.

My jaw dropped. Well, damn.

"Removing the temptation," she said. "The ward will sting a little if you decide to test it out. I wouldn't though. Herb is here to answer the door." She smiled, all teeth, in a way that was perhaps meant to be reassuring but came off as low-key threatening. "Don't look so stressed. Nothing is going to happen while I'm gone. It's been a slow week."

"Okay." I gave her my best fake smile in return, one that didn't broadcast my disappointment at being locked away from the massive book in her office that might hold the information I needed. "I can handle it. Don't worry about me. I'm great."

She cocked her head to the side. "You're a weird kid. Just call if there's trouble."

"Got it. I'll be fine."

The cursed mat didn't move a fiber as Antonia stood on it, her high heels making dents in the fabric. "I know or I wouldn't leave." She turned and strode out, the door closing behind her.

Suddenly I was totally alone in a big office space with no clue what to do. I sat heavily in my chair and twiddled my fingers. Antonia was right. I'd be fine. All I had to do was answer the phone. What could possibly go wrong?

3

SUN

Summer was such a waste of time and effort. Spring was okay. Autumn was the best. Winter wasn't bad.

I could really do without the whole summer season, though. For one, it was too hot. Especially in the city, where the asphalt baked, and the air shimmered with heat, and all of it was trapped in a suffocating concrete hellscape. It was not conducive to my aesthetic of long sleeves and jeans and dark fabric, which I was not about to abandon despite the fact that I felt positively smothered.

Sweat dripped down my spine in rivulets as I carried the box from the bus stop, and it sucked *so much* that I considered casting a spell to create my own personal rain cloud to follow me around and mist me. I didn't because I was damp enough as it was and because I didn't know the spell off the top of my head. It was clear though that I was not built for heat or the city. Because aside from the dense warmth, the city had . . . people. Which made everything infinitely worse. Too many people all packed in one place. I much preferred where Fable's cottage was located, on the very outer edge of the city, on a small lot of green acreage, with neighbors a few minutes' walk away. It was a bit of a drive from my family's home, but I dealt with it because being Fable's apprentice was worth the inconvenience.

Except for this part. Running errands and acting as a glorified gopher for a prestigious sorcerer was not what I expected when I became Fable's apprentice a few years ago, but that was what I was today. According to Fable, I wasn't experienced enough to help with the cursed piano. Even though I'd helped with worse. I was sure of it! But no, Fable called Antonia Hex for help instead and sent me with the other cursed objects to Antonia's office to drop them off for breaking or storage.

Which is why I was currently dodging people on the sidewalk while carrying a lightly warded cardboard box and sweating my ass off. I wished I'd been able to drive Fable's car, but they needed it to meet Antonia at the warehouse that had caused all this mess. Someone knocked into my shoulder and didn't even bother to apologize when I grunted and staggered.

"Watch it!" I gave them a glare from underneath my snapback, but they were already halfway down the block. I may be small, but I deserved space on the sidewalk, thanks. And if I'd dropped the box, well, that would've been bad. There was a creepy doll in there that was definitely cursed and would probably scamper off and wreak havoc if allowed. Heh. I wouldn't mind seeing that, to be honest, if said doll would exclusively terrorize jerks who ran into people on sidewalks.

By the time I'd made it to Antonia's, I had melted. Though her office wasn't as flashy as her personality, the eye-rollingly bad name of HEX-A-GONE across the door was indication enough that it was indeed hers. What an awful pun. I can't believe that she continued to operate under it. Though, anything Antonia did was automatically the talk of the community. And, well, Fable's business name wasn't much better. Fable's Curse-Breakers wasn't as creative.

If the bad pun wasn't indication enough that this was Antonia's office, the massive amount of magical power rolling off it was. It buzzed under my skin. I blinked, and my vision went black-and-white save for the thick red ley line that ran right through the building. It thumped like a heartbeat. I blinked again, and the world went back into color and the line disappeared.

Struggling with the box, I used my hip to open the door and sighed at the blissfully cool environmental controls as I stepped inside. The chilly air swept over the slick skin of my neck, and I shivered, biting my lip as I stepped over the threshold.

Despite working for Fable for a few years, I'd never met Antonia or been inside her office. I'd only seen her from a distance as she worked with Fable. Fable kept me away from her probably because Antonia was trouble and drew the ire of the Consortium more often than not. And because of what happened to her last apprentice, or what the rumors said anyway. I'd not asked Fable directly to confirm the circumstances. The rumors were enough, and I had the inkling it was a sore spot between them.

I didn't see anyone inside immediately. Just a coatrack sulking in the corner.

"Hello!" I called.

A person skittered into view, appearing absolutely flustered. He grimaced and shook his hand out with a pained hiss, as if he were a cartoon character that had just nailed their fingers with a hammer. His brown hair was tousled, and his expression was panicked and pale save for two bright-red spots on his cheeks. A purple bruise stretched across the bridge of his nose. Before he could say anything, the phone rang, and he dove into a cubicle, holding up a finger over the wall in the universal sign to wait. I sighed loudly and stood on the welcome mat, shuffling my feet.

"Thank you for calling Hex-A-Gone. How may I help you?" He reappeared, phone tucked between his ear and shoulder, brow furrowed. "Uh-huh. I'm sorry that's happening, but Antonia is not available at the moment. I can take a message and alert her that her assistance is needed right away." A pause. "Uh-huh. Well, I understand that you absolutely need hair especially for a photo shoot tomorrow. No. That wasn't sarcastic. I didn't mean it to be sarcastic. I was trying to validate you."

I snorted.

He cringed as the customer responded.

"Yes, I have your number. I'll call her right away. You want my name? To be able to complain to my boss? It's Norman. That's absolutely my name. Okay. Thank you for calling. Uh-huh. Bye."

He hung up and wilted, pressing his head into his hands. As soon as the phone clicked, it began ringing again.

"Crap," he muttered. "It'll . . . just have to ring. I guess. They can leave a message. Can I help you?"

"Your name isn't really Norman, is it?" I asked, tone a little too aggressive to be teasing, but my arms ached, and I'd carried the box all the way from the bus stop in the hellish heat. And I was tired.

He ran a hand through his hair and laughed. "Why, are you going to complain too?"

I shifted the box in my arms. "Maybe, if I don't get to set this down soon."

"Oh! Sorry. Um . . . what is it?" He walked from behind the cubicle barrier and stopped in front of me, a few feet away. He was taller than me, which annoyed me slightly, slim and classically good-looking if someone was going to notice that.

I narrowed my eyes. "Delivery of cursed objects, courtesy of Fable Page. Where can I leave them? Because this isn't getting any lighter."

"Oh, uh." His eyes darted around the room. "I don't know."

I raised an eyebrow, frowning. "You don't know? Don't you work here?"

"First day," he said. "And I'm not supposed to touch the magic stuff. I'm only office staff. Maybe Herb will know."

"Who's Herb?"

The guy, Not-Norman presumably, scratched the back of his neck and pointed to the coatrack in the corner. The coatrack shuddered, spun on its base, and hobbled away into another room.

"I don't think Herb is going to help," I said.

"Yeah, I don't think so either."

Sighing, I spied an empty desk nearby. I was sweaty and tired and frustrated with Fable and with this task and now with this clueless guy who somehow had been hired by Antonia, so I stepped off the mat and headed for the desk.

"Wait. Watch out for the—"

One second I was standing, and the next I was sprawled on the carpet, because somehow the rug had been jerked right out from under me. My chin stung with rug burn; my elbows hurt from the impact as I lay there on my stomach. The brim of my snapback jarred against the floor, causing it to flip off, and my sweaty black hair fell into my eyes. Face-planting would suck on any normal day, but I'd just done it in front of Antonia's new employee, which was so *embarrassing*. And worse, the box was on the floor, tipped over, with the contents spilled everywhere, which meant the wards were broken. Oh, that was not good, not good at all.

Most of the objects were relatively harmless, like the key chain, the bag of marbles, the jeweled letter opener, and the battered copy of an old sci-fi novel. The doll, on the other hand, rolled out with purpose.

She had a blank porcelain face with fluttery eyes, pink painted cheeks, and brown curly hair. Her dress was lacey, like a wedding dress, and she wore a wide-brimmed hat at a jaunty angle. Even if she weren't cursed, she'd be creepy as anything, but now, *now* she was dangerous as well, because she was loose.

"Oh, no, are you okay? The mat is cursed. I should've told you. It's vicious. It tripped me, and I rammed my face into the wall yesterday. Gave me a bloody nose."

There was a sound of hurried footsteps approaching, and then a grunt as the guy dropped to his knees beside me. His large hands grasped my upper arm. I shrugged him off immediately. "Don't touch me," I hissed, my eyes locked on the doll. I slapped his hands away without taking my eyes off her, because as soon as I looked away, she'd make a run for it. I'd seen horror movies. This was not my first metaphorical magical rodeo.

"Oh! Sorry. I'm so sorry."

"Don't move," I said again, voice low, as the doll slowly sat up. Her neck creaked as she turned her head to stare right at me.

"What's wrong? Are you hurt? Do you need me to call someone?"

"Will you shut up?" I bit out. "Don't fucking move, Norman. That is a *cursed* doll, and now she's free of the warded box I was carrying her in. And she's probably very unhappy at being caught in the first place and removed from her home, which she'd been haunting for the past thirty years."

He went stock-still beside me. His knees were right next to my elbow, and I saw from the corner of my eye as his hands curled into fists and pressed into his jeans-clad thighs. The doll moved again, and her eyelids fluttered as she bowed her head to glance at the letter opener, the jewels of the handle glittering in a slant of sunlight from the nearby window. Well, *shit*.

"Oh," he said, breath stuttering on an exhale. "That is so *cool*."

What? *What?* Cool? What the hell was wrong with this guy? I'd never experienced utter disbelief in my life until that very moment. I'd seen a lot of amazing things as Fable's apprentice, several of which had awed me down to my bones, but the fact that this guy was staring at a cursed doll who by all intents and purposes looked a little murderous and had a weapon within reach and thought it was *cool* triggered a feeling of overwhelming incredulity. There were many things in the magic world that were *cool*, but a cursed doll was certainly not one of them. Not even in the top ten. Ugh. I was going to die. I was going to die in front of this guy, *because of* this guy, and oh my god it was going to be much more embarrassing than nailing my chin on the floor.

The doll giggled.

My soul left my body, and my muscles locked as she lurched to her knees in horrifying stop-motion movements that looked right out of the special effects of a horror film.

"Oh, okay, maybe not so cool anymore," the guy said, his voice low and shaky.

"Yeah, no shit," I shot back.

"What do we do?"

"Get it back in the box," I answered with gritted teeth. "The box is warded."

"I actually think I know what that means."

"Good for you, genius."

"Okay, here's the plan—"

"No."

"You grab the box and—"

"What part of no don't you get?"

"And I'll—"

"It's two letters."

The doll crawled toward the letter opener and Not-Norman burst into action. "Go, now!" he yelled as he shot to his feet.

I scrambled for the box and opened the flaps wide just as he grabbed the doll by her hair and flung her into it. She slammed against the bottom, letter opener in her chubby porcelain hand, letting out a high-pitched, hair-raising shriek of indignation and evil. As soon as she cleared the lip of the cardboard, I smashed the box to the floor and crushed the flaps shut, holding them down as the box shuddered in my grasp. Thank everything that Antonia's office sat on that buzzing ley line. I reached out for it, drew the magic into me, and with a muttered spell, I reinforced the ward over the box.

The magic tingled through me, crackling like a sparkler and rushing through my hands into the established ward Fable had created earlier. I didn't know if it was necessary since the seal was intact again, but I was not taking chances with a knife-wielding murder doll. The box glowed, and the rustling slowed before finally stopping. I breathed out a relieved sigh, hanging my head, breaths coming in pants, as if I'd just run a marathon. My black hair hung around my face.

"Wow," he said. He pointed at the box. "So, she can't get out now. Right?"

"She can't. That's literally what a ward does. It either keeps something in or keeps something out."

He cast a baleful look over his shoulder, then turned back to me, smile bright. "Yeah. Anyway, that was awesome. You're awesome."

I raised my head and stared at him, incredulous. "Who *are* you?"

"Norman," he said without missing a beat.

"Yeah, right." I snatched my hat from where it had fallen, then staggered upright. My knees trembled, not so much from using magic, though it certainly did leave an aftereffect, but more from fear and adrenaline. Maybe Fable was right to leave me behind from the cursed piano this time. Though I would never admit it out loud. I leaned my shoulder against the wall, very aware of the box in front of me and the mat behind me.

"Are you okay?" he asked. "You want some water? Or coffee? I fixed the machine this morning."

I shook my head and pushed my hand through my hair, before slipping my snapback on. "I'm fine."

"Sure. You look it."

I pressed my lips together. "What the hell was that, by the way? Don't you know better than to handle a cursed object? And it had a knife."

"A letter opener. And hey, it worked out in the end." He smiled. "She's in the box and not out murdering innocent civilians. We're both alive and unharmed except for the rug burn on your face."

I self-consciously clapped my hand over my chin.

"And I got to see some cool magic on my first day. I call the whole experience a win." He smiled, wide and sunny, and a dimple appeared in his left cheek. Ugh.

"A win? We were literally just in the plot of a horror movie. Like, there are whole franchises based off murderous dolls. And also, who the hell has a cursed mat at the front of their office?"

"Antonia," he said, as if that were any explanation. And okay, it was, but come on. "And it behaves for her. I think it might be scared of her."

The mat flapped at him.

Yeah, incredulity levels through the roof. I couldn't handle it. I needed to leave before his positive outlook rubbed off on me. I pushed off from the wall. My legs shook. My heart thundered.

"Hey, you sure you're okay? Do you want to sit down?"

That was probably not a bad idea. At least it was cool in the office.

That was better than going outside and experiencing the direct sunlight, at least for a minute. "Yeah, okay."

Not-Norman—I probably should ask him his name—pulled out a chair from another desk and gestured to it. "Here. I'll get you a glass of water."

I sank into the chair and gripped the armrests.

"That *was* really awesome by the way," he called as he went into the room where Herb had retreated. "When you used the magic to reset the ward. That's what you did, right? I could see the shimmer like when Antonia did it earlier to her office door."

"She doesn't trust you in her office?" I asked, which was probably a rude question. I should've accepted the compliment first. Admittedly, my social skills were not that great, as my family and Fable liked to tell me from time to time. But he didn't seem to take offense.

He laughed sheepishly as he returned holding a bottle of water. He handed it to me, and it was cool against my sweaty palm. "No. Like I said, first day."

"Right. Office staff." I took a sip of the water. "Thanks, by the way."

He beamed. "No problem. Sorry I didn't warn you about the mat."

"You should've. It's a hazard."

The hint of a blush stained his cheeks. It was not at all endearing. "Yeah," he said, sheepish. "Anyway, who are you? Do you work for Fable? Antonia just left to go help them with a piano?"

I huffed. "It enchants people to dance themselves to death."

"Oh wow. Nice."

I raised an eyebrow. "Yeah, *nice*."

He smiled. And for some reason my lips pulled into a faint grin without my permission. I hurriedly took another sip of water and glanced away. The other objects were still scattered on the floor, and though they weren't as potentially dangerous as the doll, they could cause harm if someone without knowledge handled them. And I was certain Not-Norman didn't know what to do with them.

"Do you have another box?" I asked. "I should pick those up and ward them as well. Just until Antonia has a look at them."

"Oh, yeah. Um . . . let me find one."

He scampered away. I drank more of the water and slowly relaxed against the back of the chair. After listening to cabinets and drawers open and slam, he returned with a box that had previously housed coffee pods.

"That's . . . a lot of coffee."

He shrugged. "Antonia has a thing. She buys in bulk. Will this work?"

"It'll do."

I stood, and Not-Norman made a movement to steady me but then seemed to remember how I'd shrugged him off earlier and stopped himself.

Oh. That was . . . unexpected. And thoughtful. Usually people didn't bother to remember or respect my personal boundaries, which is why I didn't usually bother with people.

Thankfully my legs felt sturdier beneath me than they had been. I didn't have gloves with me, which Fable would berate me about when I told them later, so I pulled my shirtsleeve down over my hand into a sweater paw. He held the box steady as I lifted each object individually, carefully, and placed them in the box, until all remaining items were nestled inside. He set it on the floor next to the other, and once the top flaps were closed, I finished it off with another sealing ward. Since I had to create one from scratch, and not just bolster a ward that was already there, it took more concentration, more energy, but once the process was completed, I was proud of the job I'd done. The ward was strong, maybe stronger than what was needed, but hey, I couldn't be too careful. And maybe I wanted to show off a little.

"That was so cool," he said. "Wow."

I shrugged. "It was nothing," I said, though I inwardly congratulated myself.

"So, are you Fable's apprentice? I'm sorry, but I didn't catch your name."

"I didn't catch yours, either."

"Are you going to complain to Antonia?"

"Not this time." What was I doing? Was this teasing?

"Antonia calls me Rook."

I froze. That was weird phrasing. A specific way of saying his name. Did that mean . . . ? Did Antonia gift him a name? That was . . . that was . . . surprising. What was she up to? Was she considering . . . ? She wouldn't. She *couldn't*, as far as the rumor said. Fable needed to know about this. I needed to tell them right away.

"And you are?" he prodded. "When Antonia inevitably asks who brought the creepy doll by, what do I say? I could say 'that person who works for Fable,' but that's a little long."

"They," I said softly. "When you refer to me later, use 'they.'"

"Okay. Cool. Thanks."

The office phone rang, breaking the sudden weird tension between us. "Your phone is ringing," I said when Rook hadn't moved.

"Oh!" He blinked. "Shit." He jerked away from me, as surprised as I was at how close we were, then ran back behind the cubicle wall. He was breathless when he answered. "Thank you for calling Hex-A-Gone. How can I help you?" A pause. "Right. Hair. You need hair for tomorrow. I'm sorry. Antonia has not returned to the office, but she's aware of your situation."

She totally was not. He hadn't called her. He was a good liar.

While Rook was on the phone, I checked the boxes one last time, and satisfied with the wards, I slipped out the door and back into the heat without saying goodbye.

4

ROOK

The ward around Antonia's office did, in fact, *sting*. Not like a gentle vibration against the skin but flat-out *hurt* like being attacked by several vengeful wasps. I found that out on the first day of my employment, right before the creepy-doll delivery person arrived. I had tried to touch the door handle, and, well, that had been a mistake. After the initial throb of pain, my hand went numb for *hours*. I tried one other time with my foot when Antonia went out on a call, and, yeah, same result. Antonia was not kidding around when it came to the strength of her magic wards.

Despite my utter lack of progress toward learning more about the position of the city's ley lines, everything else was going pretty great. Two weeks into my employment, the job itself had settled to a point where nothing surprised me anymore. The incident with the creepy doll and the mysterious person who had brought it by was the peak of weird thus far. And while I didn't know their name, sometimes in the slow moments during the day, my mind drifted to them, their abrupt manner, the small pull at the corner of their mouth when I cracked a joke, the warmth of their magic, the cute shape of their nose. I'd probably never meet them again, especially since Antonia had held firm that I was office staff only, unless Fable sent them over with another cursed object that needed Antonia's expertise. Even if it meant encountering something that might want to stab me with a letter opener, I wouldn't mind seeing them again.

Nothing after that had seemed as scary or overwhelming. I'd also learned how to walk around the cursed mat to avoid any more incidents of my face becoming acquainted with the wall.

I learned about magic, even if not from Antonia herself. Mainly from the phone calls that came in each day. I'd found my groove with the customers, which allowed me to implement a few systems and processes for answering calls. Like spreadsheets and forms, which Antonia had never used before because she didn't like computers. But it was helpful to know when something was an emergency, like a hex that turned life into a scary horror movie with birds type scenario or was more routine like a jinx that made someone sneeze anytime they heard the word "cactus." Which apparently for a botanist was a real-world problem.

And in the slow hours, I tweaked the Spell Binder. I was no closer to confirming that the Spell Binder's readings were accurate, because Antonia was disappointingly consistent with warding her door, so I'd had little opportunity to snoop. However, the incident with the creepy-doll delivery person had reinforced the fact that a ley line did indeed run through Antonia's office, as they were able to create wards like Antonia. Which meant the Spell Binder was *right* about the location of that ley line. I still needed to work on other aspects of it, like strength and power radius, but I didn't yet have a plan on how. That was okay, because my hidden agenda was still hidden. And though I did harbor a little guilt for using Antonia since thus far she'd been a great boss, for the moment everything was coming up roses.

Except today, when Antonia returned unexpectedly and my

secret project that she'd probably curse me over sat conspicuously on my desk, beeping merrily as I ran a diagnostic.

"Hexes," Antonia said with jazz hands as she walked into the office, returning from field work. Her normally perfect hair looked like a nest, and she was covered in a substance that looked like mud but smelled like something entirely different. "Are a pain in my ass."

I thought she'd be out longer based on the way she'd left in a hurry, saying Fable had called and needed assistance. Now she'd returned and the Spell Binder sat on my desk, and there was no way I could subtly shove it back in my bag. That would surely draw Antonia's attention. And I did not want that. Not in the slightest.

"Oh?" I asked. "Was the hex bad?"

"Yes. And gross. Remind me to stop answering Fable's calls for the next week. Anyway, I'm going to clean up, and then we'll start your next lesson." Her gaze dropped to the Spell Binder, and her steps slowed. My breath caught. "What's that?" she asked, leaning over the screen. She reached out to tap it.

"Whoa! Hey, now," I said, snatching the Spell Binder away and tucking it close to my body. Protecting it and hiding it all in one motion. "This has taken me a lot of time and work. I'd prefer it not be fried."

She scowled. "One phone and suddenly I'm a monster."

"Three phones, a set of earbuds, a desk lamp, the coffee maker again, and a watch. Since I've worked here."

She turned up her nose. "I will not entertain slander in my own place of business."

Okay. Joking. Joking is good. Playfulness means she didn't see the ley line blinking brightly on the screen. Or if she did, didn't recognize it for what it was.

"Besides," she said, crossing her arms, "the watch was cursed." She tilted her chin toward me. "So, what is it?"

"What's what?"

"Don't play dumb. You're not good at it. What's the beeping thing?"

"Something I'm working on," I replied. "Just some tech."

"Ah, okay. Well, then." She flashed a tight smile, then walked away.

I breathed out a relieved sigh once she was back in her office. That was close. Too close. I would need to be more careful from now on, but at least this time I was in the clear.

Her office door opened. "Back here, Rook," she called. "And bring that thing you're working on."

Well, this is how I died. At the hands of the most powerful sorcerer of the last age. All for wanting to know how to access magic myself. I cast a glance at the front door, but Herb had waddled over and stood in my path. I wondered if I could take him in a fight. Except, did I really want to try to risk going out beaten by a coatrack? Oh fuck. Okay. Okay. Breathe. She obviously didn't know much about electronics. Other than how to break them. Maybe she'd buy that it was a prototype of a phone or tablet or something.

"Now, kid."

I grabbed the Spell Binder and walked to Antonia's office. She stood behind her desk. All spatters of the unknown substance were gone. Her hair was perfect. The massive spell book that resided on her desk was in front of her, opened to a page filled completely with a flowing script. Her cauldron bubbled over a hot plate on the side.

"Sit."

I plopped into the chair across from her. My pulse raced. My hands were damp. My leg jiggled. Sweat dripped down my spine, gathering at the small of my back.

"Hexes," she said slowly, "are a pain in my ass. They are more powerful than a jinx and require a higher level of skill and magic to perform. They cling to someone, and they have to be broken to dissipate. Not like a jinx, which will break on its own after a short period of time. A jinx is meant to annoy. A hex is meant to hurt."

"Okay," I said, my voice small.

She pressed her palms onto her desk on either side of the book and leaned over. "And hex is what I'm going to do to you if you don't spill right now about that little device you've been working on behind my back."

I swallowed. "Hex?"

She nodded slowly. "Oh yes. A painful one. I didn't choose this last name for nothing, you know. And before you speak, I want you to know that I'm excellent at identifying bullshit."

"It's called the Spell Binder," I blurted.

She made a truly unimpressed face. "Are you serious? I literally just said I didn't want to hear any bullshit."

"I'm not lying! That's what it's called."

"That's awful."

"Oh, and Hex-A-Gone is the pinnacle of skillful wordplay."

Her violet eyes burned. "Really? Jokes? When staring down a very pissed-off sorcerer?"

"Sorry!" I held up my hands in the universal sign of surrender.

She blew out a breath that puffed out her cheeks. "Are you ready to tell me the truth?"

I deflated like a sad balloon. Might as well face the music. At least it would relieve that pesky guilt that'd been bugging me the last few weeks. "Yeah, I am." I hung my head and pressed my fingers into my eyes. Colors burst behind my eyelids as I took a steadying breath. My heart pounded.

"Great. What does it do? Since you've kept it hidden, I'm going to guess it breaks one or more of the Consortium's rules?"

"Yeah," I said again, voice small. "It kind of does."

"It kind of does what?"

"It . . . uh . . . detects ley lines. Well, sort of. Sometimes. It's sketchy because, as you well know, magic and technology have a hard time coexisting, but I've programmed it to detect the magical energy of the lines and show them on a map so I'd know where they are. And I tried to color code it based on the energy signature, so it turns green for a robust line, yellow for a weak line, and red for a faded or dead line." I pushed my hand through my hair and met Antonia's gaze. Her violet eyes were wide. Her lips pressed into a thin line.

"It does *what?*" she said again, her tone deadly, her voice flat except for the sharp inflection on the last word.

My toes curled in my shoes. My entire soul shriveled up in my chest and tucked itself behind my ribs. "Um . . . just what I said."

"The fuck," she breathed. "So, you can use *that*"—she pointed a finger at the Spell Binder—"to see the lines? Despite not being magical."

"Yeah."

"Like actually see them like a sorcerer can?"

"Yeah." If possible, my voice got smaller.

"So if you turned that on right now, you'd see the one that runs through this building."

"Yes." Almost a whisper.

She plopped into her chair. She opened her mouth, then shut it. Her brow furrowed. She blinked several times.

And that's when I realized . . . Antonia was at a loss. She was overwhelmed. My calm, cool, capable, and frankly scary boss was . . . stunned. Stunned by something I'd created. Something I'd done. I fought back a smile at the tremendous sense of pride and accomplishment, but I couldn't help it. It bloomed across my face like a flower turning to the morning sun.

"Are you smiling?" she asked, shaking herself out of her momentary stupor. "Do I need to point out how much trouble you could bring on yourself? And me, for that matter? If I allowed the continued existence of this . . . this thing?"

And as quick as it blossomed, my smile withered. "I didn't mean to cause any harm. I just wanted . . ." I trailed off. How to explain? How to let her know that I only wanted to belong to something special again? "The only person who ever loved me was my grandmother. She was magic. I miss her. I wanted to be close to her, to be part of the community she loved. But I'm not magic. I almost contacted sketchy so-called sorcerers on the internet, but they all wanted to meet me in back alleys, and I didn't want to become someone else's cautionary tale. I can't see the lines. I can't perform a spell. I can't even feel the magic anymore like I could when I lived with her. But I know it exists. And I don't know how to live a life without it."

She stared at me with an open mouth for a second, and then her whole face scrunched. "Oh, boo-hoo. You're a manipulative little shit," she said. "Your sob story isn't going to work on me. I get it, okay. Being cut off from magic is the worst thing that can happen to a sorcerer. It's a death. No, it's worse than death. So, I can imagine how difficult it's been for you. I can even empathize. But you've been planning this since day fucking one. You were *using* me."

Right. That. She was . . . not wrong. The guilt inside me welled up into my throat. "Kind of," I said, voice going high on the last word. "I'd already developed it on my own. I was just hoping to . . . test it."

"Test it how? Is that why you touched the wards? *Twice*?"

My stomach plummeted into my shoes. "You could tell?"

Antonia rolled her eyes. "Of course I could tell."

"And you didn't say anything?" I whispered.

She shrugged. "The first time I chalked it up to curiosity. I almost fired you the second time, but I thought, what if he tripped into it or what if he was just being an impulsive teenager? So, despite my better judgment, I gave you the benefit of the doubt. Surely this kid who had tearfully begged for a job wouldn't risk it by violating my trust."

Oh. Wow. That stung worse than the wards. "What if I had touched it a third time?"

She drummed her fingers on her desk. "Remember how we started this conversation?"

I gulped. "Hexes?"

"Wow. You really are a genius."

"I'm so sorry," I breathed. "Really." I held up the Spell Binder. "I just . . . If I could show that it worked, then it could be my way back. Magic couldn't be taken from me again. I'd always know where it was."

Antonia tented her fingers. "And what would you need to test it? How would you do that?"

"Uh . . . I would need a map of the city's ley lines."

She sneered. "Like the Consortium would allow something like that to exist."

"Yeah." I scratched the back of my neck. "Then I'd need a sorcerer to confirm that what the Spell Binder was reading was accurate. That it was getting things like placement and strength correct."

She nodded. "I can't believe I'm considering it."

I clutched the Spell Binder harder in my hand. "Considering what?"

She ignored the question. "So, what else does it do?"

"Nothing yet. But I had thought about adding a spell app. You know, to have a catalog of spells. Wouldn't that be handy? To have at your fingertips? But I didn't have access to any books . . ."

"It would be handy. Better than carrying around a spell book all the time. Even the small ones are bulky. But again, kid, this goes against *everything* the Consortium allows. Everything. Non-magic folk with potential access to magic. A device that detects the ley lines. A handheld spell book. It's like their worst nightmare come true."

I gulped. "I understand."

"Which is why—"

I braced for what I knew was about to come. She'd want to destroy it. Tears pricked behind my eyes at the thought of all my hard work and my one avenue back to magic smashed to pieces. It would devastate me, much more than being cursed. At minimum, I was about to get fired. Really, that was the absolute best I could hope for.

"—we need to keep this under wraps. Understood?"

"Yes, I understand. I—wait? What?"

Antonia's shoulders were pulled back. Her fingers laced in her lap, as if she were a queen looking down on her kingdom, or the most powerful sorcerer defying the governmental organization she despised. She smirked, slowly, terrifyingly, her expression edging toward malevolence.

"Oh, come on, kid. We both know I'm not one to play by the rules. I *hate* the rules. The rules suck. I loathe when other sorcerers try to tell me what I'm allowed to do. I mean, here I am running a small curse-breaking business. I should be the most successful magic-for-hire sorcerer in the city. Better yet, I should be ruling my own country. Or the world. I could, you know. No one could stop me. They're all afraid of me. Even Fable and their little minion."

A shiver of fear lanced through me. Uh-oh. What was going on here? What had I unwittingly unleashed? Was Antonia drunk on power?

"But noooo. I'm bound by the Consortium and their"—she made air quotes again—"'rules' for the greater good. Who says I wouldn't be a fair and beloved queen?"

"Um . . ."

"Anyway, that's neither here nor there. Only a narcissist would indulge such delusions of grandeur." She laughed. "And I'm not a narcissist. Anymore. That ship sailed. And burned. These days, I'm only into"—she held up her thumb and forefinger—"tiny acts of defiance."

I cleared my throat. Utterly confused and frankly scared. "And I'm a tiny act of defiance."

"Damn right you are."

I looked down at the Spell Binder. It blinked. The thick ley line was visible on the screen in vibrant green. "Okay," I said. I swallowed. "I can be an act of defiance."

"Good. It's settled." She turned in her chair and yanked open the top drawer of her desk. The contents rattled as she searched, pulling out myriad objects, like a tiny globe, a faded figurine of a cat, a jeweled letter opener that looked suspiciously like the one the murder doll wanted to stab me with, until she found what she was looking for. "Aha!" She pulled out a small book, leather bound, about the size of a diary, and slapped it down on the desk. "For you."

"Is that a . . . ?"

"Travel spell book."

"And you want me to—"

"Read it. Use it." She winked.

"Oh, oh." I held up the Spell Binder. "Use it."

"Exactly. Only here, though. I can't let it out of my possession. It's spelled. The Consortium will know if it changes hands. And then they'll track it down and take it back."

"Nice."

"Yeah, *nice.*"

The phone rang, and Antonia shooed me away. "Go to work. And if it's Fable, tell them I'm not available."

"Right. Okay." I grabbed the book from the corner of her desk, almost knocking the cauldron off the hot plate in the process. "Thank you," I said, heartfelt and sincere.

"No problem. Now go. Phone isn't going to answer itself. Unless you have a device for that, too."

"It's called voicemail."

The look she gave me was truly exasperated. I cut my losses and ran out of the room, sliding across the floor and into my chair. I grabbed the phone. "Thank you for calling Hex-A-Gone. How can I help you today?"

5

ROOK

If there was one crucial thing I'd learned thus far while employed as a customer service agent for Hex-A-Gone, it was to keep the volume on my headphones turned low because when people called, it was usually accompanied by hysterical shrieking. Not always, mind you. Sometimes there was heavy breathing, which, creepy, and other times, dead silence, which, even creepier. Other times, a calm, collected person was on the other end who merely needed some advice on how to stop their cursed lawn chair from trying to swallow them, which somehow seemed the creepiest of the three. But 90 percent of the time, on the other end of the call was someone screaming.

This time was no different.

"Hello. Thank you for calling Hex-A-Gone. This is Rook. How can I help you today?"

A colorful expletive accompanied by shouting, then another expletive. A hair-raising screech followed by another more creative expletive. Then the problem erupted from the caller in a scream. "My daughter has a pig nose!"

Swiveling in my chair, I scooted closer to my desk and logged into my computer. "Has your daughter always had a pig nose, ma'am?"

"No! How dare you! I wouldn't be calling if this were normal!" Expletive. Shriek.

"Yes, ma'am. Thank you for clarifying." Four weeks in and I had become surprisingly adept at handling the screechy ones. "Was this an accidental cursing?"

"Yes! She's five."

"Thank you. One moment." I tapped a few keys and pulled up the accidentally cursed screening form. Which was slightly different from the purposefully cursed screening form, which was totally different from the tried-to-curse-someone-else-and-it-backfired screening form. "Is your daughter in any immediate danger?"

A pause. "She has a pig nose. A . . . a . . . snout."

"Yes. I understand. But is there a chance of imminent loss of life or permanent injury? Bleeding? Loss of limb? Anything that would require a healing tonic or an emergency department?"

A deep sigh. "No. None of that."

That was good. At least this call wouldn't be messy. Antonia would appreciate that. "Okay, ma'am. I need to gather some more information." Now that the caller had calmed marginally, I heard a distinct giggle in the background, followed by an adorable snort. I bit my lip to keep my own laughter at bay. "Okay. Can she breathe through the pig nose?"

"Yes."

"Good. Is she in any other way magically affected? Is there a curly tail? Is she turning pink? Any other signs of becoming a full pig?"

Another pause, then an angry huff. "Are you serious?"

"Yes, ma'am. Just trying to assess the situation." I clicked through the screening form, marking no for 'immediate danger of death' and 'immediate danger of causing death to others' and 'werewolf.' Which was its own column. Antonia had a thing about werewolves. "And can you explain how your daughter came to have a pig nose?"

"She was playing at her grandmother's and—"

"Is her grandmother a sorcerer?"

"No. Well, yes. She makes potions. She's my mother-in-law, so I don't know the extent of her magical ability. But look, can you help us or not? She cannot go to school tomorrow with a snout, and I can't take off work to . . . deal with this."

"Of course, ma'am. I've designated your curse as a level two incident, which means we should have someone able to come by this afternoon, within a three-hour window."

"Three hours? Three hours? Do you mean to tell me that my daughter is going to have a snout for three more hours?"

"Yes, ma'am."

"Ugh! Fine. Whatever. Just . . . get someone here as soon as possible."

"Yes, ma'am. Let me just get your address and contact information."

Antonia walked out of her office, her long dark-brown hair pulled back into a sleek ponytail, her expression like a thundercloud. Her heels added a few inches to her height, so she towered over me while I sat in my swivel chair. When she looked at me with her piercing violet eyes, she made my knees go a little weak, though I was certain I hadn't done anything to inadvertently piss her off today. It'd been a few days since our *talk*, and things had finally evened out between us. My peace offerings of coffee from her second-favorite coffee shop might have helped.

"Remember when I said the office manager was on vacation?" she asked, voice flat.

"Yes?"

"Well, it wasn't a vacation. Turns out she quit."

"How . . . ?" I said, trying to suppress a giggle. "How did that get by you? How did you not realize she quit?"

Antonia wrapped her hands around her coffee mug. It said WITCH'S BREW in fancy gold script on the side. She shrugged. "She said she needed to take some time and think about her life. I thought that meant lying on a beach in the sun with an alcoholic drink. How was I to know that translated into quitting? I mean, she did take that box of her belongings."

I ducked my head, hiding my laughter in the crook of my elbow. "Well, did you ask?"

Antonia pursed her lips. "Now, why would I pry? Ridiculous."

"Okay. Wow. Well, good thing I'm here to answer your phones. And save you from basic human interaction."

"Good thing," she agreed. "You did an excellent job keeping that mom from going full hysterical, by the way. She was almost there when she called. And over a pig nose. Can you imagine? It's not like the child is turning into an actual pig."

"That's what I said!"

She rolled her eyes. "People get worked up over the smallest things. Anyway, I guess I should do something about it. Get paid." Humming, she absently drummed her fingers on the desk. "Do you want to come with?"

I froze, unsure if I'd heard her correctly. "What?"

"Would you like to accompany me on the call? Into the field?" she clarified.

"You'd want me to come?" I did my level best to keep chill, but my voice cracked. It was . . . well, I'd been painfully obvious about my desire to join Antonia on one of her outings, but she'd been clear about my role since day one and I was positive any attempt at asking her would result in a solid no. She'd certainly not brought it up again, not even after our conversation about the Spell Binder.

My last encounter with magic, other than the simple spells she performed around the office, like conjuring a coffee stirrer, had been the day of the creepy doll and the cute person who'd brought it by, then slipped out without giving their name. And my two painful attempts at testing the wards around her office door.

She smirked, clearly reading my careful eagerness. "Sure. It'll be fun. Come out in the field with me, and we'll see how it goes."

"Are you sure? You're not, like, getting back at me for that basic human interaction comment, are you?" Antonia was mercurial on good days and downright waspish on bad. But despite my earlier missteps, she hadn't ever been intentionally mean-spirited toward me. Even when she was annoyed. And she *hadn't* hexed me over my illicit technology.

"Do you not want to join me?"

I shot to my feet. "I do. Of course I do."

"Then come on, and bring the . . . bring the thing."

"You want me to bring the Spell Binder?"

Wrinkling her nose, she set her coffee cup on the vacant desk next to mine. She leaned on the cubicle wall. "If that's what you insist on calling it."

"Hey, I don't think the person who named her magical curse-breaking business Hex-A-Gone has any room to talk."

"Touché." She walked back toward her office. "Be ready in five, Rook. We're heading out to save a little girl from a distraught mother."

I didn't have much to do to be ready to leave. I grabbed my bag, with the Spell Binder safely inside, and forwarded the office phone to Antonia's cell. Then I locked my computer. Avoiding both Herb and the cursed mat, I followed Antonia outside to her car.

I'd learned that it was in Antonia's nature to be flashy, and her gleaming red sports car was no exception. It was sleek and powerful, an exact reflection of Antonia herself. I couldn't help noticing how my ragged backpack, beat-up sneakers, and worn jeans clashed with the interior as I slid into the leather seat and carefully placed my bag between my feet. Her dark-red fingernails clicked against the steering wheel as she started the car.

"What does the"—she took a breath—"Spell Binder show right now?"

I took it out of my bag and switched it on. The light blinked green, and the map lit up with the powerful line that bisected Antonia's office.

"Interesting," she said. "Keep an eye on it as we drive. I want to see if it works."

I tried not to vibrate with excitement. Antonia was allowing me out in the field. She was letting me test out my invention. Pretty much all my dreams were coming true.

We drove through the city, bought coffee at her favorite coffee shop conglomerate, and headed to the suburbs toward the address of the little girl with the cursed pig nose. Antonia glanced at the light on the Spell Binder several times throughout the trip, her lips pressing together thinner and thinner at each reading. Her reaction didn't bode well for the Spell Binder's accuracy, and I slipped farther down into my seat with each passing minute of our drive. Defeat and dejection weighed on my shoulders.

Antonia took a sharp right turn, squinted at the Spell Binder, and hummed as the light at the top blinked a slow yellow. "Wow. That thing actually detects the lines," she said, tone slightly tinged with awe as we pulled into a gated neighborhood with extravagant houses and manicured lawns.

I sat bolt upright, spine snapping straight, all fears of failure dissipating in an instant. "What? Really? It does?"

She took a long sip of her iced caramel macchiato. "Yeah. That's really brilliant, Rook. I mean, you've proved you're smart by fixing everything I break, but this is another level altogether."

I turned my head to look out the window, beaming. I was giddy with relief and satisfaction. I felt like a flower blooming beneath the warmth of her compliments.

"Uh-oh," she said, as the GPS indicated we had arrived. She pulled along the curb, behind an old Volkswagen that was out of place in the affluent neighborhood. She set her coffee into the cup holder and sighed. Glancing at me and then the Spell Binder, she grimaced. "Better put that away for now."

My gut churned in confusion. "Why?"

"Because we have company," she said, unclicking her seat belt. "Follow my lead. Do what I say. I'll handle everything. It's your first trip in the field, so be quiet and observe. Deal?"

First trip! Potentially indicating more trips! I nodded quickly. "Deal."

She threw the car in park and stepped out. I shoved the Spell Binder into my backpack, disappointed that it wouldn't be needed. But I let those feelings surface for only a second before shoving them away. I didn't want to be left behind. I quickly zipped up my bag and tripped out of the car. Following her down the walkway that cut across the lawn, I kept half a step behind.

"Oh," a voice said. "Looks like this one has been double-booked."

I tentatively peered around Antonia's slim frame. On the sidewalk across from us stood a person wearing large glasses, curly blond hair spilling out from beneath the brim of a large, pointed hat. Next to them stood a teenager holding a bulging bag and wearing a recognizable black ball cap and a familiar attitude of exasperated displeasure.

"You!" I said, pointing at them.

"Me," they agreed with a nod. They looked much the same as they had the day we'd met. Dark clothes that covered their neck to their hands despite the heat. Their black hat. Pretty dark-brown eyes. A dour expression and a brashness that made them seem much bigger than their small frame, as if they were making up for their slight stature with pure attitude. A dour chihuahua in a room full of huskies.

At Antonia's raised eyebrow, I added, "This is creepy-doll delivery person."

"Ah, well." Antonia clapped her hands together. "Fable," she greeted pleasantly, "what the hell are you doing here?"

"We were called," the sidekick said bluntly.

Antonia smiled, all teeth. "The adults are talking, child."

They bristled. Fable gestured toward them. "Antonia, this is my apprentice, Sun. The one I told you about with the special ability. The one you've never met despite them having been my apprentice for several years." Fable said it like it was some kind of slight.

Antonia feigned a yawn. "Yes. Right. Nice to finally meet you, Sun. Maybe try not looking so sour when being introduced to your magical superiors. Next time I might think you've been cursed and try a counterspell for your personality." She wiggled her fingers.

"Antonia," Fable admonished.

"What? I'm just teasing." The thickening tension belied her statement. She slapped a hand on my shoulder, the points of her fingernails digging into my collarbone. "Anyway, this is fortuitous. You can meet *my* apprentice."

Fable's expression went utterly blank, mouth slightly dropping open. My insides mirrored them, though I valiantly kept it off my face. Because apprentice? What? I made a noise in my throat, and Antonia's grip tightened. She paused, gaze darting to me in a look that clearly conveyed "play along or die."

"This is Rook."

"Hello," I said with an awkward wave.

"Apprentice?" Sun crossed their arms. "You said you were office staff only."

I mirrored their stance, even puffed my chest out a bit, and straightened to my full height. "And you didn't even tell me your name, so we're even."

Fable narrowed their eyes. "I didn't know you'd taken an apprentice. Sun mentioned you'd given someone a name, but I wasn't sure."

"Well, I have taken an apprentice," Antonia said smoothly. "It's a recent development."

"Let me rephrase," Fable said, pink lips pulling into a deceptively sweet smile. "I wasn't sure you were allowed."

Antonia crackled with a sudden and fierce energy. "Fable," she warned. "That's dangerous territory."

Fable's eyes crinkled as they stared at me, their honeyed gaze sweeping up and down my frame. They cocked their head to the side, mouth tipping down into a curious frown. "Have you registered him at least?"

"That's between me and the Consortium. I'd advise you to keep your large hat out of it."

Fable raised their hands in a placating gesture. "Of course. I absolutely do not want to become involved in whatever you're up to, Antonia."

Antonia gave them an annoyed side-eye but nodded. "Good. Now, about this situation," she said. "I don't remember requesting your assistance on this one, Fable. Unless you don't think I can handle a little girl with a pig nose all on my own." Antonia smirked. She spread her fingers, and magic sparkled between them.

Fable crossed their arms over their frumpy sweater. "No need for theatrics."

"Theatrics? You're one to talk. I thought we stopped wearing pointed hats centuries ago. Is this work, or are you auditioning for a period movie about witch trials?"

Fable curled their lip. "Says the woman who dresses like a day-walking vampire and goes by the last name of Hex."

Okay. Wow. Not pulling any punches. I wouldn't say that Antonia dressed like a villain, because I valued my life, thank you very much, but her whole aura did scream scary lady who would stab a bitch.

Antonia scoffed. Power oozed from her. "Let's not even get into the subject of names, *Fable Page*."

I shared a look with Sun, whose eyes were as wide as my own. Good. At least I wasn't the only one who thought we might be about to witness a fight. Or would it be called a duel?

"We were called first," I blurted, my poor attempt to intervene and dispel the mounting friction. "I took the call myself."

"You gave a three-hour window," Fable answered. "Apparently that wasn't acceptable to the mother. She required a more immediate solution."

Antonia rolled her eyes. "And what? You could show up sooner, so you sniped the job? Come on, Fable. You know that's not the etiquette here."

Fable gritted their teeth. Before they could say anything, the front door opened, and a woman appeared. "It's about time," she said, taking us all in, her shrill voice unmistakable. "Which one of you is going to fix my daughter's nose?"

"I will," Fable said, stepping forward.

"Over my dead body," Antonia countered, pushing to the front. "You did call Hex-A-Gone first."

Fable curled their lip in obvious disdain. "I cannot believe you call your business that."

"With a straight face, even," Sun added under their breath.

Antonia's gaze snapped to Sun. "Watch your tongue," she said, wagging her finger, sparks flicking off the end, like a sparkler, "because it might go missing."

Sun's scowl deepened, if possible.

Antonia was taller, but Fable was broader, and it was almost comical to see them shouldering each other out of the way on the porch of the beautiful home. I stayed back, not as brave as Sun, in the face of two sorcerers with attitudes, but in the end it didn't matter who arrived first. The mother opened the door wide and ushered us all inside.

"I'm not paying you per hour for you to stand around on my lawn as a spectacle for my neighbors," she said, frazzled.

I was the last over the threshold into the magnificent entryway. The house was massive. A grand staircase led up to the next level, and a huge chandelier hovered above us. And while the other three talked with the mother, I stayed by the door, out of place in both the opulence of the home and among the three with the magical knowledge and ability.

"If it was a potion," Antonia said, voice sharp, "then we need an antidote. Not a counterspell."

Fable said something equally curt in return that I didn't understand, because my attention was caught by a giggle followed by an oink off to the side. With the four of them in deep conversation, I scooted past the knot and made my way toward the sound.

The little girl hid next to the staircase. Her brown hair was in pigtails, and she had her hands over her mouth as she laughed. And yes, she did indeed have an adorable snout.

She waved at me.

I waved back and approached her. Once close enough, I knelt to her level. "Wow," I said quietly. "That is quite the nose."

She giggled again and snorted. She pushed her finger to the center of her new nose, the pink skin dimpling beneath the tip. "Do you like it?"

"It's very cute."

"I look like my favorite cartoon."

She pointed to a sticker on the back of her hand of a cartoon pig.

"Wow, the resemblance is uncanny."

The little girl pouted, and her shoulders slumped. "Mommy doesn't like it."

"I'm sorry. But I think your mom is probably just scared."

She hummed and tapped her chin, thinking. "You're not scared," she said. "What's your name?"

"Rook," I said, parroting what Antonia called me. I'd have to ask her what the deal was with names since it seemed like an important sorcerer thing that she'd bestowed one upon me. "What's yours?"

"Zia."

She sat down on the floor and crossed her legs. Her pink designer overalls had small dirt stains on the bib and hems of her pants. A speck of dried mud dislodged from the fabric and hit the pristine floor. Then, with a quiet pop and puff of purple smoke, it vanished.

Huh. Interesting and not at all cool or disconcerting. I shifted to sit down across from her, mirroring her pose on the spelled floor. "So, Zia. Were you playing in your grandma's potions?"

She shook her head, brown hair swinging. "In her garden," she whispered. "In the stone circle."

I wasn't quite sure what that meant. Probably nothing good since, uh, pig nose. "Are you allowed to play in the stone circle?"

She bit her lip. "No," she said. "But the little blue person told me it was okay."

"Blue person?"

She nodded. "She was beautiful. With wings and sparkles. And long white glittery hair."

"Pixie," Sun said, startling me enough that I flinched. "Garden pixie."

Craning my neck, I saw Sun had walked up behind me, and they towered over where Zia and I sat, a little intimidating. Their arms were crossed, and their eyes were fixed on me. Their pink lips pressed together as they glanced at Zia, and she leaned away from them, into my side.

They turned. "Pixie magic," they yelled at the three adults.

"Pixies?" Antonia asked, hands on her hips. "Are you sure?" She leveled her gaze at me.

I did my best not to squirm. "Zia said she talked to a blue person with wings and sparkles?"

"Pixie," Fable confirmed.

"What does that mean?" the mother asked, hands twisted. "Is that different from a potion or a spell? Did a pixie hex my daughter?"

"Pixies are mischievous," Antonia said, rummaging around in Fable's open bag despite Fable's protests. "Ha!" She triumphantly yanked out a thick book and flipped through the pages. "Their magic can be stubborn to deal with, but it shouldn't last long."

"What's long?"

"A few days."

"Days!" the mom shrieked.

Antonia waved away the panic. "Yes, but we'll break it. Or at least, lessen the time. Pixies aren't malicious and usually don't mean any harm. They only want to have a bit of fun. And, ah, here it is." Antonia pointed her finger at something in the book. "This one."

Fable peered over her shoulder. "That spell requires more magic than is available here." They glanced at Sun still standing next to me. "Thoughts, apprentice?"

Sun blinked and stared off, eerily still. "There's a dead line," they said. "Very close. Another weaker one nearby, not strong, but steady." Sun shook their head as if coming out of a trance. "That's it."

Antonia pursed her lips. "Impressive, Sun. Fable mentioned you were sensitive. I'd be careful who you share that information with, however, as we all know what the Consortium does to those who are deemed exceptional. And they don't always play nice with anyone who has access to too much knowledge, especially of ley lines."

I gulped. I had no idea what Sun had done, but if Antonia was being genuine and not sarcastic, then whatever it was had to have been cool.

Sun frowned, then continued as if Antonia hadn't spoken. "If the spell pulls too much, it could deplete the nearby line. And any other spells in the house drawing from that line will most likely fail."

The mother crossed her arms and let out a high-pitched shriek. "The other spells will fail?" She looked at the floating chandelier. "That chandelier and the self-cleaning floor spell were very expensive, and I just renewed them for six months last week."

Antonia scoffed. "Do you want a clean floor or a daughter with a pig nose?"

The mother scowled. "I see how it is. This is a racket. All of you sorcerers are in league together. The Spelltorium charges me for six months, and a week later, you break their spells. Then I'll have to call them back and shell out more for a reconnection fee."

Antonia raised her eyebrow. "If you think I would *ever* work with an agency named the Spelltorium—"

"What my colleague means," Fable said, cutting Antonia off, "is that curse-breaking is a separate business than spells-for-hire. Did the sorcerer who performed those spells mention anything about the ley lines nearby?"

"I don't know," the mother said, exasperated. "All I know is that they had to consult with some agency to determine whether the magic in the area could support the spells I wanted."

"The Consortium," Antonia muttered.

"That's good," Fable said with an encouraging smile. "They followed protocol to ensure that the magic was not overtaxed."

The mother crossed her arms. "I told the Browns next door not to overuse their share with that heated pool spell. I'm going to report them to the HOA!"

Fable smiled blandly. "Well, as you choose. However, with the spells on the Consortium record, that does mean that if they fail after we fix your daughter's nose, we will contact Spelltorium on your behalf and alert them to the situation."

"You can do that, Fable," Antonia said, cracking her knuckles. "But it won't be needed. The line nearby is weak, yes. But luckily one of us here has learned how to sustain an internal reserve."

Fable huffed. "Yes. You are gifted in that regard. But we both know I'm the one with better finesse. You can't always rely on brute power."

I stood and brushed off my jeans, watching for any specs of dirt that fell to witness the magic of the spelled floor again. Unfortunately, there were none. I leaned toward Sun. "Do they always bicker like this?"

"Don't talk to me," they said back, voice low.

Wow. Nice. "Ah, so you're like that then."

"Like what?"

"A jerk."

Sun clenched their jaw. "You lied to me."

"*You* lied to *me*," I countered.

Their mouth fell open, and they spun to stare at me in surprise. "I didn't lie to you," they said, defensive, the first real bit of emotion they'd shown since they'd arrived. "How did I lie?"

"You didn't tell me your name, and you snuck out while I was on the phone."

"That's not lying."

"Not outright, but it was dishonest."

Sun scowled, eyebrows pulling together. "Whatever."

I placed a hand over my heart. "And here I thought we had shared something in those terrifying minutes when the doll was loose, holding a letter opener, because *you* dropped the box and allowed it to escape."

"I wouldn't have dropped the box if the mat hadn't tripped me."

"Maybe you should work on your environmental awareness."

A flush worked its way into the warm beige of Sun's cheeks. Their hands balled into fists. Their cute nose crinkled in embarrassment or disdain. Seeing them lose their placid and gloomy exterior was utterly delightful, and I smothered my cackle with my hand.

"Now who's the jerk," they grumbled.

"Oh, it's me. It's totally me." I grinned.

Their flush deepened. They rubbed their face with the sleeve of their sweater, as if trying to scrub off the blush. It was entirely too endearing.

"Come here, child," Antonia said, gesturing toward Zia, interrupting our verbal spar. We jumped apart, like we were caught redhanded doing something we shouldn't, though that was far from the truth.

Zia shook her head, braids flying.

"It's okay. This will only tingle."

Zia took a step back and shook her head again. "No."

"Hey," I said, crouching down. "It's okay. That's my boss. She's really nice. She just wants to fix your nose."

"She looks scary."

"Yeah, she does. They all do, don't they?" I held out my hand. "But they don't want to hurt you. Only help. Come on, we'll go together."

Zia took my hand, her little fingers wrapping around mine, and together we crossed the foyer. I made sure we were not standing directly under the chandelier, just in case. Zia shivered next to me but bravely stood in front of Antonia, her pointed chin raised, her little snout twitching.

Antonia smiled. "Don't worry. We'll fix you right up." She lifted her hand from the book, splayed her fingers, the red tips gleaming in the hovering light, and recited a series of words in a deep, clear voice.

I'd been in the presence of magic before. My grandmother's always felt like comfort, warmth, and sparkles and candy. I loved when she'd heat the house in the winter or conjure glittery butterflies for me to chase in the summer. I missed her fiercely, and the feel of her magic on my skin, in my heart.

Antonia's magic was completely different. It prickled. It made the hair rise on my arms. It was like electricity, an oncoming storm. No comfort, just power.

Zia clutched my hand. I held on just as tight as the crackle from Antonia's fingers grew, then spread. Antonia nodded at me, and I nudged Zia with my arm.

"Close your eyes."

She didn't question, just squeezed them tight. The magic shot from Antonia's hand in a flash of blue.

Zia's mother screamed.

In a second it was over. Zia blinked open her eyes and gasped, her hand flying to her face. The snout was gone, and a regular nose was in its place. She tipped her head toward me. "You were right," she said. "It didn't hurt."

I smiled, relieved. "Good. I'm glad."

"Excellent," Antonia said with a wave of her hand. "No more pig nose, and you'll notice that the chandelier is still in place, and your floor continues to gleam unnaturally. Now, let's discuss payment."

A few minutes later, I stood on the sidewalk of the nicely manicured lawn with Sun while Antonia and Fable completed their transactions. In the end, the mother forked over both of their hourly rates, the combined amount staggeringly unreal to me.

"Nice to see you again, Sun," I said, emphasis on their name. I shoved my hands in my pockets and rocked back on my heels as Sun waited next to Fable's beat-up car. The sun was blistering, but the sprinklers were turned on, watering the green grass, and the occasional mist was nice against my skin. "Maybe next time you'll wear some color."

"Not likely," Sun said, leaning on the car, arms crossed, brim of their hat pulled low. They were back to their seemingly stoic self, though I'd glimpsed the storm that brewed underneath, and I was intrigued.

"What? Are you allergic to the rainbow or something? Odd for someone named Sun." I pinched the fabric of my bright-yellow T-shirt between my fingers and flapped it for emphasis and to fan myself. It stuck to my sweaty skin.

"No. Not likely we'll meet again," Sun said. "Antonia and Fable aren't exactly friends."

"What do you mean? They seemed positively pleasant toward each other."

Sun gave a weak laugh. "Yeah, no. Fable doesn't like how Antonia flaunts her general dislike of the rules." Their gaze cut to me, piercing and meaningful.

I forced a smile. There was no way Sun could know about the Spell Binder. So what the heck did they mean? Did they mean me in general? Or the fact that I wasn't magical?

"Well, rules are made to be broken."

Sun made a face. Their whole being radiated disapproval. "Rules are created for reasons," they said, pushing off from the car, crowding into my space. They were shorter and had to tilt their head up to meet my gaze, but that didn't stop them from being slightly intimidating. My breath caught. "Maybe you should ask Antonia about her *last* apprentice."

I stiffened. The sprinkler misted across my shoulders, mixing with the sweat on the back of my neck. My mouth was suddenly dry.

"Antonia works alone," I said, though it came out soft and unsure.

"She does now. Well, she did." Sun's eyes narrowed. "Until *you*." They licked their lips, and I did not drop my gaze to stare at them. Did *not*. "I'd wonder why that was if I were you."

"I'm not you," I snapped, taking a step back, creating distance between us. "Which I'm glad for, because you seem to be allergic to color, so I couldn't wear my favorite rainbow socks, and that would be a shame. Also, I'd have to give up my personality, and whew, we both know that's my best feature."

Sun's exasperated face was a sight to behold. And it was the last thing I really wanted to see of them, so I fled as soon as I heard the front door open and close and skipped my way toward Antonia's sports car.

"A pleasure as always, Fable," Antonia said, calling over her shoulder, "but I think we should take a short break from seeing each other. You know, absence makes the heart grow fonder. It's not me; it's you. Parting will only make our reunion sweeter."

Fable crossed their arms. Their frizzy blond hair fell over their shoulder and tucked into the crook of their elbow. "Until next time, Antonia. Take care of yourself. We both know that's what you do best."

Antonia unlocked the car and dropped in. I followed and held my bag in my lap as my thoughts whirred. Antonia had taken an apprentice before. Something had happened. Antonia, though powerful, was apparently not well liked, not only by the Consortium, but by other sorcerers as well.

I felt strangely unmoored. And the realization that I didn't really know Antonia at all was like a whack to the face. I didn't like it. I didn't like that Sun knew more than I did. That maybe I'd been so worried and guilt-ridden about using Antonia for my own purposes in the beginning that I had never thought that she may be using me.

I cleared my throat. "I thought you two were friends."

Starting the car, Antonia frowned, then sighed. Her shoulders drooped. Fine lines tickled the sides of her mouth, broke into the smoothness of her brow. She pressed her forehead to the steering wheel. "We have an understanding. It doesn't make us friends." Antonia's hands trembled as she liberated her coffee from the drink holder and downed the watery dregs of what was left in the bottom of the cup.

"Uh, we can get you another one."

She shook her head. "Get the thing. Find the nearest line."

"Oh, okay." I pulled out the Spell Binder and flipped it on. I zoomed out from the map, and while the yellow line from before was still there, it didn't pick up the dead line that Sun had seen. "Um . . . we'll have to get out of this neighborhood, I think."

She nodded. "That's what I thought. There's one by my favorite coffee shop."

"I thought we hit your favorite on the way here."

"I have several favorites," she said, pulling away from the curb. "You did well, by the way. Getting the little girl to talk and tell us about the pixie was genius."

"Thanks. What is going on with you?"

"Huh? Oh, well, Fable was right. The magic from the nearby line wasn't enough to break the pixie magic and sustain the other spells. Instead of risking a shattered chandelier, I had to pull from my own reserves, and it's depleted me. That's all."

I didn't really know what that meant. Something about how Antonia was different, special, could store magical energy while others had to rely on the lines. "Oh. Okay. Sure."

Antonia's side-eye was sharp. "What did Sun say to you?"

"Nothing," I said too quickly to be nonchalant. "Nothing. They're kind of a jerk."

Antonia's flat expression told me she did not believe me in the slightest, but she didn't press. Her hands were white-knuckled on the wheel as she guided the car out of the neighborhood and back toward the city. "Well, don't worry. We won't be dealing with either of them for a while. We'll stay in our lane, and they can stay in theirs."

"Theirs is the slow lane, am I right?" I said with a forced laugh.

Antonia's mouth quirked into a smile. "The slowest."

I had so many questions. Why did Antonia gift me with a name? What did Sun mean about Antonia's last apprentice? What had I gotten myself into?

Antonia switched on the radio and murmured along to a song and offered to treat me to a coffee. And despite whatever was going on, whatever was wrong, I didn't really care. Because I was near magic again. I clutched the Spell Binder in my hand. And it didn't matter what Sun said. I wasn't giving any of it up.

6

SUN

"Once it's boiling, pour a drop of toad's tears in and stir vigorously with a wooden spoon," Fable advised from across the cottage. "Carefully now. Don't want to spoil the batch."

I checked the cauldron that hung on the spit over the fire. The potion bubbled thickly, the consistency of mud but the color of grape soda. The vial of toad's tears sat in the wooden rack on the shelf next to the stand where Fable's massive spell book resided. I plucked it from the rack and picked up a wooden spoon from the table. Pouring a single drop of anything was difficult, but toad's tears were thinner than water, and especially rare. I'd hate to waste it and make a mistake, so I went with a work-around. Using an eye dropper and a steady hand, I slowly placed exactly one drop of the tears on the end of the wooden spoon. Excellent. I capped the vial, set it aside, then lowered the tip of the spoon into the pot and stirred.

The purple viscous liquid turned teal and frothy, as it was supposed to, becoming the plant growth elixir several of the local hedge witches had ordered. The heat had been brutal on their gardens. I stirred faster, wrist and arm aching as the consistency slowly turned from mud to broth, but suddenly the potion turned black as pitch, frothy and turbulent like an ocean during a storm. It surged upward in an imitation of a papier-mâché volcano, rising faster and faster. Panicked, I skittered away, yanking the spoon out as the concoction spilled over the edges of the cauldron right onto the fire. Smoke bloomed upward as the potion made contact with the flames, the fire hissing.

"Fable!" I squeaked around a cough. I flailed my arm to disperse the smoke. "It's—"

The mixture erupted. It blasted upward and hit the ceiling. I ducked but didn't escape the splatter zone unscathed as fat drops of the potion rained all over me. It was cold when it hit my cheek, despite having just been over the fire.

I stared in confused shock, arms out, covered in viscous goo. I'd watched Fable make this same potion yesterday without a problem. What had I done wrong?

Fable clucked their tongue. "Okay, so what happened?"

"I don't know. I added the toad's tears, then stirred vigorously with a wooden spoon."

Fable didn't get angry often. In fact, Fable hadn't ever really scolded me, even when I was very new and made a lot of mistakes. They didn't yell, which was great, but they did turn everything into a teaching moment, which could become annoying after a while.

"Tell me what you did," they said on a sigh.

I licked my lips. "I put one drop of toad's tears on the end of the wooden spoon and then put it into the potion and stirred vigorously."

Fable scrubbed a hand over their long, frizzy hair. It was pulled back into a braid today. "I said, 'Pour one drop of toad's tears into the potion, then stir with a wooden spoon.' Not, 'Put the toad's tears and the wooden spoon in at the same time.'"

I grimaced. "I was worried about measuring a single drop for the potion. It's difficult, and I didn't want to waste it."

"I understand. But by trying to avoid one mistake, you made another, and wasted much more than the toad's tears, including time."

A large drop fell from the ceiling and splattered at my feet. "Sorry."

"It's all right. We all make mistakes. Just try again." Fable handed me a handkerchief for my face. "At least it won't stain your clothes."

I looked down at my ripped jeans and large hoodie, all in black. I could hardly see where the droplets of the ruined potion had soaked into the fabric.

"Do you think I should wear more color?" I asked, Rook's words echoing through my head. I shouldn't think about him. It'd been three whole days, and by this point I'd have brushed off anyone else's opinions, but he . . . he had called me awesome that first time we met.

"If you want to wear more color, that would be fine," Fable said, preoccupied with their own potion.

That was not helpful. "But would I look good in more color?" I pressed as my cheeks burned. I ran a hand over the back of my neck, fingers brushing the short hair of my undercut.

"Why?" Fable turned in their chair. "Who are you trying to impress?" They raised an eyebrow.

"No one," I said too quickly to be blasé. "I mean, well, Antonia's apprentice said something, and I just . . . Should I try to be more . . . palatable? When we go on field work?"

"Is this about how he figured out the pixie magic?"

"No," I lied. The fact that he knew to approach the little girl and engage her in conversation to gain information rankled. That hadn't even crossed my mind. Communication and social awareness were my big deficits, and to see it come so easily to someone else . . . stung.

"Okay. Did he say something else to you?"

I fidgeted, twirling the wooden spoon between my fingers. "Called me a jerk," I mumbled. Which hadn't bothered me at the time because I *was* a jerk. I recognized that, but that didn't have anything to do with him. Well, it did. Kind of. Where did he get off being all personable and smiley and carefree? Like magic was a joke?

Fable huffed. "I wouldn't worry about anything he said. He's not going to last long. He's just Antonia's latest mistake."

A lump formed in my throat. I didn't like the sound of that. Yeah, he was an asshole, and he smiled way too much, and he was too tall. And he had a dimple. But . . . he didn't deserve whatever Fable alluded to.

"Is he in danger?"

Fable pressed their lips together.

"Fable? Is he?"

"I don't know. Antonia's last apprentice . . ." They trailed off. "Well, the outcome wasn't good for her, and it was Antonia's fault. Not to mention that the new one is . . . not someone the Consortium would approve of."

I furrowed my brow. "Why not?"

"You know the rules," Fable said. They stopped work and spun on their stool, leveling me with an intense stare. "Antonia has a habit of getting on the Consortium's radar and not in a good way. She's trouble. Yes, she's powerful and she's beautiful, and if she really wanted to, she could bring the entire magical world to heel. But in the end, all that power and prestige is not worth the cost. At least, not for me."

I took a breath. Worry squirmed inside my stomach. "Whatever she's doing won't affect us, will it?"

"No," Fable said, with authority. "Absolutely not. The Consortium knows I'm on their side. And in all my years, I've never put a toe out of line. Neither have any of my apprentices." That was said as a warning. As if I had any desire to break the rules. I just wanted to learn magic, have a quiet place to myself away from the chaos of my family and the world. Magic was that for me, a reprieve, and Fable's cottage, a small house on the edge of town with a crackling fireplace and a comfy couch and warmth woven into every seam was the only place I wanted to be.

Fable nodded toward the mess. "Now, clean up and try again. And if you want to wear more color, wear it. If you don't, don't. Don't worry about being palatable for other people. Be yourself, Sun, and if that's not enough or too much for someone else, that's their problem, not yours."

My shoulders relaxed. "Thanks, Fable."

"But if you want to wear color and smile more, then do it. You'd look good in dark blue if you don't want to stray too far from black."

I huffed. "Note taken."

Muttering a familiar spell, I drew magic from the ley line flowing along the brook that babbled by Fable's home. The stream disappeared into a thick forest that Fable said I was not allowed to go into alone because it was dense with magic. The line gave life to many magical things, not all of them pleasant and congenial. But the line fed Fable's cottage, and I tapped into it, used it to clean up my mess. It didn't take long until I had a liquid globe of the black potion hovering in the air. I dumped it back into the cauldron. While I was in the middle of attempting to salvage any bit of the ingredients, the phone rang.

Fable ran their business differently than Antonia. While Antonia had an office building and a call center that apparently consisted only of Rook, Fable ran everything out of their cottage. The dedicated business phone was a cell phone with a distinctive ring tone turned up all the way so we could hear it from anywhere in the house.

Fable leaned over and grabbed the phone before it vibrated off the table. "Fable's Curse-Breakers," they said. "Uh-huh. Yes. We can handle that. We'll be right over."

Fable hung up. "Come on," they said, standing and packing up their supplies. "We have a job in the city."

I kept my complaints about going to the city to myself and grabbed my bag from the kitchen chair, throwing the strap over my shoulder. At the door, I took down my snapback from the peg, slipped it on, and changed from my house slippers to my boots before rushing out behind Fable to their small car.

"What is it?" I said, sliding into the front seat. Despite my years of being Fable's apprentice, it was only in the last year that I was allowed to join them on outings. Not until I'd turned sixteen, which was a Consortium rule. My parents even had to sign a waiver just in case. But it wasn't like anything bad would happen. Fable was all about safety.

"A mouse infestation."

I wrinkled my nose. "Mice? We're pest control now?"

"Singing mice."

"Oh. That's . . . weird."

Fable grinned. "That's business."

The drive into the city took a bit, especially in Fable's run-down vehicle, which shuddered when they went too fast. I held on to the door handle with a white-knuckled grip. Fable muttered a spell, and the AC sputtered to life. I sank into the seat, grateful for the reprieve from the heat.

The apartment block was in a residential section of the city, surrounded by identical high buildings interspersed with occasional restaurants, laundromats, and gas stations. Fable pulled in front, throwing the car into park.

I groaned when I saw the familiar red car speed by and whip into a parking space a few spots down.

"Shit," Fable said, vaulting out of the car, heading to the trunk to gather their things. I followed at a more sedate pace, grumbling about the heat that assaulted me as soon as I stepped on the sidewalk.

"You," I said as Rook approached the front of the building. He wore large sunglasses and a stretched-out white T-shirt that showed too much collarbone. His jeans had tears at the knees that were probably from wear instead of a fashion choice. His smile was much too wide, and his brown hair was too tousled.

"Me," he agreed, tone light, congenial. He pointed a finger at me. "Singing mice?"

I pinched the bridge of my nose, squeezed my eyes shut because I knew how this was going to play out. "Yes."

"Huh. Us too."

"Awesome," I said, deadpan, dropping my hand and opening my eyes. And nope, he hadn't been a mirage from the city heat. He was still there. Devastating in the bright sun.

"You know," Rook said, coming closer, circling me on the sidewalk, "when I said more color, I didn't think you'd actually take my advice."

"What?" I looked down at my clothes and oh. In the muted light of Fable's cottage, my clothes had appeared to absorb the splatter from the ruined potion, but in the bright sunlight, I was spotted with stains that glimmered a deep purple in the sunlight. I was polka-dotted, from the top of my hoodie to the legs of my jeans. My insides shriveled up in absolute mortified horror, and my cheeks heated with an instant flush that I hoped would be attributed to the unrelenting sun. I closed my eyes and hid my face in my hands. "Oh no."

Rook laughed, but it wasn't unkind. "It's okay. I'm flattered you actually listened."

"I didn't listen to you," I shot back. "It was a mistake with a potion. Those happen since, you know, I work with actual magic. But as office staff, you wouldn't understand."

Rook's smile faltered. And I instantly felt horrible about it. Embarrassed and mean.

"What's going on here?" Antonia interrupted. Rook plastered a smile back on his face, but it was utterly fake, and I was terrified Antonia would notice and jinx me for being mean to her not-office-staff apprentice. "We're not going to have a problem, are we?" she continued.

Fable came up behind me and the two of them squared off in front of the building. Antonia was all glittering violet eyes, flawless brown skin, long dark-brown hair, and fitted jeans with a flowy blouse. Her fingernails were a sparkly black, like the night sky from the porch of Fable's cottage. She looked like a model. Fable looked like a sorcerer, with tangled blond hair and wearing a long-sleeve button-down with patches on their elbows and hand tattoos peeking out from their cuffs.

"We're here for apartment 5C," Fable said evenly.

"Okay. We're 7C."

"Okay, then. No trouble at all."

Antonia gave a sharp nod before turning away and entering the building. Rook followed but tossed a smile over his shoulder at me, followed by a wink.

A wink? A wink! The audacity. My stomach twisted, and I wasn't sure if it was because of the blatant taunt or the dimple. There was no way I was going to let him figure this one out before me.

Fable's hand was heavy on my shoulder, and they squeezed. "Don't let him upset you," they said. "It's not a competition."

But it was. It was definitely a competition. That wink . . . That wink made it one.

I shrugged Fable off. "Let's go," I said, stalking into the building.

The layout of the apartment complex was the same as any other. But this was one of the older ones on the block, the interior showing age with chipped paint and frayed rugs. A foyer with a tattered couch and scuffed end tables led to a set of elevators in which one was already on its way up to level seven—undoubtedly Antonia and Rook. The second one waited for us. We entered, and my skin crawled at the small space, but I stiffened my spine. I was not a fan of elevators, but I would deal because this was a job. And I was going to do well. Rook was not going to *win* this time.

I kept myself from rushing out when the elevator dinged and opened onto the fifth floor. Breathing deep and slow, I quelled my anxiety and followed Fable down the hallway to the correct door. I rapped my knuckles, and after a moment, the door to 5C opened to reveal a young woman, who sighed in relief at seeing us. She looked to be in her twenties, and though she wasn't as distressed as the pignose mother, she was clearly uneasy. She ushered us inside.

"This is my grandmother's home," she said. "And she kept hearing things, complaining about singing. We thought it was . . . well, that she might be hallucinating." The woman wrung her hands. "But then I started hearing the same singing when I would come over to visit. Our family is not magical, and we don't have much experience with magic aside from having a few friends who dabble, but we couldn't think of anything else it could be."

Fable nodded. "Where is it coming from?"

"The walls. And then we"—she swallowed—"caught one."

She held up a lidded box with air holes punched into the sides by a pencil. I peered in and saw a little gray mouse scampering around in a panic. Fable and the girl continued to talk behind me, while I pressed my ear to the box, and sure enough, the mouse sang. The sound was high-pitched and tinny, distorted in a way because mice weren't supposed to sing, but after a few seconds of straining, I could make out the lyrics. The little mouse sang about helping its best friend, Cinderella.

I straightened. "Are there any fans of fairy tales in this building?"

She crinkled her brow, thinking. "I'm not sure. Not that I know of."

"How about musicals?"

She crossed her arms and looked to the ceiling. "Above us. Musical theater major, I think. Always dancing, always playing soundtracks. It doesn't bother my grandmother that much, but when I'm here, I constantly have to use the handle of the broom to get them to turn down the music."

"Cinderella by chance?"

Her eyes widened. "Yeah. That's all it was for several months. How did you know?"

I held up the box. "Can we take this?"

"Of course."

"Thanks. We'll be back in a bit."

In the hallway, Fable took the box and held it to their ear. "What are you thinking, Sun?" they asked.

I blinked, my vision turning black-and-white, save for the strong ley line that shot upward through the middle of the building. And beyond that, the residue of little dots moving through the walls, dozens of them, possibly more. I couldn't always see when others used magic, and I was certain that the mice were not consciously pulling from the line themselves. But they'd been spelled to sing. And whoever did the spell was still funneling magic from the line through them and into the mice.

I blinked, and the world came back into color.

"We need to go one floor up."

All we needed to do was ask the sorcerer to stop the spell and the mice would go from the singing kind to the regular kind, and the upstairs neighbor wouldn't be responsible for a magic problem, just a normal infestation.

However, we weren't the only ones who had figured it out. Antonia and Rook stepped off the elevator onto the sixth floor the same time we did and stood in the hallway.

Rook startled when he saw us and shoved something away in his bag. It looked like a phone or a tablet, but whatever it was, he squirreled it away so quickly, I caught only a glimpse of a green flickering light. Flustered, he ran a hand through his hair, forgetting he had pushed his sunglasses to the crown of his head. They caught in the strands, and he cursed as he tried to untangle them while fighting with his backpack.

Antonia ignored him. Instead, she stared at us, fingers tented. "What are you doing on this floor?" she asked casually. "I thought you were 5C."

"I thought you were 7C," Fable replied smoothly.

Antonia grinned, red lips pulling over white, white teeth. "Change of venue."

Venue. Venue was a very specific word. Venue meant concert or play. They must have figured it out too.

I held up the box with the mouse. "Cinderella soundtrack?"

Antonia cackled. "The man who called us says he regularly hits the floor with his broom handle because the show tunes are so loud."

"The girl who called us said the same but with the ceiling."

Rook finally stopped struggling with his glasses and his bag, but his shirt had slid almost to his shoulder, revealing an expanse of fair skin I had no interest in whatsoever.

"My bet is on an amateur theater director," Rook said, finally adjusting his collar, saving me from the moment of stress I was absolutely not having.

As a group, we turned and headed down the hallway. Rook stayed back, allowed Antonia and Fable to walk ahead and bicker in front of us, and slid into step at my side.

"What's in the box?" he asked, tilting his chin toward me.

"A mouse who wants to help his Cinderella."

"Wow. That's—"

"If you say 'cool . . .'"

He smiled and rubbed the back of his neck, almost sheepish. "Nice," he said instead. "It's nice that the mouse wants to help out. Usually, they're pests, but at least this little guy wants to pull his weight, assist with chores, sew buttons, or wash dishes. Whatever mouse friends do."

"You're weird."

"Says the kid in purple polka dots."

I shot him a narrow-eyed stare. How could someone be so exasperating? Literally the most annoying person on the planet?

"How has Antonia not cursed you yet?"

"Just lucky, I guess," he answered. He tucked his hands into his pockets. "You know," he said slyly, "we have a lot in common."

I balked. "We do not."

He shrugged. "Okay, not a lot in common. I'm tall, and you're short. I'm extroverted. You're clearly introverted. I'm talkative, while you prefer to communicate via glower. I'm congenial, and you're a grouch."

I mustered my best withering glare. He continued unfazed.

"But we're both apprentices to powerful sorcerers and curse-breakers. We could learn from each other."

I clutched the box in my hands. I ducked my head, kept my eyes on the ugly patterned carpet leading down the hallway to the correct door. My stomach fluttered. The back of my neck itched.

"What? Are you suggesting we be friends?"

Rook laughed, loud and obnoxious, the sound akin to a hundred different kids who'd teased me throughout my life. My shoulders hunched against it.

"Don't act like it would be the worst thing ever," Rook said, nudging me gently with his elbow. "To have a friend."

"I have friends," I muttered, hoping he couldn't detect my lie. I had siblings. I had acquaintances and classmates. The kind of friends who had to invite you to their birthday party up until a certain age, then never again when the high school cliques formed. I didn't need them, though. I had Fable and magic and singing mice. "Besides, Antonia and Fable don't even like each other. They tolerate each other because it's mutually beneficial, and it's good for the city and magic users in general to have the most renowned sorcerers as a united front. But otherwise—"

"Okay," Rook said, cutting me off, raising his hands. "Wow. Okay. I get it. You don't want to be friends."

I sighed. My stomach had become a knot. My whole body was one tense line. "That's not what I said."

"Ah, okay." Rook nodded. "I know what this means. I can read between the lines. You don't want to be friends because you want to be something else."

My heart stuttered in wild panic. That was not true. Not true at all. Okay, Rook was attractive. If you got past his personality. But I did not . . . did not want . . . that was not. We'd met three times, and each time was more infuriating than the last. I was not interested. At all. No.

"What?" I asked, voice weak and breathy despite the tumult of emotions stirring beneath my breastbone.

He smiled. "Frenemies, obviously."

I clenched my teeth, biting back a wounded noise as my soul sank to the bottom of my gut. I don't know why I felt cracked open, hurt in a way I shouldn't, because what was I expecting? That after meeting me three times, all of them in less-than-ideal circumstances, he'd do anything other than what everyone had done before? He only wanted to tease me.

"Obviously," I ground out.

"See? We understand each other. We're almost frenemies already."

I had a retort on the tip of my tongue, but Antonia's fist banging against apartment 6C's door had me snapping my mouth shut and turning my attention back to the task at hand. I stepped forward, leaving Rook behind, and joined Antonia and Fable right in front of the door.

On the other side was the sound of shuffling, and then the lock turned. The door cracked open. "What?"

"Is this yours?" I asked, shoving the box with the mouse toward the small opening, interrupting whatever Antonia was about to do or say.

"What is it?"

"A singing mouse."

Dead silence followed by a soft "Oh."

The person shut the door, and the sound of a chain link being undone tinkled from the other side before the door opened again. He peeked around the frame. He appeared utterly dead on his feet. He obviously hadn't slept in days, dark circles beneath his eyes, blond hair standing up in tufts as if he'd been grabbing fistfuls in frustration. He yawned widely and absently scratched a spot below his navel.

Antonia shouldered in, not waiting for an invitation.

"What spell did you use?" she asked, flipping her hair. "So we can break it and move on with our day."

The man blinked. "Are you the Consortium?"

Antonia laughed, her hand delicately placed against the column of her throat. She shared a look with Fable, who was less than impressed. "Do we look like the Consortium?"

He scrubbed a hand over his face. "Then who are you?"

"Antonia Hex." Antonia pointed at herself, then swung her finger in Fable's direction. "Fable Page. And others," she said, waving toward Rook and myself.

"Hex?" he said. Then his eyes widened. They were bloodshot. "Oh shit," he breathed.

Antonia smiled, sharklike. "Indeed."

He groaned as he turned and shuffled his way toward his kitchenette, like it took great effort to even move. "I bought the spell off some guy in an alleyway next to the theater. He said it would help the production."

Rook looked over at me and mouthed *Bingo*. "So, you're a director of an amateur theater production of *Cinderella*?"

"No. Theater major. This is my internship. Needed a good grade to graduate." He yawned wide, jaw cracking. "Only resorted to magic because I couldn't afford to tank this last project. I'm skilled enough to power small spells, and this one wasn't that complicated."

I'd been told by my family that smug wasn't a good look for me, but I couldn't help it when I smirked back at Rook. He shrugged good-naturedly, not at all affected by my gloat.

The guy flapped the parchment in our general direction, and Fable grabbed it before Antonia could. Fable frowned as they read over the spell. "Did you read this before you recklessly cast it?"

He leaned hard on his countertop, half-asleep. "I only needed it for one performance. The one my professor attended. But after, the mice escaped, and I was too tired to track them down. It was only five of them, and it didn't work much anyway. You could barely hear them over the music."

"Uh-huh," Antonia said, peering over Fable's shoulder. "And have you ever stopped to think about why you're so tired?"

"I'm a student about to graduate. I have exams on top of performances on top of papers. I have applications and interviews and loans about to come due. I am literally an exhausted cliché." His fuzzy gaze drifted to where Rook and I stood in the shambles of his living room. "Think hard about your life choices, kids."

I shuddered.

Antonia snapped her fingers to focus his drifting attention. "Yes, well, maybe if you didn't buy a spell off a black-market magician, you wouldn't have this problem." She yanked the paper from Fable's hands and pointed. "Do you see this sentence? You didn't enchant these mice to merely sing. You've become a conduit."

The guy grimaced and rubbed his brow. "Huh?"

"You've been pulling magic from the ley line since you performed the spell," I snapped, my patience at its limit for this bumbling fool. "Magic has been funneling through you this entire time into the mice. Haven't you felt it?"

"Sorry I'm not as adept as the great Antonia Hex and her minions," he bit back but without much heat.

Fable puffed up. They opened their mouth, but Antonia cut them off with a wave of her hand.

"As if this would be my group of minions. Please." She clasped her hands together. "Anyway, what the little minion over there was trying to tell you was that your spell made you into a conduit. You might not have noticed when it was five singing mice, but now it's much more than that. They've escaped and bred. You have a full-on singing mouse infestation that is loud enough that two of your neighbors called us to fix it. Not only that, but now you have that much more magic pulling through you into them, thus sapping the precious energy you do have."

His eyes widened. "Are you telling me that the mice are the reason I've been so tired?"

"Exactly," Fable said. "You might not have felt five, but there are dozens, maybe even hundreds of magical mice living in this apartment building, and they'll only continue to spread."

"You're lucky there was a thick ley line here, too," I added. "Otherwise, you might have drained the line and then your own life force."

"Wow." He ran a hand through his greasy hair. "Damn."

"Maybe next time leave the magic to the actual sorcerers." Antonia cracked her knuckles. She shared a look with Fable. "Now, let's break this spell."

After a quick study of the black-market parchment and a peek at the spell book in Fable's bag, Antonia and Fable agreed on a correct counterspell to sever the tie. A few words later from the pair of them, and the guy was freed. Color instantly returned to his cheeks. His eyes cleared. His posture straightened from the fatigued slump. He still looked mostly awful, but at least he didn't look like he had one foot in the grave.

I held up the box to my ear, and sure enough, the tinny voice was no longer singing about sewing buttons and finding thread. Just the squeaks of a normal mouse.

"Sun," Fable said, "check the walls."

I blinked. The vertical ley line remained, taking up most of my vision, but the little flecks of power I'd seen moving in the walls were gone. I closed my eyes, reopened them, and the world reverted to color.

"It worked."

Rook looked puzzled, his head cocked to the side as he studied me. He wanted to ask me something, but he didn't, biting his lower lip as he held on tightly to the straps of his backpack.

"Great." Fable slid the parchment over to the guy, who was much more coherent now, along with a pen. "Now, write down everything about how you obtained this spell."

After, we reconvened in the hallway. Fable held the scroll rolled in her hand. "I'll report this to the Consortium, Antonia," they said, holding up the parchment. "I know you want to have as little contact with them as necessary."

Antonia huffed and placed her hands on her hips. "Was the person who contacted you magical?"

Fable blinked. "No."

"Neither was ours."

Fable furrowed their brow. "So?"

Antonia winked.

"Wait," Fable said, crinkling the scroll in their hand. "You're not suggesting—"

"I'm not suggesting anything. Except that maybe this is an instance where the Consortium doesn't need to reap the benefits of our expertise."

"Antonia," Fable said, voice low, as close to an admonishment as I'd ever heard from them.

"What? Oh, come on. We don't tell them, and they don't take a percentage for this one measly job." She thrust out her arm. "Seriously. After their cut, is the amount left over enough to even pay for the gas it took you to get here?"

My mouth dropped open when I realized what she said. "Are you saying to not report it?" I asked, scandalized. "That's against the rules."

"Hush, minion. The adults are talking."

Fable sighed. "I can't let a black-market spell slide, especially the nature of this one. You know that, Antonia. Besides, if we don't report it, we could lose our certification."

Antonia rolled her eyes. "Fine. You do you, Fable, but I'd prefer if you kept my name out of it altogether if your moral code allows." She patted Rook's shoulder, who had remained silent during the exchange. "And his, if you'd be so kind."

"I'll only give them the information they request."

"Good enough, I suppose. Rook, head on down to the car. I'll take care of payment."

He caught Antonia's keys and headed to the elevator. Fable and I followed, going down as Antonia went up. Fable stepped off on the fifth floor, instructing me to wait in the lobby as they settled with 5C.

The elevator doors closed, then shuddered as it continued down, leaving only Rook and me in the small space. I pressed back into the corner, holding the box close to my chest, keeping a tight grip on my rising anxiety.

"What are you going to do with it?" Rook asked, gesturing to the box in my hand.

"I'm going to release it in the enchanted woods by Fable's place."

"Is that humane?" He leaned on the other wall. "I mean, you're basically kidnapping the little mouse from its family."

The elevator shuddered. My mouth went dry. "No? I mean, yes. Considering the rest of the mice here will probably be exterminated. At least this one will have a chance to live."

"Good point."

There was a grinding noise, and the lights above us blinked. I closed my eyes, pressed closer into the corner, a soft gasp escaping despite my best efforts to keep it in. My skin prickled, goose bumps blooming on my arms and the back of my neck.

"Um . . . are you okay?"

"I'm fine."

"You don't look fine." The elevator rumbled again, slowed as it approached a floor, jerked to a stop. The doors didn't ding, no sound of them opening. I heaved in a stuttered breath. The elevator shook and groaned as it continued its descent. I almost dropped the mouse. My knees went weak, and I slid into a crouch.

"Oh," Rook said. "Do you want me to keep talking, or do you want me to shut up?"

I licked my dry lips. "Keep talking."

"Okay. Well, did you know that Antonia sucks at electronics? Have you seen her phone? It's basically fried. I have to fix things she's broken daily. Like the phones in the office? She's killed three since I've been there. She keeps her cauldron on a hot plate to work on potions, and there was an entire day she didn't realize it wasn't turned on. An entire day! I just had to flick a little button on the cord. Oh, and don't get me started on computers. Or the coffee maker. I've basically banned her from using it. If she wants coffee, she has to ask me, and I'll make it, because I was constantly fixing it or cleaning up exploded grinds anyway."

I peeled an eye open. "Are you serious?"

"Yep," he said, popping the *p*. "I know she gives off this scary super-competent vibe, but when it comes to things with circuits, she's pretty hopeless. Don't tell her I told you that. She'll jinx me. Or kill me."

I swallowed around the lump of fear in my throat. "Fable can't grow plants. They have a black thumb."

Rook laughed. "Really? Fable looks like someone who should have a whole house covered in weird plants and vines."

"I know, right?" I said, with a breathy giggle. "But they suck at it. Like really suck at it. They've tried to grow them since I've known them, but our own garden won't grow. Fable says it's because of the proximity to the enchanted forest. I think it's because they're so focused on other things that they forget to water the plants, and when they do remember, they drown them."

"Nice. There are a few plants in Antonia's office, but I don't know what they are or what they're used for."

The elevator slowed again.

"One more floor," Rook said. "Anyway, I still have so much to learn. I feel like I'm always behind because I'm starting so late. I mean, you're younger than me, right? I'm almost seventeen."

"Sixteen."

"Yeah, see, you're younger than me and you've already been doing this for years. And you know things, and what was that thing you did? Upstairs? That was so cool."

The elevator dinged. The doors opened, revealing the lobby. I heaved myself to my feet, staggered toward the opening, and exhaled once I was outside in the relatively open space. Now that I was safe, I registered Rook's words.

He said I was cool.

"What thing?" I asked.

"Where you could tell that the spell worked."

"Oh, I was just looking at the ley line, tracking how the power flowed. Seeing if the mice were still spelled in the walls."

"Ah, that makes sense." Rook fidgeted. "Are you feeling better?"

I cleared my throat. "Yeah. Now that I'm out of there, I am."

"Good." He toed the carpet. "You know, elevators are pretty safe. They get yearly inspections and monthly service. And even if it failed, there are brakes and access panels to climb out. Or is it not elevators specifically but small spaces in general? Did I make it worse?"

I couldn't help it. I laughed. The sudden dissipation of fear and anxiety left me giddy anyway, and I sank onto the lobby couch in a fit of helpless giggles. I set the box with the mouse beside me and pulled my knees to my chest, burying my laughs into the ripped fabric of my jeans.

"Oh, wow," Rook said, pushing a hand to his chest. "Wow. You're laughing. You laugh. You know how to laugh. Did I break you, Sun? Are you broken?"

"Jerk," I said, tipping my head back, breathing deeply, composing myself. "I know how to laugh."

"Well, I've not seen it before."

"Maybe because you're not funny."

Rook burst into laughter, surprised and delighted. "Ouch. That hurt. I'm offended," he said, though chuckling, clearly not offended at all. "I mean, that was rude. Funny but rude. Okay. I take it back. Laughing Sun is creepy. Please return to grumpy antisocial judgmental Sun, who is cold and aloof and perpetually annoyed."

I allowed the tension to bleed out of me, and I slowly relaxed my facial muscles into my normal resting bitch face. "Fine," I said, trying for monotone with a perturbed edge. I lifted my head. "I'm back."

"It scares me that you did that so quickly and effortlessly."

"What can I say? I'm a chameleon."

Rook grinned, cheek dimpling. "You'll need a bit more color for that to be true, but the polka dots are a step in the right direction."

I groaned and pulled the brim of my hat lower. "Small spaces," I said, answering Rook's earlier question. "Though elevators are their own particular brand of hell."

"Noted."

The elevator doors opened, and Antonia and Fable stepped out, their bickering echoing through the lobby and disrupting the easy banter between Rook and myself.

"Fable," Antonia said, voice sharp, threatening, "I'm asking *politely.* You said you'd stay out of it. Remember?"

"Yes. I do, but *you're* making it exceedingly difficult," Fable snapped. "Your blatant disregard for Consortium edicts is hard to ignore."

Antonia groaned dramatically. "Just for once can you not blindly follow their rules?"

"I won't lie."

"I'm not telling you to lie. I'm asking you to not bring it up."

Fable bit the inside of their cheek. "Fine. I won't offer information, but if they ask, Antonia, what am I supposed to do?"

"They won't ask. Unless they have a reason to, and I'm not giving them a reason."

Fable huffed. "When have you known the Consortium not to pry, especially when it comes to your business?"

Antonia's violet eyes glittered. Magic crackled down her fingers. "Don't cross me, Fable."

"Well, don't do anything out of line, and it won't come to that."

Antonia shot Fable one last narrow-eyed look and spun on her high heel. "Come along, Rook. Things to do, curses to break, people to save."

Rook scampered after Antonia, throwing another wink over his shoulder at me as he pushed through the doors. My cheeks absolutely did not grow warm.

Fable sighed. "Let's go." We walked outside, back into the heat, into the sunlight that sparkled off the purple dots all over me.

That last exchange bothered me, and though I didn't like to interfere when it came to Fable's relationships with other sorcerers or Consortium business, it seemed as if Antonia's and Fable's almost playful rivalry had taken a turn.

"Everything all right?" I asked, as Fable pulled out of the parking spot.

Fable ran a hand through their frizzy blond hair. "Fine. It's fine. Nothing for you to worry about."

That didn't soothe me at all. "Are you sure?"

"Yes, Sun."

We sat in silence, the air-conditioning sputtering. The mouse in the box had regained energy and scurried about, little feet scraping across the bottom.

"Fable," I asked, gathering my courage. "What did happen to Antonia's last apprentice?"

Fable exhaled, loud and long. They flexed their fingers on the steering wheel. "You know the general story, right?"

"That she tried to use magic to take over the world. And the Consortium caught her and punished her. And the rumor is that Antonia is banned from taking on another apprentice ever again."

"That's the pleasant version for the public."

My breath caught. "What? What really happened?"

Fable merged onto the highway, heading out of the city. "When she started going rogue, Antonia didn't stop her. Antonia didn't want to stop her. Antonia loved her, ignored all the warning signs of what she was doing, and then it was too late. The apprentice cursed her way through the Consortium, killing anyone who tried to stop her. Finally, Antonia intervened and caught her and handed her over."

My throat went tight. "What did the Consortium do?"

"Bound her. Cut her off from magic forever."

My mouth dropped open.

"They threatened Antonia with it as well. But most of the community stood up for Antonia, saying in the end she was the one who caught her and kept her from achieving her goal. Antonia was powerful back then, too. And no one wanted to be on her bad side. The Consortium warned her, though. She does something else, even a whisper of rebellion, and they'll do the same to her."

"Could they?"

Fable turned on the blinker and took the exit toward their cottage. "They could. If enough of them tried. Antonia is powerful but not without weakness."

"Would they try?"

"I don't know." Fable glanced at me. "Why do you ask?"

I bit my lip. "No reason. Just . . . Is she allowed to name an apprentice?"

"I'm not sure. The details of Antonia's punishment were not made public."

"Is Rook in danger?"

"That's the second time you've asked that today. I thought you didn't like him."

"I don't." I squirmed in my seat. "He's a jerk. And he teases me. But . . ." I thought about the way he'd distracted me in the elevator. He hadn't teased me then. He'd asked what I needed and followed through. His personality may be chaotic and off-putting, but he was kind. "I think . . . he may be in over his head and doesn't know it. And even if I didn't like him at all, he doesn't deserve to be hurt."

Fable hummed. They reached over and patted my hand where it rested on my knee. "If he was in trouble, Antonia is the best person to protect him."

"But what if he needs protecting from Antonia?"

Fable's eyes caught the sunlight, glinted gold, as they set their jaw. "If he needs help, we'll get the Consortium involved. Okay?"

That didn't settle my unease at all. Fable had basically admitted that the Consortium could do little to control Antonia. And I didn't think I could protect Rook from anyone, much less Antonia or the Consortium if it came to that. But that was all hypothetical. He was just an office worker that Antonia had gifted a name and called apprentice. That didn't mean anything. Even if Antonia wasn't supposed to have an apprentice, that wasn't his fault. He wouldn't be the one in trouble. And while Antonia had proved herself a wild card, she'd never been malicious.

He'd be fine.

He'd totally be fine.

It wasn't my place to intervene anyway. Right?

ROOK

"Okay, so let me clarify the situation. You believe that after your ex caught you cheating, they cursed you to be unlucky in love for the rest of your life? And that you've been unable to get a date for the last six months since the incident? Wow. Okay. And none of your previously great pickup lines have worked since? That actually sounds more like a jinx or a hex than a curse, but semantics. Uh-huh. Um . . . could it be that your ex may have told their friends, and word has gotten around that you're a cheater? No, I'm not passing judgment." I totally was. "But no, that can't be the case? Okay. Well, let me take your name and phone number, and Antonia Hex will return your call. Please note that since this does not meet emergency curse-breaker criteria, your call may be returned in twenty-four to forty-eight hours."

I took down the cheater's information in my handy-dandy non-emergent probably-just-a-jerk form. It really wasn't called that, but I was surprised at how many of Antonia's calls were people who had done something wrong and were now worried that the consequences of those decisions were magical in some way, a jinx, hex, or a curse, when in reality they were just normal consequences. Like, oh no, I'm being held accountable for my questionable actions.

The phones had been busy the past few days, which Antonia said had to do with the full moon. I hadn't been out on any calls since the singing mice, and I wondered if it was because of the little tiff that Fable and Antonia had on their way out. Antonia had been tight-lipped about what spurred it on, but I was certain it was about me. There was definitely something Antonia was not telling me about her last apprentice. And in my blind pursuit of magic for myself, I'd let it slide. And I still was letting it slide because even if I wasn't going out on calls, I was still working on the Spell Binder.

The small book of spells had almost been completely inputted into the digital database app. I only had a few more before I could work on the big spell book in Antonia's office, and the compendium would be well on its way. It wouldn't be complete, as I'd learned that different books contained different spells and were spread across the entire world of magic so no one person held all the information. It was a fail-safe, just in case, to keep the powerful from obtaining too much knowledge. So the little book only contained a few, but at least those it did have were accurate and not risky illegal spells bought from men in trench coats hanging out in shady corners of the city. Those were dangerous and could literally drain your life force, as I learned on our last outing. It was a good thing I hadn't resorted to those when I first started on my mission for magic.

Speaking of my last outing, Sun continued to amuse and surprise me. Sun had a cute nose. Sun laughed, and when they did, their eyes crinkled into crescent moons, and their giggles were a little breathy, a little husky. Cute. Just cute. And despite their overall grumpy emo aesthetic, they were adorable. I liked them. And I was happy that I'd gotten them to at least admit to being my frenemy.

Antonia breezed out of her office, holding a cup of coffee and smiling despite dealing with a hex earlier that involved a person who belched fire.

"There's a haunted house," she said, sitting primly on the edge of my desk. "Too much for just one curse-breaker to handle, so the family contacted both myself and Fable. The plan is for Fable and me to divide the objects between us, break the curses, and return whatever we deem safe back to the family."

"Sounds fun."

"Not really. Anyway, lesson three. Curses. Curses suck. They can be aimed at people or objects, unlike jinxes or hexes, which are for living beings only. Though I don't know why anyone would jinx a dog or a cat. Anyway, I digress. Curses are meant to not just hurt but damage. And they're strong. Like cursing a family line for generations. They're serious business and take a lot of power."

"Your kind of power?" I asked.

"Fable could curse you if they wanted. There are a few others out there that I wouldn't cross. But most regular magical folk can only perform a curse if there are a few of them together or they ask someone special to perform it for them."

My eyes widened. "Have you—"

"Neither here nor there," she said, brushing off my question with a wave of her hand. "Anyway, cursed objects absorb the magical energy that was channeled from the ley line and twist it. The more power that was put in, the more damage that object can do and the harder the curse is to break. And the curse can't be broken by breaking the object; it just means what's left remains cursed. So throwing it away means some unlucky person who encounters it later will feel the effects." Antonia nodded toward the welcome mat. "Of all the cursed objects I've come across, for some reason, that mat is unbreakable. I have no idea how or why or who, but at least it only likes to trip people."

"Lucky, I guess."

She nodded and took a sip of her coffee. "I'll be heading out there shortly to work with Fable and inspect that house." She reached out and booped the end of my nose. "You'll be—"

The front door opened.

We hadn't received a visitor since Sun weeks ago, so it was unusual for someone to drop by. Oh, maybe it was them! Bringing over more cursed objects! I popped my head over my cubicle wall, and my excitement vanished to find Herb bowing to a short woman with spectacles and brown hair pulled back into a severe bun. She held a clipboard in her hand, a large purse over one shoulder, and she frowned as Herb backed away slowly under her sharp-eyed stare.

"Antonia Hex, I presume," the woman said, voice clipped.

Antonia straightened, squared her shoulders, and delicately laced her fingers together in her boss woman pose. She eyed the woman as if she were an intruder, as if she were going to walk into battle. The excitement I had over the guest potentially being Sun was sucked right out of me like water down a cartoon drain, slurping noise and all.

"Depends on who is asking."

"I'm Evanna Lynne Beech, representative of the Magical Consortium, Spire City office." She tapped the badge she wore on her chest. Her credentials lit up and projected into the air, large enough for both of us to read. MAGICAL CONSORTIUM, DEPARTMENT OF REGULATIONS AND MONITORING, SPIRE CITY. REGISTERED SORCERER, GRADE FOUR.

"Grade four," Antonia said, clucking her tongue. "Sending out the bigwigs to talk to little old me."

Evanna Lynne touched the badge again, and the glowing credentials disappeared. She pulled a pen from her pocket and clicked it. "An animated inanimate object," she said, checking a box. She peered down her nose at the welcome mat, which trembled beneath her clunky heels. "Cursed object in an unsealed location." She made another check. She glanced to me, and I snapped my open mouth shut as she narrowed her eyes. "And you are?"

"Office staff," Antonia said, placing her hand on my shoulders, nails digging in. "There is no rule against having office staff. He answers my phones since I have a very reputable business, as stated by my certificate in the window. And as you well know, I'm not permitted to name an apprentice without approval from the Consortium."

My stomach dropped as Antonia confirmed what I'd feared. She wasn't allowed to have an apprentice. Why? Then . . . what was I? Why had she called me that in front of Fable and Sun? As a brag? A show of her disregard for rules? A power play?

"Of course, there is no written rule that states you cannot have office staff, but there is an understanding that you are not allowed to mentor or teach others at this time," she said, gaze dropping to where the small spell book sat among my pile of things, including the remnants of Antonia's cauldron hot plate.

Antonia snapped it up. "I was reading it before you walked in unannounced and interrupted my afternoon." She pocketed it in her purse. "Now, may I ask why the Consortium has deemed to come bother me during my very busy workday? You do realize we've just had a full moon, and things are a bit hectic."

"Investigation," she said. She rapped her pen against the clipboard multiple times. Antonia's fists clenched, and I worried that she was going to blast the representative into oblivion. "And I wouldn't have needed to make an in-person visit except that your scrying mirror appears to not be working."

Antonia smirked. "My scrying mirror met an unfortunate demise a few years ago, and I just have not had the time to replace it."

Evanna Lynne smiled tightly in return. "Well, the Consortium will supply you with another mirror. I'm sure we can find a model that will meet your needs."

Antonia hummed. "Regretfully, that one will break as well." She gestured to where I knew the ley line ran through the building. "It's something about the amount of power in this space. Consortium objects seem to break under the pressure when they're nearby."

Evanna Lynne didn't flinch at the thinly veiled threat, which was impressive because I wanted to curl into a fetal position under my desk, and I was on Antonia's good side.

"Anyway," Antonia continued, "investigation about what?"

"An alleged black-market spell that you came in contact with recently."

The air crackled. Antonia radiated anger and magic; the feel of it prickled along my skin. Evanna Lynne didn't seem to notice, or if she did, she didn't allow it to affect her demeanor at all. Herb fled for the break room. I wanted to sink into my office chair, but Antonia gripped my shoulder like a lifeline, like I was the only thing grounding her and keeping her from zapping Evanna Lynne into a puddle of goo right there on the cursed mat.

"Well, doesn't sound like Fable left you out of it," I whispered, trying to ease the tension.

Antonia's glance was like a cut from a sword, and my soul withered under its intensity. Her lips thinned as she addressed Evanna Lynne. "And who made that report?"

"Fable Page and their apprentice used a scrying mirror to contact the Consortium when they came in contact with the spell while working a case regarding singing mice. Does that situation sound familiar?"

Antonia shrugged. "I work with Fable and their minion often. Am I expected to remember every instance we come in contact?"

Evanna Lynne made a disapproving noise. She clicked her pen

again and flipped a few pages on her clipboard. "The report states that Fable Page and their apprentice met with an individual in an apartment complex who handed over the spell, saying he purchased it in an alley from an unnamed magician. Antonia Hex and her apprentice were also present and assisted in breaking the spell. The perpetrator who cast it corroborated the story. How about now?"

"Singing mice guy? Unfortunate that Sun saved him from having his life force drained."

Evanna Lynne allowed the paper to flap back into place. "So, you were there? Acting as office staff?"

My heart sank. Oh. That would've been a good instance in which to keep my mouth shut.

Antonia blew a breath out of her nose like a bull.

"Fable and I were called by different community members. We happened to run into each other there and came to the same conclusion that the gentleman—and I use the term loosely—in apartment 6C had utilized an improper spell."

"Yes. We've gathered. Which means you failed to report your earnings from the incident, failed to report the illegal spell, and failed to register your apprentice before taking him into the field. Which is highly unusual, since, as you said yourself, you are not cleared to have an apprentice."

"Office staff," I corrected, raising my finger meekly.

Evanna Lynne huffed and made another mark on her sheet.

Antonia narrowed her eyes. The pressure in the room thickened like the air before an oncoming storm. "Let's convene in my office, Evanna Lynne Beech, registered sorcerer, grade four." Antonia spread her arm. "This way if you please."

She gave a curt nod and walked to Antonia's open office.

Antonia turned on me. "Fable likely couldn't keep their mouth shut. I didn't introduce you as apprentice at mouse guy's apartment, so they obviously did when they called the Consortium. Or their sour little gremlin did. One of them. Habitual rule followers, those two."

My throat went tight at the thought. Would they do that? Would Sun do that? We'd had an understanding the last time we'd met. We'd bonded, sort of. We were frenemies.

"Oh."

"Yeah." She grabbed a pen and paper off my desk and scribbled down an address. "This is the address of the haunted house. Meet Fable there and bring whatever small objects back to the office in a warded box. Any large ones, just catalog and tag. We'll figure those out later. I've already arranged payment with the family, but they did ask for an expedited response. I don't know how long this will take, so give me a call before you return. Okay?"

I took the paper. "Are you trying to get me out of the office?"

"Yes."

I swallowed. "Oh," I repeated. "Are you sure I should leave? What if . . . ?"

Antonia snorted. "I'll be fine."

"Okay. But what about me? Should I meet with Fable alone?"

"I will deal with *them* after we get this job done. It's important and expensive, and Fable can't not take this payday. And I can't have Fable and their minion taking all the credit and the coin. Have to keep our reputation solid, especially if the Consortium is going to be bitches about every little thing I do."

Antonia dug around in her purse and pulled out her wallet. She slapped a wad of bills into my hand. "Money for transportation. Sorry. Can't trust you with the car, but call a cab or something."

"I can take the bus. I know how public transportation works."

"Then keep the money. Consider it a bonus. Now get going, office staff."

"Yes, boss."

I quickly gathered my things, including my backpack, where the Spell Binder beeped merrily and illegally, shoved Antonia's money in my pocket, and escaped the office.

I worked myself into a fit of righteous anger on the long bus ride to the supposedly haunted house. It was all so complicated. I didn't know why Antonia wasn't allowed to have an apprentice or that she wasn't even supposed to have one until a few minutes ago. I did know that the Spell Binder was very illegal, but Fable and Sun didn't even know it existed. But they did know something about Antonia that no one was telling me, and I was going to find out. Somehow. Probably not directly because I didn't want to end up hexed.

The walk to the house from the bus stop wasn't a short one, and by the time I got there, I felt thoroughly sunbaked and epically annoyed. So much that the novelty of the haunted house meeting every cliché from every horror movie I ever watched didn't draw a smile from me. The house towered over the rest on the quiet street on the outskirts of the city, like it was there first, and then a gentle family-friendly neighborhood grew around it in spite of its brooding oppressive atmosphere. The house itself sat on a weed-filled lawn surrounded by a high metal fence with decorative spikes along the upper edge and matching ornate scrolls on top of the gate. I wouldn't have been surprised if a gargoyle perched on the roof or a single thundercloud hovered over the topmost spire. That would actually be nice at this point. It would match my mood, and I wouldn't mind a little rain as a reprieve from the oppressive heat.

I checked the numbers on the mailbox, and yep, this was the place, if I had any lingering doubt. A single car sat out front, an old mom-car, definitely not Fable's clunker. Maybe one of the family members Antonia had mentioned? Oh well, if Fable wasn't there, I'd wait or head to their cottage. Antonia had written that address on the note as well, just in case. Maybe they too were waylaid by the Consortium. Serves them right for snitching.

The gate was propped open, and I slid through, following the cracked stone path up to the front steps shadowed by a large porch. The heavy front door had a menacing knocker affixed to it. Luckily, I didn't have to use it as the front door was also cracked open.

I pushed through, suppressing the shiver that crept down my spine as I crossed the threshold and called out. "Hello?"

"In here," a voice called back. It came from the room off to the right, and I followed it to find Sun standing in the middle of a mess, a den filled with different weird objects, that were scattered around in no discernible pattern at all.

"You," I said.

Sun spun on their heel and rolled their eyes. "Me," they agreed.

Yet they didn't look like their typical Sun self. At all. This Sun wore a long-sleeved white T-shirt with a stretched-out collar that hung off their sharp collarbones. This Sun was not wearing a hat, and their black sweaty hair was pushed out of their face, slicked back, revealing the undercut beneath and a pair of simple stud earrings in both ears. This Sun wore black leather gloves and tattered blue jeans with rips in the thighs and knees, and okay, what was going on? This Sun made my pulse race and my stomach swoop, and I was just not prepared for this Sun. This Sun made the anger and annoyance that I'd stoked the whole way there evaporate in the face of . . . skin.

"So," I said, my voice cracking on the vowel. Sun raised an eyebrow, and I cleared my throat. "That's your mom-car out front."

"It's literally my mom's car," Sun said, hands on their hips. They pulled their sleeve down over their hand and wiped their face with it. "There's no working air-conditioning in this house, and no one has lived here in years, so there's dust everywhere. I've sneezed like fifteen times. I hate it here."

"Huh. Well, that kind of explains why you're not wearing your customary black-on-black ensemble."

Sun frowned, looked down at themself. They brushed their gloved hands over their jeans and dust wafted in little puffs in the sunlight streaming through the small part in the heavy curtains. "It's hot. It's dusty. I am not about to experience heat exhaustion in this decrepit house dealing with objects that may or may not be cursed. Thanks." Despite their complaints, Sun shivered. "And it feels wrong. The energy is heavy and thick and it's . . . not great."

"Nice."

Sun groaned.

"What? You don't like it when I say 'cool.'"

"How about you don't say anything, then," Sun snapped.

I mimed zipping my mouth shut as I stepped farther into the room. I couldn't really blame them for being tense. The house made *me* anxious, and I could barely feel magic. The air was dense with *something*, and all my muscles bunched together in a fight-or-flight reaction.

The room was a large den with another closed door that led deeper into the house on one side and the archway I had stepped through on the other. Sun wasn't wrong. It was dusty. And dark. Several large windows were along one wall, but they all were covered by heavy brocaded curtains. Only one was cracked, and it let in a weak sliver of light. There was a chandelier attached to the ceiling, but only a few bulbs were lit with a flickering light that cast weird shadows in the corners. There was a large couch in the middle of the hardwood floor, a desk on one wall, a bookcase, a grandfather clock, a long low shelf filled with succulents and books and knickknacks like ceramic statuettes. Two of the porcelain figurines were of ladies dancing, and one of them winked at me. An intricate sword with a jeweled hilt and a crimson-stained blade was displayed over the entranceway. It was all very strange and foreboding.

Okay, so this is probably where I died. I could feel it in my bones, things watching and waiting.

"Where's Antonia?" Sun asked, pinching the bridge of their cute nose.

I did not squeak in surprise when they broke the silence, but I did almost trip my way back out of the room. If they noticed, they didn't comment, which meant they probably didn't notice, because I couldn't imagine a world in which Sun didn't comment on me almost falling on my butt.

"It's difficult to tell what's cursed and what's not in here with all this"—they waved their hands—"weirdness. And I can't break most of the curses on my own anyway."

And, oh, right. I was there instead of Antonia because Fable ratted me out. That anger I'd cultivated surged back, despite Sun's distracting self. "Hanging out with a Consortium representative, registered sorcerer fourth grade."

Sun's eyebrows shot up. "Fourth grade? You mean grade four."

"Whatever. How many grades are there even?"

"Five is the highest."

"Great. Care to explain?"

Sun furrowed their brow. "How to explain that five is greater than four? Okay, I can, but for the record, I'm in summer school for math."

"What? No. Why a Consortium official is meeting with Antonia?"

"How would I know?"

"Wait, you're in summer school for math?"

Sun glared. "What does that have to do with the Consortium?"

"I don't know!" I flailed. "You brought it up."

Sun shrugged and fiddled with the edge of a decorative pillow. "Seemed like something a frenemy would want to know."

Frenemy. We're frenemies. Subtract the enemy and we'd be

friends. Warmth suffused me, and my heart fluttered. "Yeah. Yeah, I would." Wait, no. I was meant to be mad. Not infatuated. I shook my head. "Anyway, back to the argument at hand; the Consortium rep said Fable contacted them."

"Of course Fable did. Fable told Antonia they would."

"And Antonia asked Fable to keep me out of any report they made. Thanks for that, by the way—for telling the Consortium about me. Now I might not be able to stay on as anything but office staff, which really puts a dent in my plans, so, you know, living up to that frenemy label."

Sun blinked, mouth turning down in a pretty moue. "Fable didn't mention you. Only the black-market spell. But glad you think so highly of us that you automatically assume that we would stick our noses in Antonia's business."

"How do I know you didn't? The representative knew all about the singing mice and the spell and the guy in apartment 6C."

"Because they investigated and talked to the guy in 6C, and he said that two sorcerers and their apprentices showed up."

"Antonia didn't introduce me as her apprentice."

"Well, neither did we. Maybe he assumed."

"I'm supposed to believe that? Believe you?"

Sun slammed a vase of fake flowers down onto an end table. "Fine. Believe what you want. But it's not my fault that your boss hasn't told you about her deal with the Consortium. Maybe talk to her instead of yelling at me." Sun picked up a journal, placed their palm on the cover, spread their fingers. They went still, muttered something under their breath, then tossed the journal into a large cardboard box. "Cursed."

"I'm not yelling at you."

"Literally were yelling."

I crossed my arms. "Well, fine. Where's Fable? I'll yell at them instead."

"Fable is also talking with the Consortium. And no, not about you. Despite what you think, you are not the center of the universe."

I lifted my chin. "I don't think the universe revolves around me."

"Funny because you give off that vibe."

I didn't pout. And I didn't really want to fight. And Sun's explanation did make sense. The singing mouse guy probably did just assume I was Antonia's apprentice. And it wasn't Sun's fault that Antonia had kept me in the dark.

I dropped my defensive posture and nodded toward the box. "So, what does that cursed book do anyway?"

"I don't know. It's a journal, so it could be that whatever you write comes true but not in the way you want, or that anyone's name you write in it dies or whatever memories you write down you lose."

"That is a very bleak journal."

"Well," Sun said, eyeing the box they'd thrown it in, "it's undeniably powerful. And I definitely don't want to try to find out what exactly it does."

I walked into the room, carefully stepping around a set of candlesticks that were on the floor, a rug (I'd learned my lesson about rugs, thank you very much), and a random office chair that I swore twitched when I scooted past. "What is this place, anyway?"

"Haunted," Sun said, without missing a beat. "Some powerful sorcerer went around collecting a lot of supposedly cursed things and kept them in this house, and when she died, her family inherited it and boarded it up because they sure as hell didn't want to touch any of it. Then it all sat here for years and . . . festered."

"Gross. Scary." I paused. "Cool."

Sun sighed, but their lips twitched like they were holding back a smile.

"So why would someone curse all this stuff? What's the point?"

Sun picked up a rotary phone and shuddered. They placed it in the box with the journal. "People are jerks," they said with a shrug. "If you had the power and were pissed off, why wouldn't you curse someone's phone to alter everything they said to the other person on the line? Wreak a little havoc on someone who hurt you?"

"Wow. Note to self, don't get on your bad side."

"That presumes I have a good side."

I chuckled. I did not voice that all of Sun's sides were good, especially today, because that would only add to the creepy ambience of the situation, but I definitely thought it. I must've been quiet for a beat too long because Sun stopped their inspection of the room and raised their eyebrow at me.

"Are you going to help, or are you going to watch me do all the work?"

"I'm helping," I said, though I had no idea how to contribute. I couldn't feel what Sun felt. I couldn't see the magical energy like they could. I mean, I was definitely weirded out, but that was more a general feeling of unease from the eek factor of being in what was classified as a haunted house. "Antonia told me to bring back whatever was cursed in a warded box and tag the other stuff for her for later."

"Okay." Sun pointed to the box that held the journal. "Cursed shit goes in there."

I cleared my throat. "I . . . uh . . . I don't . . ."

Sun sagged, rolled their neck backward to stare at the ceiling. "Antonia hasn't taught you how to detect curses yet. Has she?"

"No."

"Ugh. What *has* she taught you?"

"How to answer the phone and how to catalog situations into jinx, hex, and curse. And how she likes her coffee."

Sun's mouth dropped open, looking positively scandalized. "You really are office staff."

That stung. I smiled anyway, cocked my head to the side. "Would you be willing to tell that to the Consortium? Maybe they'd believe you."

"Not likely," Sun said, rolling their eyes. "Despite not teaching you anything, Antonia did gift you with a name. That's basically slapping you with a rubber stamp that says 'Hey, this kid is my apprentice.'"

"Yeah, about that," I said, scratching the back of my neck. "What exactly does that mean? Gifting a name? I've heard it alluded to, but . . ."

Sun's expression pinched. "Did Antonia not tell you?"

"Um . . . no."

"Oh. And is your family not magical? Like, is this"—Sun gestured to the shelf with the dancing ladies, who winked at them again—"all new to you?"

"My grandmother was a sorcerer, so not all new, but I've begun to realize there was a lot she didn't tell me. Is yours?"

Sun shrugged. "A little. My dad and one of my sisters can cast a few small spells. My mom knows some potions. Nothing to warrant Consortium registration or a mandatory scrying mirror. I'm the only one adept enough to land a magic apprenticeship." They said the last part with a tinge of pride.

I knotted my fingers together. Yet another hint that Antonia naming me as her apprentice was more significant than I initially understood. "That's cool. Your family must be proud of you."

Sun shrugged again, but their cheeks pinked. "Yeah. They are. Anyway, gifting names is a sorcerer thing."

"Did Fable give you your name?"

Sun nodded. "Yeah. They, of course, considered my input, and together we decided on Sun."

"And why . . . ?"

"It's . . . well . . . it's a tradition. And it protects my family since it's a pseudonym. And . . . ." Sun's voice went soft, quiet. "I like it. It fits me."

"Ah, that's . . . that's good."

"It is." Sun made a face. "Okay, well, I don't want to spend the rest of my life in here, so first things first. You should always have gloves to handle anything."

I nodded. "Gloves. Don't have them but will get them. Got it."

"Second, you know how you can sense a ley line without really seeing it? Like, it thrums in your chest, right here?" Sun pressed two fingers to their breastbone. "Like a hum? And it might be weak, but it's warm and friendly?"

I didn't. "Sure. Yeah."

"Okay, well, curses feel the opposite. They're cold. And they're outside of you, against your skin, instead of inside your chest. And they aren't friendly. And they pulse. Does that make sense?"

I licked my lips. "Not at all."

"Ugh. Sorry. I'm not good at explaining." Sun ran a hand through their hair, giving me a peek of their silver studs again and the curve of their ear. I felt like a Victorian gentleman who had just seen their first dainty ankle with the way my pulse sped up.

The problem was that Sun could be excellent at explaining. I just wouldn't know it. Because I couldn't feel the magical energy. I couldn't feel the lines. I couldn't see them. And while, yes, everything in that room was giving me major creepy vibes, that was more situational and due to the environment than the actual objects. It was disheartening in every way. And I couldn't very well pull out the Spell Binder for help, because it could only detect ley lines, not curses.

"I should go," I said, looping my fingers through my backpack straps. "I'm not going to be able to help you." I shrugged. "I'm no use here." I tried to keep the dejection out of my voice, but even the porcelain dancing ladies could hear the disappointment.

"No, wait." Sun chewed on their bottom lip. "Don't go." They blushed, kept their gaze trained elsewhere. "At least keep me company? I really don't want to be here alone." They cleared their throat. "It's spooky in here."

"You want me to stay?"

They nodded, head bobbing like it was on a string. "Yeah. Yeah, please stay."

My heart pounded. "Okay. I will."

"Thanks. I . . . uh . . . was kind of freaked out before you got here?" They said it like it was a question. "Fable gave me the key, and I actually thought about walking right back out and waiting in the car for Antonia because the energy was so dense." Sun swallowed. "It's suffocating in here," they said on a whisper, as if the very room could hear them.

I may not have magic, but I knew exactly what they meant. I shrugged off my backpack and placed it by the door. I mustered my best grin and clapped my hands together. "That's because it's so gloomy. Let's open some curtains, huh?" I crossed the room to the nearest window, grabbed the edge of the fabric, and flung the curtains wide.

"Rook! No!"

"What? They're just—"

The curtain wrapped around my wrist with bruising force, the cloth *freezing* despite being directly in the sun, its touch so cold it burned against my skin. I cried out as the vicious fabric snaked up my arm and tightened, squeezing my limb as my fingers went numb. I tugged away on instinct to no avail, wrenching my shoulder, my human strength no match for the magic. Sun scrambled from where they stood, reached out their hand for my free one, but the curtain jerked me forward into its folds. I slammed into the windowsill so hard I grunted with the force of it, my palms banging against the window, rattling it in the frame.

I didn't have a chance to recover from the collision before I was suddenly engulfed in the heavy fabric. I yelled as it twisted around my arms, my chest, my legs, encasing me in yards of ruby brocade, until I was pinned between the folds. I could barely breathe as it squeezed around my chest, and with every stuttered inhale, the fabric pressed against my lips. I froze and burned at the same time, the curse sweeping over me, down my spine, setting my nerves alight with pain.

Sun shouted, their voice muffled by the yards between us.

Sun. Don't come closer, Sun. You'll be caught too. Use magic. Call Antonia. Call Fable. Do something. Please help. Please.

I was scared to call out, lest the curtain dive into my mouth, but I whined, high-pitched, afraid, pained. Fear crawled up my throat, and I fought. I twisted and turned, trying to break free, but with each movement, I became more stuck. In each second that passed, my oxygen became increasingly scarce. I was suffocating.

I clenched my eyes shut. Tears leaked from their corners. My heart pounded in my ears. My toes tingled, and my fingers went numb. My knees gave out, and my body went slack, the curtains the only thing holding me, pressing against every inch of my frame.

My last breath was a painful wheeze.

Then I fell. Hit the ground, jarred back to consciousness as my body flopped to the floor, shoulder first.

The curtains tore. My arm was freed. And though I was sluggish, I knew to at least yank the fabric off my head. I greedily sucked in the blessed dusty haunted house air before wriggling away. When I finally raised my head, the first sight of my new life was Sun holding the gleaming, red-tipped sword, the one from above the entrance-way, hacking at the curtain with all their might like some kind of avenging angel. An angel who cursed a blue streak.

It was the best thing I'd ever seen in my entire short life.

Then I passed out.

8

SUN

What the fuck? What the fuck? What the fuck?

"What the fuck!" I yelled as I slid the office chair across the floor to under the doorway. I stepped on it, and it tried to roll out from under me, but I grabbed the doorframe to steady myself. I didn't have time. I didn't have time. Rook didn't have time.

I reached up, grasped the hilt of the sword, and yanked it off the wall, ignoring the fact that it was most definitely cursed.

Of course it was cursed. This whole monstrous house was cursed.

I jumped from the chair and ran across the room, kicking aside candlesticks and tripping on the edge of the rug. I couldn't remember a countercurse. Even if I could, I didn't know if I'd have the power to cast it. I wasn't as skilled as Fable. I wasn't as powerful as Antonia. The ley line nearby wasn't the strongest—one of the reasons why the family of the original owner had moved away and wanted to sell the house. So I did the next best thing other than magic. I found a practical solution.

Rook was somewhere in that mound of fabric, suffocating. His cries and yells had become weaker and weaker until they'd stopped altogether. And oh no, what if he was already dead? What if the curtains had killed him? My legs trembled at the thought, threatened to collapse right from under me.

Okay. No. Don't freak out. I didn't have time to panic or to overthink. I had a sword in hand. I had a plan. I needed to act.

As soon as I was close enough, an edge of the curtain whipped out to grab me, and I swung the sword to bat it away. The bloodstained blade sliced through the cloth like it was paper, and the edges of the cut burned like the end of a cigarette, curling and blackening as the embers ate through the fabric.

Wow. Okay. Go, cursed sword. Also, I made a mental note not to touch the blade when this was all said and done.

Rook was taller than me. I needed to aim high. I didn't have time to pull the couch over to stand on it, and the chair wasn't well behaved or stable enough to hold me while I swatted at angry curtains with a stained, smoking sword. I improvised by placing one foot on the high windowsill, then jumping up and pushing off to propel me higher, swinging the sword at the same time. It gave me enough leverage to swipe at the curtain a few inches below the curtain rod. The fabric sizzled and smoked where I'd sliced, and a bundle of it *thunk*ed to the floor.

I landed, slipping on stray pieces that tried to climb my legs, as I stumbled to a safe distance. I poked the scraps that clung to me with the tip of the blade, leaving smoldering holes behind as they slid off my jeans.

Rook. He was still hopelessly tangled, but the mound twitched, and a low groan emanated from the swaddle of fabric. The curtain reached for me again, but I swiped it away and more of it caught and smoked. Luckily, Rook was at least coherent enough to pull the curtain from his face and army crawl to safety. Okay, so not dead. Thank everything magic that he was not dead. Not looking great though and still in danger.

So, I hacked and hacked until the whole curtain fell to ribbons and burned into crispy wisps. I grabbed Rook's forearm with one hand and pulled him across the hardwood. There were pieces of curtain still trailing behind him, but they were small enough that I was able to kick them away into a sad, cursed pile.

Rook didn't move. He lay boneless.

I tossed the sword across the room. It clattered away, leaving scorch marks along the floor from the smoking blade.

Dropping to my knees, I rolled Rook onto his back. His face and lips were pale. Every inch of skin where the curtain had touched was either turning blue from bruises or red from the cold. I leaned closer, placing my palm on his chest and turning my cheek close to his lips and nose. His breath tickled my ear, and his heart beat beneath my palm. Oh, thank magic. I took off my glove and touched one of the red, swollen marks on his arm, and my fingertips froze.

That was a powerful curse. Stronger than the journal. Stronger than the phone.

Dizzy with relief, I rested my forehead on his collarbone and squeezed my eyes shut. I wanted to collapse next to him, but I needed to be strong, pull myself together despite being shaken to my core. Rook had taken care of me in the elevator, so I could be what he needed right now.

I took a breath, heaved myself to sitting, and sat next to him, my hand still on his chest, where I could feel the rise and fall of his breaths. I drew my knees close and kept watch as I gathered myself. My eyelashes were wet when I blinked, and I used the sleeve of my shirt to wipe them dry. My hands shook when I reached for my phone to call Fable.

"Pick up," I muttered as it rang, pleading. "Pick up. Please, Fable. Pick up." They didn't. I hung up at Fable's voicemail. "Fuck."

I didn't have Antonia's number. But I bet Rook did. If I could find his phone. I patted his pockets and, no, he didn't have it on him.

His eyelids fluttered, and I leaned back over him as they slid open. "Hey," I whispered. "Hey. You in there?"

He stared at me, eyes glazed, a little foggy, then smiled, cheek dimpling. "Your eyes are pretty."

My stomach twisted. "What?"

"Your eyes. They're very pretty. Like the night sky. Like space. But not the scary space. But the pretty one. With stars."

"Did . . . did you hit your head?"

Rook groaned, raised his hand, and pressed it to his forehead. "Probably? I don't know." He rolled to his side, propped up on one arm.

"Don't move," I scolded. There were a thousand other things I wanted to say, like, *You really scared me*, and, *I don't know what to do with all the feelings roiling in my gut*, and, *I don't normally like people, but I kind of like you*. But I didn't say those things. I couldn't say those things. "Seriously, don't move. You've knocked over a ton of shit, and I feel like we're in a minefield right now."

"Great," he wheezed before wrapping an arm around his torso and pressing his forehead to the floor. "Sounds awesome."

"Where is your phone?"

"Huh? You put it in the box."

"No. Not the evil phone. Your phone. So I can call Antonia. Fable is not picking up."

"Ah. In my bag."

I spotted his backpack by the doorway, and with the grace of a newborn fawn, I hobbled over, desperately trying to not let my own fear show. I grabbed his bag, unzipped the main pocket, and peeked inside.

"Which pocket?"

"Huh?"

"Your phone? Which pocket?" I asked, patting the bag, trying to find a hard shape that resembled a phone. Lights lit up the inside, and I moved aside a few papers and a hoodie and found a tablet. I grabbed it and stared. It was not a phone. It was . . . What the hell was it?

"No! Not that!"

Rook had pulled himself to sitting, propped against the back of the couch, one arm wrapped around his middle. Bruises blooming across his skin. Eyes bloodshot.

I held it up. "What is it?"

He gulped. Somehow looking paler than he did when he emerged from his cursed curtain cocoon. "Nothing. Just . . . put it back. Please."

I flipped the object over, inspecting it. It had a screen that flickered on, and blinking lights, and . . . wait . . . was that a map? It was, and our location flashed as a little red dot. After a few seconds, the light at the top turned a solid yellow, and a line appeared on the screen, a few blocks away, cutting through the neighborhood, just like the nearby ley line did. Huh. It followed the same path.

I froze.

That *was* the ley line.

"Sun, *please*." Rook's voice broke, and I shook myself, sliding the device back into the bag.

"Yeah. Uh. Phone?"

"Front pocket."

I felt around and retrieved it, leaving the bag with the . . . ley finder . . . in the doorway. That was a problem for another time. If there was one thing I was great at, it was compartmentalizing.

Crossing the room, I sat on the floor next to Rook and handed him the phone. "Here. Call Antonia. You need medical attention."

Rook grimaced. "I'm fine."

"You're really not. Can . . . Can I touch you?"

Rook blinked. "Um . . . yes?"

I nodded. Tentatively reached out and curled my fingers around Rook's wrist. His skin was cold against my clammy palm. I closed my eyes, breathed, and pulled from the nearby line, letting the spark of magic flow through me. Rook shivered beneath my grasp as I searched for any residuals of the curse. It was difficult, because the whole room pulsed with unnerving energy, but I focused, furrowing my brow.

"What are you doing?" he whispered.

Energy curled around Rook, and while tendrils of the curses dimmed the atmosphere, nothing malevolent clung to him.

"Checking for residual curses," I murmured. "You're fine."

"Oh."

I ran my hand through my hair, tugged on the ends, exhaling hard. The adrenaline drop left me shaky. I rubbed my hands up and down my thighs, trying to ground myself, but it was difficult with the surrounding pulse of magic that didn't want us there, and with Rook's dazed gaze locked on me, and with whatever beeped softly from Rook's bag in the doorway.

I nudged him with my elbow. "Call Antonia."

"Oh, oh yeah. I should." He clumsily opened his contacts. Antonia's name was at the top, and he pressed his thumb against the screen. It rang and rang, and when I thought it was about to go to voicemail, Antonia answered.

"Rook? Am I on speaker?" she demanded.

"Yes," I said. "This is Sun."

"Hello, Fable's minion. Why do you have Rook's phone? What is going on? Rook? Are you there?"

"You picked up," Rook said. He was still out of it, and it worried me. Should I call an ambulance? Could he die of shock? Could we both die of shock?

"Of course I did," Antonia snapped. "You're my . . . office staff," she said, avoiding the word "apprentice" because of my presence, I was sure. "And I sent you on a task. I'm going to pick up the phone when you call."

"Oh. I didn't know if you would." I startled, head snapping up. He said it so bluntly. A fact. A very sad fact.

Antonia cleared her throat on the other end. "Are you okay?"

"No," I said, cutting in. "There was an incident with cursed curtains, and Fable is not here, either, and Rook . . . He should go to the doctor or a healer. Do you know a healer? He was trapped for a while, and he passed out after I freed him. He's awake now and breathing, but he's not quite with it."

A beat of tense silence followed by the jingle of keys and the slam of a door. "I'm on my way," Antonia said. "I'll be there shortly. Don't leave. Don't leave him. . . . Have you called Fable?" Antonia sounded worried, a crack in her cool facade.

"I tried to call them, but they didn't answer."

"Try again. Tell them I'm on my way. Don't touch anything else. Can you do that, Sun?"

It was good to have an adult just tell me what to do. I didn't like being bossed around normally, but having Antonia take control of a situation that was out of my depth was nice, freeing. Like when my parents handled things for me, so I didn't have to, because I was still a teenager, and they had life experience I didn't have. Antonia doing it now allowed some of the tension to seep from my shoulders and spine.

"Yes. I can do that. Call Fable. Don't touch anything. Don't leave."

"Good. Call me if anything else happens."

"Will do, boss," Rook said, a smile tugging at the corners of his mouth. "Hey, do you think you could bring me some coffee?"

"There you are," she responded. "Good. Okay. Be there in a few minutes. Speed limits are just suggestions anyway."

Antonia hung up. I tugged my phone from where I'd shoved it in my pocket and called Fable. Rook didn't look great, but he appeared more awake, like he was coming out of anesthesia or a deep sleep.

Fable answered on the first ring. I told them the same thing I'd told Antonia, and they too were on their way within minutes. After, Rook and I sat in silence, curved toward each other, Rook's back against the couch, my feet slid slightly under, my posture bowed by fatigue. Our knees touched. Warmth radiated from that small point of contact, where my bare skin broke through the rip in my jeans to touch the outward seam of his. I tried not to focus on it—there was so much else to think about—but I couldn't. Everything around me became background noise save for that one spot of heat.

I contemplated moving to the foyer, but we were both unsteady, and where we sat was relatively safe as long as neither of us moved too far in either direction. The couch didn't give off any energy that made me think it was cursed, and if it were, it would've already tried to do something when Rook first leaned against it.

"Are you going to ask me?" Rook said, his first offered words since I'd freed him.

"About what?"

Rook gestured limply. "Pick a topic."

"Do you want me to ask?"

He shrugged. "Aren't you curious?"

"A little."

"Then ask."

"You've just been through a traumatic experience. I don't think—"

"I call it the Spell Binder," he said, cutting me off. "It detects ley lines."

My breath caught. "That's . . ." I trailed off. Amazing? Heretical? Really cool? "Against all the rules set by the—"

"I know."

Of course he knew. He was a rule-breaker. Just like Antonia. No wonder she'd taken him on as her apprentice. "Did you make it?"

Rook nodded. "I invented it."

That was incredible but also disquieting. Why would he invent such a thing? It meant access to magic for . . . everyone. It could disrupt the whole order of our world. It was trouble. "Why? Why would you do that? *How* did you do that? It's . . ." I struggled for the right words. I was angry. I was afraid. I was in a weird head space to begin with after the whole watching-Rook-be-eaten-by-curtains thing. "It's not right."

"Who says?"

"The Consortium."

"And you're going to live by their rules for the rest of your life?"

That brought me up short. I hadn't really thought about it. But what other option was there?

The door burst inward. Antonia and Fable entered like whirlwinds, power leaking off both of them as they entered the den. Fable stopped just beyond the threshold and wrinkled their nose, while Antonia marched past, intent on where we sat on the floor.

"It's *dense*," Fable said. "Why on earth would you send your green apprentice here to begin with, Antonia?"

Antonia huffed. "You said you'd be here." She dropped to her knees and took Rook's wrist in her hand. "Why did you send your minion? They wouldn't be able to break any of these curses without you."

"Because you said *you'd* be here."

"Well, I was held up in Consortium bullshit, thanks to you." Antonia's violet eyes burned. Her grip around Rook's wrist was tight, pinching his skin.

"Don't blame this one on me. I tried to warn you, but the great Antonia Hex doesn't take advice. Your bad decisions are what led to the Consortium being involved."

Antonia snarled. "My decisions are not the business of Consortium representative Evanna Lynne Beech, Department of Regulation and Monitoring, sorcerer grade four from the Spire City office."

"You know it doesn't work like that," Fable said on a sigh.

"It's how it *should* work."

"Well, whose fault is that?" Fable snapped. "Who didn't follow the rules the first time? Which led to—"

"Hey!" They both turned to me. I gestured to Rook. "Can we have this argument later, please?"

Antonia flipped her hair, still holding Rook's wrist, and nodded. "Fine." She took a steadying breath. "No residuals," she murmured.

"Sun confirmed that earlier," Rook said. His chin tilted to his chest, hair falling into his eyes. "Sun saved me. With a sword."

"You were right," Antonia said to Sun, releasing his wrist and pressing her hand to his forehead. "He's delirious."

"No! I'm not. I'm hungry and I'm tired. I'd love some coffee? But Sun really did save me. With a sword. Cut me right out of those curtains like some kind of warrior. It was"—he flashed his dimpled grin—"cool."

I ducked my head and bit back a smile.

"This sword?" Fable asked, crossing the room, and toed the sword with their boot.

"That's literally the only sword here," Antonia answered. She stood and studied the remnants of the curtain spread across the floor. They twitched toward her feebly, like charred sentient leaves on a soft wind.

I stood as well. Rook remained on the floor, legs sprawled, seemingly exhausted down to his bones, if the way his eyelids fluttered closed every few seconds was any indication.

"Antonia." Fable's voice was even but tight. Something was wrong. "Check Sun for residuals."

Antonia didn't give me a chance to protest. She grabbed my wrist, her grasp like iron around my joint, furrowing her brow. "Something is clinging to you, Sun. I bet from that sword. It's not strong, but it's there."

What? *What?* "But I'm fine. I feel fine."

"Odds are you won't shortly."

Rook scrambled to his feet, coming alive at Antonia's statement. She grabbed his biceps, steadying him. "What? Are you okay? Is Sun okay? Sun, are you okay?"

A headache bloomed behind my eyes, and my body was stiff, but those were all symptoms of a stressful situation. The fluttering in my stomach was from hunger or adrenaline and not at all because of Rook's sincere concern. I was fine. I'd be fine. I was totally fine. "I'm fine." I took a step, my vision tunneled. I went light-headed. My knees shook. And oh. Maybe I wasn't.

"Let's go, Sun." Fable was at my side in an instant. "Let's get to the cottage."

We headed for the door. Fable guiding me. Antonia keeping Rook steady on his feet. When we left the house, the door slammed behind us of its own accord, as if to say "Good riddance." The feeling was mutual.

"Are you going to be okay?" Rook asked me as I squinted against the sunlight. My head hurt. My body ached. Like I'd suddenly caught the flu and all the symptoms slammed into me at once. He pinched the fabric of my shirt between his fingers, as if he was hesitant to break my established boundary of no touching but wanted to reassure himself anyway. Or reassure me.

"Yeah. I'll be fine. Fable will take care of me."

He nodded. "They'll let Antonia know, right? That you're okay?"

"Yeah. I'll make sure. What about you? Are you going to be okay?"

Rook fiddled with the strap of his backpack. "Yeah. Yeah. I'm good." He swallowed, shifted on the doorstep as Antonia and Fable went to their respective cars. "Guess I'll see you next time?"

"Yeah, guess so."

"Okay. Until then." He nodded, then smiled, rivaling the sun. "Thanks for saving me. Take care."

My heart pounded in time with my head. I told myself it was the residual curse, but I was lying.

9

Rook

Antonia slammed a candle onto my desk, jarring me out of a session of staring off into space and thinking about Sun while waiting for the phone to ring. Antonia had heard from Fable that Sun was fine, the lingering curse had broken, and Sun spent two days in bed with the flu but was otherwise recovered and back to their sarcastic self. We hadn't talked more than that, Antonia keeping to herself since the Consortium visit, locked in her office, presumably sulking since her hand had been slapped by Evanna Lynne. I'd been worried she might fire me, especially after the haunted house incident when I was basically almost killed by home decor. But she hadn't.

The thick silver holder *thunk*ed hard next to my elbow. The candle itself was a stub, more melted wax than candle, with a short, burned wick.

"If the Consortium is going to give me shit about your existence, apprentice or not, then dammit, you're going to be my apprentice. No more of this office staff nonsense. You're going to learn."

Apparently, she hadn't been sulking. She'd been planning her next move in her own personal rebellion. I should've known.

"Am I your apprentice?"

She put her hands on her hips. "You're not magical, and I'm not allowed to have an apprentice, so, according to them, you are merely an employee of Hex-A-Gone. But we both know that's not true."

"It's not?"

"I literally just said we both know it's not true. So no. Not true. You're my apprentice."

"Okay." My brow furrowed.

"You look confused. Why are you confused?"

"I just . . . Like you said, I'm not magical. I was a liability in the haunted house. I can't make a potion or cast a spell. The only way I can see the ley lines is with technology. So, why?"

Antonia rolled her eyes. "Honestly? A number of reasons. I was tired of hearing about how great Fable's minion is, and I wanted to be able to brag myself. But also, you're smart and you work hard, and I like you. Don't make a big deal out of it."

Oh. Wow. Antonia *liked* me. That kind of was a big deal, but I did my best to temper all the warm fuzzy feelings and my massive grin. "Okay."

"Anyway, Magic Theory 101. Magic comes from the ley lines. Ancient lines of power that crisscross the globe, which have been used by sorcerers for centuries to—"

"Hate to interject, but I literally invented a device to detect them. I know what a ley line is."

Antonia narrowed her eyes. "Someone is snarky this morning. Well, do you know where they come from?"

I scratched the back of my neck. "No."

"Well, you're in good company because no one else does, either. The leading theory is that they're natural, created from a mixture of forces like gravity and the life essence of nature. We like to hope that magic is renewable and limitless. Though we know that's not necessarily true because lines can weaken or die completely. The Consortium uses that information to keep the prices to access magic at a premium. But we also know new lines appear, and dead lines have been known to revive after a period of time. No one has figured out why because outside forces, like erosion or even urban sprawl, don't seem to affect them. Case in point"—Antonia made a motion like she was plucking something from the air, and a small ball of power glowed between her fingertips—"if the concrete of this building had any bearing on the ley line, I wouldn't be able to do that."

I smirked. "Well, you would, but others wouldn't."

Antonia held the ball of magic in her palm, her expression smug. "I always knew you were smart." The ball floated upward. "Anyway, short answer, ley lines are veins of ancient power, and they're everywhere."

I cleared my throat. "I'm aware."

"Great. Gold star. A-plus student." She crossed her arms. "Sorcerers like myself see the lines. We draw power from them through us and then use it to cast spells. Spells are many and varied, almost as unique as snowflakes. Some require a quick blast of magic and are done. Curses, for example. They require a massive amount of power, but once it's set, it's set, and there is no breaking it unless—"

"Unless someone hires you."

"Exactly," Antonia said, smiling like a shark. "Other spells require a steady stream to keep working."

"Like the chandelier?"

"Right again. The floating chandelier spell required a continuous flow of magic from the ley line. If the line were to be cut, like if it lost power or if a ward was set around the home, the chandelier would fall."

I nodded. "Okay. Got it. Some spells are a one and done and other require a stream."

Antonia nodded. "Anyway, rhetoric is that those who can't see the lines can't draw from them."

I looked away, embarrassed. I stared down at my desk and the light scratches in the surface. "I'm aware of that, too."

Antonia pushed the candle into my line of sight. "Well, here's a little secret. That's not entirely true."

I snapped my head up. "What?"

Antonia tapped the ornate base of the candle. "The history of magic is long and diverse. And despite the Consortium's control over most information, they can't keep it all from us. Even the bits they really don't want someone to know."

"But you know."

She smirked. "I do. And what I know is that there are stories of folks who were deemed nonmagical, who reportedly couldn't see the ley lines, but were able to cast anyway."

I sucked in a harsh breath. "What?"

"I've never witnessed it, but I've heard stories. And all the research is under lock and key in a Consortium vault, and that tells me there has to be some truth to the rumors."

My face went hot with fury, and my throat tightened with tears. "Who . . . ?" I swallowed. "Who else would know?"

"The higher-ups certainly. The person who told me learned it from them. But regular worker bees like Evanna Lynne probably don't."

I stared at the stubby candle. It blurred as tears filled my vision. Two times in my life I'd been tested and told I didn't have the ability to access magic. One of those times resulted in being taken away from everything I'd ever known. But if it was a lie . . . then the last lonely year of my life . . . shouldn't have happened.

"Why?" I whispered.

"Control. It's all about control. And money. Which is one reason they're so concerned that someone not magical is close to me." She cleared her throat. "I've defied their expectations before, accomplished things that were impossible, and they're worried I might do it again. Just think, if you *can* learn, their whole regime would come tumbling down."

Oh wow. I hadn't thought about it like that. I'd only thought about *my* relationship with magic. All the other consequences were peripheral. But the implications of both the existence of the Spell Binder and of someone nonmagical being able to cast a spell would change the very fabric of how society viewed and interacted with magic . . . forever.

But that was apparently only one reason the Consortium was upset. Something had happened with Antonia's last apprentice that she had not told me. Sun knew. Fable knew. But I didn't, and no amount of searching online had garnered any information. I didn't even know what time period it happened in because Antonia's age was . . . uncertain. I wanted to ask. But I also didn't.

Because, despite the potential world-altering consequences, this was what I wanted. I wanted more than just to answer phones and make coffee and carry boxes of cursed items and merely know where the ley lines existed and be adjacent to magic. I wanted to *learn*. That was my original mission before Antonia crushed it the first day we met, and I had readjusted. I had *settled* for being close to magic again because I'd missed it in my very soul. But here she was, offering what I thought was impossible. There was no way I could refuse, even if I was only a pawn in Antonia's larger agenda.

I wiped away the tears that had escaped down my cheeks and steeled my resolve. "I want to learn."

She nodded sharply. "Good. Now to put theory into practice, you're going to light this candle."

"What now?"

"I chose this location for an office because of the very powerful ley line that flows right through here. There's no better place for you to try. You just have to feel it and draw from it."

I furrowed my brow. I hadn't felt anything, even the day I first walked into the building. Sun said it was a thrum under their breastbone. Warm and familiar. The only thing under my breastbone that thrummed was anxiety, like a guitar string plucked by my insecurities on the regular. That certainly was not magic.

"How do I do that?"

Antonia's expression pinched. "When you were in the haunted house, did you feel anything?"

"Creepy."

She drummed her fingernails, green today, on the sleeves of her shirt. "Go on."

I shrugged. "Just a general sense of unease since it was a weird-ass house with a lot of cursed stuff inside."

She hummed. From her crossed arms, she tilted her first two fingers toward the candle. The air prickled. It lit.

"Did you feel anything then?"

"Not really? I mean, a . . . tingle? Maybe an itch?"

An itch, she mouthed, thinking. "And when your grandmother performed magic?"

"Warmth," I said, without hesitation. "Happiness. Love. Every grandma cliché you can think of, like the smell of cookies, a blanket tucked around your shoulders, the taste of lemonade in the summer."

Antonia's expression softened.

I cleared my throat. "What do you feel when you pull from the line?"

Antonia cocked her head to the side. "It's been so long since I've thought about that. It's instinctual now. I'm always attuned and connected. Even when I'm not here, I can feel it. Like the blood pumping through my body, magic is always flowing through me."

"That's not helpful."

Her red bottom lip stuck out in a pout. "I'm trying my best here. I've never taught anyone who can't feel magic."

"Maybe I'll ask Sun," I said, idly pushing the silver holder with my fingertip. "When I see them next."

"Don't." Antonia's playfulness dropped away instantly. "Don't trust Sun. Or Fable. I know we haven't talked about the Consortium visit, but after they ratted me out over the singing mice and the black-market spell, I don't think we can trust them with your"—she glanced at my bag—"invention. Fable already knows you're not magic, and they were all over me about it earlier. Saying it was cruel to lead you along and that it was against the rules to reveal anything about magic to you."

My throat went tight. "But Sun—"

"Sun is their apprentice. Sun's loyalty is to Fable. Just like your loyalty is to me."

A chill went down my spine. "Is that the way it works?" I asked, the words falling out like bricks in the silence of the office. "You never said. You didn't even tell me the importance of gifting me a name or what it means to be an apprentice."

Antonia looked away, her jaw clenched, her profile hard, the lines around her eyes tight. "Gifting a name is a tradition in magical circles. I shouldn't have done it impulsively like I did. The thing was . . . I didn't think you'd stick around." She swiveled her gaze back to me, her violet eyes glowing, like they did in the sunlight or when she was angry. This time it was with something else other than irritation, almost like sorrow or grief. "Fixing the junk I break, answering phones, and making coffee are not the most desirable tasks for anyone, as evidenced by my last office staff up and going on a permanent vacation. But they're especially tedious for a magical apprentice. And for those in this world, my business, the things I've chosen to do, the things that have happened, have become like a joke or a meme." She spread her arms to encompass the empty office with Herb standing in the corner and the cursed mat on the floor. "The most powerful woman in the world banned from holding office in the Consortium, reduced to curse-breaking, not allowed access to spell books. Cut out of the basic parts of our culture." She sighed. "Like you were when your grandmother died."

My breath caught in my chest. Antonia saw herself in me? Is that why she let me stay? Is that why she hadn't tossed me out when she discovered the Spell Binder? Oh wow. Antonia had a heart, a soft side, a squishy interior hidden deep beneath her tough-as-nails and indifferent exterior.

She cleared her throat. "Light the candle. It's a simple cast. Doesn't even require a spell. Find the line, pull the magic through you and out of your fingers. It'll light. Once you can do that, we'll move on to something else."

"Okay," I breathed.

Her tense posture eased, her shoulders dropping to a natural position. She reached over and tousled my hair. "You're a good kid."

"Thanks."

"We'll figure this out. I only have one rule."

"What's that?"

"Don't betray me." The words hung ominous in the silence. Antonia wore no hint of a smile, no teasing exterior. Her intense eyes bored into me, and I squirmed like an ant beneath a magnifying glass. Then she smiled, all teeth. "And things will be okay."

The quick change in her demeanor left me a little breathless and a lot scared, like I'd made a deal with a demon without knowing the full terms.

She went back to her office. "Light the candle," she called over her shoulder.

Right. Yeah. Light the candle. Don't betray Antonia. Don't trust Fable. Don't tell Sun about learning magic or about the Spell Binder. My thoughts stuck on the latter. Don't tell Sun. How was I supposed to avoid telling Sun about the invention they already knew about?

Fuck.

The candle wouldn't light. As much as I tried to reach for magic—magic I knew was *right there*—I couldn't. And as the morning wore on and the wick remained unlit, my hope that I could cast a spell died on the vine. Antonia was no help, locked in her office, probably watching me through her blinds. All she'd see would be me pointing two fingers at a stubby candle in vain while Herb did his weird coat-rack mocking laugh in the corner. (It sounded like creaking stairs.)

After the entire morning of unsuccessfully lighting the candle and not receiving a single phone call, Antonia whooshed out of her office. She slapped a wad of bills and a laminated business card into my hand.

"What's this?" I asked, holding up the card.

"How to thwart the Consortium's capitalistic exploitation of magic," she said.

I raised my eyebrow.

"Sorcerer discount card. One of the few perks of being a registered sorcerer. Since the Consortium takes a cut of profits from all magical businesses, the prices are elevated significantly to offset the cost of the required certificate in the window. Use this when you order my coffee and muffins, so you're charged the sorcerer rate and not the regular one."

"Oh. Okay," I said, sliding the card and money into my wallet. "Sounds overly complicated but sure."

She sighed. "Don't get me started. That card will only work within the Consortium's Spire City jurisdiction. If you fall outside of it into another office's sector, well, then, it'd be full price unless you have their designated card."

"Sketchy. What does the Consortium need all that income for?"

"To pay their lackeys to invent new ways to harass me," Antonia replied without missing a beat. "And other sorcerers, of course. Not only me. I'm not *that* vain."

"Right."

She frowned and wagged her finger at me. "Don't sass me. Now, venture forth to my third-favorite coffee shop and bring back sustenance." Antonia's third-favorite coffee shop was way across town by bus. I didn't really want to leave the office, but at least it was a break from my constant failure.

The ride was uneventful, and I was in a seat by myself with no one around. I opened my bag and discreetly checked the Spell Binder as I rode. There were several weak lines on the way there, but as I neared my stop, a massively thick line showed up on the screen. So big that it blocked out much of the map. Wow. Interesting.

The driver eyed me as I hopped off at the stop, the only departing passenger, despite the seemingly bustling area. I walked down the sidewalk toward the coffee shop. I made it a block, watching as brooms swept the sidewalks by themselves out in front of businesses, and markets advertised frog's tears and specialty potions along with their giant heads of cabbage and massive watermelons, and the art drawn on the sides of buildings and on the sidewalks moved and danced with bright, beautiful colors before I realized that the entire neighborhood was magical. And yeah, that made sense. If there was a ley line that brimmed with unbound energy, the magical community would be drawn to it.

I absently wondered if Antonia lived near here and that's how she knew about the coffee shop, or if she had an ulterior motive for sending me this way. I wondered if she meant for me to try to sense the ley line here; maybe it had a different feeling or rhythm or frequency than the one at the office.

No matter what her motive was, even if it was just for the special muffins, it was cool to see all the different ways magic was used here. If I'd known about this community before, it would have been where I'd spent my days instead of shuttered up in my apartment in a decidedly not magical part of the city.

The coffee shop was called Deja Brew, and a Consortium certificate was taped to the window next to the open sign. The bell jingled overhead when I entered. There was a short line, so as I waited, I looked around the shop. It was just like any other coffee shop I'd been in, with different drinks and tables, cushy places to sit, books to read, but just like the haunted house with its dense and creepy atmosphere, there was a difference in the air here, an ambience that was light and liberating. Something breezy and uplifting.

Which was why it was so weird to spy Sun sitting at a table in the corner, ballcap pulled down, wearing their signature black ensemble. Three pretty girls sat around them chatting away, drinking coffee, and occasionally bumping into Sun or tugging on Sun's shirt or laughing at something Sun said, which was undoubtedly sharp and hilarious, and I was not jealous. Not a little bit. Not even when one of them grabbed the bill of Sun's hat and tugged it off, laughing while she did. Sun muttered something, snatched it back, and dropped it to the table, smoothing down their hair with their palms.

"Can I take your order?"

"Huh?" Right. In line. Ordering things for Antonia. I stepped forward and ordered Antonia's muffins and two coffees, one of which with Antonia's specifications. Loud laughter erupted from Sun's side of the shop, and I only half heard the amount the cashier quoted, but what I did register was that it was entirely too much.

"Um? What was that?"

She frowned. "You did want two muffins and two iced coffees, right?"

"Yes. Oh, wait." I'd been so distracted by Sun that I'd forgotten the sorcerer discount card. I yanked it out of my wallet and handed it over. The girl raised her eyebrows, but as soon as she saw the laminated business card, she sighed. She tapped keys on the register, and the dollar amount decreased exponentially.

"Next time," she said, a little terse, "show your sorcerer discount card first."

"Right. Sorry," I said.

I stepped to the side to wait and slid my gaze to Sun, who was staring back at me with a single arched eyebrow, black hair a mess, looking a little tired, and a lot fondly annoyed with the girls around them. They lifted their hand and gave a small, awkward wave. They *waved*. Sun waved, and the curve of their mouth lifted into a tiny smile. Did that mean I should go over? Of course it did. Right?

Gathering my courage and leaving my not-jealousy behind, I ambled toward them, hands in my pockets, trying for nonchalant. It did not work because I caught my foot on a chair that hadn't been pushed in all the way and stumbled. I righted myself before I fell but used someone's shoulder to do it.

"Oh, shit. I'm sorry. I'm sorry. So sorry. Sorry," I said, face flushed completely red. "Did I spill anything? Should I buy you a coffee?"

The person rolled their eyes, turned in their seat in a silent dismissal, and went back to their conversation with their tablemate.

The distinct sound of giggles reached my ears, and I sheepishly turned back to Sun's table in the corner. "He's beauty, he's grace," one of the girls said to the others, chin in her hand. "And he's coming this way."

My hope that my stumble went unnoticed died a quick, unglamorous death. Okay, I could recover. I could do this. Bring it back. Once I was close enough, I nodded to Sun.

"You," I said.

"Me," they agreed.

"What are you doing here?" Excellent. I'd tipped too far in the other direction and went from endearingly clumsy to downright rude. "I mean, um . . . come here often?" Wow. This interaction had dramatically gone downhill, and I'd literally said only three sentences thus far.

Sun tapped the end of their pencil against their notebook, biting down on their lower lip to keep from smiling or laughing. Definitely laughing. Sun was so inwardly laughing at me. I could see it in their eyes. "I live nearby," they said. "I belong here. So, the question is, what are you doing here?"

"*Rude*," one of the girls said. Sun ignored her.

I pointed back to the counter. "Coffee and muffins for Antonia. This is her third-favorite shop."

"Makes sense. They do have good pastries."

The girls exchanged a glance between them, eyes wide, mouths open, surprised by our exchange. By their furious whispering between each other, it didn't appear to be a common occurrence.

"Hi to the rest of you as well," I said to the table, because it would be impolite to ignore them.

A chorus of "hellos" came back at me. "Nice entrance," the girl from before said, smiling widely.

"Oh, that? That was nothing. Just a little error that I had hoped you'd overlook and not mention under the guise of graciousness."

Sun snorted.

The girls laughed. "No. Sorry, that's not how we operate."

"Not at all," one of the others said. She had short, angled hair and a nose piercing.

I scrubbed my face with my hand, trying to wipe away the embarrassment. My cheeks were hot. "Should I walk back over to the counter and try again? Would that help?"

The girls giggled. The third one swept her gaze over me. "Sorry, you only get one chance to make a first impression."

"Did you quote a credit card commercial at me?"

She grinned and tossed her black hair over her shoulder. "Depends. Are you buying me coffee?"

"Okay," Sun said, voice gruff, pushing the girl's shoulder. "Weren't you three leaving?"

"Well, we're not leaving *now*," the pierced one said. "This is entertaining."

Sun groaned, slouched back in their seat. "Please, leave?"

I don't know what type of situation I'd walked into, but I didn't like the way the girls jostled Sun as they talked or that they were ignoring their request to leave them alone. Sun pouted at them. Sun never pouted. It was disconcerting. I didn't like it. That not-jealousy I'd left at the counter reared its ugly head.

"Sun, do you want to come join me at another table?" I said, pointing over my shoulder. "To get away from them?"

That was not the right thing to say. The girls whistled and cackled and grew generally louder. One elbowed Sun in their side, and Sun frowned, though their cheeks went pink.

"Oh, are you saving them from us?" The girl closest to Sun batted her eyelashes. "A regular dashing hero."

"Ignore them," Sun said, eyes narrowed. "They were just *leaving*."

"Fine," the middle one said as they all gathered their things. "Stay here and study your math while we go to the movie. Text Mom, though. She'll want to know that you didn't come with us. We'll take the bus and leave you the car."

Mom. *Mom.* "Oh, are these your—"

"Sisters," Sun said, long-suffering. "Older sisters." The short-haired girl stuck out her tongue and blew a raspberry. "As you can see, older but not more mature," Sun said, smacking the other girl's hands away as she tried to ruffle their hair.

"Love you too, asshole."

"Go away already."

"Come on, let's allow *Sun* to talk to their friend."

And okay, yes, upon further observation, they all looked alike, and one of the girls did appear older than the others, early twenties, while the other two looked closer in age to Sun. They grabbed their purses and cups. The youngest gave me a once-over with her eyes, from my tennis shoes to my ragged jeans, to my T-shirt, to the sunglasses perched on the top of my head. I self-consciously tucked my thumbs into my pockets, just for something to do under the intense scrutiny.

"Fine," she said. Then pointed a finger at me. "Don't distract them too long. They do have schoolwork."

I raised an eyebrow. "You were trying to convince them to go to a movie."

She shrugged. "Sisterly privilege. You're just a *boy.*"

Luckily, my name was called at the counter, and by the time I got back, the girls had vacated. Sun sat there, staring blankly down at a textbook and a notebook full of figures.

"What are you studying?"

"Math," they said. Flat and bored.

"What kind of math?"

"I don't know. The kind with numbers and letters."

"Oh, wow. Okay." I slid onto the bench seat next to them. "Mind if I?" Sun waved at the book, and I pulled it closer. "Oh, trig. Yeah, this can be difficult if you—"

"Aren't a genius, like you, right?"

I grinned. "How many problems do you have to do?"

"The odd numbers in this set."

It was only five. But by the way Sun's paper was thin from being erased several times, I could tell the first one had been a struggle. Well, Antonia's coffee and muffins could wait a bit.

"Do you want help?"

Sun eyed me, suspicious, which I admitted hurt a little. We'd survived a scary event together. I thought we were beyond this level of distrust. Though Antonia had said not to trust Sun. I wonder if Fable had told Sun the same.

"Are you going to make fun of me?" they asked, hackles raised.

And ah. Okay. A different kind of mistrust. I got that. Being teased about something that was a sore spot was different from being teased in general. There were a few things I was sensitive about myself.

"No."

Sun was still wary, if their stiff posture was any indication. And even though Antonia explicitly said not to trust Sun, I couldn't imagine that someone who would willingly handle a cursed sword to save me would want to see me hurt or in trouble. And well, I wanted to be friends. "As long as you don't tease me that I spent the morning trying to unsuccessfully light a candle with magic."

Sun sputtered, slapped their hand over their mouth as they muffled their laugh, relaxing into their seat. "What?"

Grinning, I scooted closer on the bench seat, pressed my knee to Sun's under the table. "Yeah. I'm having a hard time with it."

"At least Antonia is finally teaching you magic."

That was a fairly blasé response to Antonia blatantly breaking a rule. But Sun didn't know I couldn't see the ley lines. I certainly had not told them. "I think she feels bad after what happened."

"She should," Sun said, vehement. "Fable should too. You could've been seriously hurt."

My cheeks flushed at Sun's apparent concern. I cleared my throat. "Speaking of, glad you are okay."

Sun picked at the spiral of the notebook. "Fable broke the curse easily, but I was sick for a few days. Which is why I'm behind on this schoolwork now." The notebook flopped to the table. "You too, you know."

"Thanks to you. That was quick thinking with the sword."

"Thanks. I'm glad it worked."

"Me too."

Sun looked everywhere but at me, staring out over the coffee shop, color high in their cheeks. "And I didn't tell Fable about the . . . the thing."

"The thing?"

"The Ley Finder."

"The Spell Binder."

Sun made a face. "Ley Finder is better."

"It is not." It totally was.

"Whatever horrible name you call it. I didn't tell Fable."

My stomach twisted. "Yeah. That. Um . . . Antonia will curse me if she finds out you know about that thing too. So, uh . . . can we keep that . . . between us?"

Sun swallowed thickly. "I . . . uh . . . thought a lot about it. I was mad at first, that you'd be reckless to make something like that. It could be . . . a lot of trouble. Like a lot. Not just for you but for . . . well . . . all of us, I guess." Sun met my gaze, their dark-brown eyes wide. "But as long as it's not going to be used to hurt people or anything, then . . . I mean, it's not my place to make judgments. Is it? So . . . it's okay."

I did not expect that. Not at all. Sun came off as such a stickler, just like Fable. But maybe that was Antonia's perception that I'd unwittingly adopted. I shook my head. "No. It's not meant to harm. At all. I don't even know how it could. It's meant to help."

Sun grimaced. "I still don't understand *why*, but if you promise me—"

"I promise."

Sun blew out a gusty breath that ruffled their bangs. "Okay."

"Okay."

"All right."

"Cool." I reached across the table and picked up Sun's pencil from where it had rolled. I did have to make my way back to Antonia's office, but helping Sun was infinitely more appealing than staring at a candle that wouldn't light. And a few problems shouldn't take too much time. "Okay, so math."

We settled in and worked on Sun's math assignment. They had a good grasp of basics, but Sun had a tendency to become frustrated when they didn't understand something right away, which led to more mistakes. Numbers and math concepts had always just fallen into my head, formed the pattern they were supposed to, and that was that. Sun struggled, though they kept at it, and by the last problem, they completed it on their own with no coaching from me. Sun rubbed their temple with one hand, then wrote down their answer.

"That's right."

Sun stared at the sheet, cute nose scrunched. "It is?"

"Yes."

"Thank *magic*. I couldn't stomach doing it again."

I laughed, and Sun smiled, a real smile that showed off their teeth.

It was weird to be giddy over teeth, but I was because it meant that Sun was happy and unguarded. I liked seeing them like that, and it made me happier to know that it was because of me, because of my presence.

I checked my phone. And oh. I had several missed messages from Antonia because time had passed without me noticing. A lot of time. Two hours of time. I hadn't even realized, so focused on the way the pencil rested in the curve of Sun's hand and the way they pursed their lips when they concentrated on their paper, and their gusty sighs at getting something wrong, but their pleased little look when they came to the right answer.

Looking at Antonia's iced coffee, the ice had long since melted. Condensation slid down the outside of the cup and left a puddle ring on the tabletop.

"Oh crap."

Sun shoved their notebook into their bag. "What?"

"I was supposed to be back a while ago. And Antonia's coffee is basically diluted bean water." I sighed. "I'll have to get her a fresh one."

I stood, but Sun tugged on my shirt. "Wait. There is a reason this is her third-favorite shop." Sun held their hand out next to the plastic cup and splayed their fingers. I dropped back to the seat as warmth suffused the scant space between us, gentle and comforting, and as I watched, magic glowed from Sun's fingers. The coffee in the cup sloshed, and before my eyes, the ice re-formed and the coffee refreshed to what it looked like when I first brought it over to the table, two hours ago.

"What?"

"It's spelled," Sun said, smiling softly. "To always taste the best it can. You just have to activate it."

"That's amazing." And the reason it was so expensive. I should've realized when I saw the certificate on the door that this was a *magic* coffee shop.

"It's neat. Probably not the best use of magic, but it's great when you kind of forget about your coffee between working on math problems and being teased by your siblings."

I laughed. "Yeah. I can see that."

"This whole neighborhood is magic." Sun zipped up their backpack. "It's nice to be here."

"I wish I'd known places like this existed. I'd have spent the last year here."

"The last year?"

I shoved the bag of muffins into my own bag on top of the Spell Binder. "Uh . . . my grandmother died last year, and I had to move into the city. It's not been that great." Understatement of the year.

"I'm sorry for your loss." I didn't know if Sun meant my grandmother or the last year of my life that had been lived in a gray, dull world of loneliness, but I appreciated the sentiment.

"It's okay." It wasn't. "It's been a year." It still hurt.

"Doesn't mean it doesn't suck."

"Spoken like . . . well, like you."

Sun smirked. "I should let you go. And I should go pick my sisters up from the theater. It would be the nice thing to do, and maybe then they won't relentlessly talk about you at dinner in front of my parents tonight."

I inwardly preened. "Will that work?"

Sun's shoulders slumped. "No. It won't."

I laughed. Sun's dejected face was so cute. They were cute. Fuck, they were so cute.

"I need to get this back to Antonia anyway. She's probably going feral back at the office without it. Who knows what electronics will be destroyed when I return."

The side of Sun's mouth ticked up. "I'll see you next time?"

"Yeah. Next time."

We stood and made our way to the exit together. I tossed my empty cup into the bin and groaned when, as soon as we stepped outside, thunder rumbled, and the sky opened. The summer was notorious for late-afternoon storms. I should've known. Rain poured in fat drops, battering the small awning we stood beneath, the concrete of the street going from bone dry to a slick hazard in seconds, a small river of water already flowing down the edge of the sidewalk toward the drain. I considered going back into the shop to wait it out, but I'd kept Antonia waiting for too long already.

The bus stop was at the end of the street. Maybe if I ran . . .

Sun tugged on my sleeve as they put on their snapback. "This way. Come on, I'll give you a ride."

"What about your sisters?"

"They're mature young women. They'll figure it out."

I was not going to argue, especially after a fork of lightning lit up the sky.

Sun's mom-car was parked along the curb only a few spots away. I was mildly damp when I slid in the passenger seat and not absolutely drenched as I would've been if I had tried to make it to the bus stop. Sun started the car and tossed their bag in the back. They clicked their seat belt, adjusted their seat and their mirrors, turned on their blinker, and eased out of the spot. I should've known they'd be a careful driver and would obey every traffic rule to the letter.

It should've annoyed me, but it didn't. It only endeared them to me more.

Some pop song played low from the radio, something that fit Sun's sisters more than it did them.

"Why can't you light the candle?" they asked after they merged onto the highway that would take us back toward Antonia's.

"If I knew that, I'd know how to light it."

"Seriously."

"Are you going to tease me?" I asked, echoing Sun's words from earlier, hoping they understood that this was my sensitive spot.

They did. "No."

"I can't figure out how to harness the magic of the line." There.

"Ah," they said. "The good news, though, is that once you learn how, you don't forget, and it gets easier every time."

"Did you have trouble with it?"

"Um, no."

"Of course not."

Sun shrugged. "But my sister Soo-jin, the one with the pierced nose, she struggled with it for a while until she learned. And now she can cast simple spells." The windshield wipers beat a drum's rhythm as the rain continued. "I could try to teach you," Sun said, barely audible over the sound of the rain.

I straightened from my unattractive slump. "You would?"

"Yeah."

"When?"

"Right now."

I froze. "Right now?"

"Yeah. You just . . . um . . . so, like, you have to picture it. And think about how magic feels, to you. Right? Like to me it's a vibration, and it's gentle and warm and lives right here." Sun tapped the middle of their chest. "But for Soo-jin magic is stubborn and hard like a rock. She had to imagine chipping off a piece at first to grab ahold of it, to remove it from the line and use it. I just had to reach out for it, and it reached back. You have to know what it feels like to you and then picture a way for you to take a piece of it."

I scratched the side of my nose. "I have no idea what magic feels like other than what it felt like when I lived with my grandmother."

"Okay. And what did your grandmother do with magic that you loved?"

My first thought was how she'd cast butterflies and I'd chase them in the summer. I'd catch them in my hands, and they'd burst into sparkles. It was like the feeling of fizzing candy on my tongue, explosive and sweet.

"Butterflies."

Sun didn't laugh. Didn't sneer, didn't say anything as we pulled closer to Antonia's office. "Then catch a butterfly. And light the candle."

My throat went tight. "Okay. Yeah. I'll try it."

"Good."

"Um . . . you can pull over here. Antonia . . . I don't think Antonia should see us together."

Sun's whole attitude changed. Their warm smile slipped away into something . . . not annoyed, but not unconcerned, either. Prickly, like a cactus. They held themself stiff as they pulled over, their muscles taut.

"Antonia doesn't trust me and Fable." It wasn't a question.

"No."

"I didn't think so. You should be careful."

"Why?"

"She's not telling you everything."

"And you are?"

Sun bit their lip. "She had an apprentice before."

"So you've said."

"Something bad happened."

"So she said. How bad?"

"Bad enough that the rumors say that the Consortium banned Antonia from having an apprentice ever again." Sun swallowed. "Bad enough that she hasn't told you what happened. That she feels she has to hide it from you."

That confirmed what I already knew. But that didn't give me any additional information. And as much as I appreciated Sun's warning, it was hard to ignore the fact that I myself was considered "very bad" by the Consortium. They deemed the Spell Binder, a device that was only meant to help, as something bad as well.

"That doesn't tell me anything."

"Give me your phone."

"What?"

"Your phone." Sun made a grabby hands gesture. I passed it over. Sun's fingers flew across the screen, and then I heard their own notification ding. "I texted myself from your phone. You have my number now."

"What?"

Sun blushed. "My number. You have it. Text me. If you need to. For help with magic. Or rides in the rain. Or whatever."

"Oh." Sun gave me their number. I had Sun's number. "You might regret this."

"I already do. Get out."

I laughed, grabbing my bag. "I'll text you."

"Go. Before I change my mind and block your number."

"You won't."

"I will. Go."

I scrambled out, slipping my bag over my shoulder. "Let me know if you need any more help with math."

"I will. Go catch a butterfly!" they yelled after me as I closed the door.

Okay. Yes. I could do it. Sun had faith in me. I could have faith in myself. I could catch a butterfly. I could light a candle. I could pull from a ley line and cast. I could totally be an awesome apprentice.

10

ROOK

I could not light the candle.

I'd tried. And tried. Days of picturing the ley line in my head as a long string of my grandmother's butterflies and plucking one from the air and then flicking my fingers toward the stubby candle. And days of utter failure.

Ugh.

Maybe Antonia was wrong about those other non-magic folks who had cast spells. Maybe I wasn't cut out to be the best apprentice ever.

My real name was Edison, for fuck's sake, I should be able to solve the problem of illumination. But I hadn't. And I couldn't. And I hated life.

I texted Sun a picture of the unlit candle with the caption of DARKNESS REIGNS.

My hands did not shake when I hit send. I wasn't nervous. It was only the first text I'd sent them since the intimate car ride and the day in the coffee shop and the not-jealousy I had felt at seeing their sisters all over them when I didn't know it was actually their sisters. No big deal. It wasn't a big deal. Okay, maybe it was a big deal. I liked them. I thought they were cute, and I liked when they laughed. Sue me.

My phone vibrated in my hands, and I fumbled it in surprise.

Sun had texted back. A frowny emoji. Followed by What did the butterflies feel like?

I couldn't explain it. It was hard to put into words. I spun my phone in my hands. Sparkles. Fizzy soda, I texted back. Popping candy.

Sun read the text. I waited a few minutes. Then a few minutes more. And when half an hour had passed and I didn't hear back from them, I guessed the interaction was over. I sighed heavily. I pulled the Spell Binder out of my bag and tweaked a few settings. I opened the spell book app and scrolled through the few spells that I'd managed to input from the small spell book. Nothing overly complicated. Antonia hadn't really explained spells to me yet, but based on what I'd read, they varied a lot in structure. They were sometimes incantations or chants, sometimes hand movements, sometimes a mixture of both. Spells did a lot of different things, like enchant mice to sing or break fairy magic to cure little girls' pig noses, and sometimes they were broad and sometimes very specific. There were some that were very basic that everyone knew and didn't need a lot of magic to cast. And others that required enormous amounts of power. They were as different as snowflakes and as numerous.

There would be no way to capture them all unless I was given access to every spell book imaginable. But those that were accessible were tracked by magic, and those that weren't were locked in a Consortium library that very few had access to.

The phone rang, and I took the call—it was from someone who had walked under a ladder and broken a mirror in the same day. I took their information on my they're-just-superstitious form and emailed it to Antonia. She was currently out, handling a sentient slime situation, but it didn't sound urgent, and she could give the person a return call later.

After a few more minutes of spinning around in my desk chair, my phone vibrated.

Is Antonia at the office? Sun asked via text.

No, I sent back.

A few seconds later, the front door opened.

I shot to standing, stumbling because I'd made myself dizzy, and peeked around my cubicle wall. Herb had disappeared into the break room when Antonia left, still not pleased with my presence, but I was suddenly glad of it, so he wouldn't witness my moment of complete infatuated dorkiness.

"You!"

"Me," Sun said with a nod. They glared at the welcome mat. "If I step over it," they asked, "will it try to trip me?"

"I usually skirt around it."

Sun had a tote bag looped around one arm and was in their typical Sun fashion of black on black. Sun stuck the tip of their tongue out as they very carefully moved around the mat. It flicked them in the ankle.

"The fuck?"

"I tried to move it once," I said. "It bit me."

"It has teeth?"

"Kind of?"

"Weird."

My heart fluttered with excitement at seeing Sun. I smoothed down my wrinkled clothes, which I had pulled from the bottom of the drawer because I hadn't done laundry. At least I was showered, and I was pretty sure I'd remembered deodorant this morning. I hoped I didn't have any of my breakfast stuck in my teeth.

"So . . . ," I said, drawing out the vowel. "Do you come here often?"

Sun rolled their eyes and shuffled past the receptionist desk that was forever empty, into the office, and over to my cubicle. The Spell Binder was on my desk with the spell app open. Sun's gaze dropped to it, and they quickly looked away.

"Could you?"

"Yeah," I said, grabbing it and slipping it into my bag. I could tell it made Sun uncomfortable, seeing something so obviously against all the rules they'd been taught in the magical world.

Sun cleared their throat. "Plausible deniability and all that."

"Of course."

Shaking their head, Sun dropped the bag on my desk. "Is that the candle?"

"The bane of my existence. Yes."

Sun's eyes narrowed. They flicked their wrist as they kept two fingers pointed, and the candle lit. I sighed as the flame danced.

"Show-off."

"No. I just wanted to make sure it wasn't, like, spelled or tricked or anything." Sun closed their fist, and the wick snuffed out.

"Antonia wouldn't do that to me."

Sun shrugged, indicating they weren't so sure. "Maybe not. Anyway"—they reached into the bag and pulled out a bottle of soda—"I texted my sister, and she said this was the fizziest kind." Then they pulled out candy, the kind that popped when placed on your tongue. "Candy," they said, tossing it. "And hopefully Antonia has a fire extinguisher." In Sun's hand was a pack of sparklers.

"You brought sparklers?"

Again, Sun shrugged. "Honestly, I didn't know what they were. The neighborhood always uses magic for fireworks."

"Wow. Seriously? That's so . . . *cool*."

Sun tipped their head back and looked at the ceiling. "I should've blocked your texts."

"Too late now," I said, twisting off the soda cap, and the satisfying hiss of fizz and carbonation followed. I stepped away from my computer lest the soda overflow from being shaken in Sun's bag. Antonia destroyed electronics every other day. I didn't want to add to her already substantial office supply bill. "Anyway, what's all this for?"

Sun stared at the candle. "Magic tutoring. You helped me with math. I'll help you with this."

Oh. My stomach twisted. "You don't need to feel obligated to help me because I helped you."

Sun frowned. "I don't. I'm not. That's not what I'm doing."

"Kind of sounds like you are."

Sun went still. "Do I act like a person who does anything I don't want to?"

Well, no. The sharp bite of the words made me realize I'd offended them. Inadvertently. "Sorry."

"Don't be sorry." Sun set the pack of sparklers down on my desk. "What I say doesn't come out right sometimes. I didn't mean that I felt obligated. I just meant, well, I want to help you, because you're my frenemy."

I grinned. "Yeah. Okay."

Sun didn't look appeased. In fact, they looked sad but determined, lips pressed into a thin line. "No. No, you're not my frenemy. You're my friend. We're friends. I want to be your friend. Okay?" Sun didn't look at me, but the whole line of their body was tense, and their hands balled into nervous fists.

I wanted to hug them but remembered the first time they'd been in Antonia's office, and I didn't know how to breach that between us. The few touches we'd shared were scant and fleeting, but I really wanted to draw Sun in and reassure them. I resisted.

"We can be friends, Sun. I'd like to be your friend."

Sun's whole body relaxed, and they crossed their arms, hid their face with their hand, and took a breath. "Good," they said, voice thick. "Good."

"Good."

"Okay."

"Okay."

Sun nodded once sharply, rubbed their hands together, then picked up the popping candy. "Now, let's light a candle."

Sun was a much better teacher than Antonia. But despite their best efforts, and the soda, and the sparklers, which we lit outside in the parking lot, taking the candle with us, and the popping candy that burst into sweet fireworks in our mouths, it didn't work.

After an hour, our teaching session had devolved into both of us sprawled in office chairs, feet up on the abandoned front desk, heads tipped back as far as they could go, mouths open in a contest of who could keep the candy on their tongue the longest. Sun was surprisingly good at it, and good at not being distracted despite my best efforts of kicking my foot into theirs. It must be growing up the youngest with three older sisters. From what I'd seen in the coffee shop, Sun's sisters did not hesitate to annoy their younger sibling any chance they had.

"This is unfair. How are you so good at this? It's unholy," I said, pushing my knee into their chair, causing it to spin lazily.

Sun smirked, black hair falling in their eyes, arms draped over the chair's arms, skinny legs spread. "I have all kinds of talents that you don't know about."

My mouth went dry. I coughed, scrambling for my bottle of soda. It tasted disgusting after having the candy sit on my tongue for so long, but I needed something, because *oh my god*.

Sun's eyes went comically wide when they realized what they said. They bolted upright, hands out. "Wait, no. That's not what I meant. I meant like jumping rope and balancing books on my head. I can do a handstand."

I burst into laughter, choking on soda, on the verge of a spit take.

"A handstand? What the hell, Sun?"

I couldn't help it. I laughed, doubling over, arms wrapped around my middle. Sun joined me, laughing silently into their hands, dissolving into giggles. I hadn't laughed like that in forever, so hard that tears gathered in my eyes.

That's how Antonia found us, laughing helplessly while spinning in office chairs, candy wrappers, dead sparklers, and soda bottles scattered around.

"Interesting," she said.

Oh shit. I jumped to my feet. "Antonia. You're back."

"Indeed." She leveled Sun with an even gaze.

Sun stared back, unflinching.

"Hello, Fable's minion."

"Hi." Their response was flat and blunt.

"Ah, there's that famous personality," she said. "Are you sure you haven't been cursed? I can fix that, you know."

Sun looked away. Oh, Antonia had landed a hit right into a sore spot, unintentional or not.

"Well, this has been fun," I said, overly loud and bright. "But my lunch break is over, and I do need to get back to work." I gathered the trash quickly while Antonia watched, and Sun shrank further into themself. It was not great.

"I should get back to the cottage," Sun mumbled.

"Okay. Yeah. Thanks for coming by."

Sun put their hands in their pockets, shoulders hunched, dimmed in a way that I didn't like. "Hey," I said, knowing what I was about to say could get me fired—or worse, hexed. "I'll text you later. Really, thanks for the help."

Sun smiled. It was a small, fragile thing, but it made the butterflies in my middle take flight. And I felt like a sparkler.

"You're welcome."

They left, and I watched them through the window until they disappeared around the corner of the parking lot.

"Rook." Antonia stood by my desk, hands on her hips. "What did I say about trusting them?"

"They were helping me."

"With what?"

I gestured toward the candle. Antonia's aura darkened into a storm cloud. "You know that Sun will tell Fable I'm teaching you magic. Damn it, Rook! I lied to the Consortium, promised that I wouldn't teach you anything magical to keep them out of our business, and then you go tell the two most ardent rule followers."

"Sun's my friend. They won't say anything."

"Possibly not, but Fable will! Do you know how many people can keep a secret? The answer is two but only if one of them is dead."

"First, that's a terrifying quote. And second, do you really want to talk about secrets?"

That brought Antonia up short. She cocked her head to the side. "What?" she asked, sharp like a knife.

When the curtains had me in their stranglehold, I thought I was going to die. My short and unsatisfying life flashed before my eyes. I was terrified. This, Antonia staring me down, was infinitely scarier. But I was tired and annoyed and defeated. Annoyed over her scaring Sun away, someone who had become a rare bright spot in my life. Defeated because I was never going to light that candle, despite what she and Sun believed. And then what would happen when I couldn't be the catalyst to her own personal revolution?

"You heard me. Secrets. There is so much you're not telling me."

Antonia's jaw set. "I've taught you about jinxes, hexes, curses, the ley lines, and gave you access to a spell book. That's plenty for someone who is not magical, if I may remind you."

"Oh, I know. And that has been thrown in my face quite a few times. But that's not what I'm talking about."

Antonia went as quiet as a predator stalking its prey. Me. I was the prey. My heart raced like a rabbit's. "To what are you referring?"

"Your last apprentice. What happened? What aren't you telling me? Why aren't you allowed to have one?"

Antonia spread her fingers, turned her wrist as she gathered a ball of power that glowed her upturned palm. The energy in the room crackled. "Do you know who I am?" she asked, her voice distorted with magic. "Do you know how old I am? How long I've been magic? How long the magic has been in me?"

I gulped. "No."

"No." She clenched her fist, snuffing out the ball of power. Golden tendrils of magic seeped between the seams of her fingers. "Those are the secrets you should be concerned with, not some story that has been passed around by lesser magical beings via hushed whispers and rumors on the wind."

I froze. "I don't understand."

"Do you know that movie, the one with the evil sorcerer who tries to take over the land? She's beautiful and terrible and succeeds for a time, plunging the world into darkness? Have you ever wondered who she is based on? How the producers developed that plot? Why it might feel slightly familiar when you watched it?"

Oh. "You?" I asked. "You were the evil sorcerer?"

Antonia cackled. She shook her head, delicately placing a hand at her throat. "No, my dear. It was my apprentice."

"Your apprentice was—"

"Evil. And I taught her everything she knew. I gifted her a name. I taught her how to draw power from the lines, mold it into her veins, to become magic herself. I helped her memorize spells and create new ones. And I *defeated* her. Try as she might, she couldn't eclipse *me*."

Proud. Antonia was *proud*. Of her own accomplishments and that of her apprentice.

I gulped and took a step back. "What happened to her?"

"The Consortium cast a binding spell on her, cutting her off from magic forever."

My throat went tight. Antonia hadn't only seen herself in me, but her former apprentice, too. Removed from magic forever. I knew how that felt. Having something you love taken away, being blocked from entering by gatekeepers, always saying I wasn't enough. I didn't fit.

"That's awful."

Antonia nodded. "And that is why I'm no longer allowed to have an apprentice. For fear of it happening again." She crossed her arms. "You should thank her, you know. She's the one who entered the Consortium vault and found out a few of their secrets. She relayed them to me before they bound her and locked her away."

My knees trembled. "But I'm not like her. I can't do the things she did."

Antonia shrugged, the tense aura slipping away.

"Not yet," Antonia said. "I'm capable of anything. Don't you know? Of turning the most ardent rule follower against them. Of creating magic where there is none. Even after walking the straight and narrow for decades, I'm still the monster in their fairy tales." She sighed and rubbed her temple.

I gaped as she turned on her heel and walked across the room, grabbed one of the office chairs that we'd been spinning in earlier, and sank into the cushion. She looked tired. And I didn't know what to do, what to say. All I knew was that my heart ached for her.

"I'm sorry," I said.

She waved the apology away. Then tented her fingers. "Now, if Sun is so great at teaching, light the candle."

I tensed. I'd been unsuccessful at every attempt thus far, and being put on the spot, right after a charged conversation, did not feel great. Anxious sweat beaded along my hairline. My mouth went dry, and I licked my lips. Staring at the stubborn lump of melted wax, I wished fervently that Sun was there to offer support.

Sun. Sun. Sun, who made me giddy, quite frankly. Who stopped me in my tracks with their quick wit and wry smile and who was genuinely funny once you were able to get past their wall of defensive sourness. Sun, who had a cute nose and pretty eyes and sometimes wore earrings and other times a ball cap and other times huge hoodies and other times loose shirts, but always wore jeans. Sun, who was prickly and vulnerable at the same time, who wanted to follow rules because they were comforting, who took a chance and became my friend.

And despite Antonia's intense gaze, the lump in my throat, and the fear pooling in my veins, the thought of Sun still made butterflies dance in my stomach, sparklers set off in my chest, and candy dance on my tongue.

I grabbed on to that feeling, imagined the ley line as a migration of golden sparkly butterflies, and reached out and caught one. My fingers tingled, and warmth traveled into my core, lit up my veins from the inside. I pointed two fingers at the candle wick with intent.

The candle didn't light.

But at the tip, an ember burned red, and a thin trail of smoke curled upward.

Antonia's smug expression dropped in time with her crossed arms. Her eyes widened. She stared at the candle, then at me, pouty red lips fallen open. Shock spread across her face like butter.

"I did it," I said, as the spark still burned. My face broke into a wide grin. "I did it. I did it. Did you see it? It smoked!"

"You did it," Antonia breathed. "How did you? What did you feel?"

"Butterflies."

"That's amazing. You're amazing! I knew you could do it. I knew it." Antonia hopped to her feet and clapped her hands. In her excitement, her own magic shot off sparks. A light bulb burst overhead. The phones rang of their own accord. My computer monitor blinked out. But it didn't matter because I'd done magic. Me! I'd done it!

I staggered and grabbed the wall to keep from falling. "Wow. I can do magic. Antonia, I can do magic." Holy shit. Proof that I belonged. I belonged in the magical world. I belonged with Antonia and with Sun and with Fable.

"I'm ecstatic!" And Antonia was. Flashes of magic crackled in every direction. "Wow. I knew you'd figure it out. You're so smart, Rook."

"Hey! Calm down. You're frying everything."

"Oh, oh. Sorry. Sorry. But this, this is cause for celebration. Come on, we're going to dinner. My treat. Then I'll drive you home."

"It's two in the afternoon."

Antonia snorted. "Late lunch, then. I know you haven't eaten more than candy and soda." She pulled out her phone and sighed. "Ugh. I killed the battery again."

"Again?" I said, peering at it. "What did you do this time?"

"It must have been all the excitement at your success." She shoved it into her bag.

Wait. Oh no. I dove under the desk and ripped open my bag. The Spell Binder/Ley Finder was inside. I stabbed the power button with my finger, and it blinked into life. Oh, thank everything. It still worked. I may be able to harness the power from a ley line, but I still couldn't *see* them. I'd need the device if I was going to continue as Antonia's apprentice. I breathed out a deep sigh of relief that Antonia hadn't inadvertently fried it.

Antonia scrunched her nose. "Is it okay?"

"It's fine," I said, smoothing my palm over the screen.

"Great. Let's go!"

After our late lunch, I itched to text Sun about lighting the candle. I wanted to tell them so badly. I wanted to thank them. I wanted to tell them how it felt and that I'd been thinking of them when I did it. I wanted to kiss them. Okay, maybe I wouldn't tell them those last two things. I wasn't sure how they'd be received, since we'd only just left the enemy part of our frenemy relationship behind.

But I wasn't sure I should do any of that in Antonia's presence.

She cleared her throat. "Not going to text Sun?"

Ugh. "What? I'm not in the mood for the 'we can't trust Sun lecture.'"

"Yeah, I know."

"We can be friends. You and Fable are friends."

Antonia pulled a face. "We're not."

"You are."

"We're colleagues. We tolerate each other. I don't text Fable when I figure out a new spell or break a curse."

"You literally call Fable to gloat when you do something spectacular. I've heard you. And Fable calls you for advice and help and also to gloat when they do something awesome. So, yes, you're friends."

Antonia made a rude noise with her lips. "Whatever. But no, you can't trust Sun. Rule followers, the both of them."

"Sun literally came over to teach me how to light the candle." I cleared my throat, fiddled with a loose thread on my jeans. Antonia already knew that Sun and I were friends and that Sun knew I was learning magic. Might as well lay all of my cards out on the table. "Sun knows about the Spell Binder."

Antonia slammed on the brake, throwing me against the seat belt. Luckily, we were by the curb in front of my apartment block.

"What?" she yelled. "Since when?"

"Since the curtains. They found it when they were trying to find my phone to call you."

"Fuck!" Antonia slammed her open palm on the steering wheel so hard the horn bleated. "Rook! If Sun knows, Fable knows."

I shook my head. "No. No. Sun says they haven't said anything. And they came over to teach me magic. Sun is my friend. I know you don't trust anyone, especially anyone on good terms with the Consortium, but Sun isn't going to say anything."

"They ratted us out to the Consortium!"

"They didn't! It was the singing mice guy. Sun swears they didn't."

"Ugh. You like them. That's what this is. A love story happening in my office. Gross."

I flinched. "No," I said, too loudly for the small space. "No! No! That's not—no!"

Antonia raised an eyebrow. "Me thinks the teenager doth protest too much."

I covered my face with my hands. "Oh my god."

"Don't be so dramatic. Just . . ." She sighed. "Don't talk to them tonight. Take a break. I need a minute to think. Can you do that?"

"Yes," I said, not at all like a sulky teenager.

"Great." She threw the car into park. "I'll see you in the morning. And no trying magic without me," she said, face stern, wagging a finger in my direction. Then she peered around, lip curled. "Not like you could here. This is desolate. It doesn't feel like there is a line for miles."

"Yeah, thanks for pointing out that I live in a hole." I closed the car door.

"I didn't mean it like that!" she yelled, though it was muffled.

I'm sure. But she was right. That was one of the reasons it was so difficult to work on the Spell Binder in the first place. There was *nothing* here. No magic. No magic users like Sun's neighborhood. Only the gray concrete walls of the city, and not even the shimmering mirages of heat that rose from the asphalt could change that.

But it was okay. I only had to tough it out a little longer. And once I had enough saved, I could find a place near Sun's neighborhood, work for Antonia, and join the community where I probably, maybe belonged.

SUN

Summer school sucked. Taking the bus home from class sucked even more, especially since the ride from the school building to Fable's cottage was long, the bus interior was hot and stifling, and the seat I picked had a spring that dug into my back when I slumped. Luckily, I was the only person left, so I didn't have to endure the chatter from the other students mixed in with the loud rumble of the bus engine. I didn't think I could handle all the sensory input today.

I was only behind in math, so I only had to attend two days a week, but I still hated it. My sessions were usually first thing in the morning, which meant even in the summer I had to roll out of bed early and make my way to school. The only good thing about it was that I'd have the afternoon with Fable at the cottage, and I could spend the rest of the day working on magic.

The bus screeched to a stop, and I hopped off at the corner. I checked my phone as I walked down the sidewalk to the cottage, stomach dropping when I still didn't have a text from Rook. He usually texted me at least once a day since we'd exchanged numbers.

It didn't sting. I mean, I only spent the day with him yesterday and tried to teach him how to draw from a line and bought him candy and soda and sparklers. I only put myself out there for him, showing up despite not knowing if my presence was wanted, shoving my anxiety so far down that I was able to walk into the door with an off-the-wall idea that didn't work. But it had been fun, up until Antonia arrived and stared me down and basically told me to leave.

I knew she didn't really like me and only tolerated Fable, but I couldn't shake the feeling that Antonia was up to something. She was always up to something, according to the rumors.

And speaking of, when I turned the corner, I spotted Antonia's flashy little sports car parked right out in front of the cottage next to Fable's clunker. Raised voices emanated from the inside as I approached. Antonia and Fable yelling at each other, no doubt. It must be important for Antonia to deign to travel out to the edge of the enchanted wood. Oh no, what if she was yelling at Fable over me? Over interfering with Rook's magic lessons? Or was there something else between them yet again? They weren't friends in the way that Rook and I were becoming friends, but they had an understanding. Even if it was caustic.

Quietly, I opened the side door, slipped inside, and toed off my shoes, stepping into the pair of slippers left on the entryway rug.

"You don't get it, Fable!" Antonia yelled, voice pitching into a shriek. I hunched my shoulders. The sound was awful, spurred by magic so that it echoed in the small space of the cottage. Despite my discomfort, I peeked around the doorframe to see her throw her arms in the air. "You absolutely cannot report him to the Consortium. Not only would they attempt to bind me," she said, thrusting two fingers toward her own chest, "but they'd make him disappear. And that can't happen."

Wait. Antonia wasn't yelling. She was . . . begging. Pleading? On Rook's behalf?

Fable let out the long-suffering sigh that had been directed at me a few times over the course of my apprenticeship. "Antonia, you're forbidden from teaching magic. I didn't mind so much when he tagged along with you, but after the curtain incident—"

"He was fine."

"He wasn't. And Sun was cursed saving him." Fable stood from their chair. "My apprentice was injured saving your office staff because we both put them in a bad situation. Antonia, they could've been severely injured. Rook was lucky he didn't die. Sun was lucky that they were only cursed residually and didn't take the full brunt of what lurked in that sword."

Fable crossed the room, rested their hand on Antonia's shoulder, a rare show of empathy toward their rival.

"And what's going to happen when he becomes frustrated that he can't do it. That he can't cast. What then? He'll leave you. Not in the same way *she* did, but it'll hurt all the same."

Antonia shrugged off Fable's hand, a manic gleam in her violet eyes. "That's where you're wrong. He did it. He lit the candle yesterday."

Fable took a step back. "He what?"

He did it? He did it! Wow. He did it! I'd helped! But . . . why hadn't he texted me? I'd thought—

"The wick burned, and smoke curled. Yes, it wasn't the strongest cast, but he did it. This is the first step toward something bigger."

"But you said he can't see the lines. That you checked his palm, and he's not magical."

My head snapped up. Rook couldn't see the ley lines? Rook wasn't magical? That didn't make sense.

"He can't. But here's the thing, Fable. He's so smart. He's so very smart that he's created this device to help him. It can detect the lines for him."

Fable lifted an eyebrow. "Antonia, that's not possible."

Smirking, Antonia crossed her arms. "It is. He's made it. I've seen it. It works. He doesn't need to be able to see the lines if he has his"—here Antonia sighed—"Spell Binder."

"That's an awful name."

"I know."

"Almost as bad as Hex-A-Gone."

Antonia narrowed her eyes. "Shut up. This isn't about me. This is about Rook. And how he deserves to be my apprentice. He deserves to be part of the magical world. So please, you cannot tell them, Fable. Any of this. I know Sun has already told you that they helped him yesterday with a magic lesson and—"

"Sun hasn't told me anything."

Aw, crap. Thanks, Antonia.

Antonia blinked. Then a slow smirk bloomed across her red lips. "Well, my, my . . . Your little minion has been keeping secrets."

Oh, okay. Time to walk in and interrupt the conversation because that was not true. I hadn't kept secrets. I'd only omitted a few things. Like my whereabouts yesterday. And the fact that I'd run into Rook at the coffee shop. And the fact that we texted occasionally.

I stepped fully into the cottage's kitchen. "I have not been keeping secrets."

Antonia held a hand to her mouth. "Oops."

"He helped me with math," I said at Fable's disapproving look. "He didn't make fun of me when I panicked in the elevator. He stayed with me in the haunted house despite not wanting to be there at all. He respected my boundaries, and he doesn't mind that I'm not good with social interactions. He's kind. And he smiles. And he wants to be my friend."

Antonia winked. "Sounds like the little minion has a crush."

My face went hot. "Don't make me regret agreeing with you," I muttered.

"Agreeing with me about what?"

"That Rook should be an apprentice." My stomach twisted. It went against everything I'd been taught. Against every single rule the Consortium had, even those written down in the wake of Antonia's punishment. "He's magical. I don't know why everyone keeps saying he's not, but he is."

Fable pinched the bridge of their nose. "He can't see the lines."

"It doesn't matter."

"It's against what the Consortium has decided is the standard for sorcerers and apprentices. To access magic, you have to be able to see the ley lines, or at least sense them. He can do neither. Antonia administered the palm test, and I have not sensed even the slightest bit of magic in him."

"You're wrong."

"Sun!"

"Besides, who is the Consortium to decide what the standard is? There's not a right way to be magic, is there? Why are we keeping people out of our community who want to be here? He's one of us."

Fable shot Antonia a withering glare, who, in turn, appeared downright gleeful.

"Look what you've done, Antonia."

"I've done nothing. Sun is very smart and has realized that the barriers are bullshit all on their own."

Fable's shoulders sagged. They pressed a hand to their brow, the other on their hip, squeezing their eyes tight like they were in physical pain. "Antonia, have you forgotten what happened the last time someone you were close to broke the rules?"

"As if I can ever forget," Antonia hissed. "She was wrong, yes, in the way she went about things. She shouldn't have taken the actions she did. But she wasn't wrong in her convictions. Magic is as old as the universe and as essential as the air we breathe. The Consortium's stranglehold on it is unnatural and wrong. You cannot argue with that."

"I can, but I won't. I know it would be a waste of energy. You've put me in a bad position, Antonia. If I don't report Rook's device and the fact that you've truly taken him on as your apprentice and are teaching him magic, then I'm complicit, and I'll be caught in the Consortium's wrath when this all comes to light. If I say something, I know you'll curse me and any generations behind me." Fable cast a glance at me.

I did my best to school my expression into something blank, but Fable had been able to read me like a book for years. They could see the hope in my eyes and the affection I had for Rook as plain as the blush on my cheeks.

Fable lowered into a chair. "But I will not have you starting a full-blown revolution in my kitchen and turning my apprentice into a rebel. Do what you want, Antonia. But leave Sun and me out of it. I mean it. I don't want Sun being mixed up in anything that could result in injury or worse."

I swallowed, throat tight. "What do you mean?"

"I think Fable means that whatever little relationship you have with Rook will need to come to an end."

"I didn't say that."

Antonia crossed her arms. "Not bluntly, no. But Sun can't be Rook's friend if Rook's very existence breaks your precious rules." Antonia said it with bite. "But it also means that whatever working relationship we had is over, Fable. Don't call me when you need my expertise or my power. You'll have to turn to someone else."

Fable's brow furrowed. "All of this over a boy, Antonia? There are dozens of other young people in the city looking for apprentice-ships. Ones that are magical. Ones that fit the mold. If you're really so desperately lonely, you could fight for any one of them to be your apprentice. I'm sure you could convince the Consortium if you made a case. Can't you choose one of them?"

Antonia's violet eyes flared. Magic sparked from her fingers.

She lifted her chin. "No," she said simply. "Because Sun is right."

I startled.

"There is no right way to be magic. He lit the candle. I believe in him. I gifted him a name, so he's mine."

Fable pursed their lips. "I won't tell."

"Good choice."

"But you're right. Our relationship is over."

"Fine."

Fable's gaze caught mine. "And your friendship is done. Do you understand?"

I opened my mouth to protest.

"Or you will no longer be my apprentice."

I snapped it shut. My stomach ached. Tears stung the backs of my eyes. I tucked my hands into my sleeves, curled my arms around my body, and hunched down into my oversize shirt.

"Fable," Antonia said softly. "That's a little harsh. What if—"

"No. My decision is final."

"Fable."

Fable shot up from their chair. "I have chosen not to meddle in the affairs of your apprentice. I suggest you choose not to meddle with mine."

Antonia held up her hands in surrender. "Understood. I'm sorry, Sun."

"I thought you didn't like me."

The side of Antonia's mouth lifted. "I don't, really, but he does."

Oh. I squeezed my middle. It didn't help. "He's my friend."

"I know." Antonia very lightly rested a hand on my shoulder as she passed, heading for the door. She scratched her fingernails against the fabric of my hoodie. It felt like needles.

"I'm sorry," she said. "But Fable is right. This is best."

I nodded, unable to speak, my voice hidden in the swirls of anguish. I understood. I really did. Guilt by association. I already knew too much anyway.

Up until this point, I'd found it easy to follow the Consortium's rules. There was never really any reason to break them. But Rook was kind. He deserved a chance. He was lonely, I could tell. I recognized it in him the way I saw it in myself. I, at least, had my sisters and parents, but Rook had no one. And he deserved someone, even if it was Antonia. Even if it wasn't me.

"Don't tell him," I said.

Antonia turned on her heel. "What?"

"Don't tell him." I bit my lip. "It's better for him to think I just stopped contacting him instead of him knowing that it's . . ." I trailed off. "He'll try to break the rules." He would. Not that I thought he valued our relationship that much, but he was stubborn. He'd see a barrier and find a solution. That was the way he worked. He saw something in his way, and he either plowed through it or found an alternative route. He literally invented a whole device to secure his place in magic. "Because he's stubborn."

Antonia smiled, gentle and fond. "I understand. It's better for him to think you've lost interest than there's something keeping you apart."

"Yeah." I licked my lips. "Not that I think—"

"I hear you, kid." Antonia turned the knob. "I won't say anything."

"Thank you."

Antonia left. I crossed the room to my workstation, and without talking to Fable, took out my cauldron. The potions weren't going to make themselves.

"Sun."

I ignored them. It wasn't mature in the slightest, but I didn't know what to say. I'd chosen magic. I'd always choose magic. That wasn't the question. But it had been nice to have a friend. To have someone who liked me in return. Someone who, despite my prickliness and social ineptitude, had kept trying. Most people gave up. Even my sisters didn't fully understand.

"Sun," Fable said, tone firm.

"What?" Ugh. I didn't look up from where the fire had flickered to life.

"If you can't be civil and act like an adult, you can go home."

I took a breath, lifted my head, but still didn't meet Fable's gaze, choosing to look over their shoulder. "That's somewhat better. Sun, you have to—"

"I choose magic. I'm loyal to you as your apprentice. I understand that is what this relationship is about. Okay? That's what you want to hear?"

"No. It's not. I want you to tell me you understand."

"I understand. I understand that there are things that I have to relinquish to be in this position. I chose a different name, a pseudonym, to protect my family and myself. All my free hours before and after school are spent studying magic and being here to help you. I know that. I'm okay with that. But he is my friend." I bit my lip. "He was my friend. I liked having a friend."

"You can have other friends, Sun. I heard that Petra Moon's apprentice is quite friendly. Maybe we could—"

"No. I mean, maybe later."

"Okay. Sun, for what it's worth, I'm sorry."

Sorry wasn't worth much, but Fable was sincere. I shifted my gaze to finally be an adult and face them head-on, catching Fable's reflection in the mirror, then froze. "Fable, your scrying mirror is uncovered."

Fable startled and turned abruptly.

The mirror hung on the far wall and usually had a large drape over it unless Fable needed to talk with someone who couldn't be reached by the phone. Like the Consortium.

"Fable, what have you done?"

"Nothing," Fable said, striding across the room. They grabbed the drape and tossed it over the gilded frame. "I used it earlier. I forgot it was uncovered."

"Fable," I breathed. "Anyone could've heard that conversation."

"No one did." Fable didn't look convinced as they went back to their spell book. "Now, go ahead and work. The hedge witches have ordered more potions, and I want you to practice your spells."

My heart ached. My head ached. It was a little dramatic. But it hurt. Rook was . . . handsome, and his smile was like sunshine. And I liked him. I really liked him. He could've been someone to me.

"Okay," I said weakly. And tried not to think about frog's tears and purple polka dots in the sun and a wide dimpled grin.

12

ROOK

I hadn't texted Sun. And Sun hadn't texted me, either, which I had been counting on. Antonia had said not to reach out to Sun but hadn't mentioned Sun reaching out to me. Which was a pretty sweet loophole.

But Sun hadn't texted. Which sucked. But we had just seen each other yesterday. Maybe that was enough interaction for a bit for Sun. I'd have to ask when we talked again. Figure out those boundaries. Or I could do that now? No, calling would be right out.

Okay, maybe if I just sent a short little "Hey." That wouldn't be against the rules. Right? I wouldn't mention the candle. So yeah, that should be fine. And hey, since when did I care about rules? I worked for Antonia. Rules were suggestions.

I rolled onto my stomach in my bed, propped myself up on my elbows, and opened my contacts.

"Hey," I sent.

And waited.

No response. I frowned. Well, Sun did have a life. They had a job and three sisters and summer school. It's okay. I had things to do as well. I should do them.

So I did.

A load of laundry and a shower later and still no response from Sun.

Weird.

Fine. Not a big deal.

I watched a movie, scrounged around in the kitchen for a snack, thankful that Antonia had ordered lunch for us today when all I found was a half-open bag of stale chips. But it would do.

No response.

It was getting late. Sun was usually home by now.

A phone call wouldn't hurt, just to say hi. I mean, we hadn't talked on the phone before, but we hadn't hung out of our own accord until yesterday, either. It was a week for trying new things! Taking new steps in our friendship.

I tapped the button and held the phone to my ear. It rang once and went right to voicemail. Like Sun had rejected my call. My phone buzzed.

Can't talk.

Oh. Yeah. Right. Sun and that pesky other life they had beyond magic. It hurt a little. But okay. Yeah, that was fine. Fine.

Okay. Talk tomorrow.

No response.

I flopped back on my bed. Well, it was fine. It was late. Maybe they were already in bed. Sun seemed like the early-to-bed, late-to-rise kind of person. I would just talk to them tomorrow.

I didn't have a text from Sun in the morning, either. Or one the next day, but it was okay because Sun was busy. Sun was important. Sun had a family and summer school and a job. I texted a few times, just about the day, not mentioning the candle or anything about magic, but about the cute dog that I petted on my walk from the bus stop and a few complaints about the heat. Nothing. No response that day. Or the next. On the fourth, I texted again, just to check in, and again was met with silence.

A week later, I finally accepted that I had been well and truly ghosted. Whatever had transpired between us in Antonia's office hadn't been real, or well, had been real on my part but not on theirs. Or something. Whatever. I tried to brush it off, but being honest with myself, it felt awful, like the bitter taste of rejection I'd already experienced in different facets of my life. Like I had opened myself up, and whatever Sun had seen wasn't good enough. I thought Sun might be different, might understand what it meant to not quite fit in, but I guess I was wrong. I wasn't going to cry about it. At least, not in public anyway. Crying into my pillow was a totally different matter.

That afternoon, I walked my usual route from the bus stop to the office, phone in my hand, staring down at all the unanswered texts to Sun, especially the last one, sent in a fit of desperation and hurt.

Why are you ignoring me? Did I do something wrong?

If I could take that one back, I would. But it was out there. Sun hadn't responded, and it had been hours. So that was that, I guessed. Ghosted by my one-time rival and frenemy who had become my friend who I had kind of liked and wanted to kiss.

It didn't feel great. But I guessed that it was for the best. Maybe Antonia had been right.

Sighing, I turned on the sidewalk and headed toward the office, slipping my phone into my back pocket. The crunch of glass underneath my shoes was the first indication that something wasn't quite right. I slowed, curious and apprehensive as I took in the mess of shards that glittered across the pavement.

The front windows were blown out. The blinds were twisted and broken. There was one set that was stranded all the way in the middle of the asphalt. But the glass, the glass was everywhere, like an explosion had gone off inside the office, propelling the windows outward. Alarm bells rang in my head. All my senses went on high alert. Antonia's car was there, parked in her usual spot, but it hadn't escaped whatever had happened, either. The windshield was a web of cracks, and there were scratches all over the paint job. One of the side mirrors dangled, barely holding on by a few colored wires. Antonia was going to be absolutely pissed, if she was okay. She had to be okay. Because whatever had happened had obviously been explosive.

I stepped closer, eyes wide, heart thumping hard.

Once I stood in front of what used to be Hex-A-Gone, I saw the true extent of the damage. "What the fuck?" I whispered.

I felt a little silly pulling on the door handle, but I was on autopilot in the face of the destruction. The last little bit of window that stubbornly clung to the frame fell in a cascade.

"Antonia?" I called softly; my voice lodged in my throat. The dial on my fear and anxiety was turned up to a thousand, and I could barely push her name out of my dry mouth.

I went to hop over the cursed rug as I stepped through the door, only to find an outline of where it used to be, as if some kind of intense light had imprinted the shadow of it on the tile.

The nape of my neck prickled. I crept in, hunched like I was cosplaying a suspicious criminal from a video game, as if ducking would protect me from whatever it was that had destroyed the office. This was a bad idea and further evidence that my self-preservation skills had not improved since I started working for Antonia. In fact, I think they'd gotten worse. I gripped my backpack straps like my life depended on it as I picked my way into the building.

I reached for the light switch and flicked it. Of course, none of the interior lights blinked on because whatever had done . . . this . . . had taken out the lights as well. The silence and the atmosphere was unreal, otherworldly.

Herb was not in the corner where he normally lurked. The receptionist desk was on its side. The cubicles were flattened. My work computer was in parts, strewn across the floor. The further I shuffled in, the worse the devastation. Like whatever had happened had an epicenter that was just on the outside of Antonia's office. It was like the pictures of meteorite landings I'd seen in books, where the places closest to impact were completely flattened but the destruction radiated for miles.

Except for Antonia's door. The purple sheen of a ward shimmered across the entire wall of her office. Everything down to the windows was still in one piece. So the ward had been set before the . . . blast?

Maybe Antonia was behind the door. Maybe she had locked herself in to protect herself. I should call her. She'd answer. She'd always picked up for me.

Glass crunched behind me. I startled and spun to face the door. Voices approached from the parking lot. Someone was coming. But until I knew who they were, I should hide. I legged it behind the overturned desk and dropped to the floor, curling against the wood to make myself as small as possible. If they looked hard enough, they would see me, but I hoped in the dark and in the wreckage, I might go unnoticed.

"Still can't break the spell," someone said, walking into the office. "She really is the most powerful sorcerer of the current age."

"And yet we managed to detain her."

The other person hummed. "Not without borrowing sorcerers from our sister office in Seraph Lake. And not without injuries."

I gulped.

"Yes, how are Simmons and Frank?"

"They've been taken to a local healer."

"Good." More glass crunched, followed by the sound of an object tumbling. "We need to break this ward to retrieve her spell books and any information she has on her apprentice."

My whole body went cold with dread. My heart thundered in my ears. The footsteps came closer, and I squeezed as far down into a crouch as I could.

"If what we heard is true, he shouldn't be too difficult to capture. He's not magic, after all."

Well, thanks. Shows what you know, asshole.

"Keep an eye out. If Antonia has been able to teach him anything, he could be a threat."

I could hear Sun's scoff in my head.

The two people approached where I hid by the desk. Every muscle in my body clenched. My pulse beat a fight-or-flight rhythm. They wanted to capture me. For what?

"Hey, remember her last apprentice?"

"Unfortunately. How could anyone forget?"

"Hopefully this one won't put up as much of a fight."

Okay. That confirmed that I did not want to be caught by whoever these fuckers were. From my position, I could see when their legs cleared my hiding spot, clad in black pressed fabric with stiff creases, but luckily, their gazes were trained on the spell on Antonia's door and not on the overturned desk. Which was great, because I saw who these two were. And I recognized Evanna Lynne Beech, sorcerer grade four, immediately. The other was some tall guy who looked like a jerk in his suit and skinny tie and reflective sunglasses.

"He can't," Evanna Lynne said. She smirked.

"You met him, right? What was he like?"

"Why?"

The guy shrugged. "I guess I'm interested in who inspired rebellion in Antonia Hex."

Evanna Lynne huffed. "It's not that like she needed much of a reason. But he's a kid. Smart mouth. Smiled a lot. Wily."

A phone rang. I flinched at the sudden noise but luckily didn't knock into anything.

Evanna Lynne pulled her phone from her pocket. "It's team two. I need to take this. They should be getting into position by now."

Team two? Did Antonia get away? Why did they need a team two?

Unless . . .

No.

They wouldn't.

Would they?

Sun. I had to warn Sun.

Evanna Lynne turned around, answering her phone, and I couldn't wait any longer.

I had to get to Sun. I crawled quietly on my hands and knees toward an exit, desperately trying to stay out of sight. Pieces of glass dug into my palms. Freedom in sight, my toes caught on my keyboard, and my foot slid out from under me. I landed on my chest with an *oof*.

"What was that?"

Gangly guy turned around, and I couldn't hide any longer. I jumped to my feet. We stared at each other for a beat, like we were in a comedy crime movie, before I ran.

"Hey!" he shouted. "You! Stop!"

"Not likely!" I yelled back. Fortunately, the door he tried to block with his body wasn't my only option for escape, the blasted windows worked just as well. I ran for the nearest one and hopped through it onto the sidewalk.

And oh. There were more of them. Five more Consortium sorcerers milled about, wearing suits and ties and sunglasses like they were detectives in the video game I was in earlier, all holding large cups of coffee. Where were they when I first got here?

"There he is!"

"Grab him!"

"Nope!" I said, dodging an outstretched hand. Their fingers snagged on the hem of my shirt but that was as close as they were able to get because I took off running. They weren't going to catch me. I was the motherfucking Gingerbread Man.

I ran out of the parking lot, up the sidewalk, and back toward the bus stop.

Pounding footsteps and shouts followed me. A few muttered spells were fired in my direction. The branches of a nearby tree lunged when I passed, and a pit of quicksand opened in front of me. But I dodged and hurtled in a series of moves that would make my sophomore gym teacher proud . . . until the concrete rolled and buckled, catapulting me forward across the pavement. I fell. Pain shot up my ankle and my knees and my elbows, but I forced myself to scramble to my feet. My body protested as I ran across the street, ignoring the honking horns of furious drivers.

More shouts. More footsteps. More evading of pedestrians on the sidewalk. I had to find help.

I ran. They followed.

The hiss and groan of air brakes cut through my adrenaline haze. I jerked my head around to see a city bus slowing to a stop down the street. Perfect.

I jumped off the sidewalk. More car horns. More brakes squealing.

I didn't look back. I couldn't look back. I rounded the front of the bus, hands up, yelling at the driver to stop. I bounded on, dripping blood as I ran down the aisle and out through the back door into the nearby alley.

I kept running to the next street, then into a pharmacy on the corner. My chest heaved. My palms were sweaty, streaked with red. My ankle throbbed. I was so out of shape.

I waited for a minute at most, hiding in the aisle next to the window. No suit-clad sorcerers ran by, and I breathed a sigh of relief.

I'd managed to ditch them. They probably thought I was still on the bus. That move was a stroke of genius.

But that didn't mean I was safe. I was in a part of the city I didn't know, and I needed help. Pulling my phone from my pocket, I checked my messages. I had none. None from Antonia. Nothing from Sun.

My stomach twisted.

I called Sun. It rang and rang, then went to voicemail. Frustrated, I tried again. It rang and rang, and this time I left a message.

"Hey, asshole. I know you're ignoring me for some reason, but pick up. *Please*. Something has happened."

Then I hung up and called again. And again.

Fuck!

They weren't answering. I wandered to a nearby bench and collapsed onto it, yanking my backpack to the front. With one hand, I kept calling. Over and over again as I scrounged around and found the scrap of paper with Fable's address.

I had to get there.

"What do you want?" Sun's voice came from the line, exhausted and thin.

I startled. And looked down at the phone in my hand. "Hello?" they said. "If this is a joke, I'm hanging up."

"Don't hang up!" I shouted, jamming the phone to my ear.

Sun sensed my panic. "Okay." They swallowed. "Are you okay?"

"No. Fuck, no. Listen, something happened. I don't really know what, but Antonia—"

"Who was that calling you over and over?" Fable's voice was distant. "Is everything okay? It's not your family, is it?"

"Everything is fine," Sun replied, but I could tell it wasn't. That was the same "I'm fine" Sun used while in the elevator forever ago. The same "I'm fine" in the haunted house, after they'd been cursed.

"Sun?"

"It's fine. Look, I can't talk right now."

"No! Wait! Sun, listen. I don't know what's going on, but Antonia is missing, and there are these people chasing me that look like bad sci-fi movie cosplayers. Listen, you need to—"

A knocking sound came from the background. "Can you get that, Sun?" Fable asked. "I'm elbow-deep in this augury examination."

My heart seized. "Sun! No. Don't open the door. Listen to me!"

They were distracted. "I have to go. I'll . . . I'll call you later."

"No! Sun! Don't hang up!"

The phone went dead.

13

SUN

"I have to go. I'll . . . I'll call you later."

I ended the call and stared guiltily down at my phone as the last message Rook had sent blinked on the screen.

Why are you ignoring me? Did I do something wrong?

I hurt, like I'd been elbowed in the gut, which I had experience with because my sisters liked to roughhouse. But it didn't feel fun. I felt awful, sick to my stomach. It was worse than the few days I'd spent ill after the curse was broken. I'd hurt him, and I hated myself for it.

I had thought I could put my frustration with Fable over the whole situation behind me, but hearing Rook's voice again reignited all the feelings I'd tried to suppress. And for the first time since I'd become an apprentice, I questioned everything. Everything that Fable asked me to do. Everything that Antonia had said. Everything that I read in the Consortium's rules and regulations.

Not that I was about to throw away everything I'd worked so hard for because of a boy I liked and wanted to be my friend. But it did make me consider my relationship with magic and with Fable.

The shivery feeling when I thought about Rook was teenage hormones at work, but beyond this spell of first love, it made me really contemplate what could happen in the future. What if future Sun disagreed with a rule or a choice that Fable or the Consortium laid before me? What then? Would I be able to handle the guilt that came with making a choice that hurt someone else? Is this what Antonia had been fighting against all along?

"Sun?" Fable called, as the impatient knocks sounded a second time. "The door."

My phone lit up as Rook called again. I furrowed my brow, worry bubbling up into my throat. I'd talked to him while half-hidden in a small storage area where Fable kept their extra magic supplies and dry goods. There was a ladder that led to the attic and a window that was eternally stuck halfway open, a screen propped against it to keep the bugs out. It was the only place I could find some privacy, so I was fairly certain Fable hadn't overheard. But I couldn't risk talking to him, not at the cottage. I'd call him back after I left for the day. And just . . . check in. If he wanted to talk to me at all.

"Sun!" Fable said, exasperated.

"Yeah. Coming."

No sooner were the words out of my mouth when the door shook with magic so forcefully that dust rained down from the rafters.

Fable cocked their head to the side. They held up their hand and stopped me from leaving the back room. Grabbing a towel, they wiped off their arms and waved me away.

"Who is it?" they called.

"Open the door, Fable, and we won't have a problem."

"That didn't answer my question."

Another powerful knock, and a crack rippled through the wood, the hinges coming loose from the frame. "This is important

Consortium business, so either open the door or we will take it and the ward down."

"In a moment," Fable called.

They turned and made a gesture for me to be quiet. I nodded. My pulse raced. I clutched my phone in my clammy hands and realized that maybe Rook's call had been more urgent than me getting into trouble with my mentor. I should've listened. Rook's account of being chased by sorcerers in suits filtered through my rising unease. This was bad.

Fable straightened their shirt and trousers, smoothed down their hair, and lifted their chin as if they were bracing for the worst. They crossed the room and creaked open the door a sliver.

"May I help you?" they said as I retreated into the storage room, back pressed against the rustic wood as I trembled in fear. My phone vibrated in my hands, and I shoved it into my pocket. Whatever happened, I needed to keep them away from Rook, and if they knew we were in contact . . . they'd use that. They'd use me.

I couldn't see the sorcerer Fable spoke to, but their voices were loud and clear.

"Fable Page, you and your apprentice, Sun, are hereby detained for questioning in regard to Antonia Hex and her apprentice, Rook."

Fable hummed low in their throat. "Is this threat of force and detainment warranted? As the Consortium well knows, I have never once defied a Consortium law."

"You are friends with Antonia Hex, are you not?"

"We are not friends."

"But you occasionally work together."

"Sometimes."

"And you were aware she had named an apprentice?"

Fable sighed. My hand clenched around the phone in my pocket. "I was aware he existed, but—"

"Quit stalling, Page," a gruff voice cut in. "You may not have broken any law, but your apprentice surely did when they taught Hex's *apprentice* magic." He said the word like a sneer, like Rook wasn't worthy of the title.

I winced. Fable sucked in a harsh breath.

"My apprentice is young and made a mistake. And they—"

"Are in a lot of trouble. Now, you can either hand them over and come quietly, or our threat is going to become an action. Oh, and just know that Hex chose to put up a fight. She lost. Being as she's twice the sorcerer—"

I didn't allow him to finish. I ran forward, tapped into the ley line, muttered a spell, and pushed the magic outward in a fierce wind. It slammed the door shut in his face, but not before he saw me over Fable's shoulder.

"They're both here!" he shouted.

Fable locked the door and cast an additional ward, but it did not set in time.

The door buckled inward, breaking and crumbling before erupting into a shower of splinters. Tiny shards pinpricked my skin, while the blast left my ears ringing and my head fuzzy. But I was still sharp enough to see several sorcerers in Consortium-issued suits spill into the cottage like ants.

"Sun, run," Fable said, already alight with the glow of magic.

"But—"

"Run!"

I turned for the back door in time to see it fall inward, like it had been struck with a battering ram. Okay, front door and back door were out. There weren't many places to run, especially since I had the sinking feeling that we were surrounded.

Shit! Heart in my throat, I dodged around a suit-clad body, pushing them away with a spell before diving into the storage room. I kicked the door closed with my heel and set a haphazard ward as thuds emanated from the other side. I had no way out. None. I was only delaying the inevitable, but if I could buy time, maybe Fable could defeat them.

Until then the only way out was up. I'd seen a lot of horror movies, thanks to my sisters, so I knew it was not the smartest move to go to a second story instead of exiting the house altogether, but there were sorcerers much stronger than me flooding the downstairs. I grabbed the first rung of the ladder, ignoring the tightness of my chest at the thought of the small, square entrance I'd have to squeeze through at the top, and climbed. My hands slipped on the rungs and my legs quivered, but I pushed upward, relying on adrenaline.

My heart thudded in my ears as I climbed to the top, but the sound didn't drown out the fight below. Furniture thumped as it was overturned, dishes crashed, and the metallic clang of a cauldron hitting the ground rang out. I hadn't pegged Fable as someone who would fight. But judging by the noise and the amount of magic that itched through me, they were fighting. They were fighting hard.

The door to the storage room finally broke, and a sorcerer shoved inside. Hands shaking, I hauled myself into the attic. Magic flooded through me as I pulled again from the ley line to cast a spell, breaking the ladder behind me, leaving me without a way down but the sorcerer without a way up.

A low laugh wafted upward into the attic after me.

"Do you think that is going to stop me?"

I shivered with panic, tears springing into my eyes, as I ran along the exposed beams of the unfinished attic. One wrong step and I would go through the ceiling and back into the melee below.

Balancing on the wood, I ran toward the single window and

peered out. It overlooked the front porch roof. If I could get through, I could drop to the roof, then jump to the bushes, and make a break for the enchanted forest.

"Now, now, don't make this hard on yourself. You're no match for me, little apprentice."

My stomach churned. His voice was awful and patronizing, and it made me squirm. I grabbed for the windowsill and dug my fingernails into the wood, trying to pry it open, but it had been painted shut.

No. No. I slammed my palm against it, which did nothing except send a spike of pain up my arm.

Despair lanced through me, followed quickly by terror. I knew what the Consortium did to people who disobeyed them. At best, our spell books would be confiscated. At worst . . . well, at worst, we'd be magically bound, never allowed to practice. They'd done it before. Most recently to Antonia's previous apprentice, according to Fable.

I grabbed at the ley line, fumbling with it in my own panic. The magic slipped through me, skittering away as my breath came in quicker and quicker pants.

The beam creaked behind me. I spun around to find a sorcerer in a suit and a skinny tie approaching me, his hulking frame bending the boards beneath his polished shoes.

"Sun," he said, low and calm, though with a slimy edge. "Come along quietly, and I'll make sure no harm comes to you."

Fear dripped down my spine, along with sweat. I was trapped. I couldn't escape. Not from up here. I turned to face him, my fists balled. My chest heaved.

He smirked. "Going to fight me? You're no match for me in size or in power."

He wasn't wrong. He was tall, very tall, and the Consortium

badge that dangled against his broad chest marked him as a sorcerer grade three. He took another step and *wobbled*.

No. No, I wasn't going to fight him. I was going to do something better. I gripped the windowsill behind me and cowered as he approached, trying to make myself look defeated and meek, which wasn't much of a stretch. I focused on my breathing, calming myself. My muscles locked.

"That's good, Sun. No need to be frightened." He smiled, though it was far from friendly.

"I'm not," I said, though it came out a whisper. I swallowed and reached out for the ley line. This time it greeted me like it usually did, the warmth of magic flooding me from my head to my soles.

He took another step, this time on a cross board, and the wood bowed beneath his feet. He was suspended so precariously, all it would take would be one push.

Or one very gusty wind.

I muttered the spell and channeled all the magic I could gather.

The wind burst from me in a tornado aimed at his chest, kicking up a cloud of dust and debris. His eyes widened in surprise, and I tasted victory.

But then the sorcerer laughed as he cast a counterspell, and the wind dispersed. He didn't move. Didn't even twitch in the swirl of dust motes.

"What?" I said, voice weak. I dropped my hand. The magic leeched out of me as my soul shriveled up. His smirk returned.

"Nice try, little apprentice." He shuffled forward, the plank bending under him, as he came within arm's length. "But you'll have to—" He sniffled, rubbed his sleeve under his nose. "You'll have to—" He sucked in a sharp breath, covered his face with his hand, and sneezed violently. The sneeze unbalanced him, causing him to take a step back, off the plank and onto . . . the ceiling.

He sneezed again. The ceiling cracked beneath his girth, and his eyes widened. "Oh no." The drywall gave way, and he fell.

But not before he grabbed the front of my hoodie and pulled me down with him.

My surprised cry caught in my throat as my body smacked against the ceiling before breaking through.

I somehow landed on what was left of the kitchen table, my back slamming against it, forcefully knocking out every ounce of air I had in me. The sorcerer landed on the floor and pieces of a broken chair. I couldn't breathe, but at least I was back downstairs again.

The room was eerily silent as I lay there, stunned, staring up at the hole we'd fallen through as bits of broken ceiling, exposed insulation, and wood rained down like a drizzle. Before I had a chance to recover, someone yanked me to my feet and threw me against the wall.

Pain sparked like fireworks behind my eyes, and my head spun.

The person who grabbed me pinned me in place by my shoulders.

"Got them!"

"Sun!" Fable yelled.

I winced, blinking to get my vision to focus. Once it cleared, I surveyed the room. Fable was surrounded. They weren't bound, but it was clear they were defeated. Blood ran from a cut above their eyebrow, and they were bruised, clothes tattered. The cottage was destroyed. Every possession of ours was either broken or on the floor. Even my backpack had been opened and dumped out into in a pile on the counter.

"Fable?" I asked, reedy and thin.

"You told me you wouldn't hurt them."

The sorcerer who tumbled with me groaned from the floor, which gave me a small modicum of satisfaction.

"We said we wouldn't hurt them if they didn't run or fight. They apparently did both."

Fable narrowed their eyes. "Sun," they said, "are you okay?"

"Yeah. No. I don't . . ." Everything *hurt*. And I was scared. Scared like I'd been when I had to wield that sword and cut Rook out from the curtains. But I wouldn't show the Consortium sorcerers my fear. "I'm fine," I said.

Fable cut their gaze to me. "Do you remember what I asked you when you were first hired?"

I couldn't remember anything, not with the pain in my head and the adrenaline scattering my thoughts.

"Fable," someone warned. "Stop talking."

Fable didn't acknowledge them. They stared at me, eyebrows raised, and I couldn't for the life of me recall what they were talking about, but I nodded because it was all I could do. They nodded back, then muttered a spell.

There was a flash, and my legs gave out. I fell to the ground, landing on all fours, swaddled in layers of fabric.

I shook my head to clear it, disentangling myself from the hoodie draped over my head. Somehow, I'd fallen, or shrunk or something.

"Run!"

I realized my captor no longer held me. I was free, but low to the ground and staring at their shoes. Whatever. I could escape—that was the important part—and I scampered across the wooden floor. A commotion followed me, but I was quick, so quick, and small and . . . What had Fable done?

Okay. I couldn't dwell. I just had to escape. Despite my misgivings, I ran into the storage room again. Luckily, the half-open window screen hadn't survived the melee, and without analyzing or overthinking or worrying, I jumped onto the sill and squeezed my small body through the broken frame.

I dropped into our pathetic garden, four paws sinking into the damp earth, then ran.

14

ROOK

I hoped I wasn't too late.

The cab had dropped me off a block away at my request, and now I ran down the sidewalk and onto a long driveway. But as soon as I neared, I spotted the cars piled in front of Fable's cottage and the suit-clad sorcerers milling about.

Oh no. I was too late.

I pressed my hand against my thundering heart. What was I going to do now? They had Antonia. They probably had Fable and Sun. I couldn't save them; I could barely cast a spell. Maybe the Consortium was right, and I didn't belong. Even if I did, I was in over my head and knew no one else who could help. Should I just turn myself over? Would that make anything better?

I snuck over to the trees ringing Fable's property, creeping through the trunks in the hopes of getting close enough to hear or see anything useful. Around the back side of Fable's house, there was a small brook that disappeared into a forest. This must be the enchanted wood Sun mentioned. If I could have felt magic, I bet it would be vibrating with it.

I didn't know what I was doing. There wasn't anything I could do to help now. Hopefully, Sun had pulled their head out of their ass and heeded my warning.

A commotion around the back of the property grabbed my attention. I slid between the trees as fast as I could and watched as a small gray cat dropped out of the back window and sprinted toward the tree line.

Sorcerers spilled out of the back door, pushing, shouting, tripping over each other to give chase.

"That's the apprentice?" one of them yelled.

Another answered. "Yes! Don't let them get away!"

I gasped. The cat was Sun? No way. Absolutely no way.

Except—

Stranger things had happened.

I leaped out from behind the trees and whistled sharply.

The cat didn't break stride, but it veered toward me, running at full speed until it slid to a stop in the grass at my feet before climbing up the leg of my jeans, its tiny claws catching in the fabric and my skin. Holy shit. Was this *really* Sun?

"Hey! There's the other one!"

I scruffed the cat by the back of the neck, tucked it close into the cradle of my arms, turned toward the forest, and took off running into the trees.

I had no path. I had no plan. Judging by Sun's daring escape, Fable had been captured as well, which meant we had no mentors. All I had were my limited self-preservation instincts, an illegal electronic device, and a cat. A cat that was apparently my rival turned friend turned nothing turned feline.

The tree branches whipped at my skin as I ran. Shouts from the sorcerers followed me, so I kept going. Deeper and deeper into the forest until I couldn't hear the chaos behind me, and all that was left was my own harsh breathing and the calls of bothered birds above.

I found a carved-out den of branches and leaves next to a tree and ducked into it. I pulled my knees to my chest as I settled against the tree trunk, listening for any sound of our potential captors through my jagged breath.

After a few torturous minutes, I heard nothing, and I finally eased my arms from their curled position.

The cat stared up at me balefully with dark-brown eyes, body pressed to me in the cage of my arms, whiskers twitching in what I read as annoyance.

"Sun?"

It meowed.

"Is it really you?"

Another meow.

Huh. "Meowing in response to my questions could be a coincidence. How do I know it's really you and you're not just some poor cat that was in the wrong place at the wrong time?"

The cat dug their little claws into my chest.

"Ow! Damn. Okay, it's you."

I opened my arms, and Sun jumped out, landing daintily next to me, tail twitching. They were absolutely as adorable of a cat as a human, and it was really messing with my head that my once-friend had fluffy fur, a tail, and little gray ears that twitched.

"What the fuck?" I asked, staring at them.

Sun lifted a single paw as if to say "It is what it is," which is a phrase I knew for a fact Sun hated.

I peered around the tree but didn't spy anyone or anything nearby. I hoped I hadn't disturbed some small animal's den by hiding in this nook, but who knew. I was in an enchanted forest. My friend was a cat. Sorcerers were chasing us. Anything could happen at this point.

"So," I said, drawing out the vowel. "We have a few problems. First, you're a cat."

Sun blinked, unamused.

"Second, Antonia has been captured by the Consortium, and I'm guessing Fable has as well?"

Sun nodded to confirm.

"Right. Third, we're officially on the run. Unless we want to turn ourselves in."

Sun hissed.

"My thoughts exactly."

I dug my phone from my back pocket to check the time and to see if I could figure out a way out of the forest. My battery was low, and I had no signal, probably due to the amount of magic in the forest. Even without the signal, I wasn't expecting a message from Antonia, but it was still a blow to my optimism that there was nothing there. Only the last frantic calls I'd sent Sun today and the damning text from that morning. Sun shifted awkwardly, turned their head away, and . . . right. Sun had ghosted me. For a week. And that had hurt. And I wasn't over it, but we had bigger problems at hand than our almost-friendship, maybe-something-more that could've happened.

"We need a plan."

Sun nodded.

"Do you have your phone?"

Sun blinked again. Their tail swished. "Right, dumb question. You're literally a cat, and you have no pockets." I tapped my fingers along my lips. "I have no ideas. Do you?"

Sun walked over to my bag and placed a paw on the fabric. I slid it off my shoulders and opened it. Sun peered inside and hissed. The Spell Binder/Ley Finder was on top, and yeah, okay. I got the sentiment. It was partly what landed us in this situation.

"What?"

Sun meowed.

"I don't know what you want."

Sun meowed again.

"Seriously. Do you want me to destroy it? Turn it on? Look for a spell to turn you back?" And oh. There was an idea. Did I have a spell that could turn Sun back? I might. I did input that whole spell book. But even if I did, I wouldn't be able to cast it, not even here, where magic dripped off the foliage like dew. Unless I found someone else who could. Sun had a sister who might be able to. And I assumed Sun probably had connections to other sorcerers.

"Hey, so, uh, are you a magic kitty?"

Sun stared at me with a less-than-impressed expression at the term "kitty," then cocked their head to the side, whiskers twitching. Then they sneezed. It was the cutest, tiniest sneeze I'd ever heard, but I took it as a no, that Sun did not have access to their magic at this time.

No matter. We were still in the information-gathering part of this mission. I turned the Spell Binder on to find a spell that might possibly magic Sun back to human. The screen lit up and pulsed with magic. Not just a single line but a whole convergence of power. Oh. So that's why this place was enchanted. It sat on a massive amount of magic. I flipped to the spell app, scrunched down to the ground, and opened it up. Sun sat by my shoulder, tail curled around their cute feet, and peered at the different spells.

I scrolled through them, reading off the names in case Sun couldn't read in cat form. There weren't that many, the spell book had been small, but maybe, just maybe.

"Spell to grow larger plants." I shook my head. "Spell to turn any liquid to water. Handy, but not what we need right now." I slid my thumb along the screen. "Spell to allow animals to talk or sing. Well, singing mouse guy should've used this one instead of trying a black-market spell." Oh! "Maybe we should try to find a black-market spell."

Sun hissed.

"What? If I ended up draining my own life force, then you could just fix it when you turn back to human."

Sun hissed again.

"Fine. We'll put that in the *maybe* column." I rolled my eyes. "But maybe we could grant you the gift of speech with this one? Then you could actually talk instead of hissing at me and clawing me."

Sun didn't respond. I took that as it might be a good idea if we couldn't find a better option.

"Spell to change the color of fabric. Spell to rearrange furniture in the most pleasing order. Spell to change cat litter." I snickered.

Sun swiped at me with their claw, which then proceeded to get caught in my sock. Cue an awkward moment of Sun yanking backward trying to become unstuck and me trying to gently extract their paw without being clawed. Once freed, Sun slunk a few feet away and licked their paw, staring at me grumpily.

"Well, serves you right. You ripped my sock."

This was how we spent the next hour, running through the list with me reading out the spell names and Sun ignoring me. By the end, I was sore and exhausted and in no better mood than I was when we started.

Yawning, I scrunched down further on the bed of leaves. "Why were all these spells objectively horrible? Who needs a self-playing piano unless you host dinner parties?"

Sun yawned a little cat yawn and wiggled down to their haunches.

"I don't know what to do, Sun," I admitted, humor failing me, so the statement came out more sincere than I would've liked. "I don't know where we are in this forest. I don't know where to turn."

I scrubbed my hands over my face. "I just wanted to be part of something magical. What's so terrible about that?"

Sun sighed.

"Yeah, everything apparently." With the adrenaline gone, I was exhausted down to my bones. I couldn't imagine trying to trudge out of the forest in the dark, either, and honestly, if we encountered more Consortium lackeys, I don't think I'd have it in me to escape. "Let's just . . . stay here for the night? And then tomorrow morning we'll find our way out, and I guess we'll . . . go to your family."

Sun sat bolt upright and meowed, distressed, and shook their head.

"Oh? You don't want them involved?"

Sun paced and let out a low, menacing growl.

"Because we could bring unwanted trouble to them. Right. Okay. Got it. So, no to contacting your family. And we can't go back to the cottage. And we can't go to Antonia's office. Okay, fine, we'll have to figure it out in the morning. I don't know about you, but I'm tired and my body hurts, and I really want to try to rest for a while."

Sun agreed if curling up into a furry little ball was any indication. They tucked their face under their tail, and it was so cute I was going to die from it. That is, if the Consortium didn't kill me first.

Careful not to disturb Sun, I pulled an extra sweatshirt from my backpack, then fashioned my bag into a pillow. I tucked the shirt around me like a makeshift blanket and made sure that one of the sleeves was over Sun.

Satisfied, I closed my eyes. Even though I was exhausted, sleep was a long time in coming.

15

SUN

So . . . I was a cat. This was less than ideal.

When Fable hired me, they had asked me if I had a choice between a cat, a bird, or a dog, what would I choose.

I thought it was a personality test of sorts, to see if we would work well together, like a cat-person versus dog-person pop psychology meme. I had no idea that they were asking me as a magical transformation fail-safe if I was ever in trouble, the kind of trouble in which there was no escape unless I was one of the above animals. And while I'm glad I'm a cat instead of a bird or a dog, because cats are awesome and don't slobber or have feathers, I'd much rather be a human. As a human, I'd have opposable thumbs, the ability to communicate in more than meows and hisses, and I'd be able to access the ley lines and maybe get Rook and myself out of this mess. Though I could still feel the magic humming within me, I couldn't grasp the line or cast a spell. It sucked to feel it but not be able to touch it, but at least it was there. The thought of being cut off completely made me shudder.

Being a cat was weird. I went to sleep on a bed of leaves and woke up tucked under Rook's chin, all warm and limp, muscles relaxed.

Like some animal instinct had me seek out body heat and touch in the night, which was not like me at all. Even weirder, when I woke up and stretched, I hadn't minded being so close to Rook. I didn't mind it at all.

I needed to be human again.

The sunlight was low, as if dawn had just broken. Rook was still asleep, curled up in a ball under a sweatshirt, and I tried my best to slip away without him noticing that I had basically slept tucked close to his chest all night. The leaves barely made any sound when I hopped onto them, but they twitched in the soft breeze. The edges fluttered right in my line of sight, and I couldn't think of anything else as distracting as they were. I batted at them with my paw. One dislodged from the pile and floated upward, drifting lazily, before settling a few feet away. That wouldn't do at all. I crouched low, my tail twitching, then pounced, trapping the leaf beneath my paws. Satisfaction at catching my prey curled warm in my belly. And damn, I really was a cat.

"Sun?" Rook asked, coming around, voice rough with sleep. "You there?"

I scampered over, slightly horrified with myself, and sat in front of his face, making sure the end of my tail smacked him in the nose.

"Oh," he said, blinking awake. "Still a cat."

Yes, indeed. Still a cat.

He groaned and sat up, blinking blearily into the morning. He scrubbed his palms over his face and cursed.

"I had hoped it was all a stress dream, but I guess not. We're still in the forest and you are still cute and fluffy."

My ears twitched. Yes. Cute and fluffy and annoyed. We needed a plan.

"We need a plan," Rook said around a yawn.

Yeah, no shit.

Rook ran a hand through his hair, knocking a few twigs loose.

"Okay, so, here is how I see it. We have a hierarchy of needs here. First, we need out of the forest."

I nodded. Agreed.

"Then we need a safe place to regroup."

Also, agreed.

"Then we need to get you turned back to human."

Three for three.

"Then we need to rescue Antonia and Fable and take down the Consortium."

Wait. What? I meowed in disagreement.

"Good to hear you agree with me."

What? No. I don't—

"Okay, let's get out of here. Do you want to ride in my backpack, or do you want me to carry you?"

Absolutely neither. Balking, I backed away, my back arched, and fur fuzzed out. I hissed.

"Adorable. But I have long legs, and I don't think you can keep up. And what I remember about cats is that they sleep, like, most of the day. You're going to be exhausted if you scamper about the forest like some woodland creature."

I took offense to that. I could keep up.

"Don't be obstinate about it."

Rook reached out, and I danced away.

"Sun. Cut it out. We don't have time for you to be prickly."

Oh, fuck off. I was not prickly. I was introverted and sometimes standoffish but not *prickly*. I took a few more steps back.

"Sun, I'm serious."

So was I. I was not about to be *carried*. I loped off into the underbrush, heading in what I thought was the direction of the way out, following the breaks in the foliage and undergrowth where Rook had barreled through yesterday. It was a wonder we hadn't been found. Rook cursed behind me, and I heard him scrambling to catch me. He did so easily, striding out in front, backpack on his shoulders, phone in his hand as he searched for a signal.

We walked together for about an hour, and everything was going okay. And except for that few minutes when I'd been distracted by a green lizard, I had been able to keep pace. Until now. My paws were sore. My body hadn't quite recovered from the beating I'd taken the day before, and I hurt all over. Falling through a ceiling wasn't awesome, and if I were human, I'm sure I'd have bruises on my back.

Despite my earlier objections, I let out a pitiful meow.

Rook kept walking. Huh. He must not have heard me. I sat down in the path and meowed again, a little louder, more of a yowl than anything cute.

Rook turned, eyebrows raised. "Oh? Something the matter?"

I sighed, trotted over to him, and twined between his legs, butting my head against his calf.

"I don't think so."

He started walking again, and I had to scurry out of his way lest he trip over me or step on my tail. I ran after him, having to trot to keep up, the jerk.

I meowed again, the only way I had to converse with him, and again Rook stopped and turned to look at me.

"Well, maybe you should've taken my suggestion at the beginning. But no, the great and powerful Sun doesn't need help. They don't want help. Or friendship, apparently." He said the second part lower, as if he didn't want me to hear.

But I heard anyway. And I guess I deserved that. I had ghosted Rook. Not by choice. Well, I guess it was a choice because I had chosen magic. I had no way to tell him how much it had hurt to let him go, or how many times I wanted to reach out to him and let him know it wasn't his fault. That it was a situation beyond our control. But I hadn't. I let him believe I was disinterested. And now, without a voice, I didn't have a way to convince him otherwise.

Hands on his hips, Rook sighed.

He crouched down and opened the top of his bag. "Come on," he said. "Get in."

I didn't really want to get into the backpack, but I wasn't about to refuse a ride. I slinked over and jumped in, settling myself on the extra sweatshirt. The space was small, and when Rook went to zip up the top, I gave another plaintive meow.

"I know," he said. "Small spaces. Here, I've left a spot for your head."

I poked my head through the gap and looked out. It was a little disorienting when Rook slid the backpack onto his shoulders, but after an adjustment, I was able to rest my chin on the lip of the bag and peer over Rook's shoulder as he walked.

"Let me know if you need anything."

Not for the first time, I was impressed by Rook's kindness, and my heart warmed. He didn't deserve what I'd done. He didn't deserve to be manipulated by Antonia. He didn't deserve Fable's ire. And once I was human again, I was going to tell him that.

I must've fallen asleep in the cozy warmth of the backpack, lulled by the rocking movement of Rook's footsteps. When I woke up, we were on the edge of the forest, right in the shade of the tree line. Beyond was Fable's cottage, and there were unfamiliar cars parked around it. It was definitely being watched.

"It's being watched," Rook murmured.

I stretched and let out a sound like a *meep*.

Rook looked over his shoulder. "Awake, huh? Well, hi. Have a nice nap?" I yawned in response. "I think we're far enough away to not be seen if we stick to the trees and head for the road." Rook lifted his phone. "I have a signal now, too, so we can map our way back to the city."

I perked up. But where would we go? I couldn't go home. The cottage was being watched. We couldn't go to Antonia's, either.

Rook sighed. "Come on."

We kept to the trees, and luckily didn't encounter anyone in suits with Consortium badges. The woods gave way to someone else's property, a rustic cabin nestled in between small hills and a brook. Rook kept walking, crossing the field and back into another bunch of trees. We avoided the road until the neighborhood gave way to the outskirts of the city.

After about another hour, we were truly back in the city. The only green were the medians in the road, and even those were brown from the hot summer sun and the baked-in heat of the concrete. Rook turned down a sidewalk and found the nearest bus stop.

I meowed. I didn't really know what I meant by it. *Thank you*, for one. *I'm scared*, for two. Maybe even, *Don't leave me*. And on top of that, *I'm thirsty and hungry*.

Rook looked over his shoulder. "Yeah, I hear you." His voice was weary yet fond, and I savored the sound.

When the bus pulled up, Rook touched the top of my head with one finger and nudged me down into the bag.

Right. Cats probably weren't welcome on city buses unless they were secured. As much as I hated it, I ducked inside. Thankfully, Rook didn't zip the bag over my head.

I fell asleep again on the bus ride, snuggled on Rook's sweatshirt, nose tucked under a sleeve. I was jostled awake again when Rook hopped off the bus and back onto a sidewalk.

The area was made of ugly concrete blocks, all the same height, laid out in a grid. Each one was exactly the same as the other. But the worst part was that there was no magic at all. Not a drop of it. It jarred me fully awake to go from a place soaked in magic to one so utterly void of it. My stomach lurched. How was it possible? Most places had a least a weak line, and with my sensitivity, I could even feel the residuals of dead lines, but this place . . . I shuddered. It was like there had never been any magic here at all. It was bleak.

Rook entered one of the identical buildings, only differentiated by the rain-stained numbers on the side. He walked through the dilapidated lobby toward the open elevator. I winced, whiskers twitching, but at the open doors, Rook stopped.

"Elevators," he said, then turned to the right and headed for the stairs.

My heart fluttered.

After climbing several flights, Rook exited the stairwell and stopped in front of a door. He rested his head against it, his key in his hand.

"Don't judge. I'm not the best at housekeeping."

Oh. This was Rook's home. He'd brought me to his home.

I nodded.

"Okay."

He turned the key and pushed open the door, tension draining from his frame as he entered and kicked off his shoes.

"You don't have to worry about anyone else. I live alone."

That sounded . . . lonely.

"I'm starving. I don't know if I have any food that you can eat in cat form. Or that I can eat, for that matter."

Rook slipped into the kitchenette that was attached to the living room. He opened the refrigerator, grimaced, and closed it. "Takeout it is." He crossed to the cabinet and took a glass, hesitated, and grabbed a bowl. He filled the glass with water from the tap and took a long drink. He filled it again. "Come on, my room is this way."

Rook's mattress was on a plain frame. He had a dresser and a closet and a desk that was filled with electronic junk. He set his backpack gently on his mattress and opened the zipper wider, and I hopped out. The sheets and blanket were soft under my sore paws, and the mattress bounced when Rook sat heavily next to me.

"Okay. Being here should be pretty safe. Only Antonia knows my real name, and I only told her once when I was first hired. She probably forgot it already. I know she never wrote it down." He set the bowl on a makeshift nightstand and filled it with water from the glass. "For you."

I tiptoed over. I was so thirsty, but how . . . I glanced back at Rook, who watched me intently. Great. I eased forward, and misjudged, stuck my face in the water. I reeled back, whiskers wet, and rubbed a paw over my nose. Rook, for his part, didn't giggle, which was good because if he had, I would have been forced to curse him once I was human again. I tried a second time, hovering barely over the surface of the water, and lapped and okay, that seemed to work. I drank too much, my belly full and sloshing once I was done, but I felt much better.

"Anyway," he said, lifting the Spell Binder out of the bag and holding it up toward me. "As you can see, no ley lines. Nothing. Absolutely void of magic. It's one of the reasons why developing this was so difficult because I couldn't tell if it was working unless I left the area. If a sorcerer were to come here, they couldn't do anything spell-wise, unless they can store magic like Antonia."

I scrunched my nose.

"I know. That's an Antonia-specific ability."

He sighed and fell backward on the bed, socked feet still on the floor, arms spread. "I didn't mean for all of this to happen."

I padded over and sat next to his arm.

"I just wanted to be a part of the community." He stuttered out a breath. "I just wanted to belong. I'm sorry. This is my fault."

I stared at the pale skin of his wrist, the blue veins that spread downward. I wanted to comfort him, reassure him, but I didn't know how. Should I try to hug him? Wait, that wouldn't work. Touch him in some way? Purr? No. No, I was *not* purring for any reason at all. That morning had been a fluke. But Rook was hurting, and if it would help him . . .

Before I could do anything, he sat up. "Okay. So, we're out of the forest and we've found shelter, which were the first two items on our list. Before we move on to the third, namely turning you back into the scowly, judgmental Sun I know and like and not this cute, fluffy exterior that I don't know how to reconcile with your actual personality—"

I hissed.

"Great. That's helpful. Before we do that, let's eat and nap. I don't know about you, but I need a shower. I have no idea how you need to address that, though. Are you going to lick yourself? Is that a thing."

How dare . . . ? I stood and turned away from him and sat back down, staring at the flaking white paint on the wall.

Rook laughed. It came out a little unhinged and breathless, as if yesterday's events were all of a sudden catching up to him and breaking forth in a fit of uncontrolled giggles.

"Sorry. I'm sorry. I'm just"—he sighed again—"a little on edge. It's okay. It's fine." He pulled out his phone and reached over the bed to grab his charger. He plugged it in. "I'm ordering food. I hope chicken is okay."

Chicken was fine. He tapped on his phone, then tossed it on the bed.

"Shower time." He gathered a change of clothes and a towel. "Uh, feel free to make yourself comfortable."

Once he left, I yawned. I stuck my face in the bowl again and drank a bit. Then I experimentally licked my paw. And ugh. No, thank you. My tongue was like sandpaper, and I had fur in my mouth. Awful. How did cats live like this? Gross.

With Rook gone, I was bored, so I decided to explore. I jumped down to the worn carpet and picked my way through a pile of clothes and empty snack bags until I sat at the bottom of his desk. I looked up, and wow, that was intimidatingly tall. But I was a cat. Cats liked high places. Right? I could do this. I totally could. But maybe I'd jump to the office chair first, then the top of the desk. So, I did.

And missed.

I overshot the seat and landed on the very edge, skidding off and onto the floor. At least the fall wasn't as traumatic or pain-filled as falling through the ceiling the day before.

I glared at the chair as it lazily spun from my antics. I crouched low to the ground, wiggled my butt like I'd done in the forest earlier before I pounced on that poor, unsuspecting leaf, and jumped again. This time, I landed safely. The next jump to the desk wasn't as difficult except I knocked off a few of Rook's contraptions. They *ping*ed to the floor in a cascade. Oops.

They were not what I was interested in anyway. I walked across the desk, sat in front of a picture frame, and peered at it. The picture was fairly low quality. It was taken at a selfie angle, and it was of Rook laughing while standing next to an older woman who gently smiled at him. That must be his grandmother, the butterfly conjurer. They shared the same kind smile and dimple. Rook missed her fiercely. He wouldn't have made the Spell Binder if he didn't. He wouldn't be so desperate to find a way back to magic. And again, I was hit with the realization that under Rook's smiley exterior was someone who was hurt and lonely and, despite all that, was still able to be thoughtful toward others.

And again, I cursed Fable and Antonia for making me choose. Rook was big feelings material, and while I would never know what could've been, I would have at least liked the chance to find out.

The doorbell rang, startling me out of my reverie, and my body jerked on instinct, my fur fuzzing out. I scrambled along the desk, my paws sliding, knocking into myriad objects. I darted to the floor and ran under the bed, scrunched between a shoebox and a textbook, shivering. My claws were out, digging into the carpet, eyes wide and on high alert.

Rook hurried past the bed, bare feet slapping against the carpet. I tensed even further when the front door opened, my heart beating so fast. There was a low conversation, followed by the crinkling of a bag, and then Rook padded back into his room, stopping within my line of sight. His ankles were pale and thin boned.

"Sun?"

I slunk out from beneath the bed and peered up. Rook's hair was damp-dark and flopped in his face. He wore a T-shirt and plaid pajama bottoms that looked worn and comfortable.

"Oh!" he said. "There you are." He paused. "Are you okay?"

I meowed.

"I can't tell if that's a good meow or a bad one." He lifted the bag. "But food. Let's eat."

We ate chicken together, Rook perched on a stool in the kitchen while I sat on the counter next to him. He peeled pieces off the bone and placed them on a small plate for me. I ate messily but the food tasted so good, and I was so hungry, and I didn't have hands. Rook merely raised an eyebrow when I used my paw to clean my face. He drank soda, and I continued to have trouble with not shoving my whole face into the water bowl because I was bad at judging distance apparently.

"I lit the candle," Rook said into the comfortable silence of the apartment.

I startled and looked up from my plate.

Rook's mouth was set in a determined line. He wiped his hands on a napkin, then met my gaze.

"I wanted to tell you so badly when I did it. Because you helped me. You were the reason I was able to do it, so thank you."

I straightened from where I was hunched over my food. Guilt sat like a stone in my stomach, right next to the chicken. Again, I wanted to apologize for everything. And I would, as soon as I could. In the meantime, I could only meow and allow the fondness to sweep through me.

The corner of Rook's mouth lifted. "I'll take that as 'you're welcome.' You're a great teacher, by the way. Whoever you choose as an apprentice one day is going to be extremely lucky."

I ducked my head at the compliment. If I was human, I would've blushed, but as it was, my whiskers twitched, and then I sobered at our current reality. *If* we had a future. If we managed to evade the Consortium until we could figure out what to do. If we weren't punished and didn't have our magic stripped away.

"Anyway, after I did it, Antonia took me out to this amazing restaurant, and we ate so much. She told me not to contact you. I did anyway." He looked away.

I didn't know how to respond. Rook saved me by yawning wide.

I glanced at the clock on the stove. It was only early evening, not really late enough for bed, but Rook was exhausted. It was evident in the droop of his shoulders and the dark circles beneath his eyes. He had bruises and scrapes littering his skin, which served as a reminder that I didn't really know what had happened to him before he arrived at Fable's to rescue me.

My own body ached. And after one more instance of submerging my face in the bowl, it was time for bed.

Rook packed the leftovers away into the fridge, and I followed him back to his bedroom.

Rook didn't have a nightly routine other than just flopping into the bed and crawling into his preferred spot. "Here. You can have this pillow," Rook said, patting the pillow next to his. He yawned. "If you want."

I wasn't sure what to do, but my blinks were progressively slowing. Rook slept on his side, facing inward, with one hand tucked under the pillow and the other resting on the bed, with a blanket pulled to his shoulders. His eyes fluttered closed before I had made my decision and his breathing evened as he dropped into sleep.

I crawled close, nestling into the small space created from the edge of the blanket and the pillow and Rook's bent arm, almost like the den we'd slept in the previous night. Tucking my face under my tail, I drifted to sleep, warm and safe.

I purred.

16

ROOK

I hadn't set my alarm.

So that couldn't be the reason for the loud and obnoxious sound blaring from my phone that had yanked me from a peaceful and exhausted sleep.

It stopped after a few seconds, which great, because I didn't have the energy to reach across the bed and grab it from the nightstand. I drifted in a hazy space, the soft line between asleep and awake, leaning more toward falling back asleep. Except, the alarm went off again. This time louder and shriller and more insistent.

Cracking open one eye, I saw that the light filtering into my bedroom from the one window was thin and weak, like predawn-type light. Ugh. What was so urgent? I was warm and comfy and . . . Sun was cuddled against me. Wait. I craned my neck, and yes, gray fur was pressed tight against my chest, and their tail tickled beneath my chin. Sun cuddled me.

Sun. Cuddled. Me.

That was enough to drive me fully awake. Sun, who didn't like being touched and didn't like small spaces and, honestly, didn't like people in general and didn't like when any of those topics was mentioned was cuddled against my T-shirt. *Cuddled.*

At the very least, I needed my phone to take a picture to document this historic occasion.

Doing my best not to disturb them, I stretched my arm across the bed, my fingertips grazing my phone just enough to pull it toward me.

I grabbed it and swiped the screen to see why it decided to wake me up in the first place.

Splashed across the display was a citywide alert with the words MISSING AND ENDANGERED YOUTH. Underneath was a picture of Sun.

I sat up so quickly my head spun, dislodging Sun in the process.

"Fuck," I breathed.

Because there was no way that wasn't Sun. It was them. Smiling wide in a candid picture, black hair styled, wearing a nice sweater and a silver necklace. All of it together was messing with my brain. A scroll of text below the photo read, *Missing and Endangered. Hee-sun Kim. Last seen by their family in the morning three days ago before attending summer school at Spire City Southwest High. Last seen wearing a black hoodie and black ripped jeans and black boots.*

A small meow sounded next to my elbow.

Oh. Oh shit.

I couldn't hide this. I shouldn't hide this. But I didn't want to show them. I had to show them.

I cleared my throat. "You need to see this."

Reluctantly, I tilted the phone toward where Sun blinked sleepily, stirring awake.

They yawned and stretched, little claws popping out as they did so, before padding over.

"I don't know if you can read, so I'll read it for you." I licked my dry lips. "'Missing and Endangered Youth. Hee-sun Kim. Last seen by their family in the morning three days ago before attending summer school at Spire City Southwest High.' Followed by a description of what you were wearing."

Sun's meow was plaintive and sad.

I clicked on the link the alert provided, and a video opened. It was of Sun's sisters. Soo-jin held up a photo. "Our younger sibling is missing," she said, voice shaky, into the camera. "If you've seen them, please call the Spire City police department. We think they might be with someone going by the name of Rook."

I dropped my phone in surprise. It fell to the bed, facedown. Soo-jin's voice was muffled. Sun pawed at the case, meowing, and I quickly turned it over for them to see.

"We're really worried. It's not like them not to come home or call us. We've tried their phone, but it's run out of battery, or it's broken." She sniffled. "Sun, please contact us, if you can. Or just come home. Okay?"

The video ended with a phone number for those with information to call.

Sun pressed their paw to the screen.

"I'm sorry," I said, throat dry and tight. "I'm so sorry. This is all my fault. I didn't think how it might affect you and your family. I didn't think. Sun, please."

Sun didn't move. Didn't make a sound.

"Is this why you ghosted me?" I asked, the hot sour sting of tears hiding behind my eyes. "Because of your family? That I could hurt them? That I could hurt you? I get it. I was selfish. I didn't think very far ahead. I only thought of myself. I'm sorry. I'm so sorry." A tear dripped off my jaw onto my pajama bottoms. Then another fell on Sun's head. "Damn," I said, using my sleeve to catch the rest. "I'm sorry for that, too. And I forgive you, you know, not that there is anything really to forgive since you were doing what you thought was best for yourself and your family. But just in case you felt guilty. That's presumptuous of me. You might not have. Whatever. I'm just saying that I was hurt and annoyed, but we're good now. We're good."

I clenched my hands in the blankets, took a steadying breath. Sun hadn't moved.

"Okay. So. We need to find a way to turn you human and take you back to your family. Or at least let them know you're okay. I could text them. Could you tap out the number and I—"

Sun jolted, as if startled, then reached out and sunk their claws into my arm.

I jerked away.

"They obviously want you home, Sun."

Sun shook their head.

"Sun, be reasonable. Your family might know how to turn you back. And they miss you. It's cruel to let them think the worst when you're relatively okay."

A low growl followed. Sun's dark-brown eyes met mine, and I saw in them a hint of fear.

I sighed. Okay. This was Sun's decision, even if I didn't agree. They would know best, I guess. But the thought of having someone actually miss you, worry about you, resurrected a familiar pain. I'd had that once. I didn't have it now.

"Fine," I said, defeated. There was no arguing with a cat. "Fine. Okay. We'll continue with our plan. Which, by the way, was really vague on how we were going to return you to normal Sun. Any ideas in that regard?"

Sun tilted their head, then hopped off the bed and crossed the floor to my computer chair. They jumped from the chair to my desk, sitting right in front of the picture I had of my grandmother.

Sun batted at it.

"My grandmother? She's dead, Sun." A lump formed at the base of my throat, and again I dashed my tears away with my sleeve. "I told you that. Remember? Our date at the coffee shop?"

Sun's head snapped up, eyes wide, like they'd sniffed catnip.

Oh. I said date. *Our* date. Embarrassing. Wow. My ears went hot. I pushed on, choosing to ignore how my brain to mouth filter didn't work before 6:00 a.m.

"Uh." I cleared my throat. "What about my grandmother? She could use magic, but she wasn't powerful like Antonia or Fable. She just made potions and cast butterflies. She had this ancient recipe book that she used to make soup . . ." I trailed off. "Wait. She had books. She had to have owned a spell book. It could've been the recipe book." I shot to my feet. "She'd never mentioned the Consortium to me, and Antonia once said that there was no way they could know everyone, watch everyone. The spell book could still be in her belongings."

Sun meowed.

"But," I said, deflating, "I don't have access to her things. After she died, I wasn't allowed to return to the house and was immediately sent away."

Sun tilted their head and meowed again.

I had no idea what they were saying, but that didn't stop me from trying to have a conversation. "I mean, we could go to her house and look. There's nothing stopping me now. And even if there's not a spell book, there might be something. Anything. It's a place to start."

Sun sat primly, little paws tucked close, tail wrapped around their body, and nodded once.

"I know that I'm the genius of this relationship, but that was really smart thinking."

Relationship. Again. Slip of the tongue. I should just bury myself.

"Okay, if you think Fable's place is far out, wait until you see my grandma's cabin. It's north of the city, and it'll take some time to get to, but it's not like we have anything more pressing to do."

It was still early, but I was rejuvenated by the thought of going home. If the little cabin in the quiet cul-de-sac was even still standing. I didn't know. I hadn't been back, but it was worth a try.

I scrambled around my room, shoving some clothes into my bag for me and Sun in case we were successful in turning Sun human. I grabbed my phone charger and wallet and ensured the Spell Binder was settled safely inside. Sun watched from their perch on the desk as I ran around my room and demurely looked away when I changed my clothes.

"Okay," I said, clapping my hands. "Let's go. We'll hit a coffee shop for some breakfast and coffee, and then we'll find a bus headed that way."

Sun hopped down from the desk, and without any argument, jumped into the top of my bag. I zipped it up around them and slid the bag on my shoulders.

Having Sun this close to me again made me want to mention the cuddling. I didn't mention the cuddling.

"Ready?"

Sun meowed. That was the best answer I could receive.

Despite an incident at the coffee shop where a little girl really wanted to pet the cute kitty in my bag, the trip to the cottage was relatively uneventful. There wasn't a bus that was scheduled for a few hours, so I ended up having to use a car service, which cost a significant amount. But the job with Antonia had put enough in my bank account to cover it and whatever other expenses I'd incur on this mission.

Grandma's cabin sat at the end of a long, winding street. It was a neighborhood of sorts, with scattered houses on big lots of green and large areas with old-growth trees. Sun was pressed against my thigh, cuddling me again, a low rumble emanating from their chest. It was the cutest thing ever. But as adorable as Sun was in a gray, fluffy body with ears and a tail, I missed my Sun. The Sun who cast unimpressed looks in my direction and who smiled softly and was blunt to a fault and who, I had realized, beyond that thorny exterior, was inherently considerate and felt deeply for those they loved.

The driver pulled in front of the house. I used my phone to pay and roused Sun with a nudge from my leg. They yawned and stretched and hopped into my bag with little fuss.

Once the car pulled away, I set Sun on the ground, and they followed me up the brick path. The grass was overgrown in the front yard, tall wildflowers tangled all over what was once manicured beds and pruned bushes.

"Wow. It's still here," I said, marveling. A year away had felt like an eternity. My chest went tight with the thought. "I hope no one lives here now. That would be awkward. But judging by the lawn, I assume it's vacant."

Other than the overgrowth of the front yard, the cabin itself appeared to be in good shape, almost pristine. No leaves on the awning of the porch. No vines climbing up the sides. No evidence of weathering at all in my absence. Huh, that was strange.

As we neared, Sun suddenly hissed beside me. Their back arched.

And that's when I saw it too, an almost transparent sheen encompassing the house.

"A ward," I breathed.

Sun scuttled away, gray fur fuzzed out. I didn't blame them. I'd made the mistake of touching Antonia's wards *twice* and paid the painful price for doing so both times. Antonia's wards buzzed like live wires, but this one . . . seemed different . . . felt different . . . like butterflies.

"I'm going to touch it."

Sun growled in warning.

"It's okay," I said, curious but unafraid. "It feels like Grandma." I placed my hand flat against the magic. It tingled in my fingers and against the palm of my hand, warm and comforting. The ward rippled, wobbling outward from where my hand pressed in. The vibrating increased, and then, without warning, it popped, like a soap bubble.

I flexed by fingers and grinned down at Sun. "Wow. That was cool."

Sun made a noise that was akin to a grumble, and I laughed. Of course, when I tried the door, it was locked.

Luckily for me, the ceramic frog with the wide mouth sat next to the welcome mat. I picked it up and tipped it over, and the spare key tumbled to the deck.

Sun huffed.

"I know, right?" I said. "A ward and a key? That tells me that no one has been in here. And that means, if Grandma did have a spell book, it's still inside."

The door had always stuck, and there was a trick to opening it. Pull the handle, turn the key, push inward, and yay! It worked. We were inside.

The living room looked just as I'd left it, though the recliner, worn rug, and couch with the crocheted blanket on the back were all covered in a thick layer of dust from being vacant. The house still smelled the same too, a little mustier than I remembered, but the same. A wave of nostalgia washed over me so fiercely that my knees went weak, and I grabbed the back of the couch to steady myself. As if sensing my discomfort, Sun wove between my legs, rubbing against the fabric of my jeans. I didn't call them out on it and shrugged off my bag and set it in the recliner.

Unfortunately, the house was hot and stuffy, and when I tried to flick the light switch, nothing blinked on because, well, no one had paid the electricity bill in a year. I sighed and looked down at Sun. "Come on. This way."

To the left of the living room was the kitchen. I stepped through the archway and walked to the drawer by the oven, whose heat-swollen wood resisted when I tried to pull it out. With a firm yank, I was able to open it, and on the top was a book. Sun jumped to the counter and meowed.

"Yeah, this is the one I was thinking about."

I gently took the well-worn book from the drawer and carefully peeled back the cover. There was a recipe for soup. Right, I remembered that one, the one she'd make me when I was sick. Okay, but a recipe, not a spell. I turned the page. And there was one for banana bread. And the next page was one for peach pie. My heart sank.

Sun peered down at the writing.

I turned the page.

A casserole.

"Uh, this is not looking good, Sun. I'm sorry, but it looks like it's only recipes."

I flipped through faster, and each entry was more food and more food and an alcoholic punch, which, damn, Grandma, that called for a lot of rum. But no luck. It really was just a recipe book. I sighed and closed it, running my hand over the spine.

"Well, okay, so our first plan did not work. That's okay, though. There are other options. And hey, at least we're safe here."

Someone knocked on the front door.

I spun on my heel, heart pounding. Sun hissed from their position on the counter, ears flattened.

"Maybe if we ignore it, they'll go away," I whispered.

Another knock. "I know you're in there," someone called.

Oh shit. "Maybe if we hide?"

"I saw you go in."

Okay, so ignoring and hiding were out. "In a minute!" I called back. I turned to Sun. "What do I do? What should I do?"

But Sun was a cat and couldn't tell me, and I was freaking out.

"Come on, Eddie! I know it's you."

That brought me up short. Eddie? No one called me Eddie anymore. The Consortium surely wouldn't.

I crossed into the living room, caught the edge of a window drape with my finger, and moved it aside.

A woman stood on the porch. A woman I vaguely recognized.

I opened the door a crack and peered around the edge.

"It is you!" she said, smiling, her brown eyes shining. "I can't believe it. You're back!"

"Um . . ."

"Do you remember me?" She waved her hand. "I babysat you a few times when you were young, and then I went away to college for a while. When I came back to the neighborhood, you were gone."

I wrinkled my brow. Wait. I did remember a teenager who watched me a few times and then graduated from high school and left. She was about ten years older than me and had dark-brown skin, curly hair, bright brown eyes, and a wide smile. "Mavis?"

She smiled. "Yes! You do remember! I should've known. You were always so smart and curious! A little genius. I almost couldn't believe it was you when the car pulled up, but you have the same smile you had when you were a kid." She clasped her hands together. "I was so sad when I heard about your grandma and that you were taken away. I returned home right after it happened."

I scratched the back of my neck. "Yeah. I live in the city now. Just came back here to find something of Grandma's. Anyway, Mavis, this isn't exactly the best time—"

"Oh my goodness, is that your cat?" Mavis squealed and pushed past me into the house. She crouched down to where Sun sat in the archway between the living room and kitchen. "It's so cute! Look at those little paws."

Sun flattened and hissed.

"Oh. Yes. But be careful. They don't like to be petted."

Mavis pulled her hand back just in time to avoid getting clawed and hugged her bent knees instead, staring intently at Sun.

"Oh," she said softly. "You're not a cat at all, are you?"

I froze. Sun froze. We all froze. Then I very slowly and deliberately shut the door behind me.

"Mavis?"

She stood and turned toward me, hands on her hips, and shook her head. "You are in a lot of trouble, *Rook*."

17

ROOK

I gulped. "I think I liked it better when you called me Eddie."

She clucked her tongue. "You've messed up, kid." She rolled her neck and tipped her head back to look at the ceiling, sighing dramatically as she did so. "And you've put me in an awkward position."

"I haven't really," I said. I stayed by the door and wiggled my fingers next to my side to get Sun's attention. They caught on, thankfully, and slunk their way toward me. "Nothing to see here. Nothing to report to the Consortium, which I feel like you might have a relationship with if you know my magic name and what's going on."

She held out her hand, palm up, and a small spark of magic blazed upward, like a miniature firework, before bursting into an impressive flower of sparkles. Mavis was magic. Oh. Well. That would have been great information to have before I opened the door.

"The scrying mirrors have been lit up for days with your face and name and your darling little kitty here." She pointed. "Sun, right?"

Sun sat next to my foot. And if looks could curse, Mavis would have been swarmed with scorpions about thirty seconds ago. I glanced at the door behind me. We could run, I guess, make a break for it, but Mavis seemed unconcerned by that option, like she had a plan if we tried, or knew there wasn't much of an escape route. Also, my backpack sat on the recliner, and I couldn't leave the Spell Binder behind.

"What else have the mirrors said?"

"Just that you're dangerous and have broken a ton of Consortium laws. Luckily, they don't know anything about you other than you're Antonia Hex's apprentice, who she calls 'Rook.' Which we need to have a discussion on how you became *her* apprentice because that would be a feat for anyone in general but especially for someone who doesn't have magic." Sun's tail twitched in agitation, and it brushed against my ankle. "But I knew the real you," Mavis continued. "So, I've kept a lookout on the house to see if you would finally return. And you have."

"And what? You told them? For recognition or cookies or whatever?"

Mavis shrugged. "I didn't tell them anything. Not yet anyway."

My breath stuttered out in a relieved gasp. We still had a chance. "Why?"

Mavis slowly walked around the living room, her fingertips trailing along the back of the couch. Dust motes trailed in her wake in the weak sunlight filtering through the covered windows.

Sweat gathered at the back of my neck. The room was hot, and Mavis's attitude was not helping. What was it with sorcerers and their penchant for theatrics and moral ambiguity?

"I wanted to decide for myself. I don't take the words of those in power as absolute, especially when they are notorious for being secretive and known for their oppressive tactics."

"That's a good life policy."

She smirked. "So, Eddie or Rook, want to tell me what exactly has the Consortium after you?"

"Not really." I hooked my thumbs in the pockets of my jeans and rocked back on my heels, going for the innocent-kid look. I wasn't sure it worked. "The usual, I guess."

Mavis shook her head, her curly hair bouncing around her face. "Not good enough, kid. You have to give me more information than that."

"Or what?" I asked. "You just said you don't trust them. And the way I see it, if you were concerned about the Consortium yourself or if you wanted to earn brownie points, you would've turned us in the minute you saw us."

She huffed, unamused. "What if I was lying and I did? And I'm stalling until they get here?"

I hadn't thought of that. I scooped Sun into my arms and, for a brief second, took my eyes off Mavis and glanced out of the front window. I didn't see anything, but that didn't mean they weren't out there. Sun let out a disgruntled yowl when I held them too close, but I ignored it as I twisted back to face Mavis. My heart pounded. I could probably run past her to the back door, but there was no way I could grab the bag and keep ahold of Sun and Mavis obviously had magic and who knows how powerful she was, but the ley line was weak and—I sucked in air, chest heaving. My whole body was stiff with fear, caught between fight, flight, or freeze.

Mavis held up her hands. "Whoa. Sorry. I haven't. I promise. Don't do anything stupid."

"Why should I believe you?" I snapped, gasping, clutching Sun. "I can't trust you. I can't trust anyone. We only came here because we had nowhere else to go, and we need a spell to turn Sun back to human. Menacing ex-babysitters with ambiguous motives who call me Eddie were not part of that plan. They weren't even in the vicinity of the universe of thoughts that we had."

Mavis's eyebrows rose to her hairline, and her brown eyes went wide. "Wow. Okay. You're obviously a little stressed. My fault. Let's start over."

I bit my lip and took a step toward the door, dropping my free hand to the handle. But if we ran now, we couldn't come back. Sun might not ever be human again, and we'd leave the Spell Binder behind.

"Rook," Mavis said, tone firm, "your grandmother trusted me to watch you when you were small. Doesn't that count for something?"

"I don't know."

"It should. She loved you. She loved you so much, and she didn't trust anyone to watch you except me."

Sun meowed. I breathed out, and yeah, that was true. "Yeah, and?"

Mavis relaxed. "I'm sorry for coming on a little strong. But you had to imagine my surprise when that little nonmagical boy I knew growing up became the subject of a mirror-wide manhunt. I had to know if you were actually dangerous. I hadn't seen you in so long."

Okay. Okay. That was fair. I understood. "I'm not."

She smiled. "I figured that out."

"Okay."

"Great. Come on." She beckoned me into the living room. "Sit with me. Tell me what's going on."

Sun hissed. But as much as I agreed with their reticence, we didn't have much of a choice. And I was tired. Running was exhausting. And we needed help. "Can you ward the door?" I asked. "And the windows?"

She made an impressed face. "Okay. That's a smart idea."

"I am a genius, you know."

I shuffled in and sat on the edge of the couch, close enough to the recliner to grab my bag with my non-Sun hand. Sun imperiously eyed

Mavis, like Sun was more of a cat than they let on. Mavis pointed two fingers at the door and muttered a spell, and a purple sheen erupted and spread out along the walls until the whole room was encased. It was impressive.

"Now, tell me what has the Consortium so ruffled that they're after two teenagers."

So, I did. I didn't spill everything, that would be unwise, and Sun poked me with their needlelike death mittens anytime I skirted too close to something they didn't want revealed. But in the end, I told Mavis about being Antonia's apprentice and how the Consortium didn't want information shared with someone nonmagical and how Antonia wasn't allowed to have an apprentice anyway because of things that went down a few decades ago. And how Fable and Sun had been wrapped up in the mess by association, and how the Consortium had tried to capture us, but I'd managed to escape, and Sun had been spelled into a cat.

"I remember learning about Antonia's previous apprentice," Mavis said, nodding, voice low. "From my own mentor."

"You had a mentor?" Wait. Mavis had shown she was magic and was fairly powerful based on the ward she'd set. If Mavis had a mentor, then maybe she was skilled enough to help us. Maybe she had a spell that we could use for Sun.

She nodded. "I did. Apprenticing was one of the reasons that I stopped babysitting. I apprenticed for a person named Laurel Thrall. He was great, but it was difficult to keep up with after I went to college. And even though I still dabble in the magical world, my day job isn't based in magic at all."

"What do you do?"

She beamed. "I'm a librarian."

"Oh, wow. Okay. That's awesome." Ha. She probably would appreciate the reference app of spells on the Spell Binder, but I'd omitted that part of the story. "So, anyway, yeah, that's about what's going on."

Mavis frowned. "That's not the only reason they have people scouring the area for you two, and you know it. What's the real reason? Why is Antonia in so much trouble?"

I exchanged a glance with Sun. Sun had their ears flat, eyes narrowed.

"The less you know about it, the more you can claim ignorance if you get caught talking with known fugitives."

She squinted at me. "Fair enough," she said with a nod. "So why come back here? You said you had nowhere to go . . ." She trailed off.

"Honestly, I don't. We need help. We need a spell to change Sun back. And then we need to return Sun to their family." Sun sank their claws into my leg. I winced. "Ow. Okay. Well, first we need to change Sun back so they can communicate without resorting to pain."

Sun stared at me and defiantly licked their paw.

Mavis chuckled.

"And I don't know. I thought Grandma might have a spell book or something we could use." My leg jittered. I drummed my fingers along my thigh. "My grandma never mentioned the Consortium. Did they know about her?"

Mavis smiled, wide and bright. "Your grandma was badass. Did you know?"

"Uh . . . no. I didn't."

"I didn't really realize it, either, when I was young, but she was the original rebel. She was on the Consortium's list, like they knew she existed and was a sorcerer, but when they showed up here once on Consortium business, she broke the scrying mirror in their faces. Told them to leave her alone."

I perked up. "Really?"

"Oh yeah. They didn't return. While she was alive anyway. I doubt they were scared of your grandma, the little old lady that she was. They probably saw her as more of a hassle than anything else, but she didn't follow their rules."

Huh. Pride flooded me, made me all warm inside. *Go, Grandma.* I exchanged a glance with Sun. "What do you mean while she was alive?"

Mavis sighed. "You don't know?"

I shook my head. "Don't know what?"

Mavis frowned. "After she died, the Consortium came here to collect her things, but your grandma had spelled the house to set a ward. No one could break it. Until today, that is."

I exchanged a glance with Sun. Their whiskers twitched.

Mavis continued. "I bet they wouldn't have sent you away if they knew you could've let them in."

I stiffened. "What?"

For the first time, Mavis's self-assured demeanor faltered. "Eddie," she said, voice low, "do you know why you were sent to the city?"

I gulped. Leaning forward, elbows on my knees, I clasped my hands together. "Because I was a minor without a parent or a guardian, and so I became a ward of Spire City Social Services."

Mavis flinched. "Partly."

"Partly?" I prodded. My knuckles were white. My body trembled.

"You were a *nonmagical* minor who grew up with a sorcerer who bucked against the established rules. You were a Consortium loose end. You had to be dealt with."

Dealt with. Like Antonia's apprentice. Like Antonia herself. My mouth went dry. My body shook. To hear it so plainly, so bluntly, was a shock to my system. I mean, deep down I'd known. I had put two and two together, but I had ignored the truth in light of different concerns—Antonia, Sun, death curtains, and so on and so forth.

I swallowed. "Okay. So, they've been dictating my life a little longer than I'd initially been led to believe. I can't change that now. So, anyway, her spell book?"

Mavis cocked her head to the side. "You don't have it?"

"No. That's why we came here. We thought that if we could find it, we'd find a spell for Sun. We only managed to look in the kitchen before we were interrupted, and all that's in there are recipes."

Mavis hummed. "Well, obviously no one has been in the house."

If Grandma had a spell book, it could still be here. We were a step closer. Maybe. And we might have help, if Mavis stayed on our side.

"And after you turn Sun back? What about Antonia and Fable?"

Oh. Right. Reality check. "We don't know yet."

"Fair enough." She clapped her hands together. "Okay. Well. Time to find a spell book."

I raised an eyebrow. "You're going to help?"

"Why not?"

"We're fugitives." I gestured broadly. "From a huge magical governing bureaucracy that could make your life hell if you're caught assisting us."

Mavis shrugged. "Could be worse."

I glanced at Sun. I still didn't completely trust Mavis. The Consortium was powerful, and even though Mavis hadn't turned us in yet, it didn't mean that she wouldn't when pressure was applied. Sun stared back, their eyes so wide and deep, and meowed, and gave their kitty version of a shrug. I basically took it as an okay.

"We'll divide and conquer."

Mavis went to the kitchen, while I led Sun to Grandma's bedroom. There were only two bedrooms in the house, and they sat on opposite ends of a short hallway, a bathroom in the middle, with a linen closet on the other side. The smaller room had been mine, and I'd basically taken everything except the furniture when I was forced to leave. But I hadn't gone into Grandma's room. There was a good chance that no one had been in it after she'd died.

I placed my hand on the knob and looked down at Sun at my side.

Sun placed a paw on the top of my shoe in what I suspected was meant to be a comforting gesture, which was undermined when they batted absently at my shoelace. Which was weird. I'd noticed that Sun's catlike instincts were showing up a little bit more the longer they stayed a cat. It'd only been a few days, but Sun had already taken to napping a lot, and did I mention the cuddling?

"I'm fine," I said for what felt like the thousandth time. If I kept saying it, maybe one day it would be true.

I pushed open the door and stepped inside. The room was stuffy. It smelled like Grandma's preferred perfume mixed with heat and dust.

Grandma's room was off-limits to me as a kid. Even when I had a scary dream, she'd come into my room to tuck me back in instead of letting me climb into her bed. I never really thought about it before, just chalked it up to privacy. But now that I was inside, I knew why. Other than the heavy wooden furniture—a bed that looked like it was made for a giant with a matching dresser and mirrorless vanity—there was a large wooden stand. On that stand was a massive spell book.

"Found it," I said weakly.

Sun scampered along the wooden floor, hopped up on the vanity, and then jumped to the stand, paws landing on the thick leather-bound book. The book reminded me of the one in Antonia's office, the one I wasn't allowed near, which was spelled to be Antonia's alone and which would be collected by the Consortium if it ever changed hands. I wondered if this was spelled to my grandma. I couldn't sense magic, but Sun could. Sun could tell me.

But right now Sun was a cat. They gamely tried to flip open the thick leather cover, and as cute as it was, I really needed Sun to be human again.

I crossed the room and stood behind the sturdy podium, gently nudging Sun aside. The book creaked when I lifted the cover. The pages were full of stacked writing, the same loopy scrawl that had been on the recipe cards, from the top of the page all the way to the bottom with no space spared. Oh. This was Grandma's writing. This was her work scrawled across pages and pages. Her own creation. It was strange to know that she'd had an entire aspect of her life she'd hidden from me, and I was only seeing it now. But from what Mavis said about her, Grandma clearly had a whole backstory she'd kept from me. A story that included being a total badass rebel.

The very first page had a spell for butterflies and a note dated at the bottom. *Edison's favorite.* My heart stuttered. I swallowed hard and begged the tears to stay in my eyes lest they fall and damage the paper. I blinked several times, quickly, and the liquid caught on my lashes.

Sun meowed.

"The dust," I said, wiping my face. "Anyway. This first page is about butterflies," I said. I turned to the next page and read the spell out loud just as I had with the spells in the Spell Binder. "Next is a spell to warm the hearth. And the one next to it is a spell for music in the walls." And that's how we spent the next several minutes. Turning each page, finding more spells that my grandmother had either copied or created, I didn't know which. On some pages, there were little notes in the side, tips and tricks for the next time she'd cast them, with scrawled dates next to the notes.

As we neared the end of the book with no sign of the spell we needed, despair began to set in. Only a few pages left. We might just have to resort to the spell on the Spell Binder to at least give Sun the ability to speak until we could find one to turn them human. I was sure Mavis could cast it at least. I sighed, turned another page, and—

"Spell to transform a human to an animal." I stopped. My mouth went dry. I read it again to make sure. "Spell to transform a human to an animal," I said again. Sun perked up from where they'd formed a cat-loaf on the bed behind me.

I ran my finger over the script, following it down until I reached Grandma's notes. "To transform an animal to human, say the spell backward." I gulped. "This is it. Sun, this is the spell." I kept reading. "Two sorcerers recommended to keep the spell steady, but one could work." Oh. Okay. That might be a wrench in the plan. I didn't know how powerful Mavis was, but we'd cross that bridge. I continued reading. "A ley line of moderate strength is needed to complete the spell."

Well, at least I could confirm if that part would be a problem or not. I pulled out the Spell Binder and flicked the power button. A yellow line lit up, one that flowed on the other side of the street. It wasn't as bright as the pulsing energy of the forest, or the huge, vibrant line that ran through Antonia's office, but it was there at least. Weaker, drained. It sent my thoughts scrambling along different paths, wondering if my grandma only used smaller spells because she only had access to a weaker line. If what I had thought about her was wrong, that she was low level in talent. Maybe she'd been powerful but didn't have the energy to draw from, or maybe the energy had changed in the year I'd been gone, or maybe the ward outside had drained it, or maybe she had from living in this cabin her entire life. I'd never know, and the grief and pain of her being gone slammed into me again, like a freight train of sorrow.

Sun meowed, knocked their head against my hand.

"I'm fine," I mustered, scrubbing my sleeve over my eyes. I

shoved the Spell Binder back into my bag. "Come on, we need to tell Mavis."

We found Mavis in the kitchen with a cup of tea, waiting for us. She'd obviously finished her search of the house a while ago and had made herself comfortable. How had she made tea without power? She saw the confusion on my face and wiggled her fingers. Right. Magic. Anyway, I set the book down as carefully as I could, but the table rattled under the heft.

"We found a spell."

Mavis read it and nodded. "Yes. This will work. I can do it, I think."

"That's great. Do you know someone else that can be your second person? You know, to keep it steady?"

She blinked at me. "You want me to ask another sorcerer to break the law and assist you and hope they don't turn you in as soon as they see you?"

Right. "Oh," I said. "Forgot that part."

Sun jumped to the table. They headbutted my hand and made a noise.

"What?" I asked. They did it again. "Are you thirsty? I have a water bottle in my bag. Or hungry? It has been a while since breakfast."

Sun sat and made a weird growly noise.

"I don't know what that means."

"I think it means that Sun wants you to be involved with the spell," Mavis said, then took a sip of her tea.

Sun nodded.

"I can't. I mean, I lit the candle, but it was mostly smoke, and I haven't really practiced."

Mavis arched an eyebrow. "You lit a candle? With magic?"

I nodded. "Yeah. It was just smoke, though."

"I thought you weren't magical."

"I'm not."

Sun meowed.

"I mean, I am. I can't see ley lines, but I can cast."

Mavis dropped her teacup. It rattled in the saucer. "What? That's something that can be done?"

"It's a day for revelations!" I snapped. "Yes. I did it. Yay for me. The Consortium arrested my boss because of it."

Mavis gaped. "Well, that's amazing."

"Thanks. But, Sun, I barely made the wick smoke. I still can't feel magic like you can. I mean, I can't risk your life."

Sun stalked over to the spell book and pawed at the edges of the paper.

"They want you to turn the page."

"Do you speak cat?"

Mavis went back to sipping her tea, unbothered by my attitude.

I turned the pages, Sun nodding along until I came to the first page. Sun placed their paw there and stared at me.

Butterflies.

Like that day at the office. Butterflies. Candy. Soda.

"Catch a butterfly," I murmured. Sun placed their paw on my wrist. I sighed. "You really want me to? You trust me that much?"

Sun nodded.

I took a steadying breath. "Fine. I'll do it."

"I don't know what just happened," Mavis said, gaze flicking between us, "but it was cute. You two have a real bond. No wonder the Consortium is after you both."

I rolled my eyes. "Thanks for reminding me."

She clapped her hands together. "Okay. Let's do this."

Sun sat in the middle of the carpet in the living room. Mavis and I had dragged the podium from Grandma's room and placed it next to the couch, the spell book opened on top of it to the correct spell. If Sun was nervous, they didn't show it, save for the rhythmic flick of their tail. Otherwise, they sat demurely, gray paws together, looking more like a cat statue than an actual cat.

"Ready?" Mavis asked.

I took a deep breath and met Sun's steady gaze. "Yes. No. Wait." I disappeared into Grandma's room, grabbed a blanket from the bed, and brought it into the living room. I opened it and flapped it a bit to air it out, then draped it over Sun.

Sun meowed but didn't scamper from beneath, and from the movement I could see, they merely circled in place, then lay down.

Mavis raised an eyebrow. "Okay, focus on the line. Do you feel it?"

No. But I didn't tell her that. Instead, I closed my eyes, remembered the path of the line from the screen on the Spell Binder and imagined it as a trail of golden butterflies. And I thought of Sun, the feeling of sparks that erupted in my chest every time I thought about them, their rare wide smiles, their wit, their fleeting touches. I grabbed on to those feelings and on to the magic of the ley line.

"Got it."

"Okay, when I start channeling, steady the energy and direct it to me. Okay?"

"Yes."

I imagined the stream of butterflies breaking off, flowing toward Mavis as I reached for it. A tingle worked its way into my fingers, and warmth spread into my core, lit up my veins from the inside. With my other hand, I latched on to Mavis's wrist and directed the flow into her.

"Whoa," she said. "That's amazing. Great job."

I smiled but kept my eyes screwed shut, concentrating.

Mavis spoke the spell, starting with the last word and reciting backward, her voice growing in intensity as the magic surged. My fingers burned where they touched her skin. The hair on my arms stood on end. Magic rippled through me, pounding in time with my heartbeat. The sparkle of it rushed into my cheeks and down to my toes. The taste of fizzy candy danced on my tongue.

Magic swirled around us, sparking behind my closed eyes. I pried them open and gasped.

The small lump that was Sun under the blanket was surrounded by bright golden light. Mavis outstretched her hand, fingers splayed wide, her voice powerful, thundering in my ears along with my pulse.

She spoke the last word of the spell and pushed outward. A wave of magic swelled, then broke over the form on the floor, bursting into glitter, and between one blink and the next, the small lump was suddenly not so small anymore.

Mavis dropped her hand and bowed forward, her forearms propped on the stand. I let go and sucked in a harsh breath. The magic receded like a tide, slowly inching out of my body, until I couldn't feel it anymore. I grabbed the back of the couch to stay standing, depleted, but not exhausted. I was strangely *wired*, like I needed to run laps around the room to disperse the energy.

Instead, I sat on the couch, my leg jittering, and I stared at the blanket on the floor, waiting for some monumental reveal. Nothing happened.

"Sun?" I called to the lump under the blanket.

The lump shivered. So yes, alive. Great. That was awesome. Excellent even. We had not killed Sun. Thank everything, because I would not have been able to live with myself if I had. But I couldn't see if the spell worked. I mean, the lump was larger than Sun had been as a cat, but that didn't mean we hadn't just made Sun into a bigger cat. Oh fuck. What if we had made Sun into a bigger cat? Like a lynx? Or a panther? Or a tiger? What if Sun was a lion? Okay, the energy was messing with me, and I needed to focus. Focus, Rook.

"Sun?" I called again. A little more frantic. A little more urgent.

The lump shifted and groaned, which was a very human sound, and from underneath the blanket, a foot slid out from the end. A human foot with a thin ankle and toes and oh, thank magic, it was Sun.

I sagged into the couch cushions.

It worked. The spell had worked. I had helped cast a spell. Steady a spell. Something. I'd helped with something.

Mavis clapped her hand to my shoulder. "I think it's a human under there. So, good work."

"Fuck," I said, dropping my head to my hands, scrubbing them over my hair. "I can't believe it. It worked."

Sun still hadn't emerged, which fair. They were literally just a cat, and they had to get their bearings.

"Does that look right to you?" Mavis asked, gesturing to Sun's foot.

I nodded, utterly relieved. "I would recognize that ankle any-where."

"You have a thing for ankles?" Mavis asked.

No, just Sun's ankles.

It was at that point that Sun popped their head out from the other end. The blanket or the spell, I didn't know which, had ruffled their black hair to a staticky mess. But it was them, and oh my god, they were more adorable as a human than I remembered. Sun squinted at me, then at Mavis.

"You," I breathed.

Sun narrowed their eyes. "Me," they agreed. "Also, what the fuck?" they muttered, voice rough and disgruntled.

"You, my friend, are no longer a cat." I threw out my arms. "Con-gratulations!"

Sun rubbed a hand over their face, then stared at their hand, spreading out their fingers and wiggling them as if transfixed.

Sun grumbled something under their breath that sounded suspiciously like a thank-you. My heart soared.

Mavis eyed us both, brown eyes glancing between us. "I'm going to leave you two and get us some food. I'll be back. Don't answer the door for anyone else."

"Okay, thanks."

"Thank you," Sun said in a scratchy whisper, holding up an arm, then letting it flop back to the floor limply.

After the door closed, signaling Mavis's departure, Sun dropped the pretense of trying to get up and be anything other than a puddle of human under a blanket on the floor.

I propped my elbows on my knees. "Are you going to stay right there for the rest of the night?"

"Rest of forever," they responded.

"Feeling that bad?"

"It's more exhausting being a cat than a human," Sun answered, muffled by the blanket they'd pulled back over their head. "Need sleep."

"Not yet. Come on. Clothes, then water, then sleep. Can you manage that?"

Sun's answer was a snore.

I sighed. I gave them a few minutes, gathering up the clothes I'd packed for them and a bottle of water before easing down next to them. I didn't touch them except for one poke to where I thought their shoulder was.

"Sun," I singsonged. "Rise and shine. Come on, there's a bed that I bet is infinitely more comfortable than this floor. Let me help you to it. And I have clothes, these nice soft pajama pants and this oversize T-shirt."

Sun stuck a hand from beneath the blanket and made a grabby

motion. I handed them the bundle of clothes and they pulled it under with them.

"Yell when you're ready or if you need help," I said. "I'll disappear until I hear from you." I stood, and the lump didn't move. "And I'm setting a timer for twenty minutes."

I wasn't entirely sure that I should leave Sun but opted to give them privacy, which I knew they would appreciate. Instead, I went back into Grandma's room and changed the sheets on the bed, though the replacements were a little musty. I cracked the windows to let in the summer breeze and relieve the hot staleness of the air.

I sat on the edge of the bed and waited. Step one was to get out of the forest. Step two was to find a safe place. Step three was to get Sun back to human form. Step four? What was step four? Save Antonia and Fable? How? Despite steadying the magic for Mavis during the casting and making a candle smoke a few times, I had no real magic. And Sun was weak and tired. They needed to rest. And I still didn't trust Mavis completely. I didn't know what her limit was for this. Would she run screaming to the Consortium if she found out about the Spell Binder? And, honestly, was the Spell Binder even worth it all?

I pulled it out of my bag and stared at it. What was the point? Yes, I could now see the ley lines. If I practiced enough, I'd proven I could harness magic and cast spells in some capacity, but it hadn't made my life any easier. I hadn't been welcomed into the community with open arms, not even by Sun. I had to fight for my place, and I was pretty sure that would always be the case. The thought was exhausting. And I wasn't really sure if it was worth it.

The door creaked on its hinges as Sun shuffled in, leaning heavily against the wall. The T-shirt hung off their shoulder and the pajama bottoms dragged under their heels. Definitely human. Definitely as pretty as they were before, and my hands itched to smooth back the hair hanging in their face to see their deep-brown eyes clearly and the cute shape of their nose.

"Oh, hey," I said, hopping off the bed. "How do you feel?"

"Tired."

Sun *looked* tired. When they lifted their head, dark circles stood stark under their eyes, and their shoulders sloped downward with fatigue. "Other than that, are you okay? Everything in working order?"

Sun's brow furrowed. "I guess." Their voice was scratchy and low, and it made the butterflies in my middle flutter with a vengeance.

They took a step and stumbled. I darted forward, grabbed them around the waist to keep them standing. Sun leaned heavily into me, wrapping their arms around my shoulders, and rested their head against my collarbone.

"Oh," I breathed into their hair. "I'm sorry. Let's move to the bed and get you in and—"

"Shut up," Sun said, tightening their hold.

"What are you doing?"

"I'm hugging you."

"You're hugging me?" It had been a long time since someone had hugged me. I hadn't really thought about it, but now that Sun was pressed along my front, I realized how touch starved I'd been. How it had been ages since someone had touched me with purpose.

"Don't make it a thing," Sun mumbled, words slurring against the skin of my neck, their breath hot.

"It kind of is a thing." I hugged them back, wrapped my arms more securely around their waist. "A nice thing."

"Don't make me regret it."

I laughed. I couldn't help it. "Wow. Don't sound so enthusiastic. I might get the wrong idea."

Sun grumbled. "Already regret it," they said, but they made no move to pull away, only sagged into my hold.

We stayed that way for a year-long minute. It was nice, but the longer we stood, the heavier Sun became in my arms. Their lashes fluttered against my neck as they slipped toward sleep.

"As nice as this is," I said, because it *was* nice, "let's get you into the bed. You're going to fall asleep standing up, and I don't want to be responsible for you braining yourself on the floor."

Together we maneuvered Sun into the bed and under the covers. I pulled a blanket from the foot and threw it over them. Sun tucked both hands into the curl of their body, grabbing the edge of the blanket, black hair spilling across the white pillow like ink, pink mouth open.

"Didn't want to ghost you," they breathed. "Didn't want to leave you. Needed you to know."

I smoothed the blanket over them with shaking hands, my heart in my throat, overcome with fondness.

"Rest, Sun."

I stayed nearby until Sun drifted off to sleep, thankful they were themselves again, thankful that we had made it this far, and dreading what was next, but at least for the moment Sun was safe and happy, and that's all that really mattered.

18

SUN

I didn't know what it was that roused me, but as I slowly moved toward wakefulness, in those hazy moments before full awareness, I stretched. I pushed out my front arms and arched my back and kneaded my claws . . . wait. I didn't have claws. And I was not that limber. In fact, I think my spine popped when I did that because pain shot up my back.

Oh. Holy shit. I wasn't a cat.

I jolted into full wakefulness and found myself tucked into a bed, swaddled in a blanket. It was dark in the room, the only light a small flickering candle placed on the vanity and the soft light of dusk filtering in the window. I patted myself down, and yes, I was back the way I was supposed to be. I breathed out a sigh of relief, then immediately yawned. I was exhausted to my bones, and I ached in a weird way, like I'd been stretched out like taffy.

Thank magic I was no longer a cat. I lifted my hand to run it through my hair, but paused, had a brief thought about licking my knuckles, then shuddered in disgust. I tugged on the strands of my hair instead to ground myself. Those cat instincts had been strong.

Stronger than I'd realized. I mean, I had wanted to cuddle. I did cuddle. I *purred*.

I hugged Rook.

I clenched the blanket in my fists. The mortification was enough to send me sliding back underneath the covers to stay forever. I'd hugged Rook. As a cat, I had cuddled with him in the bed. But that was *as a cat*. As a human, I'd hugged him, of my own volition. Like, initiated it and held on. I'd *rested my head on his shoulder*. Oh no. Could I blame that on residual cat instincts? Should I blame that on residual cat instincts, or should I go with it?

Rook might not mention it if I didn't bring it up . . . Who was I kidding? Rook was totally going to mention it the second I saw him again. He'd grin and walk with swagger and tease me until my cheeks turned pink about how I'd *hugged* him. Ugh. But . . . it wasn't that bad of a thought. I liked him. I'd admitted that to myself a while ago. I just hadn't told him that yet.

I was going to, though. I hadn't let go of my conviction to tell Rook that he deserved better from the people in his life. He deserved to know what had happened and my feelings for him. Then it would be up to him to decide whether we could continue to be friends. I eased out of the bed. My bare feet felt weird against the wood, and I wasn't quite steady when I walked, used to all fours for the past few days.

Laughter drifted down the hallway when I pushed open the door, and I staggered into the dark living room. Through the archway, Rook and Mavis sat at the small kitchen table, a few candles lit around the space. They shared takeout containers while talking, laughing like they were old friends. I guessed they were. I paused and watched. I wasn't sure about Mavis. She'd come through when we needed help, but she seemed convenient. It was unlikely that someone would be willing to help two fugitives on the flimsy premise that she too had problems with the magical governing body that ruled our world. It wasn't that I wasn't grateful for her help, but I didn't think we could count on her for whatever our plan was going to be next.

"Sun!" Rook yelled, standing so quickly his chair skittered across the floor.

I flinched at the sound.

"You're awake." He smiled widely, his cheek dimpling. "Come sit down. Mavis brought us some food. I'm sure you're hungry."

Rook reached out his hand, and I stared at it, not comprehending. After a moment, his fingers curled in on themselves and his bright smile dimmed. And oh. Oh. I should've taken his hand. I wanted to take his hand.

"Forgot," he said, mumbling.

But he hadn't. I knew he hadn't. Rook hadn't crossed any of the boundaries I'd set once he knew they were there. He was thoughtful like that. The gesture was . . . That was because of the hug.

Mavis watched us with a knowing look and eyebrows raised, and yeah, I was not sold on Mavis.

I hobbled to the table and sank into the chair that Rook pushed out for me.

"Nice to meet you, Sun," Mavis said with a nod. "You're looking . . . human."

I looked awful, from the reflection I caught in the window. Which was not great in the face of Mavis's pretty manicure and curled lashes and deep-brown eyes and bouncy curls and flawless brown skin and . . . Oh no, I was envious. Jealousy bubbled like acid in my gut.

"Thank you," I managed, though my throat was dry. Ugh. I had drool crusted in the corner of my mouth, and I hastily rubbed it away.

"Here." Rook offered me a bottle of water, which I took gratefully. He pushed a carton of food toward me as well and a set of plastic utensils. "Eat all you want. We saved it all for you."

"Thanks."

"You're welcome."

I dug into the food, unaware of how hungry I was until the hot and delicious smell of it hit me, and I sighed heavily after swallowing my first bite, inadvertently blowing out a candle.

"Oh. No worries. Watch!"

Rook went still, narrowed his eyes, and held out his hand, then flicked two fingers toward the wick. The candle lit.

Mavis clapped with enthusiasm.

"You did it," I said, watching as the little flame danced happily. He'd done it. With ease.

Rook beamed. "I did. It's easier the more I do it. Like you said it would be. I think assisting Mavis with steadying that spell really helped."

Stunned, I set down the carton. "Like I said—"

"Yep. When you came by, and we had our office study date."

I jerked and knocked my knee into the table. Everything rattled, and the candle went out again. Date. *Date*. He'd referred to it as a date at his home too, when I was a cat.

Rook blushed. He scratched the back of his neck. "I mean, when you came by that day, and we ate candy."

"I remember." Why was my voice so low and scratchy? Why was it doing that? I was no longer a cat. I cleared my throat and took a long sip from the water bottle.

"Anyway," Rook said, plowing through the awkwardness like a pro, "Mavis was also kind enough to lend me a battery charger so I could recharge my phone." He smiled again, something soft and fond. "So, if you want, you can contact your family."

I dropped my water bottle. Luckily, I'd screwed the cap back on, so I avoided a potential water volcano when the bottle hit the floor, but the plastic *thunk* of it was still loud. "What?"

"Call your sisters and your parents. Tell them you're okay. You remember the missing person's bulletin, right?"

"Yes. I was a cat, but I understood everything that happened."

"Right. Well. Now that you're no longer a cat and can actually speak, rather than meow, you can let them know you're fine."

"No!" No. *No*. What was Rook thinking? I couldn't contact them. "I thought I'd made it clear. I'm not involving them in this. Not until we've figured out what we're going to do next."

Rook frowned. "As you pointed out, you were a cat. Nothing was clear."

Oh. Good point.

"Anyway, you should eat."

I shook my head. "I don't want to call my family because they will try to rescue me from you."

Mavis glanced between us. "Okay, well, I am third wheeling here, obviously." She stood and gathered her things. "I'll come back in the morning. Until then, stay out of sight. And think about what you want to do."

Rook and I stayed stock-still even after the front door closed behind her, signaling her exit.

Rook wouldn't meet my gaze. His eyebrows drew together, his lips pursed. "I've been selfish from the start, Sun. You don't need to stay here with me. You don't need to help me figure out the mess I pulled you into. They *should* rescue you from me."

I sighed and pinched the bridge of my nose. "I ghosted you."

Rook winced. "Yeah. You did."

He pulled no punches, which was fair. "I didn't want to. Fable said I had to choose magic or you, and I chose magic. And I don't know if it was the right choice or not, but I know that cutting you off wasn't fair. It hurt you. I'm sorry."

Rook looked up. "They made you choose?"

"Yeah." I flicked a piece of noodle that had fallen on the table. "Antonia came by after you lit the candle. I overheard them talking, and Antonia told Fable how proud she was of you and how smart you are and how much she wanted you as her apprentice. She even told Fable about the Ley Finder."

"Spell Binder."

"Whatever. Fable was upset and told Antonia they couldn't work together any longer and that included me and you."

"I didn't know. Antonia didn't say."

"I asked her not to. Because I knew that if you thought rules were breaking up our friendship, you'd just break the rules." The corner of my mouth lifted.

"I would've."

"That's why you had to think it was me just being . . . me." I ducked my head. "Weird awkward antisocial Sun was an easier excuse."

Rook sighed. "I never thought you were weird."

"Just awkward and antisocial."

He knocked his foot into mine under the table. "Hey. I liked awkward and antisocial. Let's just say you grew on me. Like a fungus."

"Ugh." I hid my face in my hands, smothering my laugh. "Gross." Rook chuckled.

A moment of silence settled over us.

"The point is that I'm choosing you right now. Okay? I didn't fall through a ceiling for nothing so I'm not leaving. I'm going to stay and help. Is . . . that okay?" I unclenched my fists, rubbed my palms on the soft fabric of the pajamas. "Unless you want me to leave?"

"No, I don't want you to leave." Rook smiled, relaxed in his chair, the tense line of his body easing into his regular sprawl. "But if you want to contact them, let me know. I won't bring it up again until you do. Okay?"

I nodded. "Thank you. And I'm really sorry for what I said."

"It's okay."

"It's really not. You deserve so much better, Rook."

Rook fiddled with the hem of his shirt. "Thank you."

"You're welcome," I said, then yawned.

Rook's smile grew. "Come on. You're still tired, and I'm tired. Let's get some rest and talk about everything in the morning. Maybe we won't be so irritable."

I did my best to hide another yawn, but it broke forth anyway, thus quelling any argument. Together we collected the trash and the food and blew out most of the candles. Rook locked the front door.

"I'll take the couch."

I stiffened. "No!"

Rook raised an eyebrow. "Um . . ."

"I mean . . ." I trailed off helplessly. How to explain to him that I didn't want to be alone? That I was still a little scared? That I hadn't minded when we shared the forest floor and the bed in his room? I twisted my hands together. "Uh, the bed is big."

"Yeah. It is."

I frowned. Okay. That didn't work. I'd have to be clearer. "It's comfortable."

"Okay. I'm glad. Oh, by the way, did you really fall through a ceiling? Did you land on your back? That had to hurt. Are you bruised?"

Not the line of questioning I was going for but okay. "I'm fine." I wasn't. I had spied a bruise on my shoulder that wrapped around to my back, but I wasn't brave enough to squirm and actually look.

"That must have been frightening."

I nodded.

Rook bit his lip.

And oh. Ugh. "You're going to make me say it, aren't you?"

"Yeah. Waiting on it."

I sighed heavily. "I would really like it if you shared the room with me."

"Just the room?"

I narrowed my eyes. "You know what, never mind. Have fun on the couch."

I stalked off, albeit wobbly.

Rook laughed. "Wait. Sorry. Okay. Sure. We can share the bed."

"I don't know if I want to now."

"You do," Rook crowed, following me into the room, carrying a candle. "You totally do."

"Nope. Request revoked."

"Fine. How about I ask you? Sun, can we please share the bed? I don't want to sleep on the lumpy couch that is right next to the door."

I sighed, tipping my head back. "I regret everything."

"Life choices, friend. Come on, like you said, it's big, and we won't even have to touch in the night. Unless your inner feline decides it wants to cuddle again."

"So much regret."

In the room, I settled in the place I was before, head on the pillow, blanket pulled to my chin. Rook blew out the light on the vanity and carried the other candle to the far side of the bed. He set it on the nightstand, then blew it out, bathing the room in total darkness. There was a rustle of fabric, then the bed dipped, and Rook slid in. He was right. There was enough space to fit a pillow between us, but that didn't ease my sudden case of nerves.

In fact, everything that had happened over the course of the last couple of days slammed into me all at once, like it all had been waiting on the fringes for a moment of stillness to creep in. It was like a floodgate had opened, and all the fear and anxiety and worry that I'd been able to compartmentalize because I was a cat and more worried about being not a cat crashed over me. It was like being pressed down beneath a wave, water spilling over the top, unable to move, to breathe. I sucked in a quiet breath, tried to keep my breakdown to myself, to allow Rook to sleep. Tears gathered behind my eyes, slipped out the side creases, and slid down my face, into my ears, onto the pillow.

What had they done to Fable? To Antonia? How had they been able to capture the most powerful sorcerer in an age? What would happen to us if we were caught? How were we going to resolve any of this?

"Sun?" Rook said softly.

"Yeah?" My voice was thick with fear, quiet because it had stuck in my mouth.

"You okay?"

I pressed my lips shut. More tears spilled. My chest hitched. No. I wasn't okay. My body ached with remnants of my escape. My hands shook where I clutched the blanket. I wanted my sisters.

"Because I'm not," Rook admitted into the quiet dark. "I'm really not."

I closed my eyes. "I'm not either." It was easier to confess than I thought it would be, probably because of the pitch-blackness.

"I'm scared," Rook said. "For Antonia. For Fable. For us. I don't know what to do. Well, I think I know what I need to do, but it's not a fun thought."

I didn't know what Rook was thinking. He had mentioned something about rescuing Antonia and Fable, but that would be the two of us against a whole consortium of sorcerers. We wouldn't stand a chance.

"We'll figure it out," I said, but without much conviction.

Rook huffed. "Whatever happens, I'm glad we're back to being friends. And I've done the best I could. I mean, I kept us alive, right? I escaped sorcerers who were really after me. Kind of can't believe I was able to. And hey, you're not a cat anymore. I know that not having magic was more of a hindrance, and if I was able, we wouldn't have to be here, in a house with no power, relying on someone that I knew as a kid, but . . ." He trailed off.

"Rook?"

"Yeah?"

I shifted, rolled to my side, facing him. In the dim light, I saw the outline of his profile, but not much else, his features obscured.

"I'm sorry about what the Consortium did to you when your grandmother passed."

"Oh," he said. "Uh . . . it's okay."

"It's not. It sucks. And I'm sorry."

He didn't answer straightaway. Silence stretched between us, broken only by the distant sounds of summer on the other side of the window. I worried I had overstepped, but just as I was about to apologize, he spoke again.

"I know I said this when you were a cat, but I really didn't know that creating the Spell Binder and learning magic would cause all this trouble. I thought I could prove that I belonged, you know?"

"You don't have to prove your worth to be my friend."

Rook's breath left him in an audible exhale.

It must have been the right thing to say. The mattress squeaked as Rook shifted, rolling over to face me. He didn't say anything, but he didn't need to.

"You're my friend no matter what, if you have the Ley Finder or not. If you can cast a spell or not. I think you're a good person, and my opinion wouldn't have changed if we'd been caught. You're kind, and you try hard." I swallowed back the "I like you" that wanted to follow, but I left it hanging in the air between us. There was no way he didn't know. "And I don't think enough people have said that to you."

Rook sniffled. Oh no. Had I made him cry? Had I made it worse? "That's easily the nicest thing you've ever said to me. I need a calendar to mark this day down. So I can remember it for always." I recognized the flippancy for what it was, Rook's self-defense.

Despite myself, I laughed, a raspy, whispery sound. "Why are you like this?"

"My charm, I guess." He shifted again, the blanket slipped, and he tugged it back up. "Thank you," he said, voice lower, heartfelt.

His sincerity punched me in the gut, made me want to squirm, hide my face in my hands, and run around the room at the same time. It was unbearable. I liked him so much.

For one of the limited times in my life, I wanted to give comfort via touch and take comfort in it too. I'd needed that in a few instances, like leaning into a hug from my mom after a bad grade, usually in math, or Soo-jin's arm around my shoulder when in an unfamiliar place, or even a pat on the back from Fable after a good day of magic. I'd even given touches every once in a while, when I recognized they were needed. I tolerated accidental touches or touches within social constructs, but I wasn't one to seek it out or offer often. But now I wanted to show affection. I wanted to curl into Rook and soak in the comforting physical presence of him and show him I trusted him. That was a scary feeling in and of itself, so I went with something small.

"Can I hold your hand?" I whispered.

Silence from Rook's side of the bed. I thought and slightly hoped he'd fallen asleep. He hadn't. He shifted closer, and I barely made out the line of his arm and his upturned palm.

"Yes."

I didn't hesitate. I grabbed his hand in mine, despite my clammy skin, and threaded our fingers together.

"Thank you."

"You're welcome. For the record, I like it."

My heart raced. "Me too."

"Good night, Sun."

"Good night, Rook."

I lay in the dark, eyes closed, exhausted to my marrow, the fear of the morning hovering nearby. I squeezed Rook's hand. He squeezed back. And I slipped into sleep.

19

ROOK

Loud knocking on the front door woke me from the best sleep I'd had in ages. The bed was comfortable, my pillow soft, and while the sheets were a little musty, they were warm in the cool breeze coming from the windows. It had to be early, because the heat of the summer had yet to permeate the air. The gentle pitter-patter of rain on the windowsill alerted me to a morning shower.

Sun was still asleep next to me, face slack, mouth slightly open. We'd shifted in the night. Sun had curled toward me, like a parenthesis, their feet lightly brushing mine, our hands still clasped. If I had the time, I would've stayed like this, admiring the way the morning light highlighted Sun's cheekbones, pouty lips, and the dark sweep of their eyelashes. The way their hair fell across their face and ears.

But someone pounded on the door.

Sun's brow creased. I resisted the urge to ease it with my fingers. Because we had to get up. Someone was at the door. It could be important. It could be the Consortium.

Oh shit! It could be the Consortium!

"Sun!" I whisper-shouted.

Sun came awake in a second, staring at me with wide eyes.

The sound reverberated again.

We scrambled. I slid into my jeans. Sun fell off the other side of the bed before popping back up and shoving the hoodie on over their head, hair standing up everywhere.

Together we crept into the hall and paused. I nodded to the linen closet. Sun opened it, and I grabbed a broom. Sun took the dustpan. Good choice. It had a sharp edge. Armed with cleaning supplies, we made it into the living room.

The knocking hadn't ceased.

I cleared my throat, froggy from sleep and the open windows. "Who is it?" I called, using a light, high voice that was maybe supposed to sound like someone other than me.

Sun made a face of incredulity.

I shrugged.

"It's me," Mavis called. "Your favorite neighbor who has news and needs you to open the door like fifteen minutes ago."

I slumped with relief. Sun did not. They kept the dustpan held like a weapon. After crossing the room, I peeked through the window just in case, and okay. Mavis was alone, on the porch, and held a canvas duffel and a fast-food bag that I hoped contained breakfast.

I opened the door, and she breezed in, dropping the heavy bag at her feet and tossing the sack of food in Sun's direction. Sun dropped the dustpan and caught the bag without a problem. They must have still had access to some of those cat reflexes.

Mavis eyed my broom. "Doing some light cleaning this morning?"

I leaned it against the wall. "Maybe."

"Uh-huh. Anyway, news came over the scrying mirror about ten minutes ago."

"I'm guessing it's not good?"

Mavis shrugged. "Well, depends. Do you like your mentors with the ability to cast spells?"

Sun dropped the bag. The contents, which happened to be wrapped breakfast sandwiches, spilled onto the floor.

"What?" they asked.

Grimacing, Mavis sat on the couch, crossing her legs at the knees, her flowy blouse spilling around her. "The Magical Consortium has decided to bind both Fable's and Antonia's magic for the rules they've broken."

Sun staggered, then collapsed in the recliner, eyes wide. "What?" they said again, breathless.

"Binding."

I crossed the room, picked up the sandwiches, and settled on the couch next to Mavis. "That's bad, right? That's what they did to Antonia's apprentice?"

"Yeah, it's bad."

"It's death," Sun said, rubbing their chest. "For a sorcerer, it's like a death. Rook, remember how you felt leaving here and moving to the city? To the apartment with no magic?"

I nodded. It had been awful, like a piece of me had been sliced away. I swallowed. "Yeah."

"Binding is like that but a thousand times worse."

I could imagine. "Okay, well, this is not good news."

Mavis leveled me with a look. "There's more."

"More?"

"If they catch Sun"—her gaze flickered to where Sun had collapsed in the chair—"they'll do the same to them."

Sun turned shockingly pale, and their lips went bloodless.

"Unless," Mavis continued, "Rook turns himself in."

I nodded. It was what I had figured, anyway. There was no way around it, no way out. I had already planned to turn myself in, with the Spell Binder, and submit to the Consortium in exchange for letting Fable and Antonia free and pardoning Sun. It wasn't what I wanted, and I was scared beyond belief of doing it, but Sun had a family, and Fable and Antonia had magic and helped people. I was superfluous. I'd accepted that last night. Honestly, that possibility had been in the back of my mind all along, but I wanted to have Sun back to themself first before I even broached it.

"Okay. Then. Well. Not much of a choice, is it?"

Sun's mouth dropped open, eyes wide, fingers digging into their knees. I met their gaze and winked.

"Guess I'm turning myself in, then."

Sun shot to their feet. "No!"

I sighed. "Sun, it's for the best."

"Don't patronize me," Sun snapped. "The best for who? For you? Did the scrying mirror say what they would do to Rook? If he turns himself in?"

Mavis shook her head. "No."

"So they could do anything, right? They could bind him?"

Mavis shot Sun an incredulous look. And, honestly, I was a little confused myself. "Bind him?" Mavis asked. "Rook can't see the ley lines. By Consortium definition, he doesn't have magic. That's one of the problems of him being Antonia's apprentice."

Sun crossed their arms. "I keep hearing everyone say that, but I don't understand. How could he not have magic? He lit the candle. He steadied the spell yesterday."

Shaking my head, I stood and faced Sun. "The first day I met Antonia, she took my hand and looked in me, and she didn't find any magic. She didn't see the spark or whatever it's called that would allow me to be a full sorcerer like you. And if the most powerful sorcerer in an age can't find it, then it's not there. And that's okay. I can't see the ley lines. I can't *feel* magic like you can. Remember in the haunted house when you told me what the curses felt like to you?" Sun nodded. "I couldn't feel any of that. That's why I touched the curtains. I didn't know they were going to try to suffocate me to death."

Mavis made a high noise of surprise.

I plowed on. "Antonia and I thought, correctly I might add, that with training, I might be able to learn, but it will never be easy for me. I'm not magic. Not like you."

Sun threw out their arms, exasperated, and stomped their foot. "That's where you're wrong. Fable and Antonia can't see it, but it doesn't mean it's not there."

"I can't see it in him, either," Mavis offered.

Sun shot her a glare. "You can't see it, but I *can*." Sun tapped their fingers on their breastbone. "That's my gift."

The world tilted on its axis, jarred to a halt so hard I thought I might have been thrown off. The songs of the birds outside, the patter of the rain on the roof, the creak of the house as it settled stopped instantly. My vision tunneled until all I saw was Sun, their pleading expression, the bright spots of red on their cheeks. I swallowed. "What?"

"Don't you remember the singing mice? I saw the magic in the walls, pulling from the ley line. I saw the weak and dead lines in that neighborhood with the rich lady and the pig-nose kid." Sun deflated and gestured toward me. "And I see it in you." They stepped forward, grabbed my hand, and pushed their finger into my palm. "I see it. It's small, underdeveloped, but it's there. You can't see the lines, but that doesn't mean you're not magic. It doesn't mean that you don't belong. You've always belonged."

"You see it?"

Sun nodded. "Yeah. I've seen it the whole time. That's why I never questioned that you were Antonia's apprentice. Why I was confused when Fable listed their objections against you. Why I didn't understand why you needed"—Sun's gaze flashed to Mavis—"the thing. And they kept saying it, and I didn't know what they meant because I could see you, Rook."

I blinked rapidly to keep the tears from falling. I bit my lip. "You could see me?"

Sun nodded. They reached out for me, took my hand in theirs, laced our fingers. "Since the beginning."

I didn't want to cry. But I couldn't stop the tears that slipped down my cheeks. "Wow. This is intense," I said with a laugh.

Sun squeezed my hand. "Even if you weren't magic, you belong. You've always belonged. Anyone who barges into Antonia Hex's office and demands to be her apprentice has a place in our community."

I laughed again, wiped the tears away with the flat of my hand, smearing them more than anything. "That literally is not what happened. I freaked out at Herb the coatrack, banged my knee under her desk, and tripped over the cursed mat on my way out, giving myself a bloody nose."

Sun shrugged. "I like my version better."

I looked down at our entwined hands. It had felt good last night. It felt even better in the light of day, but that didn't change anything. Magic or not, I still had a duty. I still had to face the consequences of my actions. I disentangled our fingers and gently let go of Sun.

"It doesn't change anything. The fact that I can actually be bound doesn't change my decision. I have to turn myself in."

Sun's face was a thundercloud, but I cut them off.

"Sun. There's no other way. What are we supposed to do? Fight them? Hide forever? We can't do either of those." Sun couldn't argue. They knew I was right. "Mavis, how long do we have?"

"They're planning the binding ceremony for tonight. It's to be broadcast across all the scrying mirrors."

I closed my eyes. "We shouldn't waste time, then."

"I'll get my car. There are clothes that my younger siblings don't wear anymore in that bag. They should fit both of you. And bottles of water, toothbrushes, et cetera. You can at least wash up a bit before you face down the Consortium."

"Sun's not coming."

Sun stopped in their tracks. "I'm coming."

"You're not. I'll turn myself in, negotiate for your pardon, while you stay here or go home. You can even watch it on Mavis's mirror."

Sun clenched their hands into fists. "I'm coming. I will speak for myself."

"Sun."

"No! You're not leaving me behind. You're my friend, and I'm not letting you go alone."

"It would be safer—"

"Fuck safer." Sun grabbed the bag. "If you leave without me, I'll follow. So, you might as well just save us both the trouble and give in now."

And that was the prickly Sun I was used to, that I had fallen for weeks ago. "You can't follow me if I tie you to a chair!"

Sun flipped me off as they walked away and disappeared into the hallway.

"Fine! Come with me! Risk your life and your magic!"

"I will!" they shouted back.

In spite of it all, I grinned.

"I don't know how your mentors stood it," Mavis said, leaning in the doorway.

"Stood what?" I asked.

"The crackling tension between you two. I've known you two days, and I don't know how you two exist in the same space without kissing. It's like watching a rom-com."

Heat rose in my cheeks. "Shut up."

"I'm right, though, right? You want to kiss Sun? I mean, you were just holding hands, and Sun totally wants to kiss you." She put her hand to her mouth. "Wait, are you already together?"

"I thought you were going to your car?"

"What? In a rush to turn yourself in?"

I hooked my fingers in the pockets of my jeans and cleared my throat, hoping for nonchalant. "You think Sun wants to kiss me?"

"Honestly? I can't tell if they want to kill you or kiss you, but as they've had ample opportunity for murder and you're still alive at this point, I'm leaning toward kiss."

"Helpful."

"I aim to please." She patted me on the shoulder. "Oh, and for the record, I'll drive you to the Consortium main office, but that's as far as I'm going. The rest of this shit, and whatever other piece you're not telling me, is between you and them."

"Noted. And thank you, for all you've done for us so far. You didn't have to."

"I know I didn't, and honestly, I didn't do it for you. I did it for your grandmother. She was amazing and slightly terrifying in her own right, and I knew she'd haunt me if I didn't help."

I laughed. "She wasn't terrifying."

"To you maybe, but to the rest of the neighborhood, she was not to be trifled with." Mavis lightly punched my arm. "Anyway, I'll be back soon."

She left, and I wandered toward the back of the house intent on freshening up and changing my clothes. Sun was in the bathroom, the door slightly ajar as they brushed their teeth using bottled water, a borrowed toothbrush, and a travel tube of toothpaste. They'd found a pair of black jeans, a black shirt, and a pair of slides—I'd totally forgotten about the need for shoes. I was glad Mavis had at least thought about that so that Sun wouldn't have to go barefoot into the city.

Sun looked up while they rinsed their mouth, water swishing, pink lips pressed hard together, eyelashes and fringes of their hair damp from where they'd washed their face. They spit into the sink, then took a towel and patted their face and mouth dry.

It was weirdly domestic and intimate, watching them complete their morning ritual.

"What?" Sun asked.

"Huh?"

"You're staring."

"Oh, uh, sorry." I scrambled into the bedroom and found the duffel on the bed. I changed my clothes, slipping on a pair of jeans and a loose shirt, then took my turn in the bathroom.

I emerged to find Sun waiting for me on the couch.

"I heard what Mavis said." Sun perched on the edge of the couch, spine straight.

"Which part? The one where she's going to bail on us as soon as we get there, or that apparently my grandmother was a formidable and scary magic person?"

Sun's cheeks turned pink. "The other part."

I crossed the room and sat next to them on the couch, turned slightly toward them. "You'll have to elaborate. We've talked a lot in the last few minutes."

Sun grimaced. "Why are you like this?"

"It's fun," I said with a wink.

"Fine. The kissing. How she thinks I want to kiss you. Or you want to kiss me? That part."

My heart thumped. "Ah, that part," I said with a nod. I tried for nonchalant but knew I'd failed when my own face flushed. I clasped my hands in my lap.

"Well?" they prodded.

I licked my lips. "I wouldn't be averse to kissing. We're literally about to confront a bunch of sorcerers, so, I mean, if we're going for bucket list here, I wouldn't mind a first kiss—"

Sun made a face that let me know that was exactly the wrong thing to say. "Really? If the only reason you want to kiss me is because you might not get a chance to kiss anyone else anytime soon, then—"

"No!" I said, laughing at their positively affronted expression. "No. I'm sorry it came out like that. I just . . ." I fisted my hands on my thighs. "I like you. I've liked you since the doll incident. And it's only gotten worse, to be honest."

"Oh," Sun breathed. "You like me? Since the doll incident?"

"You were cute."

"I was grumpy and sweaty."

"What can I say? I have a thing for introverts with brusque attitudes."

Sun blinked. "What is wrong with you?"

"Are you questioning my taste in people? Because I like *you*? I think the more appropriate question would be what is wrong with you that you think you're unlikable? Have you seen you? Not that I'm basing this completely on looks alone, because that's not cool and also not true. I like you. All of you. Even the rough pieces."

Sun ducked their head, rubbed a hand over their face, but I caught the small smile that curled the corners of their mouth.

"Okay. So, I've said I like you and you've left me a little out here by myself. Is that a no? You're not into it? Which is fine. Or is this a maybe? An explore after we get this Consortium business figured out? Or should I find a spell to erase the last several minutes of this conversation or find one to create a hole in the floor that will swallow me because—"

Sun leaned forward and, without any warning, planted a kiss on my open mouth, stopping me midsentence. It was soft and sweet and fleeting, but it was definitely a kiss. My first kiss. They pulled away just as quickly, leaving me stunned, speechless, my mouth still half-open, but now with the soft phantom pressure of Sun's lips lingering there.

"Was that okay?" Sun asked.

Was that okay? It was more than okay. It was unexpected and amazing. I cleared my throat. "I guess? I think I need more empirical evidence to make a sound judgment. A second set of data, if you will."

Sun smiled, one of their rare full smiles, beautiful and radiant. They leaned in again, fingertips against my jaw, present and comforting as they pressed their smile to my mouth. My eyes fluttered shut as I melted into it. The kiss lasted a little longer than the first one, and I sighed shakily, overwhelmed by the feeling of Sun's lips moving against my own, the whisper of their breath, the devastatingly cute sound they made in their throat as I kissed back, as fumbling as it was.

Sun broke away first, and I did not embarrassingly follow no matter what they said at a later date.

"How was that?" Sun asked, not pulling away, staying close, their hand now resting against the side of my neck, thumb sweeping across my rapid pulse.

"How are you so good at that?" I asked, eyes still closed.

"Obligatory middle school boyfriend. We dated for, like, a week. It was awful."

I scrunched my nose. "A little jealous of him but also feel like I should send him a gift basket."

Sun huffed a laugh. "For the record, I like you too," they said.

And then we were kissing again. I sank into it, slow, dragging kisses. Sun surprised me with how assertive they were when it came to making out, and I would've gladly stayed on the couch with them, leaning into their touches, welcoming their kisses, and learning what it meant to be with them, but as it was, we ran out of time.

"I knew it," Mavis said as she breezed in the door, twirling her car keys on her finger.

We sprang apart. Sun's face was flushed, and mine was not any better if the heat in my cheeks was any indication.

"We'll be right out," I squeaked.

She laughed. Turning on her heel, she flounced back outside.

Sun's forehead dropped to my shoulder. "Embarrassing."

"For you, maybe," I said, running my fingers through their hair. "But not for me. I was just caught making out with the hottest person I know, so, if anything, I'm feeling pretty good right now."

Sun snorted. "Regret," they said. "So much regret."

"You like it."

Sun lifted their head and smiled. "Ugh. I do. It's maddening."

Mavis honked her horn. We separated and stood, adjusting our clothes. I grabbed my backpack, the Spell Binder inside, and I took one last look around the cabin, not knowing if I was going to be back anytime soon. I hoped I would, but my future was uncertain.

Sun took my hand, laced our fingers together, and squeezed.

I took a breath. "Okay, then. Let's get this over with."

Together, we walked out the door.

20

ROOK

Mavis drove us into the city, straight to downtown, where the towering glass office buildings scraped the sky, all the streets were one-way, and there was no parking anywhere to be found. Where the sidewalks were shaded due to the height of the structures, and people herded along the crosswalks, dead-eyed and lifeless, as they went about their busy workday even in the midst of the summer heat. I hated going downtown, just because of the bustle and how everything made me feel smaller.

Despite myriad horns honking at her, Mavis stopped abruptly in front of a building that I assumed housed the offices of the Magical Consortium, Spire City branch. It appeared more like a museum, with wide white stairs and fluted columns holding up an ornate pediment. I stared out the window, my mouth hanging slightly open in awe.

"Wow."

"What?" Mavis asked, leaning over me to look out my window. "Oh, that's the city museum," she said. She tapped my shoulder and pointed across the street. "That's the Consortium office."

I blinked. "Oh."

It didn't look at all like I thought it would. It didn't have the cottage-core feel of Fable's place or the bleak business office park chic of Antonia's. It was a lonely wooden door set into a tall, skinny gray stone wall with a single pane of glass and white letters that merely said SPIRE CITY OFFICE. The building itself appeared wedged between the structures around it, like some architect took it as a challenge to build on the smallest piece of land they could, so they did, and the result was a vertigo-inducing stone block.

A horn bleated behind us, and Mavis huffed. She turned to me, her seat squeaking. "Look, whatever happens"—her gaze cut to Sun in the back seat—"make sure you come out of there. Okay? Your grandma's ghost will haunt me forever if you don't."

I nodded once, heart in my throat, palms sweaty. I rubbed them on my thighs. "Yeah. Whatever it takes. We'll be walking out of there. Sun with their magic and me with, whatever."

Mavis smiled grimly. She patted my arm. "Don't take so long to visit the old neighborhood again. And until you do, I'll keep watch over the place."

I squeezed my hands into fists. "Thanks." I took a deep breath. "Okay. This will be fine," I said, voice high and not at all genuine. "Fine. Totally fine."

I exited the car and slammed the door shut, hanging my bag over my shoulder. Sun scrambled out, and we stood on the wrong side of the street, staring at the door as Mavis drove away.

Sun held out their hand. I took it, laced our fingers together, and squeezed. "Come on," they said, slightly tugging me. "Let's get this over with."

"Right."

"It'll be fine."

I laughed, slightly hysterical. "You, the optimist? What's happening?"

Sun rolled their eyes. "I was trying out that whole positive outlook thing."

"Cool."

"Regret," they said, with a slight smirk. "So much regret."

I laughed again, but this time it was sincere. "You do not regret it at all."

Sun blushed, looked down at our joined hands. They tightened their grip. "Yeah. I don't, but at least let me keep the facade."

"Sure," I said with a nod. "Okay. Enough stalling. Just, no matter what happens, you were the best part of this whole magic adventure."

Sun looked up from where they had studied the pavement. They cleared their throat. "You too. I'm glad I met you, even if you annoyed me."

Smiling, I ducked my head and ran a hand through my hair. "Thank you."

Despite the overwhelming fear and every bit of my limited self-preservation instincts telling me to run the other way, we crossed the road and stood in front of the simple door. I lifted my free fist to knock, but the door swung inward before I made contact. I yelped in surprise.

Sun raised an eyebrow.

Together we leaned in and looked around. It was a very small space, about the size of an elevator, with brown paneled walls, a white tile floor, and nothing else except for another door. Sun and I exchanged a glance. We shuffled inside. The door slammed shut behind us, and Sun's breath hitched, their fingers tightening around mine. But as the door behind us closed, the one in front opened.

"Well, this is fun," I said, as we peered into another room that looked identical to the one we were currently standing in.

We stepped into the next foyer. The door closed behind us, and the next one opened. We walked in, and the previous door shut behind us. I sighed as the next door opened.

"They're fucking with us," Sun said, clearly annoyed.

I nodded. "Maybe."

The pattern repeated and repeated, and as each new door opened, both of us became bolder, stomping in instead of tentatively entering. I lost count of how many revolving rooms we went through before Sun stomped their foot. Sun seemed to lose their anxiety around small spaces in the face of utter frustration.

"Wait," they said, jerking me backward before I stepped through the next door. "It's a trick."

"I figured," I grumbled. "I am pretty smart."

Sun huffed. They let go of my hand and walked around the tiny room we were in, looking at the tile floor and the paneled brown walls. There was literally nothing in there with us other than walls and floor.

Sun scrunched their cute nose and blinked.

Oh. "What do you see?"

"Magic everywhere. This whole room is soaked in magic. I can't see beyond it to make out any ley lines."

"No worries." I took my bag off my shoulder and pulled out the Spell Binder.

"Rook!" Sun whisper-shouted.

"What? It's not like they don't know it exists, and I can't get into *more* trouble than I'm already in. Besides, I want to know how much power is coming through here. It might help us out in the long run."

Sun grumbled but nodded. I flicked the switch, and in seconds, the screen lit up. A huge dot took up most of the screen. It had to be vertical, since it didn't cross the map, but the diameter was massive, and that wasn't all. Other lines, smaller but just as strong, fed into the large one. Sun peered over my shoulder.

"That's a lot of magic."

"Makes sense, I guess. Have you ever seen this before?"

Sun shook their head. "I avoid downtown like the plague. I hate the city, as you probably guessed."

I nodded. "I do seem to remember how disgruntled you were the first time we met at Antonia's office."

I shoved the Spell Binder back in my bag. "But you can't see it now?"

Sun shook their head. "No. I can't discern the lines, but I can feel them"—they touched their breastbone—"humming like a livewire. It's especially strong over here." They walked to a corner, reached out their hand, and pressed their palm flat to one of the panels.

The walls jerked, a low rumble of gears and mechanisms emanated from around us, and then the whole room plummeted.

It happened so quickly, I didn't have time to grab for Sun before my stomach knocked against the roof of my mouth as the whole room fell like an elevator with no brakes. As quickly as it began, it ended, the room juddering to a hard stop.

I was breathing hard when my feet hit the floor, and my knees crumpled. My head spun, but as soon as I had my bearings, I unglued myself from the paneling and crawled to where Sun crouched on the ground, arms over their head, face tucked into their knees.

"Hey," I said, stopping beside them. "You okay?"

They trembled, wiped their face with their sleeve. "Fine," they said, but their voice was thick. They shuddered. "I thought you said elevators were safe."

"Well, this one is obviously not. I'm going to write a strongly worded letter. Leave a nasty voicemail. I may even wag a finger or two in someone's face. Because that was not okay. That was really not okay. I think I lifted off the ground? I think I may have thrown up in my mouth too. So no kissing until I have a chance to brush my teeth. Like wow." I rested my hand on Sun's back. "Seriously, you okay?"

"Yeah." They stood, and I followed. Their legs were wobbly. "Fuckers," they said, as one of the paneled walls slid open, leading us into another room, at least not identical to the one we were in.

I agreed immediately. "Sadistic fuckers." I took the hand Sun offered and held on. "If they thought I was annoyed before, I'm pretty livid now."

Sun bit their lip. Their face had drained of color, but they were determined, even if fine tremors ran through them. "Me too."

The next room was larger and had a receptionist desk, as if we walked into a business office instead of a magical consortium that was about to punish our mentors with a metaphorical death. A very bored-looking person sat behind a large round desk.

We walked up to it, and I cleared my throat.

He glanced up. "Yes?" he asked, annoyed.

I peeked over the desk and found that he clutched a paperback, a finger holding his place, the cover obviously a historical romance.

"Uh, hi. My name is Rook, and this is Sun. We're the apprentices to Antonia Hex and Fable Page, and we're here to turn ourselves in."

He blinked, then nodded toward a line of chairs along the wall. "I'll let them know you're here. Sit and wait."

"Um . . . we're, like, wanted for crimes."

He rolled his eyes. "And I'll let them know you're here." Then he pointed toward the chairs.

We shuffled over and sat down. The receptionist tapped the large mirror on the corner of their desk, and the surface shimmered. "Hey," they said into the suddenly cloudy reflection. "So, I have two kids here saying they're apprentices to Hex and Page. Uh-huh. Yeah." He rolled his eyes. "I know, right? They let anyone be magic these days."

Sun bristled next to me. I rested my hand on their forearm where they gripped the armrest.

The receptionist looked over at us, then turned back to the mirror. "Yeah, they match the description. Mostly. Uh-huh. Okay. Yeah." They tapped it again, then went back to their romance novel.

I leaned into Sun's side. "You know, this is turning out to be really anticlimactic."

Sun nodded, brow furrowed. "Agreed. This is weird."

"Have you ever been here before?"

Sun shook their head, black hair falling into their eyes. "No. We always use a scrying mirror to talk to the Consortium."

"Maybe we should've done that instead of coming here."

Sun's eyes widened. "Wow. That . . . We should've done that. What were we thinking?"

I shrugged. "We know for next time."

Sun spluttered. "Next time?"

I nudged my shoulder into theirs. "Positive outlook."

"How is that positive?"

"It means we make it out of this and have a second adventure—"

The door behind the receptionist banged open, and a group of suit-clad sorcerers filed out and surrounded us, followed by Evanna Lynne Beech, sorcerer grade four, of the Magical Consortium Spire City office. Her heels clacked as she strode across the room and stood in front of us, clipboard in hand, every inch the woman who had interrogated and then captured the powerful Antonia Hex.

She looked us over and snapped her fingers.

Four of the sorcerers broke off from the half circle surrounding us and yanked us to our feet. "Hey!" I yelled, as they broke the connection between myself and Sun. "Hands off."

One ripped my backpack from my hand and passed it off to someone on the side, while the others jostled us as they patted us down. One took my cell phone from my pocket and handed it off as well.

Sun struggled next to me as one of the sorcerers gripped their arms and another snapped a pair of manacles over their wrists. The metal shackles glowed green, and Sun gasped, doubling over.

"What are you doing?" I twisted away from the person who held me. "Take them off. What the hell?"

Evanna Lynne leveled a gaze at me. "Don't waste a pair on him. He doesn't need them."

As they dragged us toward the open door, I fought to get closer to Sun, digging my heels in against the carpet, fighting the sorcerers who held on to me.

Evanna Lynne whirled around. "I thought you were turning yourself in," she said, voice clipped.

"I am, which is why you don't need to manhandle me. And you don't need to do whatever it is you did to them."

She nodded to the two people who held me, and they let go. I didn't waste a second, shouldering through the crowd until I was next to Sun, and hooked my arm through one of theirs. They trembled. Whatever those cuffs were doing was not pleasant.

"Take these off," I said, yanking on the chain between Sun's wrists.

"They're a necessary precaution. They dampen the ability for the wearer to cast. Which is why you don't need them."

Sun glared. If looks could curse, Evanna Lynne would be covered in spiders while trapped in an elevator.

Evanna Lynne smirked.

"Fine. But you're not separating us. We stay together."

"I'm agreeable to that," she said, chin lifted. "Now, come along like good little apprentices, and this will all be over shortly."

I did not like the sound of that. I gulped and clutched Sun's arm, pulling them as close as possible.

Sun leaned over. "Well, at least it seems like we're getting our climax."

"Way to stay positive," I said, as we followed Evanna Lynne through the door and deeper into the Consortium office.

21

SUN

The cuffs didn't hurt per se, though they did pinch my skin when they were first snapped on. They were mainly just cold and prickly. I shuddered as I realized the last time I'd felt cold and prickly was when we were in the haunted house. The shackles were cursed, and they muted everything. All the magic I could normally feel, the ley lines and spells I could see when I used my ability, all of that was . . . dampened. Not completely gone, not the death that binding would be if that were to happen, but definitely disconcerting. Like I was hearing music underwater. It was there but too muffled to understand the words. I tried to reach out for magic, but it didn't reach back like it normally would. I didn't like it at all.

I also didn't like how they were treating Rook. First the receptionist and now Evanna Lynne.

They led us farther into the building, where the rooms bloomed into large spaces with high ceilings and marble floors. Paintings and sculptures of past sorcerers lined the hallways. Orbs of light floated in the air, casting a warm glow. Badge-wearing sorcerers in suits and ties and dresses walked past us, carrying clipboards, too busy to watch our weird parade. This was exactly what I thought the Consortium would look like, and Rook's awed face mirrored the sentiment. At least I finally knew where all the fees we paid went.

Evanna Lynne opened another door and revealed a dizzying spiral staircase that plunged downward into gloom.

"Court is this way," she said, gesturing.

"Court?" I asked.

She nodded. "Your trial. We've been waiting for you. We're all set and ready."

"Trial?" Rook squeaked. "Trial? We've turned ourselves in. I'm here to negotiate."

"No," she said, her patience stretched thin. "You're here to stand trial and accept your punishment alongside that of Fable Page and Antonia Hex."

"What?" Rook shouted, face going dangerously pale. I'm certain mine matched. "I was told you would let them go if I came. I'm here. I've turned myself in so that Antonia, Fable, and Sun would be released unharmed."

Evanna Lynne sighed. "You'll have to discuss that with the judge."

My heart sank. With a judge. A Consortium judge. Any little bit of hope I had clung to went up in a puff of smoke. We weren't getting out of this.

"You tricked us!" Rook yelled.

She smirked. "We did what we needed to apprehend two dangerous individuals."

Rook scoffed. "Dangerous. Seriously? Do I look dangerous? Why didn't you cuff me if I'm so dangerous?"

Evanna Lynne didn't deign to answer and instead turned on her heel and led us down the staircase.

Undeterred by the dismissal, Rook added, "Antonia was right. You are a bunch of hypocrites."

Evanna Lynne's back stiffened, but she kept walking. Rook's eyes narrowed, and he bit his lip, remaining silent as we descended. The air grew colder, the staircase widened, and the landing was in sight. Beyond that appeared to be a large room—the courtroom.

I sucked in a harsh breath as the reality of the situation hit me full force. Despite the awkwardness of the shackles, I reached for Rook's hand. He grabbed mine and squeezed.

Rook cleared his throat. "For the record," he said, his voice full of false bravado, "your laws suck. And the Consortium sucks. But especially you, Evanna Lynne. You suck so much that I can't wait for the second Antonia is released and has access to a ley line because that is going to be *amazing*."

Evanna Lynne spun to face us. For the first time since we'd entered the Consortium, her expression showed something other than arrogance. It looked a lot like unease.

"Opinion noted." She turned to me. "And what about you? Do you agree with him? Or are you smart?"

I licked my lips. Our fates appeared fairly solidified. There was no way she would allow the judge to sentence either of us lightly. If I wanted to, I could disagree, maybe save a little face, but what was the point? "I, too, cannot wait for Antonia to have access to magic again."

Her expression pinched and she turned away. As I watched her descend the last few stairs, her shoulders were tense, her fists clenched. She visibly seethed.

I looked to Rook. He smiled, dimple showing.

"Be careful, Sun," he said, voice low. "Someone may get the idea that you're a rebel."

I couldn't help but smile. "I learned from the best."

That was all we could say to each other before being marched into the courtroom. The room was round, with a raised wooden seat for the judge and a gallery high up that circled the room for spectators. A few people milled about above us, but it was far from full. There were no seats on the floor, only markers that designated where we should stand, and we were pushed into a rectangular area. As soon as we were inside, a ward sprang up, boxing us in. It reached only to our waists, so it wouldn't be used to block out magic, but it was enough to keep us from trying to run.

Evanna Lynne snapped at another sorcerer, who scurried away through another door. Then she tugged at her blouse before moving to stand in the center of the room. She eyed us like we were bugs she wanted to crush as she tapped the toe of her shoes against the stone floor.

A few moments later, there was a commotion, and another door opened. Several Consortium sorcerers piled out, and in the middle of them walked Fable and Antonia.

"Antonia!" Rook yelled.

"Fable!" I echoed.

They both looked up. Fable looked worse for wear, their frizzy blond hair all over the place, their complexion washed out by the weird jumpsuit they wore. Antonia didn't look much better, haggard but fierce. Both of them sported the dampening shackles over their wrists. Antonia broke away from the crowd, amid shouts, and after a struggle where she elbowed a sorcerer in the sternum, she ran across the room, bare feet slapping on the paving stones.

"Rook!" she said, colliding with the ward around us. It didn't stop her. She reached over the low barrier and wrapped her arms around Rook, hugging him tightly, the chain between her shackles pulling taut over his chest. In the jostling, I dropped Rook's hand, but I couldn't begrudge the loss of connection when seeing the naked affection on Antonia's face as she clutched Rook.

"Antonia," he said, voice choked.

"You're okay," she said, grasping him. "Right?"

"Yeah. I'm okay."

She disengaged and reached out and grabbed me, too, pulling me close and cupping my cheek. "Minion, are you okay too?"

"I'm fine."

"Good. Listen," she said, low and urgent, "if you have an opportunity to get out of here unscathed, I want you to take it. Understand? Don't worry about me or Fable. We'll be fine, and—"

A Consortium sorcerer grabbed Antonia's arm and jerked her back before she could finish.

Antonia shouted as they dragged her across the room, where she was unceremoniously shoved into a similar warded box to ours, along with Fable. They couldn't run, pinned in as they were with the magic barrier, and with their cursed shackles, they certainly couldn't cast. Fighting was useless, but it didn't stop Antonia from yelling and Fable from testing the ward by kicking it in various places.

Evanna Lynne stood in the middle of the spectacle. She impatiently tapped her foot, hands on her hips, as another sorcerer maneuvered a floor-length mirror into place at the front of the room.

Right. The punishment was to be broadcast across the mirrors. It was the first time in decades that something like this was public for all to see. My heart sank as they turned the mirror to ensure that the four of us would all be captured in the frame.

"A public execution, then," Antonia shouted. "How medieval."

Rook winced next to me, and I shared his sentiment. We were about to be infamous throughout Spire City and the rest of the magical world. That thought brought me up short. Wait. Scrying mirrors needed a continuous feed of magic, especially if this farce was going to be live from beginning to end. Which also meant the Consortium sorcerers couldn't ward the entire room, or the spell source for the broadcast would be blocked. A little flare of hope lit in my chest.

The shackles may have dampened my power and kept me from pulling from a ley line, but they didn't limit me entirely. I blinked, and my vision went black-and-white. Indeed, the room was not warded. And there were ley lines all around, humming and accessible. Faint in my limited vision but present, the strongest in the uppermost right corner.

Evanna Lynne rolled up her sleeves, spread out one hand, and said a few words. The thrum of the magic shuddered through me, despite the dampeners, as the spell set. The magic flowed from one of the lines into the mirror, powering the transmission. The mirror wavered, then lit, and we were connected. The sorcerers watching appeared as floating bubbles meandering along the glass, all of them connected to this moment.

The buzz of chatter filled the courtroom.

"If you would please mute your mirrors during the trial," Evanna Lynne said with a smile far softer than anything she'd shown to me or Rook.

The flame of hope in my chest burned brighter in the face of her total one-eighty for the mirror. Everything that happened in this room would be broadcast throughout the magical community. The Consortium, though undeniably powerful, still needed to portray themselves in the best possible light. We could use that. I could use that.

I turned my back to the mirror and nudged Rook with my elbow. "Smile for the mirror," I said. "We're live. There's no ward around this room, so when the time comes, upper right corner." Rook's eyes widened, but before he could respond, the judge entered and took her seat at the top of the dais.

"Order," she said, and the hall immediately quieted under her hard tone. "Court is now in session."

22

ROOK

As soon as the judge called order, Antonia scoffed.

"May I remind the judge that I've already been convicted and sentenced to binding," she said, flicking her hair over her shoulder. "And I would rather not sit through another mockery of a trial." She cast a glance at the mirror. "Even if I will bring amazing ratings."

I bit my lip. As much as I appreciated the fact that capture and imprisonment hadn't fazed Antonia one bit, now was *not* the time.

The judge narrowed her eyes. She was a short woman with gray hair, wrinkles, and an air of "I don't give a fuck," which was particularly worrying.

"Be quiet, Hex. Or you will be removed."

The judge slid her gaze over to where Sun and I stood.

"You two," she said, addressing us. "How do you plead?"

I cleared my throat and straightened my shoulders. "It would be helpful to know what we've been charged with," I said.

Evanna Lynne looked unimpressed. "Apprentice Rook is charged with creating an illegal spell book and violating our laws regarding electronic information. Apprentice Sun is charged with teaching magic to a nonmagical individual."

Sun opened their mouth to retort, but I cut them off before they could incriminate themself or piss off Evanna Lynne or the judge with their classic Sun personality.

"Look, I'm here to turn myself in. I was promised that if I gave myself up, Antonia, Fable, and Sun could all go free. So that's what I've done. Here I am."

"And you are?"

Oh. "Um, I'm Rook."

"And you are Hex's apprentice?" the judge asked.

I didn't know how to answer that. It felt like a trap.

"He is," Evanna Lynne said from her place on the floor, standing between our two warded boxes. "Hex gifted him the name Rook and taught him magic."

The judge hummed. "Yet Hex is not permitted to have an apprentice. And even if she were, our laws are clear that the apprentice must meet certain specifications."

"Point of order," Sun yelled. "Rook *is* magical, and he can cast spells."

A low murmur rose through the crowd. The judge raised an eyebrow. I knocked my elbow into Sun. "What are you doing?" I asked between clenched teeth.

"Trust me."

The judge leaned forward, intrigued. "You can cast?"

I licked my dry lips. The bubbles of sorcerers' faces swirled around the mirror. They all watched. They'd tuned in to see Antonia sentenced. To witness her demise. And that, well, that made me angry. I hardened my resolve and nodded. "Yes. I can," I announced without hesitation. "I can pull from a line and light a candle, and I steadied a spell to turn my friend here from a cat back into a human."

"We were led to believe that you cannot see the ley lines without your little device," Evanna Lynne said. "And we have on record that you were deemed nonmagical a little over a year ago."

A chill swept down my spine at the memory, and I crossed my arms, defensive, uncomfortable under the scrutiny and also very aware of how volatile this could become. "You're right. I can't see the ley lines. I've been tested twice, and both times I've been told that I don't possess the ability to access magic."

The judge raised her eyebrows. "Then it's impossible that you can cast."

"It's not impossible," Antonia said. She frowned down at her fingernails, feigning nonchalance, as if she weren't about to rock one of the very foundations of Consortium law. "He is my apprentice. Of course he can cast."

Another wave of conversation, this time not so quiet as before. Some of the sorcerers watching via the mirror unmuted themselves and voiced their disbelief, chiding Antonia for her theatrics and her lies.

The judge pounded her gavel. "I'll have order," she shouted. "Fine. If it's not as impossible as you claim, then show us."

Nervous sweat broke out on the back of my neck. This was a crack in the Consortium's carefully crafted rule of law, an attack on their long-held beliefs. This was dangerous. But it was worth it. Antonia was worth it. Sun was worth it. Fable was worth it. And every other person who had been kept from magic because they didn't fit the mold, the standards the Consortium had set, it was worth it for them, too.

"Fine. I will."

Sun had said the upper right corner of the room. That must be where a line ran. I lifted my hand. Spread my fingers. Imagined the trail of butterflies. A stream of them broke off, fluttered toward me, and I felt the magic thrum beneath my skin. I pointed two fingers toward a piece of parchment on the judge's desk and—

"Objection, Your Honor," Evanna Lynne cut in, voice high-pitched and panicked.

My concentration shattered. The butterflies slipped away, as did the warmth of magic.

She tugged at the sleeves of her suit dress in agitation, casting me vaguely wary looks. "He's admitted he cannot see the ley lines, and we have records that show he's nonmagical. That should be enough."

Antonia scoffed. "You're right, Evanna Lynne, it *should* be enough. If the Consortium rules weren't based on a bunch of falsehoods, but as they are, I demand you allow my apprentice to continue. He was about to cast a spell."

"For what reason?" Evanna Lynne snarled. "You still weren't permitted to mentor him."

"No, I was not," Antonia said with an agreeable nod. "But it would exonerate both Fable and Sun."

Evanna Lynne rolled her eyes. "How unlike you to be concerned for others, Hex. But my objection stands. Any so-called magic he performs is surely to be a parlor trick that Hex has taught him. She is known for her dramatic personality. So I humbly suggest that we move forward and address the issue of the illegal electronic device."

"Parlor trick?" Antonia straightened from her almost disrespectful slouch against the ward around her. "Parlor trick? How dare you?" She lifted her shackled wrists. "Take these off and I'll show you some parlor tricks. Let's go a few rounds of real magic and settle this like in the old days."

Evanna Lynne arched an eyebrow. "I've already bested you once, Antonia. That's enough for a lifetime."

"Yeah, you and twenty of your friends. It took *all* of you. Admit you're scared of a true one-on-one match."

The judge banged her gavel again. "Hex, one more outburst and you *will* be escorted out. And there will be no removing of the dampeners until after the sentence is carried out."

Antonia changed tactics and pouted. "Please, Your Honor? I promise I'll behave. I've worn them for days, and they itch."

"No," Evanna Lynne said evenly.

"At least take them off Sun," Fable pleaded, the first time they'd spoken since the trial began. "They're a child, and it's hurting them."

I snapped my head around. Sweat beaded along Sun's forehead. Their face was void of color. Their body trembled. Their breath was fraught.

"Sun?" I asked, catching the crook of their arm.

They swallowed thickly. "I'm fine."

They were not fine. "Take them off." I turned to the judge. "Please, take them off. Sun has done nothing wrong. Let them go. I take full responsibility for all of it."

"May I remind Apprentice Rook that he does not give the orders in this courtroom."

I stiffened. "Yes, Your Honor. Just let me cast. Let me show you I can do it, and then Sun's charges can be dropped."

The judge sighed. "I'm afraid I must agree with Sorcerer Beech. You've admitted you cannot see the ley lines, and the test records are clear. You do not meet the qualifications required of a member of the magical community, much less that of an apprentice. Even if you could cast, which I doubt you can, your existence is against the law."

My stomach dropped. The judge's words rolled around in my head, pinging against every insecurity that lived there. Another confirmation of all my fears, of everything I'd worked against. But worse, all hope I had of maybe, possibly, allowing Sun to walk free was dashed. There was no way out. No way any of us would be getting out of this.

"Now." The judge drummed their fingers. "I want to know more about your device. The illegal one."

I grimaced. "It's in my bag. Wherever that is."

A sorcerer from the side handed my backpack to Evanna Lynne. She walked it over to a table next to the judge's desk, which was already filled with several objects, and dumped the contents on the table. The Spell Binder fell out, along with my clothes and my wallet and other sundries. Evanna Lynne picked through my belongings and hefted the Spell Binder from the midst. She studied it, then handed it over to the judge.

"What does it do?"

"It detects ley lines," I said.

"It also has an electronic compendium of spells," Evanna Lynne said, poking the screen. "Which is against our rules of unauthorized spell books."

I sighed. "Yes. Thanks for pointing that out. There is an unauthorized spell book in an app as well."

The judge examined the Spell Binder and the furrow in her brow deepened. Her lips pursed. "That is a dangerous gadget."

"Why?" I challenged. If there was no way out, at least I'd go down swinging. "Because it would allow people like me to see the ley lines? Because supposed folks you deem nonmagical might know what magic looks like? Where it is and how it works?"

The judge frowned. "You're out of order, Apprentice Rook."

"So what?" I said, channeling my inner Antonia. She looked on, fingers tented, hopefully impressed. "You've already said my existence is outside your rules. How much worse can it get for me?" I gestured toward the mirror. "And you've robbed the people watching at home a chance to see something you've said was impossible. I may need that device to see the ley lines, but I can cast. I am magic. Because Antonia and Sun said I am. So, fuck you and fuck your rules. I'm tired of defending myself to gatekeepers like you."

Silence. Utter deafening silence. The sorcerers gathered around gaped in dismay. Many on the mirror looked away, the uncomfortable truth hanging between us all. I figured I'd done more harm than good, but at least I'd said what I needed to say. And once it was out there, all I felt was *relief*.

"He's not wrong," Antonia said into the damning quiet. "You enforce arbitrary rules to line your pockets. Let's be absolutely blunt about how allowing access to magic to everyone would affect the Consortium's bottom line. How would this organization afford such a nice underground courtroom if just anyone could cast a spell and didn't need to seek out the overpriced spell workers with Consortium certificates in their windows?"

"Hex, this is your last warning," the judge threatened. She set my device on her desk. "Well, this has been enlightening, but you've all given me no choice but—"

Sun gasped and swayed.

"Sun!" Fable yelled.

I tightened my grip on their elbow. "Okay. That's enough. Destroy it. Do what you have to. Just take the dampeners off Sun."

The judge's expression hardened. "I've already cautioned you once. You do not give orders here."

Sun stumbled to the side, lurching out of my grasp, leaning hard on the edge of the magic box, almost doubled over the edge. Their knees buckled, and they slid to the floor with a cry.

"*Please*," I said, my voice cracking.

Fable and Antonia shouted. More voices joined them from the spectators around the room. The sorcerers on the mirror unmuted and yelled for Sun to be released. Demanded that I be given a chance to cast. A cacophony of angry voices, but instead of berating us . . . they sided with us.

Evanna Lynne looked stricken, panicked as she lost control of the situation, realizing the crowd had turned on the Consortium fully the instant Sun fell.

The judge pounded her gavel, bellowing for order. But it was too late. The Consortium had to act or lose.

She handed the Spell Binder to Evanna Lynne. "Destroy it quickly. Then release the apprentice."

I tore my gaze away from Sun's wan face to watch as Evanna Lynne smiled at the Spell Binder in her hand. She smirked at me, held it out at arm's length as a taunt, then opened her fingers. She didn't break eye contact as it dropped like a stone, watching my expression as my creation, my once solitary tie to the magical world crashed to the ground. It landed hard, the screen cracking, bits of metal and circuits breaking off and skidding across the floor.

All the hard work. All the worry. All my hopes and pain had been molded into that device, and now it was destroyed. Gone. It didn't hurt as much as I thought it would.

"Are you done?" Antonia shouted from across the room.

Evanna Lynne tilted her head and stomped on the broken hardware again and again until all that was left of the Spell Binder was a mangled mess of circuitry.

"Yes," she replied calmly, smoothing down her pencil skirt. "It's done."

"Then see to Sun," Fable demanded.

Sun. Oh shit, Sun. I whipped back around, and Sun lay propped up in the corner of the magic box, panting and sweating and grimacing, cute nose scrunched, teeth sunk into their bottom lip.

I reached out, but Sun squirmed away from my touch. "No," they rasped, curling up into a ball. "Don't."

"Sun," I said, soft, low. "Sun, what can I do? Tell me how to help."

They peeked out from beneath their crossed arms and . . . winked. Wait. What?

The sorcerer with the key crossed the room to unlock Sun from their dampeners, but Sun cowered in the corner of the box, making themself small and oh . . . *Oh*. My heart thumped wildly as the sorcerer stopped at the barrier. They frowned down at Sun, key in hand. He leaned in as far as he could, hand outstretched, but couldn't reach them as they huddled.

He stood, frustrated. "Get them up," he barked.

I lifted my hands in surrender. "I can't. They won't let me touch them."

"Then they won't be unlocked."

A chorus of shouts rose from the spectators and the mirror at the front.

"*Please*," I said, laying it on thick. "They're hurting."

"What's going on?" Evanna Lynne called from her place by the judge and the remnants of the Spell Binder. "Is there a problem?"

"No," he said with a grunt, bending at the waist over the magic boundary. Off-balance, he all but climbed in with us, one knee perched on the edge, one hand wrapped around it, reaching as far as he could until the key slid into the cuffs.

My muscles bunched, pulse thudding in my ears, as I waited for whatever Sun had planned, whatever Sun wanted me to do. I hoped I knew it when I saw it, or else this was going to be a very short-lived escape.

I shouldn't have worried.

As soon as the shackles fell, Sun slammed one hand against the ground and thrust the other toward the upper back corner of the room. In a blink, the magical barrier around us disappeared.

The sorcerer fell from their precarious balance and dropped the key. It went skidding along the stone. The key. The *key!*

I scrambled after it, snatching it from the ground before anyone knew what was happening, and made a break for Antonia.

The room was in chaos. Evanna Lynne shouted. Sorcerers lunged after me, but I was determined. As I ran, the sorcerers who tried to catch me tripped and fell before they even touched me, the floor heaving beneath their feet.

I was almost to Antonia and Fable. Almost. A step closer and—

I was jerked backward by the collar of my shirt, the fabric snapping right across my throat.

"Rook!" Antonia yelled.

Fuck! I fought, but they were on me, all over me, hands grabbing my clothes, my legs, and I wasn't going to be able to break free, not from the several sorcerers who had pounced and were intent on physically stopping me if they couldn't with magic.

I did the only thing I could.

I threw the key.

23

ROOK

I went down in a tumble of limbs. The back of my head cracked against the floor. Someone kneed me in the stomach, and I lost all breath. Hands held my arms down, and someone sat on my legs.

Everything was a blur, the faces above me and the shouts from all around and, ugh, someone had forgotten to brush their teeth that morning, but I still struggled, still tried to break free because I didn't know what would happen otherwise. Fear drove me. Fear for Sun. Fear for Antonia. Fear for Fable. And to be honest, I was angry. So angry at Evanna Lynne and the Consortium and feeling alienated for the last year of my life and all the deception and the hurt they'd caused.

I kicked out and caught someone, who grunted in pain. I wrenched my arms free and rolled to my side intent on getting to my feet, but it was to no avail. A foot stomped on my back, and I flopped down again, this time my chin scraping along the stone. I was losing. I heard Sun's yells above the cacophony of noise and Fable shouting amid the utter chaos.

Sun! They were hurt! I had to get to Sun. I crawled to where I'd last seen them, but I made little progress with all the sorcerers holding me down. But I had to—

The distinct sound of metal hitting the stone rang out. The hairs on my arms lifted. A prickle of magic swept down my spine. I lifted my head and, through the wall of bodies, caught the sight of Antonia raising her arms, free from the dampeners, fingers outspread, reaching for the back corner as Sun had, and relief flooded through me. Relief quickly followed by panic as I caught the expression on her face and the flicker of her violet eyes, and the pressure of an oncoming storm filled the room.

Oh. Oh no. I took the warning, curling into a ball and covering my head with my arms.

The blast of magic that followed rocked the very cornerstones of the building. The floor buckled under my body, cracking and groaning, the reverberations of it shaking my very bones. The whole room shook, like an earthquake. Plaster rained down from where the ceiling cracked. Furniture toppled over. Wood splintered. Stone shattered. Everyone around me fell. The sound of bodies thudding to the floor was ominous and weird, as if they all fell at once, like puppets with their strings cut.

But the strangest thing that happened was that after the release of whatever Antonia had done, the room went utterly silent and still. The only sound was the ringing in my ears, my own harsh breaths, but all movement, all sound, ceased.

I lay there, unmoving, panting, afraid, my head tucked between my arms. After about a minute, I moved, straightening from my defensive curl. I pushed a body off of me that had fallen across my torso and hoped they were alive. Really, really hoped they were alive, because if not, I had just touched a corpse. And that meant Antonia had killed everyone, and though I was furious with the Consortium, I didn't wish death on them. And I didn't want Antonia to be a murderer.

Tentatively, I sat up. My head spun and my vision was blurry, but I was alive. And, for the moment, free.

I stood, and someone caught my arm to steady me. My instinct was to pull away, but the touch was soft, not hard, not grasping. I looked over my shoulder and found Fable, also unbound. They didn't look at me. Instead their gaze was locked on action across the room. I followed it and found why.

Antonia stood in the center of the destruction, glowing with power, hair fanned around her as if she were underwater, hands raised, magic crackling along her fingers.

All the other sorcerers were on the ground, struggling against Antonia's spell, which held them down. All but the judge and Evanna Lynne, who stood across from Antonia, frozen in place, arms pinned to their sides, eyes wide.

But Sun. Where was Sun? Sun had been faking their illness, kind of, because they couldn't fake the pallor of their skin or the sweat or the trembles. Something had been wrong. And I'd left them. Oh fuck, I'd left them. I wanted to search for them among the bodies, as they were infinitely more important than the confrontation happening between Antonia and Evanna Lynne.

Just as I thought it, a figure sat up amid the bodies, and oh, thank magic, Sun was alive. And though they appeared the worse for wear, and tired, so, so tired, they were the most beautiful person I'd ever seen.

Antonia quirked an eyebrow. "My, my, Evanna Lynne. Outwitted by two little apprentices. How embarrassing for you."

"Release them," the judge demanded.

Antonia tilted her head to the side, considering. "No."

"Hex, you're making a grave mistake," Evanna Lynne said. "There is no way you're leaving this room with your magic intact. You knew that. But now you've compromised the futures of Rook and Sun as well."

Antonia cackled. "Don't lie, Evanna Lynne. You're not good at it. You and I both know that their futures were dictated the minute they walked into this building. You had all four of us, and you weren't going to let us go, not with any abilities intact."

Evanna Lynne unsuccessfully twisted against her magical bonds. "Fine. They were going to be bound. Even the magicless brat. Happy?"

Magic crackled. "Ecstatic," Antonia said. She muttered something and snapped her fingers.

Evanna Lynne gasped and fell to her knees. "What are you doing?" she cried.

Antonia feigned contemplation. "Hmm, what am I doing?" She took a step forward. "Exacting revenge for my apprentice? Both apprentices? You remember the first one, don't you? The one you bound. The one you couldn't detain. The one you begged me to stop, and when I did, you killed her. Do you remember her?"

Evanna Lynne gulped. "She's alive. Last time I saw her, she was alive."

Antonia *tsk*ed. "You know that's not true. Binding is death. Everyone here knows that."

"It's not. It was necessary. She was evil. She needed to be controlled."

Antonia took another step. "What about you? Are you evil? Do you need to be controlled?"

Evanna Lynne paled. "You wouldn't."

"I wouldn't?"

"Antonia Hex," the judge yelled, "you have been sentenced to—"

"Oh, shut up." Antonia stuck out her chin, and the judge's

mouth clamped shut. "I've heard enough from you."

Antonia took another step. She radiated power. It dripped from her in golden sparkles. It filled the whole room. It was amazing and *terrifying*.

"It's my turn to talk," Antonia said to the room at large, to the sorcerers watching on their scrying mirrors. "It's no secret that I've been at odds with the Consortium for years. Decades even. And why shouldn't I be? They control our lives. They control our livelihoods. They control our knowledge. We work hard breaking curses, making potions, casting spells for others only for them to skim money off the top. We have to jump through hoops for our Consortium-approved certificates to place in our windows. And why? So they can dictate our choices?" Antonia prowled, stepping over the sorcerers on the floor, until she stood right in front of the mirror. "Why do we allow it? What have they given us in return for our loyalty?"

No one answered.

Antonia smiled. "That's what I thought." She shrugged. "Loyalty must be earned. And I for one am finished playing by rules that are fixed against me. I for one am ready to burn it all down."

Antonia spun on her heel and stalked to Evanna Lynne. She crackled with magic and power. No one could stop her. Not the sorcerers all stuck to the floor. Not Evanna Lynne on her knees. Not the judge. Not Fable, who stood silently beside me. Not the people shouting on the other side of the closed doors and not those watching via a cracked mirror.

No one.

Maybe not even me.

But I had to try.

"Antonia," I said, picking my way over a few bodies to move closer to her. "Boss," I said softly.

Antonia turned her head and smiled. "There you are, Rook. My apprentice. My nonmagical who is actually magical apprentice. My very smart and devious apprentice. Are you okay?"

"I'm fine."

"You have blood dripping down your neck."

Oh. Right. The back of my head did throb, but I thought that might be the oppressive magical atmosphere. I gently touched the spot and my fingertips came away slightly bloody. And the scrape on my chin burned. I pushed the pain aside to focus on the matter at hand.

"I'm okay though."

"Good." She cast a glance over her shoulder. "Minion, are you okay?"

Sun swayed where they stood. "I'm fine."

Antonia hummed. "I don't believe you, but it's okay. I'll have you both checked out by a healer very soon." She turned her attention back to Evanna Lynne. "I'm almost done here anyway."

"Yeah," I said, hesitant. "About that. Um . . . can we just go home?" I cleared my throat. "I really want to go home. Not my home, not the apartment, but maybe the office? Or my grandma's home? Or even Fable's cottage? Somewhere safe where we can talk?"

"We will. Shortly."

I swallowed. "Antonia, we can't if you do what I think you want to. I mean, if you bind Evanna Lynne, or if you hurt anyone, I don't think I can be your apprentice anymore."

Antonia froze. "What?" She glared at me. "What do you mean?"

"I'm sorry they hurt you. I'm sorry it was because of me. I mean, I made an illegal device. I wasn't magical. You should've never taken me on as your apprentice, but you did because I guess you wanted to break the rules a little bit. Small rebellion, right? If I'd known it would end up like this, I would've said no."

Antonia's hands lowered slightly. "Don't blame yourself, kid. I'm the adult in this relationship. I'm the one who made those choices. I knew what I was doing."

"Maybe," I said. "But I would like to think I was more than a pawn?"

At that Antonia's arms dropped completely. "Of course you're not a pawn. You're Rook. I wanted you as my apprentice."

That was nice to hear. I smiled. "Thanks. I . . . uh . . . I don't want you to do something you will regret. You've proven your point. You are the most powerful sorcerer in ages, and this whole group of sorcerers can't even touch you in their own home base. Like, it just took a little misdirection on Sun's part and you've brought the whole Consortium to heel. I think you've made your point without having to do the whole . . ." I waved my hands. "Death thing."

Antonia's expression darkened. "You don't understand. They'll never leave us alone. And even if they did, what about the others they've bullied? People like you who they've shut out?"

"You're right. Their rules are awful. And they need to be changed. But that doesn't have to be up to just us." I glanced at the mirror. "Others have seen. And maybe they can burn it all down and we get a chance to relax, instead. I don't know what will happen now, but I do know that hurting Evanna Lynne will only make it all worse. I don't want you to become the person they think you are, because you're not. As much as they want to paint you as the villain, you're not. You're not." I didn't realize I was crying until the tears slid down my cheeks and mixed with the tacky drying blood on my chin. "You're the closest thing I have to an adult who cares about me. I haven't had that in a while, and I can't lose that. Please."

Antonia's expression softened. She cupped my cheek, slid her thumb through my tears. "Rook," she said, voice soft. "You're not going to lose me, okay? You're not."

I nodded. More tears slipped out. "I've been so scared. Sun and I . . . we've . . ." My voice caught.

"It's okay," Antonia said. "It's okay. We'll be okay."

I took a shuddering breath and wiped my cheeks. "Thank you."

"Listen to him," Evanna Lynne blurted, still on her knees, breaking the moment. "You bind me, and I'll make it my mission to hunt you down again. And don't for a second think I will hold back against Fable or Rook or Sun."

I sighed, shoulders slumping, soul wilting. "Why couldn't you keep out of it?"

"I'm sorry, Rook," Antonia said, turning away from me. "That I can't ignore. I can't abide threats to my family." She closed the distance between her and Evanna Lynne. She slapped her palm onto Evanna Lynne's forehead. She leaned in close, lips right next to Evanna Lynne's ear. "I warned you."

Magic gathered like a storm. The air was dense with it. I backed away, accidentally stepped on a sorcerer's hand, apologized, and shuffled over to Sun. Sun leaned into my side, and I wrapped an arm around their shoulders, pulling them close.

They looped their fingers through my belt loops as Antonia said the spell, magic swirling around the hand she thrust into the sky, traveling down her arm and through her body and into Evanna Lynne's.

Evanna Lynne screamed. I hugged Sun closer, tucked my head into their shoulder, not wanting to witness the spell. It lasted only seconds before the scream choked off, the swirl of magic receding in pulses, until the spell was over. I lifted my head.

"What have you done?" Evanna Lynne cried. She trembled on

the floor. She thrust her hand out, over and over again, to where the ley line would be and cried out. "I can't feel it! What did you do to me?"

Antonia clucked her tongue. "Oh, don't be like that. I didn't bind you. It's only a little *curse*. It'll break . . . eventually."

She straightened and leveled her gaze at the judge. With a snap, the judge's mouth fell open, and the frantic mumbling they'd been making the whole time turned into panicked words.

"Antonia Hex, you have made terrible mistakes this day, and you will be punished—"

"No," Antonia said, tenting her fingers. "This is what will happen. Rook will remain my apprentice. He has the ability to cast. I understand you might need proof. Show them, Rook."

Oh.

"Um . . ."

"Light something," Sun said in a whisper. "You can do it." They squeezed my hand, lending support.

"Yeah, okay." I shuffled forward and picked up a piece of paper that had been swept away in the whirlwind of magic and fighting. I imagined the line in the corner of the room, the migration of golden butterflies, and I guided a few to break off from the stream, welcomed them to me. Concentrating on the fluttering in my middle, I held up the paper in one hand and pointed two fingers at it with the other. The corner lit and burned.

Antonia's expression turned smug. "He belongs with me, with us, in this community. And you're not going to keep him from it, understand?"

The judge begrudgingly nodded.

"Good. Now, as for myself and my good friend, Fable." Antonia licked her lips. "I've paid my penance for what happened decades ago. I hereby request the Consortium lift their unfair restriction on my ability to have an apprentice. What do you say, Evanna Lynne Beech, sorcerer grade four, Spire City office?"

"No."

Antonia hummed. She turned to another sorcerer, one who was still stuck to the ground. "Who are you?"

"Clyde Waters, sorcerer grade three, Spire City office."

"And do you, Clyde Waters, agree to lift my restriction?"

"Yes," he breathed. "Yes. Just let us go."

"There, restriction lifted. You've all witnessed it. The Spell Binder has been destroyed," Antonia said, nodding to where the remains of it lay in a pile. "And we promise to stick to spell books from this point forward. Those were the three complaints against me, correct? And they've been resolved. So, I see no reason for a sentence for myself and Fable and, of course, for Rook and Sun. I believe we should be free to go."

The judge's face looked like she'd sucked a lemon. Her eyes narrowed. Then she cast a glance at the mirror. The faces of hundreds of witnesses glared back, unhappy, unfriendly, and fractured. "You will submit to monitoring by an approved Consortium sorcerer."

"Fine," Antonia said, frowning down at her nails, as if bored.

"I know one!" I said. "If she'll do it."

The judge scowled. She banged her gavel. "Court adjourned."

Antonia smirked. "You've all heard. And you've all seen what I am capable of. And if any of you so much as blink wrongly at us in the future, you will know my wrath. You will be released once we have left the building."

Antonia nodded to Fable, and the doors swung open. It was then I realized that Fable had held the doors shut the whole time, keeping a deluge of sorcerers on the other side.

They flooded in, and I squeezed close to Antonia, tugging Sun to my side with Fable pressed along our backs.

Before it could all go south again, the judge stood from her bench. "They're free to leave," she shouted.

The Consortium sorcerers came to a halt at the words. They eyed us suspiciously but didn't argue with the judge or try to intervene as we made our way to the door. As we walked past the table of objects, Antonia reached over and snagged a plain black mat.

"This is mine, thank you," she said, tucking the cursed rug under her arm.

I gaped. But then I understood when we shuffled by the remnants of the Spell Binder and, against my better judgment, I scooped up the small bit that was still intact and held it.

"Hey," Sun said, standing close. "Leave it. You don't need it."

I sighed. "It was so much work. It was my only hope for so long. It's hard to let it go."

Sun rested their hand on mine. "Rook, you don't need it anymore. Okay?"

"But how am I going to see the ley lines?"

Sun knocked their shoulder into mine. "I'll be your Ley Finder."

"What?"

Grinning and blushing, Sun turned my hand over, and the device fell to the floor in a series of *ping*s. "You know my special ability is to see magic, even the smallest amount. So I'll do it. I'll be your Ley Finder."

"That means you'll have to be with me all the time."

Sun shrugged. "Not really a hardship."

"Wow. Wow. That's the most romantic thing you've ever said to me. I just . . . need to live in this moment and kiss you. I need to kiss you right now."

"Kids!" Antonia yelled from the doorway. "This isn't the best time."

"Outside," I amended. "I'm going to kiss you as soon as we get outside."

Sun hid a laugh in my shoulder. "Can't wait," they said. "No regrets at all."

24

SUN

True to his word, Rook kissed me as soon as we stepped onto the dirty downtown sidewalk. It was a quick wet smack to my mouth, and he probably bruised both of our lips, but it was still good. Good because we were outside, and Antonia and Fable were free, and we could go back to our lives.

Despite not having phones or wallets or money, Antonia magically hailed us transport, and before I knew it, we were in a car driving somewhere. Exhaustion pulled at me. While I'd exaggerated what the dampeners did to me, they weren't without side effects. They did sap every bit of energy I had, and by the time Rook and I were seated next to each other in the back of the car, it took everything to stay awake.

"Hey," Rook said, leaning toward me. "It's okay."

That was all the encouragement I needed. I rested my head on his shoulder and gave in to the fatigue that beckoned.

When I woke up, the car had pulled into the driveway of Fable's cottage. The adults must have been talking to each other while I was asleep, but when I pulled away to exit, Rook snorted himself awake. It was not at all endearing.

Fable's cottage had showers and food, and even if the door was knocked in and we had to usher out a raccoon family, it was still the safest I'd felt in days, once Antonia set a stable ward across the doors and windows. I showered, changed into a pair of clothes I kept there—my own jeans and shirt and hoodie, which smelled like familiar fabric softener—and I was content.

Fable made soup on the stove, and I washed the few bowls that hadn't been broken. There were only three, so I ended up drinking soup out of a large cup. As we slurped, we talked. Rook and I talked about our escape, and sleeping in the forest, and my few days as a cat, and Mavis, and Rook's grandmother. Antonia told us how they'd caught her unaware, overpowered her with a cadre of sorcerers, and how she'd been unlucky.

"It won't happen again," Antonia said with a fierce nod.

"No," Fable agreed. "It won't."

Once the soup was eaten, I pulled the cuffs of my hoodie over my hands. "I have to call my parents," I said.

Rook nodded. "I know."

"Don't worry, Sun," Fable said, lightly brushing my shoulder with their fingertips. "I'll explain everything, and, remember, they signed the waiver."

I pulled my knees to my chest as I balanced in the kitchen chair. "Still, they're not going to let me out of their sight for a while."

Rook traced the grain on Fable's kitchen table. The one I'd landed on that was somehow not broken. "I know. It's okay. I'll text you."

"I don't have a phone anymore, and neither do you. The Consortium has them."

Rook laughed. "Right. Um . . . scrying mirror?"

"Absolutely not," Antonia said, cutting through our conversation. "In fact"—she nodded toward the covered one across the room—"I know it was unintentional that they heard everything,"

Antonia said evenly, "but I don't want to be near one ever again."

"I agree," Fable said. They crossed the room, took the mirror from the wall, and slammed it on the floor. It shattered. "There."

Wow, I mouthed to Rook with wide eyes. Fable had never openly broken a rule before. But I had a feeling everything was going to change. Everything already had. Maybe even for the better.

Rook took my hand in his. I didn't mind it at all. In fact, I wouldn't mind curling up together on one of the beds in the cottage and sleeping for a year, holding hands, touching, kissing. But as it was, I'd take the way Rook laced our fingers.

"I like you," Rook said. "So much."

"Even if I'm grumpy and antisocial."

Rook laughed. "Yeah. It's kind of my favorite thing about you."

My face heated. My heart stuttered. And yeah, the situation may have been difficult and tense, and I'd spent a few days as a cat, but things had definitely turned out for the better.

25

ROOK

Watching Sun be fawned over by their sisters was endearing and cute and a little heartbreaking, but I was happy for them. Happy that they had a family who had worried about them and happy that they promised to keep in touch even as their sisters tugged them into their mom's car to drive them home to their worried parents.

I waved to them from the front porch of Fable's cottage as the car pulled away, and I stayed there until they were long out of sight, arms crossed over my middle. I missed them already, but it would be okay. Because, as Antonia had said so succinctly in the face of the judge and Evanna Lynne, I belonged. I *belonged*.

"What about you?" Antonia asked, coming to stand next to me on the porch while sipping coffee. She'd complained of a caffeine-withdrawal headache, and Fable had made a pot that Antonia was quickly drinking her way through.

"What about me?"

"You said I was your only adult. Back there at the Consortium." She drummed her fingers, her nails clinking against the ceramic. "Is that true?"

"Yes. Yes, you are."

She hummed. "Okay. Well, I have a place in the city. My home. And I want to go there. Do you want to come with?"

I snapped my head up. "What?"

Antonia held her coffee cup in both hands and looked over the landscape. "As much as I adore Fable's cottage"—she made a face as she said it—"and the quaint magical woods that are right next door, I have my own apartment. I have plants that need water. And I have an extra room that has nothing in it but a bed."

A lump formed in my throat. "Are you asking me to stay with you?"

"For a while," she said. "Or forever. Either. Or. We could try it out, and if you like it and if you want to stay, we'll make it happen."

"Are you serious?" I couldn't take it if she wasn't. My heart squeezed.

Antonia finally met my gaze. "Of course."

I nodded quickly. "Yeah. Yeah, I'd like that."

"Good. We'll go after I finish this cup of coffee. And we'll get more coffee on the way there. And then I'll buy us both new phones. After we have more food and a long nap."

"That sounds amazing." It came out watery, a little disbelieving, but earnest, so sincere there was no way Antonia could take it as anything but genuine.

"You're not going to cry on me, are you?"

I shook my head, frantically trying to rein in my utter happiness. "No," I said, my voice a rasp, tears burning behind my eyes.

Antonia smiled into her cup. "It's okay if you do."

I laughed. My heart soared. And all the fear of rejection that had followed me around since the very beginning, since I'd walked into Antonia's office all those months ago, that plagued my every step and cast a shadow over every decision I'd made, all of it merely dissipated, fluttered away on the backs of butterfly wings.

26

ROOK

"Hello, thank you for calling Hex-A-Gone. How can I assist you today?" I asked as I clicked through documents on my computer. "You think you might be jinxed? Okay. Can you provide me with some more information?" I listened as the caller rambled about tripping over curbs and dropping their brand-new expensive phone on concrete and walking into a doorframe while on a date. I gathered all the information and typed it into my handy-dandy non-emergent maybe-just-really-clumsy form on the computer.

"Okay. Thank you for your call. I will pass the information along to one of our capable sorcerers and they will return your call before the end of the business day. Thank you."

I saved the form and emailed it to Antonia and Fable for review. They would decide what to do with it and whether it needed any magical intervention. They'd taken to working together much more closely than before, practically merging their businesses. Apparently, a new understanding had passed between them while locked together in the Consortium dungeon, and while Fable still was more rule-driven than Antonia, both were more prone to being flexible.

Antonia didn't automatically buck at every Consortium-approved practice for magic and curse work, and Fable had taken to breaking a lot of mirrors. With all of us, we were able to repair the damage to the Hex-A-Gone office and to Fable's cottage quickly enough to be back at work within a week of the whole Consortium mess.

I spun in my chair and went back to studying the open spell book that Antonia had gifted me earlier that week. It was bigger than the field book but much smaller than the one in her office and smaller than my grandmother's book, which we had retrieved from her home. That one stayed in my room at Antonia's . . . our . . . place. I was still getting used to thinking about Antonia's home as my own, but since the plan was for me to stay for a while, I would eventually refer to it as such, I'm sure. It felt more like a home than the old apartment, anyway.

I'd been staying there since we broke out of the Consortium's Spire City office. And the past few weeks had been the best of the last year. Antonia had talked to my caseworker, and it hadn't been a hard sell for me to move out. We worked well together. She taught me magic and took care of the adult things. I fixed all the appliances she kept breaking.

As for the Consortium, the organization was pretty much in shambles, and reinforcements from the other offices around the world had to be brought in for a massive restructuring. Many sorcerers around the city demanded reform, and some had even taken to just not following the rules. Magic was in a weird state of flux, and the Spire City office scrambled to address complaints and keep magical life stable. It wasn't going that great for them. But it didn't seem to bother us much. Other than the addition of Mavis being our court-appointed magical monitor, it was business as usual. Curses still needed to be broken, and Antonia was happy to do it now that she didn't feel forced. And Fable not only worked with Antonia, but they had been appointed as a lead member of an action committee, advocating for changes to the Consortium's policies on behalf of sorcerers in the city. They seemed to enjoy it.

"Are you studying that spell book, or are you mooning over Sun?" Mavis asked as she breezed in, hopping over the cursed mat. She'd learned her lesson a few days ago when it tripped her, and she ended up facedown in the reception area. Herb shuffled over from his place in the corner and offered to take her bag, which Mavis declined with a shake of her head. Amazingly, Herb had survived the Consortium's destruction of the office. Unfortunately, his dislike of everyone but Antonia had also survived.

"Studying, of course." I had been. I could light the candle so much easier now. And I'd even been able to conjure my own butterflies. They'd been weak at best, but I could do it, and the more I practiced, the better I'd become.

"Uh-huh," she said, twirling her car keys around her fingers.

"How was the outing? Did that person really accidentally curse themselves to have a lizard tongue?"

Mavis full-body shuddered and crinkled her nose. "Yes. It was weird. But easily fixed, and they paid in cash." She winked. "Got any more for me?"

"A few more came in today," I said, clicking through the documents I'd saved on the calls. "I've sent them all to Antonia already, but let's see. A cursed game controller that won't allow the person holding it to rest until they beat the entire game. A person who may just be really clumsy. Oh, and a person who wanted their dog to like their new boyfriend and now the boyfriend can't go anywhere because they attract every dog in the vicinity."

"Oh! Give me that one!"

I nodded and emailed her the file, and her phone pinged in her pocket. Mavis had left her job at the library and had moved back into magical work full time. I had to admit that I was glad she was on our team, since she was able to balance that tight line between Fable's and Antonia's personalities. It also helped that she remembered my grandmother—it was nice to have that connection again.

"Good choice on the dog file, Mavis," Antonia said, emerging from her office. She wore a black tailored pantsuit and high heels, and her fingernails were painted a light blue, like the sky outside. "I'm more of a cat person myself, so I will gladly yield that job to your expertise."

Mavis laughed. "You? A cat person? I never would have guessed."

"I don't know how to take that, so I'll ignore it." Antonia opened her hand. "The cash, please."

Mavis pouted but handed over the envelope of money.

"Don't even," Antonia said. "I know you're being paid by the Consortium to monitor our activities and you're being paid a generous hourly rate by Hex-A-Gone for your services."

Mavis smiled. "Gotta love a good old conflict of interest."

"And capitalism," I added.

Antonia crossed her arms with a snort. Then she eyed me, tilting her head to the side. "Rook," she said, "isn't it date night?"

"Yeah."

"Don't you think you should get ready?"

I checked the time on my phone and oh! It was already close to five. "Crap."

Antonia sighed and reached over to ruffle my hair. "Clothes are hanging in my office. Use the attached bathroom to freshen up."

I jumped out of my chair. "Thanks, boss."

I ran into the office, grabbed the clothes hanging from the back of the door, and changed in the small bathroom. It wasn't much of a change. I still wore jeans, but I replaced my T-shirt with a button-up and styled my hair. Antonia had put a black skinny tie in with the clothes, and I didn't know if I wanted to go that far. It was just date night, and while I was taking Sun to a fancy restaurant in the magic district, I didn't know if that warranted a tie.

I walked out of the bathroom to find Antonia standing by her desk.

"Put on the tie," she said.

"Really?"

"Sun is already here. Put on the tie."

Oh. "Um."

Antonia strode forward and looped the tie around my neck and expertly tied it, leaving the knot slightly loose. "There."

"Thanks."

"Use the credit card I gave you."

"Antonia, I have money. You've been paying me to work for months now, and I've banked most of it away."

She shrugged. "Consider that your college fund. Use the credit card. Be home at a reasonable hour but not too early. It still is the summer. And make sure to walk Sun home."

"Sun's sisters will torment me."

"It will be good for your character."

I laughed. "Fine."

I walked into the main office area and found Fable and Mavis talking. Sun was with them, hands in their pockets, and okay, I understood why Antonia had me put on the tie. Because Sun looked amazing. Well, Sun always looked amazing, but they had styled their hair for date night and wore dangling silver earrings.

"You," I said.

Sun looked at me and grinned. "Me," they replied.

Sun held out their hand, their signal that it was okay to touch, and I immediately took it, threading our fingers together. They leaned in, pressing close along my side.

"Ready to go?" I asked.

"Yes, let's go before one of them does something embarrassing like taking pictures."

"Too late!" Mavis singsonged, holding up her phone. "You two are too cute. I can barely stand it."

Fable nodded. "Sun, be sure to text your parents, and be back before your curfew."

Sun muttered under their breath about being smothered. They were still very much under restrictions due to being missing for several days, which was understandable. But at least they'd been allowed to continue as Fable's apprentice. And they were permitted to go on the occasional date night because they'd scraped a passing grade out of their summer math class. They managed a C+ thanks to their sisters having no compunctions against chaperoning Sun to the coffee shop, which allowed our math tutoring sessions to continue. Soo-jin blabbed all about it to their parents, which is why Sun's mom and dad actually kind of liked me and had even stated that I was a positive influence. I wouldn't say that was true, but I would say that Sun and I complemented each other, and we made each other happy.

"Don't worry, Fable. I will be responsible and make sure that Sun arrives home on time."

Sun grimaced. "My sisters will destroy you."

"I've heard it builds character."

Sun huffed and rolled their eyes. "Let's go. I don't want to spend all my free time at dinner, if you get my drift," they said, voice low.

A shiver went down my spine. "Okay. Message received. And absolutely no complaints here, but just, give me a moment? This is . . . kind of nice." And it was. Mavis and Fable bent over my spell book on the table, flipping through and talking about the dog issue. Antonia clanged around in the employee break room, trying to make another cup of coffee. Herb sulked in the corner as always. And even the mat waited for us to try to leave, though hopefully it would not succeed in tripping either of us because I did not want a bloody nose before my date that could hinder any potential making out that was going to happen.

Mavis said something emphatically, and magic burst from her hand in a shower of sparkles. Fable flipped through the pages of the book unperturbed. Antonia cursed from the other room, and the sound of a shattered coffee mug followed. Sun squeezed my hand, and I smiled so wide my cheeks hurt.

Sometimes a family was a mischievous magical boss, her magical rival turned friend, a magical girl who used to be a babysitter and now was like an older sister, and the person you didn't understand in the beginning but liked so much now. And sometimes it was arguments and sometimes it was hugs and sometimes it was banding together to fight a morally corrupt government body and sometimes it was just existing in the same space together as friends.

But whatever this family was right now, whatever it was going to be, and however it would turn out, it was mine.

And I knew that I belonged.

ACKNOWLEDGMENTS

Of all of my works thus far *Spell Bound* feels the most personal. It addresses several insecurities I had as an adolescent and young adult, and, let's be honest, still have to some extent. Rook has grief and loneliness etched into his soul. He has been told that he doesn't belong, and he is desperately looking for a place to fit. Sun is hesitant and unsure when it comes to relationships because they are painfully aware of how different they are and how others perceive them. Both Rook and Sun attempt, to varying degrees, to reconfigure themselves, mold their beings, their personalities into what they think others want. It doesn't work because, in the end, they were *enough* the whole time. They learn that being their authentic selves is more important and more fulfilling than being accepted by those who would have them change. And that there are people in their lives who will love and cherish them as they are.

I feel this message of self-acceptance is one many of us need to hear several times for it to sink in. And I'm very grateful to all the individuals who have supported the creation of this book and have shaped it into its best version and have been instrumental in getting it into the hands of readers who may need to hear it one more time.

I'm eternally grateful to my best friend, Kristinn, who continues to be one of my biggest supporters and who is my forever writing buddy. She encourages me in my moments of self-doubt and graciously handles my author imposter syndrome with more kindness and patience than I deserve. There were several anxiety-fueled emails this time around that were the embodiment of the scream emoji that she patiently handled. Also, many thanks to the other Christin who stepped up in a big way under a time crunch to assist. Thank you so much for all your help.

Next, I want to thank my agent, Eva Scalzo. Thank you, Eva, for taking a chance on that suspect merman book that showed up in your inbox years ago. And thank you for continuing to champion my work and for being an amazing person who supports my vision for my career and who handles slightly panicked phone calls and understands my weird sense of humor. And thank you to the team at McElderry Books / Simon & Schuster especially my editor Kate Prosswimmer, who worked so hard to bring out all the potential in the storytelling and character arcs and made this book the best it could be. Thank you to the cover illustrator, the amazingly talented Sam Schechter, who once again knocked it out of the park with their stunning work and the cover designer, Becca Syracuse, for this beautiful, beautiful cover. And thank you to both Nicole Fiorica and Alex Kelleher for also being amazing members of the team. It really has been a dream to work with you all.

Thank you to the authenticity readers who consulted, provided feedback and assistance, and who were integral to the creative process including the development of characters and the narrative. I appreciate your time and your thoughts and your work so much. Many thanks to Dani Moran for their expertise and insightful feedback. And thank you to Kiana Yasuhara for the time, effort, and assistance.

I know I always thank my fandom life mate and my pocket friends who are the greatest, but they all really were my support system during the whole development of this novel. Specifically, Jude, Amy, Cee, Renee, Asya, BK, Emi, Dani, Cori, and Trys. My internet family always comes through, and I can't thank them enough for sticking with me this past decade.

I'd like to thank a group of authors who are not only my friends, but amazing colleagues, and who are my cheerleaders, beta readers, support group, confidants, and convention buddies—CB Lee, DL Wainright, Carrie Pack, and Julia Ember. Special thanks to Julian Winters, Steven Salvatore, & Ryan La Sala for their support in launching the last book and I look forward to all your upcoming releases!

I'd like to thank Malaprop's bookstore in Asheville, which is my local amazing indie store. Malaprop's has been so kind to me the past few years. The booksellers are awesome and if you are ever in the Asheville area, please drop by and say hi to the staff—specifically Katie and Stephanie.

I'd like to thank my family, especially my spouse, Keith, and my three kids, Ezra, Zelda, and Remy, who bring joy and excitement into my life every day. I'd also like to thank my brother, Rob, and my sister-in-law, Chris. If anyone is wondering where my weird jokes and puns originate, blame Rob for gifting me *The Hitchhiker's Guide to the Galaxy* for my thirteenth birthday. I would like to thank my nieces and nephews, who tell their school librarians about my books and talk them up to their teachers and friends. And I'd like to thank my niece Emma for joining me at conventions and my niece Lauren for all her support.

Lastly, I'd like to thank everyone who reads this book, who either purchased it or borrowed it from a library. Thank you for allowing me to entertain you for a few hours. I'm very appreciative of your time. I hope you enjoyed reading this story as much as I enjoyed writing it. Until next time, I hope you stay safe and happy.

Thank you,

FT

DIVE INTO MORE SWOONY ADVENTURES FROM F.T. LUKENS!